The
True & Splendid
HISTORY
of the
HARRISTOWN
SISTERS

The
True & Splendid
HISTORY
of the
HARRISTOWN
SISTERS

MICHELLE LOVRIC

BLOOMSBURY

LONDON · NEW DELHI · NEW YORK · SYDNEY

First published in Great Britain 2014

Copyright © 2014 by Michelle Lovric

The right of Michelle Lovric to be identified as the author of this work has been
asserted by her in accordance with the Copyright, Designs and Patents Act 1988

Bloomsbury Publishing Plc
50 Bedford Square
London
WC1B 3DP

www.bloomsbury.com

Bloomsbury is a trademark of Bloomsbury Publishing Plc

Bloomsbury Publishing, London, New Delhi, New York and Sydney

A CIP catalogue record for this book is available from the British Library

Hardback ISBN 978 1 4088 3341 4

Trade paperback ISBN 978 1 4088 3342 1

10 9 8 7 6 5 4 3 2 1

Typeset by Hewer Text UK Ltd, Edinburgh
Printed and bound in Great Britain by CPI Group (UK) Ltd, Croydon CR0 4YY

to my caravan of nymphs

The first show

October 1865

Joe the seaweed boy jolted us on his cart through the rain towards Kilcullen Town. High sodden hedges and our damp bonnets foreclosed on the sky. The rich mud sluiced through our wheels, uttering long vulgar kisses. Our feet pressed down on rags of dead seaweed, perfuming the air with sourness and a faint memory of salt.

Enda held Oona's hand and mine; Berenice clutched Ida's and Pertilly's.

Darcy held no one's hand, of course.

The slow crows wheeled above us, sonorous in their derision for the seven Swiney sisters in their threadbare finery. Most of all they lifted their beaks against me, Manticory, for they had witnessed my disgrace on Harristown Bridge.

'Would you look at that!' Oona pointed at a sheet impaled on a pair of rakes, her finger blurring with fear.

In letters draggling in the rain, it announced:

The Swiney Godivas
Seven Singing Sisters with Seven Sweet Throats
First ever show tonight

Old Kilcullen brooded like a beetle around the next hedge and in the heart of its black streets lurked Ladysmildew Hall, where we were to be sacrificed.

We had a bare hour's rehearsal before tea.

The hall's wooden floor rose up to trip our tapping heels in a way the dirt of our barn floor never had. And plump Pertilly landing from a leap was a thing you could hear quite loudly in the next county, according to Darcy.

Outside, the rain beat down like a blacksmith.

Inside, the gas lamps commenced to whisper.

We broke for bread-and-dripping with tea, consumed in the silence of bare terror. Pertilly dressed our hair one last time, cleverly coiling and balancing it on the strength of two stout pins.

As the second hand of the clock strutted round to five minutes before six, Darcy herded us back to the stage. Peering out through the mothy curtain, Oona and Pertilly reported on an audience of fifty sniffing matrons and two dozen sorry-looking youths who shuffled in with their hands in the pockets from which they had just extracted six hard-won pennies for the pleasure we had promised to give them.

'Nobodies, noodles.' Darcy paced up and down behind the curtain. 'And a good thing, too. No one to bother with if you bosthoons make fools of yourselves, as you undoubtedly shall.'

She'd neglected to whisper. Mrs Godlin from the Kilcullen dispensary tutted loudly from the front row. Pertilly waggled a hand through the curtain, greeting Mrs Godlin in our local fashion, 'To you.'

Mrs Godlin just had time to nod, 'From you,' before Darcy had her fingers around Pertilly's throat and was dragging her away for punishing.

Oona whispered that the seaweed boy Joe had settled himself into the very front row, like royalty.

'I shall die of fright if you make me go out there,' Oona told Darcy, over Pertilly's sobs. 'How shall I bear it?'

Darcy was not your woman for 'how'. She was more your woman for 'when'.

'Don't be talking blethers,' she growled. 'You'll be lying in your straw bed tonight dying of nothing to eat if you don't do this now.'

'Or maybe sooner, if you cross her,' I said.

2

'You are the worst thing on two feet in Ireland, Manticory.' Darcy stamped hard on my left one. Under her breath, she muttered, 'You and your goings-on on Harristown Bridge. Is it worried you are, that *he*'s down there in the audience?'

My heart dropped into my belly that she'd said those things aloud.

The curtains were already creaking apart. We stood still for a moment in a state of fossilising fear. Then Darcy swept to the centre of the stage and began to sing. The hall filled up like a milk pail with the goodness of lovely noise, for the throat of a nightingale was in Darcy's neck, even if a viper's tongue was in her mouth.

From the wings, I ran my eyes over the audience. He was not there, himself, the man.

Only Darcy knew of him. The oldest of us she was, nineteen at that time, Darcy of the Ethiopian-black hair, coiling and crinkling like the sea in a sunless cave. With her hair came a serpentine muscularity of body and will. Darcy's rages could encircle and choke the life's will out of you.

Darcy retired from the stage, applause clattering behind her.

Next were our twins, lively Berenice and my most darling Enda, who had matching shades of soft brown – Madonnacoloured – hair. They sang a tense duet, each gesture in perfect harmony, as if they did not hate one another worse than a devil and an angel.

Could I tell Enda what had happened to me on Harristown Bridge? So soft, so tender, Enda would cry a well for me, but could she help me?

Could I tell Berenice? I could not, brave and bold as she was. She was my enemy, because she was Enda's.

Now chestnut-tressed Pertilly bumbled out in front of the audience, perfectly sure, as ever, of disappointing. Poor Pertilly was not pretty at all. Not quite thirteen, she did not have even that freshness of youth we in Harristown called 'pig-beauty'. Her nose loomed too large and her fleshy upper lip hung unbecomingly over the lower one. Worst of all, her eyebrows drooped the wrong way like the dispirited tails of two dead mice. She laboured away at her stanzas.

Could I tell Pertilly? No, Pertilly would carry it hard. She would sag with the sorryness of it. The secret would seep out of her, somehow. And Darcy would pummel her for that.

Pertilly's song was mercifully done away with. Then Oona stepped up on the stage to refresh the desire of the audience for Swiney sisters. Oona, fairy-featured and amiable, had blonde hair, thick and soft as mounds of fresh butter churned in a moonlit barn. Like Oonagh, Queen of the Fairies, she had a fey, coaxing way about her. But even at eleven she spoke in a strong bass voice and could pass for a man in the dark. When she opened her mouth on her ballad of first love, the audience sighed with shock and delight.

Could I tell Oona? I could not. The nerves on her were so delicate and eleven was too young to take on my burden.

Next on stage was Ida, christened 'Idolatry', the dark-brown baby of the Swiney sisters, with dark-brown moods to match, and an irrepressible tendency to pluck the hairs from her head and wind them round her wrists and ankles. She lisped her lines about a beloved dead kitten with a furrowed brow and wandered uncertainly from the stage in the wrong direction.

How could I tell Ida? She hadn't ten years on her yet. I prayed she would not even understand the goings-on upon Harristown Bridge or in the copse beside it.

Although I am the middle sister, Darcy had left me to last.

Myself, I am called Manticory, tiger girl, on account of the red hair that is fierce upon my head. Darcy wanted me last on the stage, to give me the longest agony of anticipation, as a punishment, and because of my hair, the redness of it, which was enough to have got me into the heinous kind of trouble that I could not tell my sisters about.

Aware only of the pins and needles in my hands and the shame that clothed me tighter than my bodice, I gave them a song of a red-haired shepherdess. Darcy's drilling served me well, galvanising my legs and arms, drawing the songs out of me, as if I were still in the tumbledown barn. I danced. I bowed. I

4

walked off the stage in a wind-up kind of fashion and into Enda's arms.

'You're stiff as a corpse,' she whispered, kissing me. 'Calm yourself. It's a done thing now. Nearly.'

For we had still the ensemble piece to perform. It had nothing to do with music, or dancing, or young Irish girls singing their Famined hearts out.

It was the thing upon which Darcy pinned the whole show and our fortunes.

We filed on stage, carrying seven wooden chairs. We set ourselves upon them with our backs turned to the audience.

Simultaneously, we raised our white arms, extracted the crucial pins from our chignons and lifted our loosened hair high above our heads.

And that was when the Swiney Godivas of Harristown slowly liquefied the fat of every heart in Ladysmildew Hall.

Slow, it was, because hair bunched by hand and then let to drop does not do so in a single moment. It falls in sighing increments, a first flump, a gradual unwinding, to twists of blunt ends slithering against the neck, the hanks still smooth and unified from their confinement. Finally, each separate hair finds its appointed resting place.

The hair of the seven Swiney sisters took a long sweet time in falling, not just because of the great weight of it, but because of its unreasonable length. You see, between us we'd already grown forty feet of the stuff, enough to swaddle twenty babies or wind ten grown corpses; more than enough to cover our Swiney bodies and to caress our heels.

Our hair fell with a palpable breeze that touched the faces of those in the front two rows, turning them bloodless or coralline.

And still it kept slithering and sidling and tralloping down to the dust of the wooden floor.

Just like the thin geese, the slow crows and the kittens who had witnessed all our rehearsals, the matrons and boys watched us in breathtook silence, their heads as stiff on their necks as the stump of the round tower at Yellow Bog.

5

When all the uncoiling, rustling and falling was done, we presented a shimmering waterfall of hair, black, brown, red and blonde, a quantity of hair to terrify you and to knock your beating heart across you, and make you wish you'd been born with two of them just to take in all that hair without fear of a rupture.

'Is that the kind of thing you're after wanting?' Darcy turned and asked our audience.

The boys threw their caps in the air and the women shrieked.

The men leaned closer and breathed like undersea creatures, like the man on Harristown Bridge.

Part One
HARRISTOWN

1

We Swineys were the hairiest girls in Harristown, Kildare, and the hairiest you'd find anywhere in Ireland from Priesthaggard to Sluggery. That is, our limbs were as hairless as marble, but on our heads, well, you'd not believe the torrents that shot from our industrious follicles like the endless Irish rain.

When we came into this world, our heads were not lightly whorled with down like your common infant's. We Swineys inched bloodily from our mother's womb already thickly ringleted. Thereafter that hair of ours never knew a scissor. It grew faster than we did, pawing our cheeks and seeking out our shoulder blades. As small girls, our plaits snaked down our backs with almost visible speed. That hair had its own life. It whispered round our ears, making a private climate for our heads. Our hair had its roots inside us, but it was outside us as well. In that slippage between our inner and outer selves – there lurked our seven scintillating destinies and all our troubles besides.

Back in the very beginning – long before Darcy ever marched us onto a stage or a man laid a hairbrush on me upon a bridge – we Swineys were born into the full melancholy of the Famine and lived in hungry and ungenteel seclusion on the Harristown estate in County Kildare, fatherless and befriended principally by the lice. In those days, when the Swiney sisters sang, our only accompanists were the slow crows whose constant keening hung in the ribbons of Harristown's rain.

And it was remarkably fond of the rain where we were born. The sky was always weeping; the earth was a greedy sponge for it; the rain flowed down through our hair, inserted itself under our smocks and slid down to our feet. The thin geese were always slick with water; their eggs were slippery with it too and dropped through our hands, leaving all too few to trade with the travelling hagglers who passed through Harristown selling dusty semblances of tea and flour. The rain eased itself through the gutters and overflowed the barrels under the eaves.

You may be thinking now that my words are very and too much like the rain, pelting down on you without particularity or mercy. And I shall say that perhaps it is the rain forever scribbling on our roofs and our faces that teaches the Irish our unstinting verbosity. It's what we have, instead of food or luck. Think of it as a generosity of syllables, a wishful giving of words when we have nothing else to offer by way of hospitality: we lay great mouthfuls of language on you to round your bellies and comfort your thoughts like so many boileds and roasts, or even a lick of Finn MacCool's finger dipped in the milk that simmered the Salmon of Wisdom.

The little Swiney girls of Harristown occupied themselves not with wise salmon but with foolish geese as thin as a fat goose's feather. When we were smaller than them, we were chased by the thin geese. When we grew a tint bigger, we chased them back. Darcy wrung their necks for them at Michaelmas, my sisters' mouths candidly awater at the thought of goose fat on slices of Saturday's little soda loaf baked in the turf stove that cast such a devilish light on our few pieces of pewter. Only I myself and our mother Annora had a scruple, and never laid a hand on a thin goose's throat or even tasted a morsel of warm white friend. From each hatching, my mother always chose a favourite goose; it was invariably christened 'Phiala', meaning 'saint's name'. Annora would frequently call out to that saintly goose in a cooing voice, particularly in the dewy sadness of the evening.

And Darcy would mimic Annora's voice mockingly, and then Enda would protest, 'Where's the harm in a goose, bless her?'

And Berenice, always contrary to her twin, sneered, 'Don't you sicken on yourself, being so sweet?'

But it was Berenice who sickened with the whooping cough, and filled our cottage to the rafters with her unearthly howls.

Annora resorted to the folk remedy of a hair sandwich, cutting a curl from Berenice's nape to put between two precious slices of bread that she threw out of the front door for an animal to eat. I saw Enda creeping outside later to rob the fox or stoat of his supper and Berenice of her cure. But Berenice recovered well enough to beat her when Enda boasted of it later.

The turf stove smoked in the kitchen that doubled as sleeping quarters for the youngest Swineys – Pertilly, Oona and Ida – who muddled together in a press bed unfolded every night. Some winters, our kitchen hosted the sourest cow in County Kildare, and her occasional spindly bracket calf, who usually died quite promptly on her curdled milk.

Sheets and shirts festooned our roof-beams, a constant virginal parade day. Our mother Annora laundered and ironed like a desperate woman to keep us in potatoes and Indian meal, but never enough of either. The Famine lasted longer in our house than it did elsewhere in Harristown. Many days we lived on turnip tops, or sand eels and seaweed brought by Joe on his cart from the coast. There were mornings when Annora gave us young hawthorn leaves to chew as there was nothing else. Or we breakfasted on the smell of rashers snorting out of the La Touche kitchens as we marched past their stone mansion's rear end on our way to school in Brannockstown.

'And sausages they're having for themselves this morning.' Pertilly could always tell what we weren't eating.

'With sage and apple gravy,' she'd add wetly, for the hunger pumping through her body filled her mouth with saliva.

Like our next potato, the shelter of the cottage was uncertain. The rain made our floor dribble foaming mud, and whenever it happened to wax dry, our bodies baked under the rat-eaten thatch like little loaves ourselves. Whenever the wind blew bitter, it rifled the tired petticoats that served as curtains or searched out the fissures in the walls and came scything through our clothes to murder any living warmth on our skin. Then we took turns to lay our haunches on a perforated pot under which some precious coals pinkened. Otherwise, seated on our stake-legged stools, we competed with the thin geese for

11

the warmth of the fire, taking a short heather besom to their roasted doings every morning.

Yet we were not the worst off. Our landlord John La Touche showed no sign of evicting us. Some days there was a whole potato for each of us in the straining basket – barely boiled 'with the bone in' so that our young teeth had something to learn on – and a kitchen of buttermilk in which to dip it. The Hunger had taken one in three in County Kildare. All around houses stood empty, except of rumoured bones. Certainly no Swineys but ourselves had survived the cull. The poorest children of Harristown were born with Famine's imprint, like a bruise from a fist dark under their cheekbones and a startled look as if they'd just been kicked from behind towards their graves. Their mothers carried baby corpses around, begging for coffin money even at our poor door. Older children starved quickly and quietly; we came to know the pitiful signs of it and turned our heads from the sight of a boy or a girl whom we'd not see the next day. The adults went about it in wilder ways. You would not want to go to nearby Naas, the priest warned us, for fear of the mob that might lynch you for the meat on your bones, and its streets lined with those who'd delivered themselves to town just so that someone could witness them dying. They lay down in the street so they must be walked over.

Sometimes a living skeleton still stumbled into our hovel, violently soliciting a heel of bread. And one time Darcy came flying into the house with the news that, when emptying the chamber pot, she'd found something that had once been a man lying dead near the privy midden. I trotted to where the slow crows were wheeling like a doleful, graceful flight of mourning fans. Darcy parted the fronds of dripping grass and pointed.

I'd just four years myself then, and it was my first close-up corpse. I kneeled to look. I sobbed to see the grin stretched over his face and the grey skin that clung to the hollowness of his throat. Moths flickered on his collar. The rain sluiced tears into his open eyes.

12

'Too weak to strangle an old goose for himself,' Darcy concluded. 'Though doubtless that was his plan. Manticory, stop that snivelling and close his eyes.'

'Me? But—'

'It shall be the worse for you if you do not.'

I laid my fat little fingers on his grainy lids and raked down his harsh lashes. Then Annora came out and commenced keening with the slow crows. I cried long shouting tears into her apron. She called down the blessings of the Holy Virgin and St Brigid upon the corpse and sent Darcy for the priest.

'Is he our daddy then?' I hiccoughed, looking carefully at the dead man's hair.

Our father was a sailor, Annora always told us, and he came back solely in the night once a year, when we were sleeping.

'Why then and only then?' Darcy would lament. 'For why did he not wake us?'

'He did not wish to do so, but he gave you loving looks from the doorway, God is my witness.' Annora's words whistled through the teeth that were always especially prominent whenever she talked about our father. She added, 'And the Blessed Virgin too.'

The Pope had not long past declared the Virgin Mary free from any stain of Original Sin, a promotion popular with the Catholics in Ireland and particularly with Annora. As if to prove the point, the Virgin had quite promptly made a personal appearance at Lourdes.

'Away with your Virgin!' Darcy scowled. 'It's a dirty damned lie about the Da.'

I would push my small hand into Annora's then, for I hated to see how her head dipped under the hard fists of Darcy's words. Even in happy times, our mother's low forehead was creased, with the air of a slap perpetually hanging around her face.

'But, Darcy, you've the pennies for to prove it is God's truth, may I never die in sin,' Annora insisted. For our after-midnight papa also pressed salt-smelling pennies into the bib-pockets of our gathered-yoke smocks, which hung in a row by the door. The appearance of pennies was infallible after one of his visits, as tangible as a new sister three seasons later. Unfortunately our father had nothing more by way of money for us, his luck being perennially down on him, according to Annora, whose luck was none too sweet itself despite extensive applications on her knees to God.

In our cottage, the Almighty lived on a crucifix in the window with a spoon-sized stoup of holy water at his feet. Apart from the pennies, the only token of our nautical father was a seashell that hung from the rafters above the deal table. I loved to stand near it and imagine the sound of the sea that had beaten and rolled it to perfect smoothness. Inside that seashell burned a tallow candle on days when Annora could afford us that luxury. On the more frequent skinny evenings, a rush light fed on stinking fish oil pooled in the pearly well of its secret stomach.

All the Swiney riches grew on our heads. Perhaps those waterfalls of hair were our true paternal gift, for Annora's greying plaits were limper than boiled string, a result of starving penances like those of her favourite saints. And there was paternal wealth in the wonder of our names: another of Annora's tales was that our father chose each one.

Darcy objected to this too. 'Is it mad you are? How could he know when we were babies how we would be in ourselves?'

'He named you,' said Annora tranquilly. 'And you grew to suit.'

Certainly Annora herself would for choice have named us for some mutilated martyr of the Faith, and raised a flock of Brigids and Teresas. Instead, our names were pagan, and as rich and fine as we were not, yet written in a pen dipped in Irish ink for all that.

Would we ever have taken off so well if we had been named Brigid or Teresa and thuslike? The 'Swiney' part of our names did us no favours. The Eileen O'Reilly, the Brannockstown butcher's runt, regularly hog-snorted Darcy on Harristown Bridge. Our surname carried a whiff of manure with it and also madness, the greatest Swiney of them all being a pagan poet-king from ten centuries past who broke a bishop's bell and threw a precious psalter into the sea and was thereafter cursed to live bird-brained and bird-hearted in a tree.

*

15

The dead man by the privy midden turned out to be a tenant evicted by the Tyntes of Dunlavin.

He was not our father.

Our village, of course, had long since made up its mind that no single sailor could have fathered both Darcy's coaly coils and Oona's milky floes. Our neighbours did not believe in the 'Phelan Swiney, Mariner' named on Annora's treasured marriage certificate and each subsequent birth entry in the parish register. Years later, even after we buried Annora in her self-laundered winding sheet, we seven hairy sisters never discussed among ourselves those whispers that followed us down the road. Yet we knew ourselves condemned as the seven bastard daughters of as many late-night sailors, a sorry fact that was said to explain our mother's stark penances and her exiled existence in the back of beyond of Harristown, which was already far, far beyond the back of beyond. For all her fervid piety, Annora did not attend Mass with us, but stole into chapel for confession only when it was deserted. Our supposed variegated paternity also accounted for the fact that the cadaverous Father Maglinn, the hungriest priest in Ireland, never called on us to claim his tea and slice of soda bread.

Our papas were as likely bailiffs or rake-makers as mariners, tutted the villagers. They must have speculated: were only exceptionally hirsute men attracted to our mother?

'A great sadness of it is that poor Annora Swiney never does her sums,' I heard a woman whisper to Mrs Godlin in the dispensary. 'They won't be paying golden guineas, the men, the creatures. And a shilling won't feed the new mouth born after.'

When she saw me staring, she clapped her hand over her mouth. But the idea was sown in my head, and images began to burn behind my eyes. I felt pity for my mother. I was all of eleven then, but mature as country children are, in earthy knowledge.

I imagined the shilling clinking on the table – and the man and Annora hurriedly re-dressing with their backs to one another, she nervously chattering, 'And if you were ever to be blessed with a little daughter, what would you dream of calling her, God increase you?'

Perhaps she hoped that each man's heaving back – I pictured it pelted like a bear's – hid her from the sin-seeking eye of Our Lord and His retributive gift of fecundity. And a few weeks later, alone, retching into the wooden bucket, it would never occur to her to betray her faith and her loving heart by putting an end to the starting of one of God's children, even though there was a Church of Ireland baker's wife in Kilcullen known to have a pair of murdering knitting needles and a delicately bloodstained basin.

I hated the brackish talk about Annora. I wanted to believe in Phelan Swiney, Mariner, even when Darcy boldly pronounced him 'a great fornicator and a feckless fellow himself' every time Annora's bucket announced a new sister. And she declared that she would set up a fierce trap for the sneaking-away legs of him, if only she were ever given notice of one of his arrivals.

But even I could see that a multiplicity of fathers might account for the dire lack of sisterly harmony among us Swineys, it being seldom that we were not at deadly combat, either one upon another, or in conspiring alliances. There was never a thing Annora could do or say to keep one of us off the neck of another.

From the grimed windows our tiny cottage issued some of the largest noises you'd hear in Ireland – noises of gnashing, squealing, screaming and weeping, as if Hell had opened a private fissure in our earth floor and a section of the Devil's congregation was taking the air in Harristown.

'Mine!' was the most frequent word shouted.

There was precious little a small Swiney might call her own in that bare cottage, and the only privacy was under a blanket. Even there, we could still hear our tormentors. Our abuse and our rejoinders were as threadbare as ourselves.

'You're a stupid scrattock.'

'No, *you're* the stupid scrattock.'

'It's you yourself who is the scrattock.'

'Scrattock!'

17

'Leave me alone, why don't you?' was next in our lexicon, followed by, 'Just close the mouth on you and be done with your ceaseless maundering.'

The fiercest portion of tears and screams issued from our twins Berenice and Enda. Darcy had taught them to hate one another in their cradles, she boasted, always feeding one at the expense of the other.

'It was never right,' Annora said, 'the way you teased those babes with the bottle, Darcy Swiney, and now look.'

With each new inch Berenice and Enda were growing to hate one another more than tenant and landlord's agent, or certain shades of yellow and purple. But like tenant and land-lord's agent, the twins grew into themselves living solely for their epic enmity. They would be nothing without it, or with-out one another; they were like the tongs and griddle by the hearth, which were themselves frequently deployed as weap-ons by Berenice and Enda, for their vendettas had a simple brutality to them.

Enda explained the little puckered birthmark on her neck by saying that Berenice had tried to gnaw her head off when they still shared close quarters in Annora's belly. One of Enda's revenges was to unpick every stitch in Berenice's drawers, fastening them with flour paste so that they fell off on the way to school. Berenice was not lacking in devices of her own. She was a genius for an ambush by the water butt, where she would hold Enda's head down until her twin nearly gurgled her last.

Darcy seemed to thrive on the twins' troubles. So much the worse for any sister who tried to make a pious peace or mend a rupture between her siblings.

'Let them be or be having you,' she told us, even after Enda left a dead crow, quickening with maggots, under Berenice's pillow.

'It's a relief to them to beat on one another,' she assured me, when Berenice retaliated by trying to stuff the crow's beak into Enda's mouth, shouting, 'Did you ate your enough of poultry yet?'

Not satisfied with Enda's bleeding lip and the great blackness of feathers she was spitting from her mouth, Berenice marched up to Father Maglinn and informed him that her twin had perished of her throat in the night and required a pit dug for her grave.

The passions of the twins toppled their siblings into two camps. You were either for one or the other. Plump Pertilly and feverish little Ida followed vivacious Berenice; blonde Oona and I were with Enda, who had a natural elegance about her. Enda was tender and sweet, brushing her favourites' hair and saving us morsels from her plate.

So Oona was guilty of leading Ida into the estate woods and leaving her there with a promise of a visit from a leprechaun. Berenice found her only when the moon was high and Ida's imagination had confected a wolf crouching in the bushes. The beast was so real to her that Berenice had to beat the bush with a stick before Ida would consent to come home. The next morning Ida herself hid by the woodpile, reaching out a sly hand to trip up Oona, leaving the pretty ankles on her flailing in the air. Then there was Oona stuffing straw under the blanket where it lay atop Pertilly so the Dunlavin banshee or the horned Witch of Slievenamon, when those ladies called on our cottage in the dead of night, would see the grand mound, think it a fine fat girl, and devour Pertilly first. Nor was I innocent. I earned Ida's little fists windmilling at my hip after she saw a piece of mischief I wrote about her on the barn wall.

The only one not aligned was Darcy, who feared no one but relied on everyone to be afraid of her. She did not scruple to give any man, woman or rabid dog the length and breadth of her tongue at any time at all, and the flat of her hard hand might win prizes for its warlike prowess too.

'It is ashamed you should be of yourselves,' were the words that most frequently issued from between Annora's gapped teeth as she gave us a clatter on the rump or shoulder or whichever fleeting bit of us she could catch. Ashamed? We rarely were that. My sisters' tempers and their fears were generally too much aroused to allow for any quiet contemplation of our

19

faults. Seven is too many for that: even if one of us had a moment's pause, she'd soon be distracted by Ida's war cries or a foaming fury of Berenice's.

But there was also the Devil's match in plain love. When I sat on Enda's warm lap, even when I was far too big for it, with Oona's gentle fingers braiding my hair, I felt safe from all the world, except for Darcy and, until the troll came to meet me on the bridge, God.

Annora raised us in the True Faith, the true faith of poverty and Irishness and oppression, not to mention illiteracy. Annora herself, like fully one quarter of the Catholics in Harristown, could not read. But she could still enforce the Lord's word like a soldier and insist that we spoke 'educated, like the ladies your father intended'. She faithfully beat us for our many sins, including the dipping of our fingers in the broken jar where she kept her donations for the poor Pope in Rome and the uttering of tongue-lovely but forbidden words like 'bejappers'. Or for mocking imitations of her voice when she wandered the garden calling and keening for the latest goosely incarnation of Phiala.

Our mother kept us clean, laundering our skin and hair in thin suds left over from the washing she took in. In the summer she brightened the grey water with the squeezed haws of the wild dog-roses. She eased our knots and molested the lice with a series of wooden combs she whittled herself by the fire of an evening – no luxury of horn, gutta-percha or rubber for the young Swiney sisters.

The creamy elegance of the Church of Ireland's spire at Carnalway was not for us either. The ruined old chapel at Harristown's Catholic graveyard served as our place of worship, and a wretched walk it was too, with the rain beating on our heads most Sundays and the slow crows making pessimistic comments all the way, and the coldness reaching up out of the earth to clutch at our legs. The fat estate sheep lifted their docked tails as we passed, reserving their most derisive choruses for us.

'Bah!' they sneered at every passing Swiney. 'Bah!'

We kept our heads down as we walked on toes that never saw a shoe except on Sundays. And when those shoes died, they were given ragged dresses and seed eyes, and served as faithful dollies. Their glory was of course their hair, for each of us placed our nightly combings in a crude wooden crib that Annora grandly called a 'hair-receiver', until there was enough to wig a dolly in our own real curls. Our mother insisted that the hairs of our heads were all numbered by the Almighty, who would expect us to account for every one on the Day of Judgement. None must ever be thrown away. In the meantime she permitted us to lend them to our dollies.

One day we would do better than our shoe darlings – grander and better – but at that time we loved our rough honeys and danced them through balls attended by swarthy foreign dukes confected from boots and briar. I regret to mention that, when not romancing dukes, the shoe dollies also fought a sight of Swiney wars: in our doll family there were no amicable feminine tea parties but rather regular slayings and grisly beatings. There were at least two full scalpings and my darling Enda's baby – always dressed the most fashionably of all our dolls – suffered her wooden head cracked in two by her twin's.

For all our internecine strife, we Swineys were clannish and secretive. We did not like to be looked at. We were chary of strangers, hiding our drabness in the tall weeds if one set foot on the sparse Swiney soil.

Only one personage regularly encroached upon the land of Swiney: the Eileen O'Reilly, the butcher's runt, who continued year on year a sworn enemy to Darcy and yet was unable to tear herself away from Swineys all the same.

It was as if she were an eighth, ghostly sister, living on the margins of our scrap of land. Though she'd never taken herself a step inside our deal door – for fear of Darcy's fists – I often found her lingering outside it, with a finger and 'shhh' upon her pale lips. I would nod and keep her secret. No matter how Darcy threatened her, or beat her, the butcher's runt would return. Her light reddish hair gave her away when she hid in the long grass; so did the single eye, blue as a cornflower, she pressed to the window, watching us, even late at night. No one missed her at home: her father drank and her mother ran to sloe gin too.

So the Eileen O'Reilly was free to spend all her time a-haunting Swineys.

3

I cannot remember a time when there was not war between the butcher's runt and Darcy. Enda always said they were born bellicose, being the same age within a week and a day. The legend was that there was a constitutional inability in each one of them to stand the sight of the other, and this from the first time they were laid side by side on the counter at the dispensary at Kilcullen where mothers took their babies to be weighed. In a minute both babies were in a mortal tangle on the floor, and the only reason they were not gnashing and biting was because they didn't have the teeth for it.

They were only eight in the summer of '54, when the Eileen O'Reilly dared Darcy to meet her at midnight in Byrne's Hollow at Cowpasture, where ghosts were known to cluster after dark. When Darcy did not appear, the butcher's runt had it all around the school that Darcy Swiney was a coward whose fierceness stretched only as far as the end of her tongue.

'Not a hair I care,' said Darcy, but she lay in wait after school and rolled the runt down the mossy bank into the Liffey.

The next day the Eileen O'Reilly crept up behind Darcy at school and hoisted the back of her skirt. Before Darcy could turn round, the butcher's runt had pinned a note to her drawers. It said: *A Penny a Look at the Forked Tail Under Here.*

Then Darcy nailed a lurid paper to a tree outside the school. It proclaimed that the runt's butcher da was wanted for digging up Famine bodies and selling their meat as rashers. She had illustrated the detail in red pencil.

The Eileen O'Reilly ripped the poster from the tree and carried it all the way to our yard.

'Come out, ye great arse of a swine!' she yelled.

Darcy was not going to be resisting such an invitation.

There followed, by all accounts, a great tournament of insults and threats that ended with the both of them dried out in the mouth and tottering on glass legs. Some of the curses that Darcy and the butcher's runt smelted in the ferocious heat of their two brains that day became general currency in Harristown for years after. They were frequently heard in our cottage, as Enda and Berenice, who witnessed it all, showed a precocious talent for tucking grand insults away in their memories for future use.

Darcy commenced it, by wishing a smothering and drowning on the butcher's runt. 'May the fishes eat you, you dirty little spalpeen! And then the worms eat the fishes. And the worms wither their guts on the nastiness of your bits inside of them.'

'Here's at you! A burning and a scorching on ye!' was the runt's retort.

'I will plant a tree in your dirty ear,' shouted Darcy, 'and slap you in its shade.'

'It is yerself that's filthied me ear wid the great black tongue on ye, so it is.'

'Stones on your meaty bones!'

Then the runt wished black sorrow on Darcy's guardian angel, 'all red-eyed from shame at havin' to do wid ye!'

According to Darcy, her guardian angel was presently sending her regards to the Devil who would carry the Eileen O'Reilly around on his pitchfork till she was putrid and dropping off in lumps.

The runt replied, 'Your heart wouldn't even make a sausage, so small and shrivelled it is, Darcy Swinehead, with seven drops of the Devil's blood inside it. Soup made of Jesus's dead bones wouldn't choke *you*, ye bold black torment.'

'Is that the way of you? You are a grand mouse-sucker and a rat-friend and a knock-knee thing besides.'

'No need for them poor sisters on yours to go hungry when ye could haunt houses for a living, great unnatural-lookin' baste that ye are.'

Darcy replied loftily, 'When I look at your face, I am proud of my rear end.'

'The sheep drop dead when they see ye, Arsey Swiney. They are happy to die.'

The beggarly brains on the runt, Darcy now suggested, could barely keep her skinny legs walking.

The Eileen O'Reilly countered, 'Three hundred hairy things to ye. May your black hair strangle ye wid its great tendrils in the night till ye're found hangin' dead from the rafthers.'

'May every maggot in your father's shop crawl up your nostrils and the dead pigs rise up on their trotters in the night and trample you flatter than a wafer.'

'I hope the lightning sthrikes ye in the privy midden so ye fall dead and mulch there, and not a dry stitch on your whole carcass.'

'May a famined dog lift its leg on you,' replied Darcy, 'until you turn entirely dirty yellow like your toenails. It wouldn't bite you, of course, for fear of getting rabies.'

'A high windy gallows for ye and a nail in the knot that hangs ye by your trembling throttle till the eyes jump out of your head and visit your cousins in the pigsty, ye great pig of a Swiney thing.'

Darcy wished that a great wave would wash the runt away to Australia, 'And a great whale kick you back to America until you are killed and cut and smashed to bits on the rocks of the shore.'

'May the Divil lep out of Hell to roast the lips off ye for a divarshin.' The Eileen O'Reilly wrinkled her small nose. 'I'm smellin' the sulphur already, so I am.'

'The crows will drink the slop of your brains. And spit it out for bitter muck.'

'Baptised bears wouldn't pray for ye, Darcy Swiney, and you lying in your pit. The Divil will play marbles wid your black eyes and take two slow days to beat your curabingo till it's raw.'

'Then he'll use your tripes for skipping ropes.'
'He will wipe his nose slime wid your liver, so he will.'
'Your mother!'
'*Your* mother!'

Then Darcy poisoned the Eileen O'Reilly.

Annora was unwell that week and had taken to her bed. Darcy had set herself up as arch-duchess of the kitchen. She was more arch-duchess than cook, and terrorised us into eating her black messes, declaring, 'If you don't like it, there must be something wrong with your tongues.'

She hounded a few drops of peppermint oil out of Mrs Godlin and some daft from a black-toothed pedlar who was shunned by everyone in Harristown. Daft was a wicked powder used to stretch out the rare quantities of sugar that anyone in County Kildare might afford themselves. You could find anything in daft, so long as it was white. Sulphate of lime, arsenic, powdered limestone and even plaster of Paris might make their way into a white dust that had the glitter and faint sweetness of sugar.

With angry hands, Darcy mixed the peppermint oil into the so-called sugar, as she had seen Mrs Godlin do when making lozenges in the dispensary. Not having gum, she added in some goose doings to make a texture you could chew on and rolled the grey-white dough into long tubes that she sliced into small pungent patties.

She laid them on a window sill to dry. She gave out ghastly threats to the rest of us for touching them. So it must be allowed that Darcy never wanted any of us hurt. But the little row of sweetums was exactly in the eye line of the Eileen O'Reilly. The girl's hands were red with all the meat she was given, but she almost never had a taste of sugar, and of course she was craving it in the desperation of her heart, as Darcy knew full well.

The lozenges had been on the sill for less than an hour when the Eileen O'Reilly was under the window, reaching up to rake a handful, which she crammed directly into her mouth.

At first they gave out that the Eileen O'Reilly had the cholera. For everything in her turned to foul liquid that issued without cease from either end of her body for seven days altogether.

No one mentioned poison but that black-toothed pedlar did not dare show his face in our village again.

When the Eileen O'Reilly had recovered enough to totter to Harristown on her twig legs, she bussed on our door and demanded that Darcy come out.

Darcy leaned out of the window instead – the very window on which she'd laid the peppermint lozenges. She asked, 'What do you want, you gobaleen?'

'Look at how I lived, though ye tried to kill me wid the daft,' shouted the Eileen O'Reilly.

'True enough it's a disappointment to me to see you living at all.'

'I rose from the dead just to curse ye, so I did. I was dead longer than Jesus, for he had only three days in his grave.'

'Prove it that I tried to kill you,' Darcy said. 'And was not the first crime a case of thieving fingers at my window sill?'

'As well ye are knowin', the evidence agin ye's in the privy,' said the butcher's runt, leaning against the wall, so weak she was.

'So why are you here?' Darcy yawned.

The feud continued year on year by way of petty violence and verbal assaults. I grew into childish consciousness always knowing the Eileen O'Reilly as part of my family, the most despised part.

Yet even the poisoning could not keep the butcher's runt away.

Perhaps the Eileen O'Reilly's furtive presence drove us even more into ourselves. Living amid the hair, our brains turning over within its springy coils, we developed a tribal identity, a faithful interiority, even amid our battles. Other people were less than real to us, or must be translated for our understanding. We Swineys came to a rare silent agreement that hair, the one thing that united us, was good, wise and strong. An individual with sparser hair than ours – nearly everyone – was looked upon with pity. The one time we encountered an entirely bald man, a visitor to our congregation, we disgraced ourselves with disbelieving laughter in seven different keys. Ordered out of the chapel, our early arrival home and Ida's round eyes gave us away. Annora lined us up for beatings, after which she had me read aloud from II Kings about the forty-two children torn to pieces by a pair of bears for mocking the bald head of Elisha the Prophet.

Only Darcy escaped the beating – Annora dared not lay a finger on her. By her late teens, Darcy was spoiled not just rotten but spoiled putrid. You could see it in her eyes, in which she was very deficient, the two she had being both small and lacking in pleasant lustre, except when she set herself up as Medusa, and stared you to petrifaction. Darcy was also taller than our mother and fierce-skilled at killing the rabbits she snared in the south field, where sweet clover grew as thick as Swiney hair. Those rabbits died in bad ways. From the noises which came from that field, it seemed that Darcy chose to skin them before they were dead.

Darcy was the goose-strangler too, of course. Days before Michaelmas, she'd be giving the chosen goose the glad eye and telling it how she'd soon be savouring a mouthful of its breast. She would always choose a Phiala if she could, to Annora's tearful distress. Once, too young to know better, I lured the latest Phiala with a trail of Indian meal and tried to hide her for her own safety under a splintered barrel I'd ringed around with branches. But the goose had no care for her own safety, and gave out a mighty cackle when Darcy called. Darcy guessed the branches were my handiwork, and escorted me by the ear to the water butt, where she plunged my head over and over again into the cold liquid, until Annora dragged her away.

That night, the late Phiala hung from the rafters. Darcy tucked two of the bird's feathers in her hair. The seashell lamp threw her magnified shadow against the wall, the feathers lending horns to her monstrous silhouette. Ida, who was clever with

28

a pencil, paused in her sums to sketch Darcy's devilish shadow. Ida's heavy breathing drew Berenice's eyes to the page. An involuntary giggle escaped from Berenice: the image was so evidently Darcy and yet so clearly Satan at the same time. A second later we were all caught in a dangerous, wild hilarity – tribal alliances briefly forgotten as we for once laughed out loud at Darcy. It took her one short moment to understand what had happened. Then we saw the dark light of her eyes, and the uncertain rumpling of her lips. We all caught our breaths. Darcy was never mocked. We had ventured upon an unknown path and we cringed away from her, holding tight to the corners of our smocks.

But instead of beating us, Darcy snatched up the row of our shoe dollies from the mantelpiece and marched out of the house. We followed her at a craven distance to the privy midden, and watched her plunge each of our darlings deep into its noisome mud. Even after copious laundering, a faint smell of manure would ever after rise from those dollies when we hugged them to our chests.

We did not laugh at Darcy again.

The Eileen O'Reilly, who had witnessed the dirty drowning of the dollies, took to warning all the Harristown children to keep away from us Swineys and our cottage. 'Ye'd be amazed and murthered at just the smell of it!' she would relate, raising her thready arms like a prophet's. 'Even their poor dollies have a stink to burn the eyebrows off ye. Not enough food to feed a worm on their table, noight on noight. And as for the clatther of tongues and the screamin' and the gnashin' and huggin' and kissin' what makes no sense alongside! A din ye might aizy hear in Dublin,' she told our schoolfellows. 'And worse nor all, that Darcy Swiney. Madder nor a sack of snakes, she is! Have ye ever seen her kill a rabbit?'

She spoke with the certainty of truth about our cottage, and she wasn't having anyone but herself getting near us. As she so often did, the butcher's runt then handed out crubeens from a basket to those children who dutifully expressed themselves substantially amazed or disapproving about all things Swiney.

'Listen to me. Don't you be having any dealings or doings wid yon hairy horror Darcy Swiney, and those ragged sisters she keeps running scared and starving!' she'd tell the boys and girls gnawing hungrily on the crisp pig's feet.

And no more they did, leaving us sisters to seethe alone in our Swineyness, increasing the concentration of it in our natures.

4

I was and ever shall be the scribe and storyteller among the Swiney sisters, a thing that started, of natural course, with reading. The words arrived in me by fate and in the form of our schoolteacher, Miss Finaughty, a romantic reed of a woman. On my very first day at school, she happily diagnosed an 'active fancy' in me and nourished it with a succession of poems and fairy tales rising very quickly to the heights of Mr Moore and Mr Dickens. Miss Finaughty watched over my reading habit with a benevolent eye, slipped pencils into my smock and saved oddments of paper for me.

'Write,' she told me. 'It's in you. I see the words twitching in your slender throat. All the tongues of dead poets in the Famine pits, someone must carry on the words that died with them, or Ireland will parch. And why not a girl to do it?'

Her eyes misted. It was said that Miss Finaughty had loved a poet who starved in the Hunger. I loved her and I wanted to serve her dead poet, and all of the everyday poets – for every Irishman is one in the roll of his tongue – whose bodies had fattened the wild dogs and whose bones whitened under hedgerows all around Harristown. Ida had to be stopped from pulling them up when she saw them.

'Yet you mustn't just write,' Miss Finaughty warned, frowning over some of my early effusions. 'You must *be* someone in order to write something.'

'Who can I be?' I asked.

'Bless you for a sweetheart,' she answered gaily. 'That is to be your adventure.'

While waiting for my own adventure, I read those of others: sailors, fairies, royalty and robbers. I was a termite among the books Miss Finaughty lent me, burrowing through them as if someone were chasing me. I loved a rich phrase if I could find one, and nursed a secret admiration for a finely tuned curse or a well-stacked piece of abuse. I tucked the words and sounds into my memory, and wrote the best of them on dry leaves that I hid in a barrel in our barn.

Fluent by six, it was I who read at bedtime to my sisters both upwards and downwards of me in age. So it was I who put us in our place from the start. Those much-fingered books of fairy tales soon gave up their heartscalding truths – that we Swineys were but humble characters, the hungriest girls in Harristown, a place where competition for that title was fierce. Once we knew about princesses and gilded goblets, we were embarrassed for our clothes of indeterminate colours with the worst patching hidden by our white smocks gathered at the yoke. We were ashamed of our bare dirty feet and the stirabout we scooped out of wooden bowls and the clucking visits from the Relief Committee bearing stern gifts of grey calico and tough blankets. Worse, even the woodcutters' children in the fairy tales had visible or respectably dead fathers, unlike the little Swineys.

A great event for Miss Finaughty was a delivery to Brannockstown school of *Bible Stories for Children* dispatched by one of the many London societies for the improvement of the incorrigible Irish. The books were bound in black and reeked eloquently of cheap leather. Red ribbons grew from their spines like the tongues of sleek eels. The very ends of the pages were dipped in gold. Such a luxury had not been seen in our bare schoolroom before. But of course there was a little drawback. Those *Bible Stories* had nothing inside but creamy-white pages. The printer had forgotten himself, which was why these grand books were deemed fit for Irish schools. Or perhaps the London doers-of-good thought that we Irish, always choking on the words gushing out of us, had no need for more of them printed on the page.

I begged two blank books from the crestfallen Miss Finaughty, and took them home, thinking their pages a fine place for Enda's pastime of drawing the clothes of great ladies and pasting fashion pictures from the newspaper. The other one was for me, to practise my letters in.

But when Darcy saw the books, and heard the story, she wheeled our barrow to the school and scooped up the entire stock. Miss Finaughty hovered about her like a blur of wind-blown grass, trying to protest until Darcy silenced her.

'Saw your dead poet blethered and blasted to a stagger in the Brannockstown shebeen last night, and you grieving all these years for him. He'd rather say he's dead than be seen with a long drink of water like yourself.'

'Your . . . your mother is much to be pitied,' was all Miss Finaughty could stammer out in reply.

'Manticory,' the teacher asked me the next day, 'for what would your sister Darcy be using those black books?'

'It is more like to be a question of wanting them, than of using them,' I explained.

But it turned out that Darcy had eloquent plans for those books.

Along with Darcy's black hair and black eyes, there came a black-and-white mind. On the side of white were all things that were pleasing to Darcy, such as presents, praise and money. On the black side you'd find household chores, too-small potatoes, recalcitrant sisters, incursions by the thin geese, empty rabbit traps.

The empty Bibles became her black books, in which she recorded all crimes and offences against Swineys and most particularly against herself. Darcy kept her black books for years. So much the worse for you, and twenty pities beside, should you find your offending self inscribed there. Those Bibles were indexed and cross-referenced, so Darcy could always find an old offence to nurse or an historical insult to avenge.

By the time I was thirteen and Darcy was nineteen, Miss Finaughty's promised adventure was writing its opening pages.

I was every taste as much in love with books as I had been at six, when all the words and sounds were newly knitted in my brain.

I'd learned something perhaps unintended from all those high-told tales of ladies and gentlemen and poor little peasant girls. I'd learned this: whoever writes the words owns the story, and whoever owns the words writes the story.

So it was with words that I now began to extract my own identity from the hot churning soup of Swineyness.

UnSwinily – for my sisters lived for the next bashing or the next potato – at teatime you'd find me still spreadeagled in the clover with a book of verses making honey in my heart. The thing is, it was my own Manticory honey – not Swiney honey. It had its singular taste and texture. Instead of bashing my sisters or their dollies, even when they grandly deserved it, I was now more than likely to write a bashing poem or song about them. It was safer that way, too, so long as they never cast an eye on my productions, which joined the dry leaves in the barrel in the barn.

As it was, Darcy tried to asphyxiate my love of poetry as soon as she detected the tendency: she would simply sit on me if she caught me reading it.

I had also to worry about Annora finding me anywhere with any book that was not the Bible or a hymnal, for she'd quickly sprinkle so much holy water on the volume that the pages would blossom with damp flowers and I'd be in sore trouble with Miss Finaughty, who regarded every printed poem as tenderly as the baby she would never have.

Darcy had a particular hate on my reading in the sweet clover of the south-facing field where she baited her rabbit traps. She made sure I had a bad memory of every time she found me there, and a bruise too. I remained stubbornly fond of the place, however, and for several reasons. The Harristown rabbits and I shared a fondness for sucking the sweetness from the clover heads that massed there. I had also a preference for that spot for it delighted me to free the little brown beasts from Darcy's traps before the slow crows wheeled in to peck their eyes, and before Darcy herself came to deliver a worse fate.

She never caught me in the act of liberation. But one hungry summer afternoon she surprised me in the field before I could release a trapped rabbit. I clutched my book to my chest. Darcy took out her suspicions on my reading matter.

'Is it reading you are? Some old poems, is it?' She slapped me on the ear, none too lightly. 'Here's poetry for you – "Manticory" rhymes with "rancid boring". Away with the verses. Better use the pages for candle-spills. If I catch you here again with a book, I'll knock the priest's share out of you.'

She opened the cage and put her hands on the rabbit I'd been too slow to save. 'This is what will happen to you if I find you here again.'

She grasped one back leg and swung the beast against a tree trunk so hard that its little head flew right off its body, blasting me with tepid blood and brains.

It was in that same field and in that same hungry summer that I found the most likely reason for Darcy always chasing me out of the clover.

I'd just freed another rabbit and was carefully resetting the snare when I saw what seemed to be a wooden spoon raising its curved head amid the tall cow parsley on the edge of the field. Although I'd not noticed it before, the spoon had clearly been standing there for years. It was grained like driftwood and had begun to give itself up to the rot and moss. I parted the cow parsley for a closer look and saw that a second spoon had been tied horizontally across the vertical one, bound by tattered rags into a small cross. The letters *PS* were carved into the bowl of the first spoon. Under them: *November 1854.*

Ireland was full of such improvised graves. We Catholics were not allowed to bury our dead with the old rites. Few could afford coffins or headstones. The fields, dense with Famine corpses buried too close to the surface, were frequently reaped by wild dogs.

PS, I thought. *Rest peacefully. I'll not disturb you.*

I patted the cow parsley back into shape and thought of how Darcy was forever driving me out of this field, and always throwing back in Annora's face her story of our father Phelan Swiney, Mariner, and his salty pennies.

35

I did my sums. Ida had been born in late 1855, and there'd been no more daughters to follow her.

Could that have been because our father was dead?

The rest of us had been tiny in November 1854 – myself aged two, Pertilly one, Oona just a baby, Berenice and Enda a mere six.

Darcy, though, had been eight by then: Darcy who had always towered like a Gorgon over the rest of us. Even as a child she'd had a pair of terrible weapons hung at the end of her arms, always ready for a beating or a throttling. Darcy had already poisoned the Eileen O'Reilly with daft that very year. Even then she'd had a black violence at the core of her, and at the same time a lack: a lack of what reins in violence, whether shame or sympathy or a mixture of both.

Too many stories entirely, you will say, and myself with an imagination over-ripened by the lushness of fairy tales. But in the frightening country of our Harristown childhood, who else – my fever of logic rampaged – could have killed *PS* but Darcy?

Even if she was just a child, even if she couldn't smite his head against a tree like a rabbit's, Darcy could have found a way. She always did.

It was not true that Ireland was devoid of venomous reptiles, I thought. The Eileen O'Reilly had said Darcy had seven drops of the Devil's blood in her body.

Had Phelan Swiney, Mariner, crossed his eldest daughter in some way, and suffered the horrid consequences? If only there'd been black books back then in 1854. I could have hunted them out of their hiding place and read what she had scribbled inside.

Perhaps Darcy had laid a snare for our father, as she had threatened to do. And poisoned him after, to stop him breeding more babies on our frayed mother? She'd practised, after all, on the poor Eileen O'Reilly, who'd barely survived. Annora could have put the dead man secretly in the ground. As no one ever saw him, no one in Harristown would have missed Phelan Swiney, Mariner, thinking him away on a ship in New York or Australia. Annora would of course have kept the secret; she would not want her eldest daughter carried off for correction in a lunatic asylum. She would not want the rest of us growing up with a murderess for a sister.

It all fitted, was all of a piece. No wonder Darcy did not believe in our father! She *knew* he no longer lived on this earth!

And it made sense and more sense of Darcy's own fascination with anything to do with death, particularly bloody and untimely death. She'd told me herself that she had learned to read only so as to peruse the handbills about grisly homicides in Dublin, a habit to which she owed her grandiose vocabulary for threats and violence and her repertoire of ripe gallows curses. Her only regular use for books was in throwing them at misbehaving sisters or thin geese. Darcy was in love with her own death, too, and a romantic spectacle she made of it. She was always collecting grave-goods to be buried with her in the coffin that she endlessly redesigned under the speckled marble tombstone she'd already picked out from the Clery's catalogue that Mrs Godlin kept at the dispensary in Kilcullen. Despite being the most dangerous thing in County Kildare, Darcy cherished a sentimental inkling that she herself would make a young corpse, which put her in a hurry for her rights and deserts. When Annora denied her an extra penny for a ribbon, she'd hiss, 'Well, put it in my coffin, when you're sorry. Perhaps you'll tend to me properly then.'

And Annora would flinch, cross herself and weep beyond consolation.

That Sunday I watched Darcy singing in the chapel, her black hair billowing like a black shroud. She caught my eye and sent a murderous stare back at me.

Darcy's hymn-singing had for years drawn people from all the hamlets around to our tiny ruin of a chapel of a Sunday. Father Maglinn encouraged Darcy to leave her hair loose, and he had her stand where the morning light fussed through the one stained-glass window, conferring an oily sheen on her black crinkles. In fact, none of us Swiney sisters was without a pleasing voice, and a good head of Saturday-washed hair, or a smock so white that it would hurt your eyes, thanks to Annora's laundering. And so, as each of us was confirmed, we took our places beside Darcy in the gaudy light of the chapel window, and would have almost enjoyed the sound of our voices in rare harmony, had it not been for the Eileen O'Reilly in the third pew, and her remarks about Darcy.

'It'd be one on them the black-horned witch of Slievenamon up there,' she would observe, 'that old Arsey Swiney conceitin' herself an angel from Heaven when she's just a murthering hairy harridan, so she is.'

No one shushed the Eileen O'Reilly for everyone owed her father the butcher.

Murthering hairy harridan, I thought. Could the Eileen O'Reilly know something of the *PS* buried in the clover field?

Now I asked myself, what would happen to me if I mentioned what I'd found? I feared that it would likely end in a pair of crossed spoons and cow parsley above me and the Harristown worms busy below.

5

By then I knew already there was *something* about our hair. Those books of fairy tales, which once taught us we were humble characters, now had other information to impart. At exactly the same time our Swiney hair was lengthening and thickening beyond anything reasonable, there was a reawakening of interest in those pretty old stories. Scandalous artists away in London were painting tableaux of long-haired maidens. Fashionable poets were remouthing the old hairy folk tales. Women with sumptuous hair were being defined as goddesses, princesses even, as models and muses for these great young men with great thoughts about hair: hair and love, hair and death, hair and more hair filling up the margins of books and the frames of paintings till they were fit to burst, wrapping itself around the necks of helpless men, choking them.

Like Rapunzel's prince, the artists' models – girlish nobodies like ourselves – were climbing their own ropes of hair to a higher state. Their very names were known, alongside the artists': girls born in dubious circumstances and with nothing and no more morals than were necessary. We Swineys were already being pointed at and frankly remarked on for the hair our vanished papa had left in our blood. As that summer dwindled into autumn, I began to straighten my back and walk on my bare feet with my head held higher. I did not know where my hair would lead, but it seemed that a great story lay in store: it simply was not yet legible to me.

But, as the fairy tales taught, whenever womanly parts draw eyes to them, young women shall also know danger. Our Swiney hair also aligned us with Rapunzel, betrayed, hurt, confined in the frail frame of her own helpless body as much as in the tower from which she so badly needed to be rescued. Our hair knitted us to vanquished Medusa, tongueless mermaids, the stripped and shamed Lady Godiva.

At Mass, my sisters and I would kneel in front of Father Maglinn, our hair aflow, the trembling in his hand communicated via the wafer on our tongues. Then we would rise to see his eyes crooked with a queersome madness and his fingers still aflitter. What I did not realise then was this – it was the Swiney hair that did that to him. At confession in the little shack he'd contrived in the ruins of the chapel, he always asked me to thread a single hair through the grate for him to hold, so he could 'know the truth' of my sins. By the end of my confession, he'd invariably futtered it right out of my head. I watched it disappearing through the grate like a very slender baitworm.

And I for one was about to be made to feel the power and peril of my red hair in a most personal and startling way, and me as yet nothing at all but a red-haired schoolgirl of thirteen thin years with calluses rasping on her chilly feet as she ran towards Harristown Bridge with a book of stories slapping in her pocket and no thoughts at all of troll gentlemen with ivory hairbrushes wanting to get going with her in a copse.

If I'd been detained by a pebble between my toes, or had rested on a stile to steal the read of a tale, and I had never crossed paths with him, then I'd never now be asking myself if there's a market for dried tears in handkerchiefs sold by the square inch to those who prefer their heartbreaks worn and second-hand.

He was waiting for me on the bridge as I pelted home late and solitary from school, a man tall as a standing stone, with the last of the sun pulling a great shadow out behind him.

It is the troll of the bridge, I thought, *and me with my pockets empty of tribute. Unless it is a book of stories he's after.*

But this was not one of Miss Finaughty's fairy tales. It was Harristown, and it was Ireland, and it was my undersized self. A lilting way with words was of no use to me now. I felt the heat of the man's eyes on my face, my hips and the nakedness of my feet. My scalp hedgehogged; little pinpricks bit the backs of my hands and numbed my tongue.

My feet kept walking, however, for home lay on the other side of the troll and behind me lurked a glooming copse and then a mile of bare autumn field before the next dwelling. My sisters had long since gone ahead of me while I havered over the lending shelf.

My legs faltered a yard in front of him. He was a stranger of middle years, full-bellied and fine-dressed; not some Famined local fellow. In elegant English, he stated politely, but with no expectation of a refusal, that he would give my hair one hundred strokes of the handsome ivory brush he now produced from his pocket.

'It would give me a sizeable drop of pleasure,' he said simply, like some sober, regular gentleman. 'I saw you coming from a way off and I told myself, "This is a girl worth waiting on a bridge for. A girl with hair like that." '

'I'd thank you kindly not to, sir,' I pleaded.

He took two steps towards me and lifted my plait, grinning like a fox.

'Now that is something like hair!' he shouted. 'Is it four foot long this thing and thicker than my leg, and red as blood, and you still not fully grown underneath its great weight?'

He wrenched my plait high above my head, spinning me around on it.

'So?' he demanded, when he stopped.

'I am thirteen, sir,' I told him, my eyes dizzied and hot with pain.

'And is it a woman you are yet?'

'I do ... do ... not think so, your honour.'

He slackened his grip on my hair but he did not release it. 'Better and far better,' he gloated, rubbing my plait against his cheek. 'And look at the eyes on you, girl. Green as glit.'

This last was no great compliment, for glit was what we in those days called the weed that crusted the summer-stale ponds. But the fact that he paid me such attention was what kept me standing in front of him, just as a doe-rabbit may patiently await the ministrations of the fox whose golden eye flatters her with a stare, even if the fox thinks of her not as a fine specimen of an Irish rabbit but as tender meat and his only interest is to part her from her fur and her life.

My knees shook and my wits began to tick. Of course I dared not ask, 'Who are you at all?' From his clothes, I was beginning to suppose this man a very great personage of the kind I had never myself met – a landlord. I was as awed as if receiving a Visitation from God.

The man pocketed his ivory brush and caught up the end of my plait with both hands. Now he was unravelling it fast, the white fingers on him furrowing deftly through its redness. He grunted.

That grunt I knew for a sin.

Yet still I stood still, mesmerised.

'That's a fierce amount of hair you have there, now I see it all undressed,' he said. 'And is it not a shocking hour of the evening for a girl to be walking abroad completely alone in nothing but a smock and such a plain grey calico dress, and poor, patched stuff at that?'

He pinched a piece of it between the fingers of his other hand and then lifted my skirt so the cool of the evening was suddenly sharp around my thighs. 'And a linsey-woolsey petticoat so thin and so very short.'

I swayed, inebriated by his clear sense of entitlement. Perhaps this was what gentlemen did, I thought. I had never been addressed in any manner of means by a gentleman before. Phelan Swiney, Mariner, our absent father, had not supplied anything by way of knowledge as to how to deal with men. I knew only that I was less than this gentleman and that therefore I should serve him as best I could. I feared to mortify Annora with uncivil behaviour on my part.

Certainly his voice was so sure and steady that I was a tint persuaded by the implication that both the hour and the shortness of the petticoat were grievous offences I myself had foisted upon him. I felt a shameful creature entirely. I blushed, for it was five days since my last confession and the sins must have been piling up in me. And even if they weren't, the man's hands were mighty paddles and he had two feet of height on me. He had already shown that he did not scruple to hurt me.

Slowly, he lowered his nose to my hair parting, and took himself a deep relishing sniff and let out another great grunt. 'There must be something in the rain hereabouts,' he mused. 'I have . . . *seen* . . . a ten-year-old prodigy of curls in Ploopluck and a creditable head by Jigginstown House. But *this*,' – he raised a hank of my hair to his mouth and bit on it – '*this* is the best yet.'

Seen, was it? And was he also so unkind to their hair?

My heart swooped and rolled like a mill wheel so that I was sure he must hear its clattering. Its noise woke up my sleeping senses. I had mistaken myself to trust that a gentleman was always a gentleman. But I had left it too late to object to his landlordly ways. By allowing them, I had fallen in with him on the way to some fearful kind of badness.

I began to raise my trembling, ineffectual fist. He took hold of my arm. 'Look at this little nub of an elbow out at the sleeve! Shall we retire now to that copse over there?' he said thickly. 'And I shall lie down in that pleasant soft grass and you will hang this hair like a tent all over me. And I can put some manners on its great wildness with my brush.'

He wound his other hand around my hair and used it to drag me towards the trees.

My scalp afire with hurting, I whimpered, and flung my eyes around. The rat-grey back of Harristown House hunched in the distance, its blank windows indifferent to me. The lane was deserted in both directions, with nothing but eddies of the dust rising that we in County Kildare deem 'fairy-blast'. It was, for a rarity, not raining, though the slow crows hung like widows' laundry on every still-sodden branch. The light was dimming and the lowering sky took on a magical, churning quality, half of silvery gnats and half of my own giddy terror, by which the clumps of moss that beetled the parapet now seemed to commence to crawl and swarm. Below me to the right, the limpid Liffey flowed into the seven maws of the bridge, which mashed its composure into foaming ruin on the other side.

No more could I hold back that man's desires than the river could resist that bridge. He was back at my parting, sniffing like a dog and moaning like a sick person asleep. His arms snaked round to press me against his thighs, where something thrummed against my unwilling chest as if he swished a fox's tail before the fatal lunge.

'I'm going to have you now,' he told me.

6

That troll gentleman and I were halfway into a bush when a horse's clop struck the road from Brannockstown way. A scorch of a swear roared out of the man. I shook his teeth off my hair, rolled my whole weight upon the elbow whose fist was far up my skirt and sprang to my feet. I stamped hard on the hand that tried to claw at my ankle and kicked the ivory hairbrush deep into the bushes. Then I ran up the path towards home, a madness of tears puddling down my face. Apart from my own breath and pelting feet, everything was suddenly so quiet you could hear the milky grass stems parting the earth and the slow crows crunching the snails' shells for their flesh. It was too much quietness; it forced into my head an idea for evading trollish attentions for evermore.

'You're that late coming home with yourself, and looking like something pulled through a hedge backwards,' growled Darcy when I erupted through the cottage door. 'Mooning over the book stack, was it, Manticory? Your potato's gone cold waiting for you—'

'But I saved it for you,' Annora assured me. 'It's still got God's goodness in it.'

Averting my wet face, I lunged straight at the press drawer where Annora kept her mending scissors. I was out of the door in a moment, with Darcy complaining, 'And now what is ailing the creature?'

Behind the woodshed, I held the iron beak open over my unravelled plait, still slick at the ends with the wetness of the troll gentleman's mouth.

Poison to kill, I thought, *those slavers of his on my hair. No amount of washing will see them off.*

In my shaking hands the scissors chattered in the manner of a cat who sees a bird. I rehearsed in my mind the sound of the metal shearing through my hair. I let the beak close an inch, and a single curl whispered to the ground. Then Berenice came bustling round the corner and stopped dead to see me there like that. She screamed.

Berenice could not scare it out of me, the reason for my flirting with the scissors, for I knew there was shame in what had nearly happened by Harristown Bridge and feared the most of it being pinned upon myself. I feared blame and a beating. Berenice ran for Darcy. Then I had the cruelty of her hands on my hair until my sight crumbled at the edges. Only when she placed her knee upon my neck did I mutter an incoherent confession that included my vision of the troll swishing a fox's tail and the moss seeming to crawl across Harristown Bridge in the giddy twilight. Still Darcy's hands did not leave the hurting heat around my scalp. Faintly I heard her laughing, 'Not a troll but a foxy rich gentleman then!'

Soon she was berating me. 'What have you got the feet for? Sure you could outrun an old man in breeches, and you with divided drawers and skinny legs like a chicken, you miserable bliggard. What is it you are? Now tell me what he looked like, exactly.'

She left me sobbing by the privy midden. As she walked off, she made a swishing motion with her right hand behind her. 'Like this, was it, the old fox's tail?'

I sobbed harder.

She turned and swished her left hand in front of her thighs this time. 'Or was it like *this* instead? Don't you know the difference between the front and back of a male creature yet, and you brought up in Harristown, you tralloping great cretin!'

She laughed again and went on her way, waving a threatening finger over her shoulder at me. 'Don't tell anyone else, do you hear? It'll be the worse for you if you do.'

I rolled myself into a jointy ball and wept until I fell into a recurring dream in which the parapets of Harristown Bridge rolled open to devour me in a hungry leer. My dream feet kept approaching, for I had nowhere else to go, and each time I was swallowed up and crushed by its stones.

It was fully dark when I was awoken by a rustling near my head. A hand reached out of the long grass and offered me the corner of a smock on which to blow my nose.

The Eileen O'Reilly, the butcher's runt, squatted down beside me, so close that I smelled the manure of frightened beasts on her shoes.

'What is it, Manticory Swiney? Is ye took sick on yourself, is it?'

I nodded, whimpering, 'But shouldn't you be at home, and the moon high up now?'

'Sure they're that busy they never miss me so. Or scuttered with the gin so it's better to be out of sight.' Her voice caught on the last words. I gave back the damp handful of smock and she blew her own nose on the other corner. We sat together in the companionable misery of silence punctuated by little tearing sobs.

'Is that a book in your pinny?' she asked me presently.

'It is,' I said, showing her my tattered little volume of stories.

'I wish I could fill a page like ye do, Manticory Swiney,' she said. 'And read. But the words do swim in front of my eyes like tadpoles themselves.'

Popular among the pupils for her crubeens alone, the butcher's runt was generally in disgrace with my beloved Miss Finaughty. She was still at school, despite the nineteen years on her. They were masked by her slightness and the fact that she had failed to master her letters beyond a young child's clumsy runes. The Eileen O'Reilly was a proud one, though. There was no other girl who could approach her in that respect. So she pretended that she had her letters: she pretended bravely, evidently having a good ear and a memory to match. But I had noticed how, when called to the blackboard, she always struggled to place her 't's and 'h's in appropriate conjunction; her 'p's were back to front and her 'h's sometimes somersaulted upside down.

'I'll teach you to read,' I offered. 'There's a great pleasure in the thing once you stop suffering over it.'

47

'See the big words trippin' out of your mouth, even in the state ye are in,' she marvelled. 'Big but worth the money.'

The Eileen O'Reilly commenced to cry again. 'Would you really be so kind, and me always raggin' on your sister Darcy?'

I murmured, 'It is the greatest comfort to me that you do. Consider it by way of thanks to me.'

Darcy's voice boomed out of the dark, 'Well isn't this so very cosy? And is it the runt having herself a little old snivel? Perhaps she'd like something to snivel about?'

'Bad manners to ye, Darcy Swiney. Ye are a baste of a girl for wanting to be fought wid—'

I felt the blow to the Eileen O'Reilly's ear as if I had taken it myself. She stumbled off into the darkness of the lane, howling, 'I'll call the consthables on ye, Darcy Swiney. And up that arse on ye with a crooked stick besides.'

Darcy harrumphed and pummelled me to my feet. I watched her face anxiously for any sign that she had overheard the part of my conversation with the Eileen O'Reilly in which I promised to teach the girl to read. But Darcy was muttering cheerfully again about the foxy gentleman on the bridge. Then she stopped short and glared into my face.

'Were you telling the butcher's runt about him at all?' she demanded. 'Is that what you were moaning and weeping about?'

With the full force of truth, I answered, 'No, I would not tell her any more than I would tell . . . the seaweed boy.'

Satisfied, Darcy hauled me inside the cottage, where Enda folded me in her arms. 'Manticory, I was that worried! Hours, you've been out there. Come here, sweetheart, you're wet as dew! For why do you look so sorry?'

Annora poured me a thimbleful of buttermilk and kissed the top of my head while I drank it. She wiped the tears off my face with a clean rag.

Then, and every stretched minute afterwards, I longed for the solid comfort of confessing everything to Enda and it was sorely lonesome to keep a secret from her. I longed for Annora to take my part and bring down God's wrath on the troll. But I was too afraid to disobey Darcy's injunction of silence, especially because

I could not fathom her delight in the situation or her calculating look every time she laid eyes on me for the rest of the week.

Nor could I meet Miss Finaughty's eye the next day or rejoice in the volume of Thackeray she pressed into my hand.

'Are you sickening for something?' she asked.

The Eileen O'Reilly was not at school. I worried that Darcy had deafened her for life with that blow or put some great hurt across her brain.

I managed to keep the secret of the man on the bridge until Sunday. By then I had decided that not even Darcy would have me withhold him from God. I calculated finely, finding I was slightly less afraid of Darcy than of a long slow roast in Purgatory. For my confession, I struggled to assess whether my part in the incident constituted a venial, grave or mortal sin, so I listed it as an evil that was a tint worse than a sharp word to Ida, somewhere between grave and mortal.

When I mumbled my little rigmarole about how I had disobliged a fine gentleman on Harristown Bridge, Father Maglinn tugged hard at the single hair I'd fed as usual through the grate for him to hold.

'So you tempted a man away to a copse?' He began to ply a welter of questions as to the disposition of various bodily parts, the man's and my own. I could not force myself to revisit the scene in such detail; I cried silently.

'But is it a good girl you still are yourself?' Father Maglinn demanded squeakily.

Was I still a good girl myself? I assured him in sobs that I was, but the fact was that his very query had just possessed me with the opposite of goodness. I was suddenly seething with black anger from my scalp to my bony behind numbing on the wooden bench.

For should not the priest have asked, 'Were you grossly imposed on, poor child? Where is the divil that did it? You shall be comforted and the evil done unto you shall be dealt with!'

I was reminded of my confession by a rasp at the grate. Father Maglinn was huffing like bellows.

'Is there any other sin you'd like to be telling me about?' he asked greedily.

I blurted, 'I think Darcy did away with our father and buried him in the clover field.'

'What's that you're blethering? Phelan Swiney dead?' asked the priest. 'Your mind is running away with you, child, tugged along by that heathen-coloured hair on you. 'Tis round the village that you've your nose in some book every second minute. The stories are breeding in you like worms, child. Don't be trying to load your sins on your poor sister Darcy. She's very frightful in herself, that girl, I'll give you, but your wanton slander is the worse evil. Ten Hail Marys just for that alone. And for the rest . . .'

He laid a clatter of penances on me.

I did not say them. I had some other words for God and his henchman Maglinn. God had sent the English and the Famine down on Ireland. He had allowed Darcy to be the way she was. And as God saw all, so He had seen the troll on Harristown Bridge. Had He sent down a fork of lightning to spear that man through his dark heart? No, He had countenanced the evil quite tranquilly. Bad luck to Him! I shouted my thoughts out loud to the hedgerows on the way home, half expecting them to wither at the root. They did not, just to prove my point.

I brooded a week on His failings, until Darcy beat the back of my legs with a rake, 'To put the smile back on you, which would be a small improvement on that sad puss you're wearing.'

Annora dosed me with something swarthy in a bottle from the Kilcullen dispensary. When Miss Finaughty asked me what was ailing me, I simply shook my head.

'And where is the Eileen O'Reilly?' she asked my assembled schoolfellows. 'Does anybody know?'

Two dozen faces answered her with hungry silence.

Mass, the following Sunday, merely confirmed me on my Godless path, for I received the additional revelation that half the men in the chapel, while watching the Swiney girls at song, were doing the same thing with their eyes as the gentleman had done on the bridge. I even saw some fingers coiling and uncoiling in their laps as they mimicked my Harristown Bridge gentleman's unravelling of my hair. I imagined foxtails swishing behind them in their pews. There would never be any getting away from them. The men would be doing the same at St Joseph's Chapel over in Yellow Bog and at the Sacred Heart in Kilcullen. The whole of County Kildare, no – Ireland – was full to the brim of men who loved to prey on girls' hair, the brutal-looking foxy devils! I clamped my teeth down on the communion wafer and crunched God's Body in angry bites.

Was it only the Catholics? The third Sunday after the troll, on the way to chapel, I told my sisters I was cramping in the belly. Darcy eyed me sharply. I felt her black gaze on my back as I hobbled away, theatrically resting against the sodden trunks of trees from time to time until I believed myself safe from scrutiny.

Instead of returning home, I ran down the back paths to Carnalway where the Anglicans kept their so-called Church of Ireland establishment. Annora would have wanted me exorcised merely for standing in its graceful shadow. I hid behind the La Touche family crypt by the graveyard and crept into the outer vestibule only after the service had started so that I might observe proceedings while the congregation had its back to me. I peered up at the polished wooden barrel of a roof and read the words *Holy, Holy, Holy* picked out in Gothic gold script over blue in an arch above the altar. Annora's frail influence proved stronger than I'd thought it could be for I began to shake. The heretics chanted their unholy songs and I felt myself close to fainting. A shaft of sunlight gilded the clean heads of the men in the last row, the one closest to me. I emitted a quiet sob and one of those heads turned to me. It was the man from Harristown Bridge, holding his hymn book in the hand he'd laid on me.

At the same moment, Darcy's hand clapped the back of my neck.

'That's him, is it?' she hissed in my ear. 'Your foxy old troll?'

She rubbed her third finger against her thumb. Then she pointed to me, struggling in the custody of her other hand. She pressed her finger to her lips.

51

He nodded, bloodlessly.

Darcy grinned like a snake and dragged me outside. When the service was over, the man emerged quickly, ahead of the congregation.

Darcy impaled him on the trajectory of her stare. He writhed a bit and then his morale settled down to die. Behind the La Touche crypt, with me crumpled at her feet, he counted the coins into Darcy's hands until she unfixed her eyes from him.

When my sisters came tramping home from chapel, I was sitting on the bob-seat by the fire, stirring seaweed soup in the three-legged pot on the backstone, and reading a Bible verse to Annora. The tears had stiffened on my cheeks and my chest had ceased its heaving. Darcy was out in the yard, patting down the soil under which she had just buried her bounty.

She's a good one for burying things, I noted sourly.

7

How much Grey Manchester, White Richmond, White Duchess and Drab Sateen lacing passed through Annora's wet hands in those thin years? She was nearly transparent with the taken-in washing and with the wringing of her hands over the state of her purse.

Like many Catholic girls, Darcy and the twins were earning now, crocheting Thornton lace panels and boudoir slippers, seated around a single candle with three bottles placed in front of it to magnify the light. But they had come into the business too late. The rival lace-makers of Clones were in the ascendant. And the thin geese were overly fascinated by the lace-making. Every so often, one of them caused a great commotion by flying up to the window and launching itself through a lace flounce in its frame, ruining the work of three days. Poor tousled Ida was kept home from school to chase the geese away. School was not doing for her what it should, anyway, on account of what Annora called her 'airy fits'.

Evenings, I myself was put to work writing missives for the many Harristown folk who did not have their letters. Joe the seaweed boy brought me commissions from his own village on the coast to supplement my earnings. Unbeknownst to Darcy, I did Joe free favours for his mother. His brother was a Fenian who'd run off to America on her. Joe's mother relied on me to read his letters to her boy, who memorised them and repeated them all the slow way home. The journey took Joe an age because his horse had been bled too many times in the Hunger and walked like the corpse it nearly was.

The united labours of the Swiney sisters did not provide

enough to feed us. And all the while we were trying to grow, and our prodigious hair wound like a voracious parasite around our heads, seeming to consume all our small helpings of food before it reached our stomachs.

'The Lord will open a gap for us soon,' Annora promised, and she offered up novenas for the rich ladies of Dublin to prosper in their love of lace and for a long-distance romance to bloom between an illiterate Harristown labourer and a girl away in Dublin to keep me in love letters.

Darcy wanted more than seaweed soup and the barley stir-about, which was no longer made with buttermilk since the last cow died, but was thinned to skilly with water. The troll gentleman's bounty had soon been spent on a new hat. Darcy wanted the best of everything, and plenty of it.

Even as the poorhouse in Naas pointed a finger at the Swiney cottage, Darcy was after elegance, and cream. And salted herring from Mrs Diarmid, who sent to Cork for a barrel of fresh from time to time.

'Phooey! And is the Lord going to see to the new dress I deserve?' Darcy would demand. 'Does the Lord personally expect me to go in rags, is it? And eat skinny slops? So much the worse for Him!' She swung a fist at the seashell lamp.

'You've always had an extra ruffle round your smock more than anyone else. And the biggest of the potatoes. God shall see that your bad temper brings you great sorrow, to be sure, Darcy,' warned Annora.

Darcy was not long about an answer. 'My temper shall bring sorrow to others, I believe.' She grinned at me and I cowered in my seat.

'Don't you care to bring a drop of happiness to your mother?' whinnied Annora. 'Out of daughterly love, Darcy?'

'I have seen you trying to bring happiness to a goose by giving her a bowl of oat mash. But that is not for the love of the goose. It is for the love of her old drumsticks when she's dead.'

Annora wrung her hands some more. 'Don't be plaguing me, I beg you. You know I never eat the poor Phialas. And if anyone deserves a new gown it is Ida, for she's scarcely decent.'

She pointed to Ida's sorry crumple of a dress that had been worn by six sisters before her. Each of us had intensified its humbleness with rips, stirabout and goose doings. Ida had added a new injury to every faded insult.

'Ida is a dull dog. She suits a rag. Better not to draw attention to her with fancy clothes,' observed Darcy. 'But I'm a different case. Poverty hates me. I must *dress*.'

'Poverty is afraid of you,' whispered Annora, 'the divil you are. Well, has it come to this then?'

She rose and rifled through a drawer of the dresser, producing a smeared business card. 'It is a wig-maker from Dublin who called here last week when you were in chapel. He wants to buy your hair. He said he'd give cash money for it.'

Darcy snatched the card, roaring, 'And why did you keep this from me?'

'I ... I ... don't want to sell my hair,' whimpered Ida.

'Would you prefer to starve to death and use it for your shroud?' Darcy asked. 'For all you'll get to eat here, that's your choice. No, it's not your choice. Your doting mother already chose to let you starve, hiding this card away.'

Then Annora had to avert her eyes, and put her hands over her ears. She tried to fold her thin mouth over her large teeth, while Darcy gave her a punishing verdict on her mothering. But just as Darcy was warming to her rant, and had begun to enjoy the creature, she stopped suddenly and looked at her sisters one by one. Each of us dropped our eyes and mumbled something apologetic, as was always best in such a case. She didn't hear us. Darcy's lips were creased in an awful smile and those hooded black eyes were sequinned with rare, happy highlights.

'Wet the tea,' she ordered Annora. 'And all sit down. Manticory, fetch me some paper and a pencil. No one talk.'

Annora crossed herself. I was relieved to see the Eileen O'Reilly's blue eye bulging at the window for the first time in a fortnight. The left side of her head was bandaged.

'I'm freckened,' whispered Ida, plucking a long strand from her head and winding it round her wrist for comfort.

We all were, brimful of fear, and me most of all that it was something to do with the troll on the bridge.

For all the signs were there.

Darcy was in possession of an idea.

8

Darcy would have gone out on her own, I'm sure of it, if she hadn't smelled more money in our joined-up attractions. Your first thought might be that she'd set us up as female prize fighters, given the twins' proclivities for war. There was fuel enough in the bad blood among the two Swiney tribes to deliver a rampant spectacle on the stage. In the absence of food and pleasant weather, there was moreover a great appetite for bashing in Ireland in those days – boxing matches and street fights were the bloody joy of the poor.

But that was not Darcy's idea for turning a penny.

She drew deep on her cup of tea, settled back in her chair and announced, 'We can sell our hair and keep it too.'

Fearful thoughts stumbled through my mind, bumping into one another and falling asunder. Thanks to my troll gentleman, Darcy now knew that men would hand over money in exchange for what the Swiney hair did to them.

'The more hair we show, the more they'll pay,' she said. 'Seven times over.'

Annora protested, 'I'll not have you doing anything immoral, Darcy Swiney.'

'Very far from immoral it shall be,' said Darcy loftily. 'We shall make something of ourselves by way of the very singing voices and the hair that God gave us. What could be more moral than that?'

'There's a stupendous mass of lying somewhere in those words there,' fretted Annora. 'But I cannot find it.'

'You cannot,' Darcy agreed.

A performing septet, 'the Swiney Godivas', was conceived that day in Darcy's tempestuous brain, where it buzzed like a headache until she had written it all down – laboriously, in her bat-wing script – on a large piece of brown paper, including diagrams, lists of dances and sisters matched to solo songs. We sat in silence, watching her while our tea cooled undrunk. As her plan unfolded before us, I knew that I would never now be safe from troll gentlemen with foxtails, for Darcy was planning to deliver me to them again and again, and for profit.

The following week Darcy devoted to scaring new shoes for us out of neighbouring children. There was a rumour at school that Darcy sharpened her considerable elbows on a plough-share every night. Only the Eileen O'Reilly stood up to Darcy, kicking both her shins for her with a sharp black boot, and letting fly with a stream of blasphemy that would flay the Devil's rosy ears and give Him pause for thought. For good measure, the butcher's runt concluded, 'The curse of Black Cromwell on ye!' – this being the very worst of our Kildare lexicon at that time.

Darcy beat the Eileen O'Reilly with a hawthorn switch and left her welted, snivelling and shoeless in the dusty road, crying, 'And if Beelzebub don't take your rotten heart straight to his fiery bower for roasting, Darcy Swiney, it's a wonder.'

No wonder, I thought, *for the Devil would take one look at Darcy's face and know it for His own likeness, and blow it a kiss on Sundays.*

Darcy marched me past the Eileen O'Reilly, and I kept my eyes lowered as if I cared nothing for her pains. Winking would have seemed to make light of her injuries, so I tried to shame her less by seeming not to notice them.

I had to content myself with Darcy's black straw hat, which she'd hung up to dry in the yard after a drenching. I lowered the line a discreet amount and filled the hat with Indian meal. The thin geese obliged me by leaping up to rifle the hat's crown with their sun-coloured beaks until it hung in shreds from its peg.

'And that is one for the Eileen O'Reilly,' I whispered to myself.

And the next day she and I began meeting in a hedge near Harristown Bridge for lessons after school. I watched her bruises bloom and fade as she bent over the writing primer I'd borrowed from the schoolroom for her. Her stub of pencil pressed hard into the page. She proved quick and lively beyond my expectations. Within a few weeks we had tamed her consonants and taught her verbs and nouns to live in harmony with one another. Her spelling showed signs of wanting to be achieved.

It was as well that the Eileen O'Reilly prospered speedily in her learning, for soon our lessons were abbreviated to snatched quarter-hours.

Our time together, so contented and peaceful, was stolen from us, by Darcy, of course.

I had to run home from school now. Darcy's plan was being drilled, slapped and scorned into life. Every afternoon, we Swiney sisters donned the bullied shoes and practised in the barn, to the bemusement of the geese and the kittens, and also of the Eileen O'Reilly, who watched from a crack in the back wall. Annora stood at the barn door, wringing her hands and continually being told to be off with herself to mend our stockings.

Every time Annora wailed, 'This is not right, as God is my witness,' my heart echoed her. I very fervently did not wish to move my body to Darcy's direction, or to lift my voice in songs Darcy chose.

There was the cruelty of our hurting limbs too. The shoes Darcy had appropriated were not the same size as our feet. They either pinched like Darcy's fingers or flapped like goose beaks until we stuffed them with scratchy straw. Our blisters filled, scabbed, itched and filled again. We danced on our pain, grimacing when Darcy screamed at us to smile.

But in just a few weeks, each girl of us could sing and dance in harmony, even little lisping nine-year-old Ida; even stout twelve-year-old Pertilly who you'd think too thick about the ankle for grace; even eleven-year-old Oona, who'd always been too embarrassed by the deep bass of her voice to speak above a whisper. By the end of a month, we sisters could dance an Irish jig for you in perfect synchronicity, though

Enda – despite her seventeen grand years – could never be allowed to stand next to Berenice, because she could not be stopped from chanting 'Brown Bitch Heifer' to her in time with the music, to which her twin would reply, 'I'll choke you for a dog!' Once the twins were safely separated, the seven Swiney sisters worked like a fourteen-flanged mechanical toy cut from a single piece of tin. Our voices rose and fell in melodious plaitings and unravellings. We could break your heart with ballads and wash your soul with hymns. We'd finish you off with a dirge.

We could eke out our talent to fifty minutes.

That sufficed for sixpence a show, opined Darcy, over the rare luxury of a potato-and-milk supper with a scrape of butter on top. 'We'd be wasting our time working harder than for sixpence, and us already crusted with the sweat of rehearsing. Who's to afford more than sixpence round here? And in the meantime,' she hectored, handing out ghostly white bandannas with eye holes, 'not a one of you is to show a bare face or arm to the sun, even if it should visit for a rarity. If I see a solitary brutal-looking freckle, I'll have your life.'

'Why?' dared Berenice, who liked to garden, although her chiefest joy was digging deep holes to push Enda into. Enda was short-sighted and never anticipated these attacks. Oona and I would brush the dirt from her hair after her falls.

'Yes, why?' asked Pertilly, who dearly loved to chew a stalk of grass warm from the soil.

Darcy sighed. 'Is it more ankles than brains you have? For the sheer drama of it is why. Because if your stupid complexion is as white as a sheet, Pertilly, then your fat arms and ugly face will be a better contrast to the hair on your useless head.'

Even though she was not one of Enda's sorority, I felt a tender pity every time I looked at Pertilly. It was only her fifty-two inches of chestnut hair that lent any air to her at all. She had a nun's face, Darcy always said, born for a wimple instead of a bonnet. Pertilly's was one of those Irish smiles that's never more than an acknowledgement of hopeless adversity. Her face was rhomboid rather than heart-shaped, with spare folds where there should be none. Nor was Pertilly gifted with wit, a subject on which Darcy now expanded at length.

'Pertilly's an ignoramush!' Ida chipped in joyfully, and then clapped her hand over her mouth. 'Sorry so,' she whispered to Pertilly.

Over Pertilly's tears, Darcy instructed Annora to sew us seven new black silk shawls, also to emphasise the pallor of our complexions and the whiteness of our forearms.

'What in the earthly world are you thinking, Darcy? With what money shall I be paying for black silk shawls?' whined Annora. '*New*, is it?'

We had never in our lives worn clothes that had been made for us.

'With credit money. I'll pay it back with interest after the first show.'

'*First* show?' whimpered Ida. 'But—'

Annora protested, 'Haven't I been trying to tell you that the credit is at the tether's end? Silk's an awful price. And what if—'

'Away with your what-ifs, you stupid woman!' thundered Darcy. 'And aren't there six or seven pewter dishes just begging to be sold? It wouldn't hurt you to take in a few extra sheets for mending either.'

'Is that your manners, girl? She's a terrible girl for manners! She has a snake's manners. It is not her fault, no. But she is the Dark One's snaky minion, the serpent that she is, with that sharp tooth on her for biting at you.' Annora crossed herself and bent over her needle, invoking seamstress saints in tearful whispers.

'Is this a good stitching?' she'd moan, answering herself, 'Faith it is no such thing: it is very poor, the creature. It is the Dunlavin banshee who has put her cold hand on my fingers.'

Despite her Catholic faith, a staunch belief in fairies coexisted in Annora's confused and beaten heart. To hear her tell it, our fields were thick with fairy forts, fairy stones, fairy trees that must be scrupulously avoided. She frequently insisted Ida's 'airy fits' were brought on by the Little People who were known to infest the air, earth and water around Gormanstown Hill. Or she blamed the elfin spirits of Ratharigid and the fairies of the moat at Tournant who regularly put a dangerous excitement on the herds at Dunlavin. The two tribes of Little Folk were constantly at war; droplets of red blood would be found on the roadway after their battles. In the evil February wind – or when Darcy raged – Annora always swore she heard the cries of the banshee of Dunlavin, an ancient crone who combed her hair and pronounced scintillating curses, especially on laundresses and seamstresses. On All Souls Day, the time when the other world was deemed to be closest to ours, Annora spent every daylight hour on her knees praying for mercy on the souls in Purgatory, alternating with whispered asides begging mercy from the Sidhe of Gormanstown on their rampages.

While Annora chanted hymns to save her stitching from the Dunlavin banshee, Darcy wrenched the lice and the lice-nymphs and egg casings from our hair with the wooden comb, boiling the kettle so it whistled to cover our screams in case a constable happened to pass by. The face of the Eileen O'Reilly at the window grew round-eyed and pale as a laundered sheet.

Darcy announced our first show was to be two Monday evenings hence in nearby Kilcullen's down-at-heel Ladysmildew Hall. She ensured that a snowfall of handouts lay thick about the streets the week before. She had us up all night copying them from an example she fixed to the larder door.

THE SWINEY GODIVAS
SEVEN BEAUTEOUS FLOWERS OF OLD IRELAND
In Their Very First Bloom
Songs to open your heart
Tresses and faces never to forget . . .

Annora begged some dye from Mrs Godlin. The uniform black hid the patches on our worsted bodices. She sponged the grease and mould from our Sunday skirts with holy water. Enda, who had a natural way with these things, showed us all how to tie the black shawls in graceful folds.

Meanwhile, I pleaded with the Eileen O'Reilly not to come to our show, for I knew she'd never resist calling out some horror up at Darcy on the stage. Reluctantly, the Eileen O'Reilly agreed. 'It would be hard for a body not to abuse Darcy Swiney and her setting herself up in all her great grandeur like a queen.'

When the day came, Annora professed herself unable to attend. 'It is destroyed by my nerves, I am.'

She waved us off, murmuring, 'God and Mary be with you. And the Holy Infant.'

'Why wouldn't they be?' demanded Darcy.

Joe the seaweed boy jolted us in his cart towards Ladysmildew Hall. Somewhere between Harristown and Kilcullen the seven poor fatherless sisters became the Swiney Godivas, one of whom was half sick on a secret about a man on Harristown Bridge.

9

When it was all over, our round-bellied mayor tottered up to the stage and told us, 'But that was the grand singing intirely! It done a body's heart good just to be hearin' the sound of it.'

But everyone knew that what had made his knees shake so was not our voices but our hair and its long, slow tumble to the ground. We curtseyed until our knees rattled. Finally Darcy let us off the stage. We stood against the walls of the wings, panting. Only then did the audience straggle reluctantly from the Ladysmildew Hall, still looking over their shoulders.

Pertilly swept our hair back into chignons. Enda retied our drooping shawls.

When we came outside, we found Joe's grin waiting for us. A great Irish rainbow had bloomed over all County Kildare with its fogdogs crouched right on the road back to Harristown.

My sisters tumbled joyfully into the cart. They were full to the neck of the wanting looks they'd been given.

'Did you see the face on the mayor at the end?' asked Oona.

Even my beloved Enda was alight with having herself eaten up by the eyes of men while she stood in her naked hair in front of them.

We were not out of Kilcullen before the twins commenced to argue as to which of them had sung out of tune.

'Next time you'll *both* do it properly,' said Darcy.

Joe had to stop for Ida to vomit her bread-and-dripping in a hedge.

Holding Ida's head gently in her hands, Berenice wiped her face with a corner of black silk shawl and soothed, 'It shall be well, it shall be well.'

'No it shall not,' Ida wept, the thick tears of a nine-year-old undiluted by compromise.

I looked up at Darcy. 'Ida does not want to do this again,' I translated boldly. 'And no more do I.'

'The paper-worm Manticory doesn't want to do it again?' Darcy's voice mocked mine. 'Poor Manticory. 'Tis a pity so to vex her. Would she rather do something else to earn money then? Let me guess. Something with a man on a bridge?'

She swished one hand in front of her and one behind. 'Now get back in the cart. Ida! Berenice!'

Oona worried, 'What is all that about a man on a bridge, Darcy? And that's not a nice way to be carrying on with your hand, is it, playing about your rear end like that, and for why are you crying, Manticory honey?'

I could not unburden myself even to Oona's tenderness or in the shelter of Enda's arm that soon encircled me as we continued on our way back to Harristown. I did not want to tell anyone what had happened on Harristown Bridge, because I did not want it to have happened at all. I could not be going on breathing with the knowledge of it in the minds of all my sisters and the pity on their faces.

I nodded to Darcy and she smiled. I had betrayed myself twofold. For Darcy had my obedience now and also the means to secure it any time she wanted it. I had dared to crunch God's Body in the chapel, but I had seen the grave in the clover field and I had no means, hungry as I was, to devour my fear of my sister.

I was too ashamed even to tell the truth to the Eileen O'Reilly when she asked me, 'For why are you so sorry and heavy in yourself, Manticory Swiney? How is it, and you so clever in your brains, that Darcy keeps you so black afraid?'

Unlike the coins dropped in the chapel collection plate, the Ladysmildew Hall takings were all for us. They paid the arrears for the silk shawls. They also ran to an orange and a peppermint sugar-stick for each sister, eight pounds of candles for the seashell lamp, five jars of treacle and a grand settlement of Annora's account at the general store in Kilcullen. There was even an extra shilling each and yet another new hat for Darcy – a preposterous funereal confection of raven feathers and tortured black straw. I quietly dedicated it to Phiala the goose at the earliest possible opportunity. With my shilling, I bought a true silver locket on a black velvet ribbon. I'd coveted it for years as the store window's dust had slowly dimmed its brightness.

There was a favourable notice in the *Wicklow News-Letter and County Advertiser*:

> *Seven sisters of lustrous locks and charming voices – the oldest a bare nineteen – could not fail to entertain, and frequently gave delight. As did the hair, which you'd never ask to take your eyes from.*

At the next show, there were as many husbands as wives in the audience, and twice the number of shuffling boys.

'Dregs!' sniffed Darcy. For the finest flower of Harristown's young men – accepted only on the production of a good-conduct letter from Father Maglinn – had long since departed for the Pope's Irish Brigade in Italy: the remnants were not well thought of.

'I just pray that the Eileen O'Reilly is not out there.' Oona plaited her long fingers. 'There isn't a girl in twenty parishes I'd less rather see.'

Enda kissed the top of her head and stroked mine. At the thought of the butcher's runt in the audience, Ida took a hank of hair in her mouth to suck, as she always did in moments of difficulty. As *she* always did, Darcy twitched the hair out of Ida's mouth, gave it a good yanking, and promised a mention of it in her black book, plus a dose of Gilsol Indigestion and Wind Pills, the latest free samples from Willis's Medical Hall in Dublin to be had at the Kilcullen dispensary. The familiarity of the threat comforted us all for a moment.

And once more we found ourselves on stage, one at a time, severally and all seven together.

*

Within a week, we were booked through the autumn, winter and spring, all around County Kildare and even into west Wicklow. There was not a parish councillor who'd deny Darcy, got up in her new hat, whenever she offered us for his wooden stage. Hoteliers requested us for their lobbies, big shops for their windows. We did country fairs at Ballymore Eustace and Baltinglass, shocked the sweet-faced Quakers at Ballitore and convulsed the sturdy residents of Dunlavin. We performed a soirée at grand Russborough House at Blessington, attended by all the members of the Killing Kildares, our local hunt. I strained to see the man who had wanted to brush my hair on Harristown Bridge – and I saw Darcy's eyes questing for him too, and her anger at his absence. She wanted to extract some more money from him, I guessed. Her eye met mine; she read the agony on my face, and smiled.

After our show at Russborough, the Pennefathers of Rathsallagh House invited us too. And then the Tyntes of Tynte Park. The foxy troll was not there either, but I never stopped looking for him, not when we sang at the stark stone Grand Canal Hotel at Robertstown, nor when the Crehelp Brass Band welcomed us into town for a concert in the square.

Our names were on everyone's lips. And the word was that we could bring in the customers, and whet their thirst for paid-for refreshment. But when we were asked for at the public houses, Darcy decreed that such a setting was not suitable for the Swiney Godivas, whose morals were as pure as their voices.

Darcy lied. Pure is not what we were.

Oh yes, we were adequate little actresses and creditable warblers. There was charm in our highly commercial mixture of English and Irish, enunciated in clear girlish voices. On a good night, our voices played lightly with your feelings, but they did not line your heart's memories. Our dancing was not the most graceful you ever saw, and our feet were far from the most delicate. There was no great unloosening of wild Celtic joy to our performance, informed not by art but by a fear of Darcy. Indeed, Ida would sometimes fall body-lilty off the stage, purely so as not to have to be upon it, a phenomenon that Darcy deftly incorporated into the act as a comedy turn, with Joe the seaweed boy, our driver, at the ready to receive Ida's quivering body. Onstage, I myself devised a functional mental mechanism for pretending that I was in the midst of a recurring nightmare and that I would shortly wake up.

All the while we sang we were offering something much more alluring than songs. The flower of our show wasn't what was advertised. We sang and danced the paid-for hour, but the people handed over their sixpences and shillings for the single silent thing that we did in the final moments of our act, when we sat with our backs to the audience, and let down our hair.

Then the people leaned forward in their seats or took to their feet without realising it. Their mouths fell slack and their eyes widened in an effort to take in the wall of hair in front of them as it rippled from one side of the stage to the other.

You might have thought simple human hair unworthy of such commotion. After all, the hair on a person's head is not usually kept hidden like that which nestles in the private places of our bodies. Head hair is generally exposed to view and therefore generally unremarked on. The length of Swiney hair was no secret in County Kildare. You might have thought that the sight of seven bald girls would have excited much more interest. But by the cunning choreography of the hairfall ritual, Darcy conferred on each bare stage the breathless intimacy of a wedding night. She made everyone our bridegroom.

And so we made freedoms with men we did not know to speak to, and with a hundred men at a time, and with women and boys too. We collected them in a mass, and we teased them until Darcy smelled the hunger on them. And she would give them our hair, just before they pleaded for it, always by surprise, when they didn't expect it. On the Zambezi, David Livingstone had discovered a thousand yards of water smashing over a precipice. A parish letter from Naas drew the inevitable comparison: the Victoria Falls – they were the Swineys too. *The mighty power of the torrent*, the clerk wrote excitedly, *that is in the Swiney Godivas' heroic hair, engulfing our imaginations in a tumbling fever.*

In those early days, even young Ida had a fine growth well beyond the lower tips of her chicken-wing hips, though it was thinner than it might have been because of her constant plucking of it to make wristlets and anklets. The rest of us hadn't seen our knees behind us in some time for the heavy rain of hair that covered them. But now success seemed to stimulate our hair's growth – or perhaps the better dinners we were presently eating thanks to our earnings had something to do with the extraordinary spurt of extra follicular inches we experienced in those first months on the stage. We were able to do away with the chairs for the final curtain of curls. When our hair dropped down our backs, we had only to incline our knees so that the hair fell near the ground or touched it.

Even if they knew what was coming, the audience drew breath, made moans, threw flowers and money. Hats were waved, handkerchiefs thrown up in the air. Darcy had us pick up the flowers and tuck them in our hair as we bobbed and smiled with downcast eyes. The money, we collected only after the audience had departed.

On the last day of summer, we gave an outdoor concert, letting our hair cascade down the stone parapets of the bridge at the Poulaphouca Waterfall. A clap like thunder and a nightmare of white light broke our pose.

Ida screamed, 'We are exploded! It is the Fenians come to murder us!'

Down in the crowd, a man lifted his head from under a shrouded box on stilts and waved at us. It was the first time we'd been photographed and it was without our permission.

Darcy was already mumbling that now anyone could have a good look at us in a newspaper without giving her a penny. But I was tormented by a notion of all the years that had gone into growing our hair suddenly severed and our living curls ceasing to live, dispatched into eternity in a puff of magnesium smoke. All the photographs I'd seen were lifeless and flat. And there was no undoing or owning a photograph of yourself, as I understood it. Your image was etched, irrevocable as a wrinkle, on a glass plate that belonged to someone else. Now the photographer had taken our likeness, he would take it away, and there would be something abroad that did not belong to us, yet was us.

In fact, as grainily printed in the following Thursday's *Freeman's Journal*, the photograph was hard to make out. The Eileen O'Reilly came to school with her basket of pig's feet. Brandishing the newspaper like a shotgun, she declared, 'Now you have it. That Darcy Swiney's hairs is jest like the divil's claws clutching that poor bridge to tear it up by the roots.'

The other children clustered around, nodding. 'Claws,' they murmured. 'Roots.' 'Crubeen?'

Our hair projected from the highest points of our personal topography – it was the stage up to which any eye was drawn. By virtue of its volume, our hair staked a great claim in the space around us. Yet the Eileen O'Reilly could tell Darcy's as Devil's claws, and Devil's claws it was. What of the rest of us? The clearest thing about us had become suddenly negotiable.

'Still' – Darcy gave the Eileen O'Reilly a poke in the face – 'I noticed that you your great self bothered your hide to trudge three miles out of Brannockstown to see us there.'

'Me and your da!' shouted the Eileen O'Reilly. 'Did you see all them men gawping at the sight of ye? Come to guess who was cursed enough to call Darcy Swiney his everlasting daughter.'

The butcher's runt loved to make up stories about Darcy's father. At different times, she put it about that Darcy's da had been transported for seven years for goat-stealing and sheep-hurting, that he'd personally disseminated the fungus that had caused the potatoes and the population to rot and had then run away to America with their goods in a cart. She also said that Darcy's father was no Phelan Swiney but a Dermody from Knockandort, or a Doody from Forristeen or a Rorke from Rostyduff or a Galbally from Crehelp or a Fahy from Corncrake's Hollow. She had it that he was the local Fenian, Denis Downey, a mad, gun-running Catholic tailor from Baltinglass who'd fathered six on his own wife. 'And ye've seen the man's picture in the papers!' she crowed, 'wid a great tufty head and a wild

70

black beard on him thick as thatch. Bound to be the Darcy Swiney da!'

I never asked her to stop, because I loved it that she dared. And her scorn was reserved for Darcy. She did not torment the rest of us. Our hedgerow lessons continued in fits and starts, depending on the Swiney Godivas' engagements. Soon the Eileen O'Reilly and I spent less time learning, and more time talking. She told me how it was in her home, how it felt to be an only child, and yet still not much noticed except to be fed. I explained to her about my tribal allegiance to Enda and Oona, and the alliance of Berenice, Pertilly and Ida.

'That would be explaining it,' she nodded, 'what I see and hear at yon window or yours. There's no sense in all that niggling and gnashing, without. I allus thought Enda the pretty one of the twins. She knows what to do wid a ribbon anyhow.'

'She does.' I smiled, rose and stretched my legs. The sun's rays hung at a guilty angle: I had to rehearse a new song.

'And Ida?' the Eileen O'Reilly asked. 'I think she is no great things in many respects. But she's a dear girl in herself all the same?'

'A dear girl, yes.' I smiled and waved her goodbye. 'You would like her, if Darcy allowed it.'

'If she could walk across a field wivout pickin' a fight with a blade of grass,' the Eileen O'Reilly agreed. 'If she can't be bashing, she jest doan feel herself, do she? She'd druther foight than breathe is what she'd druther.'

The Poulaphouca picture brought us new and bigger audiences. Darcy became a convert to photography when she saw what it could do. Now our shows were attended by policemen, priests, gombeen men, county councillors, governesses, clerks, members of working men's clubs and prosperous farmers in their swallow-tailed coats, breeches and high-crowned hats. They paid without a murmur for what fell out of our heads; a terrible sight of money they paid for it.

71

10

Hymns, old songs and hair were fine and good to open hearts and purses, but Darcy decreed that the Swiney Godivas needed special songs made to order if we were to become a 'living sensation', a much more profitable kind of enterprise. It fell to me to compose our ditties, with new words constructed around traditional Irish airs, snatches of dialogue, banter.

Darcy also insisted that Ida should learn to play the dusty fiddle that Phelan Swiney, Mariner, had left hanging by the back door on one of his invisible visits.

'It takes Ida five mortal hours to memorise the words of a song,' Darcy grumbled. 'Let's see if she can play dumb notes.'

Ida took to her instrument with joy, hugging it to her shoulder. The music flowed through her with a rude ease that words never managed. She drew from the violin a sound of something ancient that had poured out of the earth unfiltered by the normal decencies. The thin geese were hypnotised by her playing and I sometimes saw the Eileen O'Reilly, narrow-hipped as an Irish stoat, swaying to it outside the window, her eyes closed, and bliss on her face.

Annora allowed Ida and myself to stay home from school sometimes to work on our songs. When he could, Joe the seaweed boy took me in his cart to the library at Naas. I was fourteen now, and had exhausted Miss Finaughty's lending shelf. To her sorrow, I had not been so avid an attender at school since I'd met with the troll on Harristown Bridge, and always made sure I walked home with a sister or two. I was happier as the mouse in the corner of the cottage, quietly nibbling on a pencil in a nest of paper.

Since what happened on Harristown Bridge, I'd withdrawn into myself. My hair was the noisiest thing about me. That hair, which had drawn the troll and danger and shame to me, felt like a betrayer that lived upon my body. Why had it fallen to me, of all the Swineys, to wear hair that looked like stabbing or a spilling of blood? A bolt of red velvet flung down? A colouring allegedly infused with melodrama and lust? I would have been more suited to the soft russet of a deer, trying to stipple herself to invisibility in the shadows of the grass. Indeed Annora often said of me that my ankles were so delicate that I trotted about on deer's feet. And my arms in the summer would dapple with freckles like a fawn's back.

Now I was silent as a deer – except when I conducted my secret hedge lessons with the Eileen O'Reilly. The rare times I went to school, I never raised my hand to answer a question. Miss Finaughty gazed at me with troubled eyes. I did not return her look.

My tongue was silent but my pencil was busy and bold. Darcy wanted our performances invigorated with a wild and sparkling malice now that the local press had begun to froth about the marvellous salty banter that poured out of the Swiney sisters between their songs.

Like forks of lightning, those pretty tongues. It is like being caught in a storm. See the Swiney Godivas for that excitement alone, said one writer. *And the hair of course. The inimitable hair.*

Into my sisters' mouths, Darcy ordered me to put words that raised passions that led to words they made up all by themselves. Fighting words. Words that flashed and glinted as the Swineys ate the heads off one another; Oona carping at Pertilly; myself shamefully teasing Ida for the romancing of her mind. Most of all, it seemed, Darcy wanted to hear Enda chant under her breath 'Brown Bitch Heifer!' to Berenice, and for her twin to reply, 'I'll choke you for a dog!'

A few heifers and dogs later, and I was imagining myself clever enough to deploy Darcy's malfeasance against her own stormy self. I was wrong.

'That Medusa is not me!' shouted Darcy, for whom I had concocted the lines:

> *And should you meet my snaky eye*
> *You'll turn to stone and, sorry, die.*

Pertilly replied, 'But that is you to the bone, Darcy!'

'It's true, Pertilly honey,' declared Oona.

Both earned a slap. And in revenge, Darcy selected Pertilly for the role of Medusa, reserving Lorelei for herself.

'The Lorelei had yellow hair herself!' protested Oona of the milk-blonde curls. 'She sat on a rock in *River Rhine* there, luring *German* fishermen to their deaths. They are a *fair* race, those Germans. And look, Manticory's written it that way so.'

In her bass voice, she chanted:

> *'I sing and comb my golden locks*
> *and lure men in boats onto the rocks.*
> *Then as they perish in the water*
> *I sing and comb and watch the slaughter.'*

Darcy sneered, 'And who is *Manticory* to decide the colour of the Lorelei's hair?'

She poked my thigh with her hairbrush.

The audience loved pairings of our twins, who were indeed decorative as crystal bookends or twin kittens, though only if you didn't know the sweet rottenness between them. As well as tensely perfect duets, Darcy had them perform riddles, a different one every night, to make it more interesting for the increasing number of regular customers. I was kept busy concocting them – always with the same answer, one that would make the audience call out, 'Your hair!'

'What is delicate as a cobweb but lives on after death?'

'What is the material border between life and death?'

'What is the only human thing that lasts longer than love?'

'Your hair!' the audiences cried. 'The lovely lovely hair on you! Bless you for long-haired, darling angels!'

But given the twins' spite for one another, even the brief exchanges of riddles frequently turned barbed. Whatever Berenice's

74

response, Enda would raise a cynical eyebrow and drawl, 'If you say so, sister.' Which threw a delicate but sorry doubt on whatever her twin had just uttered. Berenice could devise no adequate answer for such a subtle slur. Whenever she tried to banter back, it fell heavily.

It came to the point, one night in Kildare Town, that, when Enda supplied her, 'If you say so, sister,' Berenice supplied Enda with a black eye, in front of an audience stunned to silence. Enda then commenced to wail, and Oona rushed onstage and wiped the tears with her own hair, crying, 'Oh, let's not make *great bones* about it, shall we, Enda honey? Divil a taste you're freckened of a little slap!'

Fortunately the audience took this speech as a punchline to the mystifying violence, and applauded. And that encouraged Pertilly to lumber onstage too with a rendition of, 'I am sorry I made you cry, but at least your face is cleaner now,' soothing away anyone's niggling suspicion that what they had just seen was not choreographed comedy, but war.

The review in the *Wicklow News-Letter and County Advertiser* was admiring of our *daring physical routines*, before settling down to a long and excitable description of our hair.

The Eileen O'Reilly, who saw the show, was full of pity for Enda. She knew what a punched eye felt like, of course.

'You make that Berry-Kneesie pay!' she urged me, 'next time you write her.'

We busied ourselves about our lesson. I was teaching her the use of the conditional, for which she had small aptitude. The Eileen O'Reilly had a contempt for nuance and, like Darcy herself, was generally more comfortable with what was black or white.

Nothing escaped her scrutiny and consideration. Those blue eyes on her were always watching me. Even in chapel, she watched me.

'Why do ye not pray any more?' she asked me now. 'I watch your lips and ye say other words. Bad words. You take your clothes to chapel, Manticory Swiney, but not yourself.'

I was tempted to confide. The Eileen O'Reilly was black good at outrage, having rehearsed her tongue on Darcy many a time.

75

She knew what it was to be knocked about by a man's large hand. I could imagine her in the flower of a rant against the man on the bridge.

'We shall have that troll trussed and flogged on Kilcullen Hill,' she would surely shout. 'Where is he at all for his punishing?'

But I could not bring myself to share my shame with her. I needed her to think me finer than that.

So I laughed. ' 'Tis true I'm not much in the way of thanking God. He has never looked in on us Swineys except that He's laughed down His sleeve at us and sent new troubles to destroy us.'

'True enough,' she said. 'Darcy being as she is, and that bold Berry-Kneesie winning the war with Enda and all.'

I nodded.

'Should be fixed, that,' she added thoughtfully. 'Ain't I just after telling ye?'

Enda's punched eye swelled and closed. The left side of her face took on the colours of putrefaction. She was for several days deaf in that ear, though not deaf enough to miss Berenice chanting 'I'll choke you for a dog' at her every time she was allowed near. Enda was offstage a fortnight, causing Darcy to cancel bookings: without our much-vaunted full seven-ness, the Swiney Godivas were in danger of being nullities.

After that, the twins both had Darcy's eye on them at all times. Now that she had seen how profitable it might be, she sought to deploy their bellicosity to best effect. Each of them was allowed one good slap in the course of the show, but strictly no improvisation. For once the extra slap, pinch or kick was inserted, no one could know where it would all end. Whenever that happened, things always got difficult, not least for the offender after the show.

'A quiet pinch for Enda, was it?' Darcy would tower over Berenice. 'Would you be so condescending to my ignorance as to tell me why you felt so entitled to ruin our future profits and make an untidy spectacle of yourselves?'

The truthful answer would have been that each twin believed she owned the pain of the other, but they had no way of articulating that to Darcy.

'We're alike, so,' was as much as Berenice could explain.

'So doing unto others must be done alike too,' ruled Darcy.

And Enda would then be permitted to administer two outright slaps for Berenice's furtive pinch onstage. Thereafter the twins developed a cunning means of communicating insults by cracking their knuckles at one another so that no one beyond the first row could hear.

And my continuing part in all this? It was a negative role, like a depression in an acquiescent cushion. To placate Darcy, I invented and inserted the subtle slanders, and even those commas that could make a twin draw a breath that might be construed as a sneer. Of course, I belonged to Enda's tribe in the great division of the sisters, and so my writing favoured her in subtle ways, just as the Eileen O'Reilly had suggested, which naturally led to more brute frustration on Berenice's end, and so to Enda receiving the larger number of pinches and blows.

I cannot defend myself, except to say that I was afraid of Darcy and that I was conveniently not fully sensible to the pain of all those pinches and blows. Darcy also flattered me, feeding me odd specks of praise that turned my head. She saw that I was taken up by my new discoveries about the power of words, and the joy of how mightily a tiny phrase could shake the shabby village halls of Kildare with laughter; how a certain ordering of adjectives and a wily insertion of unexpected syllables could turn a sentence into a success. Although I was no great writer, Darcy had inoculated me, like a snake bite, with the writer's disease of separating my stories from my conscience, disingenuously accepting no responsibility for any hurts to third parties. If there was blame to be had, I found it convenient to lay it at Darcy's feet. It was easy to blame Darcy; she made it easy by being impervious to guilt. Berenice grumbled but dared not do more. Sweet-natured Enda forgave me every time, and told me it was not my fault. Shamefully, even this empowered me to do more damage.

I can no longer evade my share of blame for all the horror that was to happen between Enda and Berenice. I should have seen the way of things to come that memorable night in Kilcullen when Enda's blow, scripted by me, fell harder than ever on Berenice's ear. The hair lifted from Berenice's scalp, disclosing a carefully concealed bald circle – caused by the incontinent feasting of a ringworm.

Winded, Berenice hovered for a moment on the ball of one foot and then crashed downwards. She landed on her back with her hair drizzling down the front of the stage, and the naked circle on her scalp exposed inches from the eyes of three girls from our school, including the Eileen O'Reilly herself.

Pertilly and Ida pulled her from the stage by her ankles. Berenice was not badly hurt, I was relieved to see, but the tears would not stop flowing out of her.

Perhaps she understood better than I did that the truth was we were all grievously hurt in that moment.

For wasn't it the Brannockstown butcher's runt, the Eileen O'Reilly, who rose to face the audience and called out in ecstasy, 'Here's Berry-Kneesie Swiney for ye, yer graces, ladies and jintlemen, the ganky great girl wid a brutal-looking case of the baldy-worm and the great big nits!'

Only the first few rows could possibly have seen the tiny eggs in their flight, but the runt's words had been clear and loud as the bell on Carnalway Church. People rose hastily and backed away.

In the confusion, I slipped from the wings and down into the audience, hiding my hair under my black shawl. The hall was emptying rapidly, a great sea of dissatisfied murmurs flowing out like a tide. The Eileen O'Reilly was standing alone staring at the closed curtain, her colour high.

'Manticory!' She showed me her crooked teeth in gladness.

I hissed, 'How could you betray me after all our pleasant lessons?'

The light went out of her eyes. 'Betray ye? But that was one against Berry-Kneesie, weren't it? So it were *for* your Enda.

Here's me thinking ye'd be pleased. Don't ye put the snout on . . .' Her voice trailed away uncertainly.

Then I saw that she had misunderstood, and yet also understood the Swiney Godivas all too well. I knew not what to say, so I spun on my heels and walked away from her.

'Don't ye be turning your back on me, Manticory Swiney,' the butcher's runt shouted. 'Not now, don't be doing it. Is this the way you're leaving me, ye brute?'

11

I lay no claim that the Swiney sisters of Harristown were exceptional in the great battles waged on our heads between nit and comb, or in any of the attentions we paid to our hair.

The first duty of any decent morning is to devote oneself to amending the hair that so often looks as if it has gotten wrong-footed by fairies who have passed the night prancing their orgies in it. And so it continues from waking to sleeping: any moment of the day there will be a hundred thousand souls washing, greasing, dyeing, plucking, pinning, snipping and otherwise aggravating and interfering with the one piece of our anatomy we mortals have the power to alter. It must be tamed and punished with a hundred strokes. It must be inspected for vermin. And purged of the stubborn creatures who inhabit it.

So all the while that we were becoming the Swiney Godivas, the four youngest of us – Ida, Pertilly, Oona and myself – still presented ourselves from time to time at Brannockstown's poor little school, and were so subject to the migrations and massings of head-lice that plagued every educational establishment in Ireland in those days. The beasts had a clear preference for young girls and a strange distaste for the boys once their blood was beating with manhood.

Our hair – which should have been private to ourselves alone – had become public as soon as the Swiney Godivas were born. And now we sisters also caught the imagination of our fellow pupils, who had simply given us the wooden eye for our poverty until celebrity painted us with gloss. Specifically, our burgeoning fame made our schoolmates look at our hair more closely, and with critical expressions. They considered it logical that our prodigious heads must nurture not just rampant follicles but wriggling camp-followers as numerous as cottoners in Corktown. Our new predicament was that Berenice had just proved it up on the stage.

It was at the schoolhouse in Brannockstown that the rupture between the butcher's runt and myself was grievously enlarged.

The Eileen O'Reilly brought the tale of that dreadful night back to school. All the next day she cultivated a high popularity with increasingly exaggerated accounts of it. Everyone wanted to be big with the butcher's runt, for this was the most wonderful outrage ever offered up to our schoolfellows – an explicit enactment of their own secret fears, for they were none of them innocent of vermin. And the Eileen O'Reilly spoke her story in the present tense so that it seemed to be still happening and our schoolfellows hung on her words like ragged sheets on a hedge.

'So that Enda beats on yon Berry-Kneesie with her fist, so she does. Such a slap that her nose couldn't help tumbling down. And if that Berry-Kneesie doesn't scream the rafthers off the roof, leave it till again. And it is a great shame, so it is, for the beasties are flying off of Berry-Kneesie like bats out of a cave, and then the whole audience – thousands of them, I belave, hignorant gommochs the lot of them – are in uproar and they're running for the doors when they realise that there's a naked knob of skull big as your fist hidden under all that dirty Swiney hair.' She snorted like a pig, for emphasis. 'I mean, I've had a nit myself, so I have, bad luck to them, but nothing to compare wid that great dirty nest on Berry-Kneesie's head.'

'No, but did you?' asked Mrs Godlin's granddaughter. 'And are they still there in among those Swineys, those nits and worms, the creatures?'

'Would a duck swim?' replied the Eileen O'Reilly with scorn. 'Because auld Arsey Swiney's too mean to allow her sisters the cost of a steel nitting comb.'

In the dew of a single evening, our reputations had been smashed.

Not one girl would sit next to us in the classroom after that, no matter that Annora went at us every Sunday with the lice comb and the petroleum under the malodorous light of the seashell lamp. No matter that we inspected one another daily with enquiring fingers and worried eyes. Still the lice loved us Swineys as a wasp loves children's screams.

We younger ones wept and ran to hide in the long grass whenever Annora showed us the lice comb, until the evening that Darcy came out into the gloaming to read aloud from an article in *The Nation* about the life cycle of the human head-louse:

'Unless evicted, the benighted creature spends its entire life on the human head, born in an egg attached to a hair shaft and dying not far away from it. And being born again.'

Darcy improvised, 'And again. And again.'

When we stayed hidden in the grass, Darcy threw down the paper, bellowing, 'Your silly, stubborn heads are currently supplying those greedy nits with all they could want by way of pleasant shelter and delicious blood. Do you want to stay out there, letting them grow fat and multiply upon you, is it? And getting yourself a fine burrowing tick or two for your pains? All the worse for you, then. Well, we'll not bother bruising any potatoes for you tonight, seeing as you're wedded to staying out there to starve and be feasted on by the nits. Enda! Will you give that mutton stew a stir? Fine and tender with little sweet carrots, is it? And the gravy rich and brown and shining like an officer's boot? Ah, the smell would carry you to Heaven on its back!'

Hunger drove Ida, Oona, Pertilly and myself back into the cottage, our sore heads hanging low. We never hid again. But despite Annora's tender, violent ministrations on the Swiney heads, the lice still would not be parted from us on a permanent basis, apparently well satisfied with our hospitality and recommending it to their friends.

We were at war on two fronts – not just with the lice but with the ringworm, *Tinea capitis*, which Annora, in her typical hardworking ignorance, constantly redistributed among us by the use of a single comb for the nits. In the library at Naas, I found Doctor Rowland's treatise on *The Human Hair* and was amused, saddened and black angry in quick succession to read that the ringworm:

> *usually appears spontaneously on children of feeble habit, who are ill-fed and not sufficiently exercised; and originates, in great measure, from uncleanliness . . . a medical man should always be consulted.*

But a visit from a medical man would have cost money and Darcy hated to open her purse, despite its swelling contours from our earnings on the stage. And so we continued, pomading our hair over the increasing bald patches, ever unable to comb out all the nits because of the burning inflammation of our scalps.

Two weeks after the disaster, Pertilly, Oona and myself arrived at school to find a sign posted on the door:

THEM BASTARD SWINEY SISTERS SHALL NOT BE LET IN UNTIL THEY IS PROVED FREE OF INFESTERATION. STREELING ABOUT CONCEITING THEMSELVES GREAT LADIES. BUT DO THEY KNOW WHO THEIR DA IS? A WASH WOULD DO THAT HOOR'S MELT DARCY SWINEY NO HARM NEITHER.

It was not just the spelling but the handwriting that gave away the Eileen O'Reilly as the perpetrator. I felt a rueful pride in my former pupil's vocabulary and spelling.

'Darcy would give her Ballyhooly if she saw that!' whispered Oona.

'Then we must go and get her so that she does,' Pertilly declared, setting off for the dispensary in Kilcullen where Darcy now helped Mrs Godlin in the afternoons. 'It will be a thing to see and hear.'

I hoped against hope there would be no violence in it for the Eileen O'Reilly, so thin and small that she was. In spite of our quarrel, I did not wish more hurting on her. I was too sad to be angry, and knew full well that it was my snubbing her at Ladysmildew Hall that had put the spine in her pencil. And after all, I had fed her with the information that made her denounce Berenice, out of misguided loyalty to me and my tribe. She had thought, because of our friendship, that she might prove herself part of Enda's tribe. Now she was part of nothing, and naturally considered herself an enemy to everything Swiney. And she had just forcibly sealed our enmity: I could betray Darcy in secret with satisfaction, but I could not befriend a girl who mocked my beloved Enda's paternity.

Of course, Darcy marched straight up to Brannockstown school with no apparent bending of her knee the whole way. She always walked like that whenever she had a crow to pluck with someone. She tore the paper off the door and balled it up in her hand. It was presently to be seen thrust into the bruised mouth of the Eileen O'Reilly, still mumbling indistinctly, 'Ye doan frecken *me*, Darcy Swiney, great Divil that ye are, with the very feathers in your hat fightin' with one another like bastes. Leastwise, the great nits on ye frecken me more, the creatures. You should be ashamed on yerself. Never givin' yer poor sisters a chance to better themselves over the baldy-warm. And makin' them sisters behave themselves discreditable wid the naked hairs down their backs.'

'They'll do all the behaving I want,' snarled Darcy.

But after that she used two evenings' takings to consult a medical man all the way from Dublin, the result of which was the precious knowledge that we sisters might no longer promiscuously snatch at whichever bonnet we found hanging on the peg. Nor might we share the hated wooden lice comb. Darcy had Annora embroider our names in red on seven new linen caps and seven separate pillowcases. And each of us was bought our own fearsome steel comb, tied with a ribbon of a different colour. Applications of Worm Water twice a day soon cured us of the ringworm, though the Eileen O'Reilly would not let us forget the shame.

'The jinteel Swiney Nitsters,' she called after us in the street, or, 'The Seven Wormy Wonders of the World, so they are, laudy daw, laudy daw.'

Nor did she hesitate to scribble such on our show handbills if she passed one on a wall, and even on the door of our own barn, where she was still to be found very often with her eye pressed against a crack while we rehearsed.

Under siege from the Eileen O'Reilly's slanders, we had to stiffen into saints at school, on the stage and anywhere in public. At home, of course, it was deeply otherwise. Our cottage door became like Harristown Bridge when it divided the Liffey's temper between serene and foaming. The door had the magical property of changing our natures, sluicing us from one state to another. Outside it, we were in compulsory harmony, singing and dancing in immaculate time. But once we came inside, all was the accustomed turbulence among us again, with the usual symptoms of Swiney passion breaking out in a clatter of slaps and embraces. The remaining pewter on the dresser was almost never at peace, constantly jangled by the slamming of the door. The seashell lamp swung from side to side, whispering urgently of shipwrecks.

Through it all, I sat quietly writing at the deal table. The insults that my sisters shouted at one another were soon woven into their roles on the stage, as were, when Darcy permitted it, the touching affection between Oona and Enda and myself and the tender bonds that fixed Berenice to Ida and Pertilly.

After the incident when Berenice's lice massed like a halo around her head, we could no longer perform at Ladysmildew Hall, or anywhere within a cheap omnibus ride of the Eileen O'Reilly's butcher shop.

Of course Darcy had a different account of it: our hair was too big for Harristown now, or at least her ambitions for it were. She told Annora, 'We cannot make the most of it here at the back of Godspeed.' But the truth was that we were forced to set our sights wider and higher, not out of ambition but as a result of our shaming.

While we smiled on increasingly large stages, and we hefted our hair in more elegant salons, my heart was impacted with fear and a persistent sense of our poor inferiority – our 'feeble habit', as Doctor Rowland would have said of us, despite the fact that our earnings were now lining our stomachs with better food than we'd ever eaten before and we now danced in shoes that fitted our own feet. We might now be dining on grand handsome potatoes and Indian meal without a weevil; Annora might even braise a shank of mutton once a week; when Enda embraced myself and Oona, we might breathe on bought lavender water; but we younger sisters were as far as ever from the sight or smell of money. Darcy alone held the purse, and the reins.

As for the rest of us, all we really had was hair, the hair that every woman grows upon her head and at her nostrils, eyes and the entrance to her womb. (Even above her mouth there is a down; in Darcy's case, pronounced.) At those portals to our bodies, hair offers but fragile resistance. It does little more than *remind* those with a mind to brush it aside that there is a boundary transgressed, as I knew from my encounter with the troll on Harristown Bridge. And there were some who found that transgressing the boundary only added to their pleasures.

In the Swiney Godiva shows our hair became our tongues, telling stories for us, situating us ever more grandly at the heart of the myths and legends I wrote into our songs. Our brave talking hair was tasting new things for us – certainly, we were being led by the hair into a different kind of life, seeing places and people that we backwoods backward girls hardly had the wit to engage with.

And if any sister dared to voice a misgiving or a fear, then Darcy would silence her with a smart blow or a threat, depending on which side of the table she was.

'Do you want to be the nothings you were before you were the Swiney Godivas?' she raged. 'The hungry barefoot nothings?'

Every time Darcy said that, I dreamed of flight. I wanted away from the sniggering disdain of our schoolfellows, from the staring and the craving in chapel and from the fear of happening upon my troll gentleman once more, the mysterious grave in the clover field, the insoluble enmity of the Eileen O'Reilly that I had brought on myself. Most of all I wanted away from the Swiney Godivas and the increasing shame I felt every time I exposed my hair and my blushing nape to a crowd of men whose breath was close enough to feel.

But with each new show, it seemed that it would be harder to separate the Swineys from the Godivas. Some lamentable process, almost chemical, had cemented us together as an act. Darcy cared not a buttered crumpet for me personally, but she'd see me dead before she'd let me retire from the show.

There was not even the luxury of a new chapter of my imagined adventure in which I escaped from Darcy and the Godivas. Reality fenced me in. Escape into what? I'd never been further than Naas on my own. I was not yet fifteen. Darcy loved to read aloud from newspapers about girls younger than us who sold their bodies on Dublin street corners and frequently got themselves butchered for it.

I did not want to imagine the loneliness of a life without Enda's petting and Oona's tenderness. And if I found the wherewithal to run away? How would Darcy punish my tribeswomen if I defected? What kind of shows would she get up without me to try to retain a bit of modesty and dignity for us?

Darcy would go where she smelled money, and that opened us up to risks she refused to see or think about.

We had arrived at a delicate moment. It could have gone so badly for the Swiney Godivas, with immoral pits gaping everywhere for innocent Irish girls to drop into, girls who had physical characteristics that made them stand out and get noticed, and noticed in a way that had men dragging them into copses.

So it was 'very fortunate, better than you bliggards deserve' – as Darcy put it – that this was the very moment when our highly telling hair (and its much-abused tenants) attracted the eye of an entrepreneur who would require the Swiney Godivas – late of the long grass, the thin geese and the slow crows – to transform into irreproachable ladies of Dublin fashion. And so, to hear Darcy tell it, we Swiney sisters owed it all to her that we were now to neatly sidestep those immoral pits and the haunting horror who was the Eileen O'Reilly, and place our fourteen feet firmly in the sturdy, respectable empire of Retail.

12

M r Rainfleury was a manufacturer of dolls. He had found his way to County Kildare when news of our show reached Dublin via six lines in the *Freeman's Journal*. Every word of those six lines was a joy to Mr Rainfleury, for they spoke of nothing but our hair. He was on the train and at our show in Ballymore Eustace that night, in the centre of the front row. After his first taste of the air that wafted from our hair waterfall, there was his round belly and his moustache jutting out of the front row at our every show, the dust straining the glitter of his pale hazel eyes through his pince-nez, and his lips apart to inhale and swallow deep into himself all the different flavours of our Swiney hair as it came down.

The small man with the ravening great mouth on him made me hate my hair as I had not hated it since I met the man on Harristown Bridge.

Darcy had our admirer under observation from the wings. 'There it is again, the old moustache. Comes like the bad weather, uninvited.'

The moustache sent his catalogue – *Little Princess Dolls* – backstage. We crowded around the handsome volume, marvelling at the illustrations of dolls who looked so much like ourselves, though somewhat finer in the complexion and a tint larger and rounder about the eyes. All his dolls boasted the most delicate feather eyebrows and luxuriant hair that tumbled down to their bisque or wax feet.

After reading his descriptions in that catalogue, I knew the moustache for my certain enemy, as one more of those men who abandoned a healthy interest in the entire person of a girl in order to fix their appetite on just the one hairiest part of her. If you wanted to see a full-grown man to whom female hair was ambrosia, you had only to watch the way the doll man's mouth worked whenever we sisters let down our hair at the end of our act. I always stared at it accusingly when I cast my look over my shoulder into the silent audience. An oyster, moistly engorged with blood, wriggled under his moustache. Not yet knowing his real name and having no desire to do so, I had privately christened him 'Mr Chops'.

He was a florid barrel of a gentleman with around forty wistful years visibly sagging around his middle. He himself was but sparsely endowed with head hair, perhaps naturally or maybe due to it rotting at the roots by the application of too much bear grease. For a man who loved hair, he must have had a desperate time of it: he'd evidently been eating to compensate. His capillary deficiency was especially unfortunate because the lack showed up his big ears and the quaint angle at which they stuck out from his head. Those perkers were pink and triangular like a pig's. They were soft enough to flop slightly as he walked. As did the drooping moustache he'd managed somehow to deliver himself – I could imagine the straining and praying that had gone into that.

It was after the fifth night of watching us that the gentleman had sent his card backstage with a note: *I trust that my catalogue was of pleasant interest?*

I fingered it. *Augustus Rainfleury* and a Dublin address were embossed in dull gold copperplate. My own 'Mr Chops' still seemed more appropriate to the man than the picturesque romance of 'Rainfleury'.

I suggested, 'Perhaps we should invite the gentleman for tea and a scone with butter?' This was not inspired by a spirit of hospitality – I nursed a repulsive interest in seeing Mr Chops' rosy oyster closing around some actual food instead of dream-nibbling on our hair.

But Darcy tore the card in half and sent it right back. 'He's just another of your men for the hair. He cannot do us any possible good.'

'I'd like one of those dolls.' Ida would not be parted from the catalogue and would not be done with whining about wanting a long-haired wax princess for herself.

'Did you see the prices?' shrieked Darcy. I stared fixedly at her latest new hat.

The next night Mr Chops was there once more. Unchastened, he sent his card round again, this time with an envelope and a letter. Darcy ripped it open and read aloud to us:

'Dear Young Ladies, do not be alarmed at my enthusiasm for your follicular attractions. It is above all of a professional nature. Allow me to present a business proposal that could prove the making of you. Respectfully yours, Augustus Cecil Rainfleury.'

A business proposal was a horse of a different colour for Darcy. Within minutes, Mr Chops was laying his pendulous haunches upon a handkerchief he'd spread on the backstage ottoman, and Darcy was doing everything but sitting on his knee. Ida was squirming with pleasure, whispering that there was to be sure a doll in it for herself. The rest of us sat at respectful intervals on stools and stage chairs, staring. The air was redolent of Breidenbach's Violet Mouthwash, for Darcy had insisted that we quickly swig and spit before the arrival of the business proposal.

Close up, I could see that there was more to the man than his mouth. Despite the nerves that quite naturally beset him, being seated so very close to Darcy, his hazel eyes were alert and shrewd as they scanned our faces and hair, still flowing loose from the end-of-show cascade. Darcy stared pointedly at the attaché case by Mr Rainfleury's feet.

'May I?' trembled Mr Rainfleury, his fingers fluttering above her hair.

'Touch my hair, is it?' asked Darcy. 'Well, just a very little, and you must stop directly I say so. Stop!'

'But I didn't touch it yet at all.'

'You can touch Pertilly's or Manticory's if you like.'

Darcy darted across and wrenched us forward, one by each shoulder. 'Well, have your feel, though don't be doing anything that would interest the Royal Irish Constabulary, mind. And then let's be hearing your plan.'

Mr Rainfleury hesitated deliciously over his choice. Pertilly's swelling nose and damp overbite must have swayed him.

'The red-haired girl,' he said thickly. 'The young tigress. Miss Manticory.'

'Not so much a tigress,' purred Darcy. 'More of a forest fawn, really. Or a reddish-brown rabbit. Go to him, Manticory. See how biddable she is?'

This was not what I'd intended at all by inviting Mr Chops backstage. Bile churned in my throat and the cheap prints blurred on the wall. But Darcy gripped my elbow and put one of her large feet down on mine, pinioning me to the floor directly in front of the man.

Mr Chops stood and raised his pink hand at me. I looked up at his mouth, working away. I sniffed his feminine cologne. With light fingers, he turned me round by the shoulders, so that my back was to him. Darcy repinioned my foot and fixed me with her black eyes. He started at the crown of my head, running his finger along the parting. It was too lightly done, like a sick spider dancing down my skin. With all the same uncertainty, he traced a curl past my cheekbone, his moist thumb grazing my lip, before he proceeded flitteringly down my shoulders, back, lifting his hand just at the last minute before it slid into the indecent tracts below my hip. The dressing-room mirror showed me that he was trembling all over himself, his face like a pulsing lump of living coral. Then he bent to stroke my hair down past my knees. Pale and beaded on his forehead, he kneeled to caress the ends. Only then did he finally relinquish his loathsomely delicate hold.

The man on Harristown Bridge was less horrible than this, I thought. There had been sharpness and quickness to that danger, not this sanctioned, havering, prolonged unwholesomeness.

A long shudder ran through my body. The pink hand was gone but I still wanted to shake the haze of Mr Rainfleury off my hair and skin. On a warning glance from Darcy, I stayed motionless, rejoicing in the clean fresh air around my hair where his hand had been and was no longer, while the man recovered himself down there on the floor. Some moments passed before he was capable of rising to his feet.

'A curl sometimes does that to a man,' he murmured. 'You can taste, touch, smell and even hear a curl. It is the essence of Romance. Such a curl is, after all, what makes a woman different from a man. The softness of your hair has surpassed my most roseate expectations, Miss Manticory, being that red hairs are the stoutest individuals. There is nothing so pleasant for a man to run a finger down as a red curl – it always gives a teasing bit of resistance, so delightful to overcome.'

He smiled at Oona. 'Your blondes have the finest kind of hairs, each with a fairy diameter compared to those on redheads like Manticory here. And those fairy hairs grow in the densest number, do they not, my dear?'

She nodded silently.

'But red hair! Red hair is the rarest kind. It's fashionable to say that redheads are hot for conflict, and that among highway-men and murderers you'll find a disproportionate number of that persuasion. More red-haired witches were burned at the stake than any other variety. Judas Iscariot, they say, couldn't help his crimes: he was a redhead. Cleopatra and Nellie Gwyn were red in tooth, lip, claw and hair.'

Of course, he knew his hairs and his hair histories. In that moment, the humour was on me – again to cut every one of my curls off. I would never think of him as 'Mr Chops' again. It was too good for him. Furiously, I experimented with other titles in my mind: 'Mr Disgustator', 'Mr Flittergoblin' and 'Mr Fingerlimp'.

'Business proposal, is it, your honour?' drawled Darcy, her eyes tricksily downcast. 'There is nothing so pleasant as a pot of money, as we say in Harristown.'

'There is nothing so pleasant.' He tore his eyes from my hair, and reached inside his case for a roll of closely written paper.

Then he stood up, announcing, 'Miss Darcy, aged twenty, sixty-two inches of hair; Miss Berenice and Miss Enda, aged eighteen, sixty-eight inches of hair apiece; Miss Manticory, aged almost fifteen, sixty-nine inches of hair; Miss Pertilly, aged thirteen, sixty-four inches; Miss Oona, twelve, sixty inches; Miss Idolatry, eleven, sixty-three inches.'

He nodded to each of us in the correct order – of course, in attending all our performances he had long since matched face to name, and inches to ages.

'No doubt there are desires and yearnings in you ladies for bettering your lovely selves,' he began.

'We're not free of desires and yearnings,' conceded Darcy acidly.

'No more you need be, my dear young ladies, because God's gifts to you can be turned into a fortune, if skilfully rendered through the mill of industry.'

'Mill? I don't want—' whimpered Ida.

'It's nothing to me that you don't want—' Darcy began.

'I speak metaphorically, my dears,' he intervened. 'The Swiney Godivas shall never toil in a menial manner, not when they have in superabundance exactly what the world craves. The world is starving for hair!' he cried. 'Starving!'

'Yes, yes, yes and—' Darcy tapped her foot impatiently.

'Which part of his adored wife may a man gaze at equally in public and in private?' demanded Mr Rainfleury. '*Only* her hair.'

There are whole religions and whole continents, I thought, *where the men would not agree with you, Mr Pig-Eared Ignorant.*

But my sisters were staring with their mouths open as Mr Rainfleury continued. 'So how highly charged with *looking* is this softest part of her that a husband shares with others? How that hair soaks up the looks of men . . . Other men see it bound up, coiled on the head – but all may own the *fantasy* of it let loose, rippling over the shoulders in private. But what need I teach the Swiney Godivas about *that*? Your gifts have already been showered on thousands of men. But you need to understand that a certain kind of man needs to see only one curl

94

... ahem ... This is why women must cover their hair in chapel. There is so much more to explain to you blessedly, magnificently endowed girls—'

'I hope not,' interrupted Darcy. 'That was already quite sufficient. Ida and Oona are still children, you know.'

'Indeed, I was coming to children. The little dears. Who doesn't love a long-haired little girl?'

'You'd be surprised,' snapped Darcy. 'And?'

'And this brings me to the subject in hand, that is, children's playthings that even a grown person may love and fondle. In this climactic epoch of hair-love, there is no more perfect and economical way of a lady possessing her private acreage of hair than to own it in miniature on her very own doll. For every hair-love, there is doll-love – for what woman or girl does not want an immortally tressed beauty on her dressing table? What husband or father does not long to purchase it for her?'

Darcy snatched the paper from him and read aloud, '*Rainfleury & Masslethwaite*—who's Masslethwaite?'

'My late partner.'

Darcy nodded and continued, '*Rainfleury & Masslethwaite shall, on payment of an agreed fee*—'

Darcy interrupted herself, 'What fee? No! Whisper to me alone.'

Mr Rainfleury leaned over and gave her a breathy sentence in her ear.

Clearly, he didn't affront her by that sentence. Indeed Darcy looked like a woman in receipt of a bouquet. Wordless, she handed him the contract and waved at him to continue with the reading:

'Rainfleury & Masslethwaite shall, on payment of an agreed fee, produce a set of seven different dolls, each to the full likeness of one of the Swiney Godivas, complete in verisimilitude as to the eye colour, comparative height and the colour and texture of the hair. The dolls, named for their muses, shall be sold separately so that they may be collected by an enthusiastic feminine public.'

He lowered the paper and let his eyes pass over us again. 'There is, ahem, also an opening for the gentleman collector in this new line.'

I imagined a gentleman, not dissimilar to Mr Rainfleury, gazing avidly at a long-haired naked doll seated on his grand mahogany desk. Surely, I thought, Darcy would never allow this obscenity, but she nodded as Mr Chops continued, '*The Swiney Godivas shall agree to show these dolls in all their future acts, and to endorse them at every opportunity.*'

'Endorse?' asked Pertilly.

'Personally recommend, associate yourselves and generally show admiration of,' supplied Mr Rainfleury.

Pertilly began to weep in earnest. 'I don't want to cut my hair off for to have it stuck upon a doll so. You cannot make me—'

'Neither I need, you ass,' bellowed Darcy. 'Will you stop battering the ears of our man here and listen? He'll not take a hair off *our* heads. Will you, Mr Rainfleury? You'll need hundreds of heads of hair. Your men'll cut something off a silky old horse, no doubt. Or buy it from a French maid. Am I not right, Mr Rainfleury? You'd not shave our heads and spoil our show for us, is it? Not when there's hair being sold by the bale in every poor street on the Continent.'

My mental teeth ground out, 'Mr Scissorthief!' 'Mr Despoilerator!' For everyone knew about the trade in women's hair. There were even hair markets where impoverished girls lined up to sell the only treasure they had. Poor women's hair was refashioned by other poor women – the lowly *posticheurs* and boardworkers – into convincing fake pieces to amplify heads of rich ladies of fashion. If you read the newspaper editorials, the hair trade was generally considered shameful – a kind of capillary cannibalism – and it was also deemed filthy, as if poverty endowed the sold hair with disease and vermin.

Yet the hair trade was outstandingly profitable – so much so that there were regular outbreaks of hair crime in London. Girls with visibly abundant hair had been set upon in the street and barbered by men who sold their booty for profit. I flinched from our supposed benefactor. Didn't Darcy realise that by making us famous he would also be making us targets for 'hair despoilers', as these thieves were known?

Mr Despoilerator stammered, 'Well, of course the bulk will be from ... a special source of my own. I'd not for the world compromise your own personal splendours. I am ... in the process of ... patenting a new form of artificial hair spun from silk and extracts of rare plants. It imitates real hair to a nicety and totally obviates the need to dabble in the unwholesome human hair trade, where a respectable businessman like myself would never in any case dip a finger.'

'The bulk?' Darcy glanced down the contract. 'Oh, I see. *"Rainfleury & Masslethwaite will guarantee to customers that each doll contains one genuine hair from the head of a Swiney Godiva."* '

She sneered. 'And is it also an unmentioned condition that Mr Rainfleury himself must choose that single hair?'

He nodded eagerly.

'In other words,' said Darcy, 'he may spend as long as he likes handling the full lengths of our hair while he chooses those single strands at leisure. Is that it, Mr Rainfleury? Do I have it nutshelled here, is it?'

I mentioned quickly, 'But we can collect the hair ourselves in our hair-receivers whenever we comb it. There's always plenty there, especially after a wash. He doesn't need to—'

Ida said, 'And what about the Day of Judgement? When we must assemble all our lost hairs? How will we get them back then? Mam will—'

'We won't be plaguing Mam with such details,' said Darcy firmly. 'And God will be too busy to account for every single Swiney hair on Judgement Day.'

I thought, *No, He'll be busying Himself with looking into how PS got buried in the clover field.*

Now Berenice and Oona were crying. 'We don't want to have our hair handled either.'

'So much the worse for you, then. You'll be made into a doll, and you'll be handled if I tell you to,' rapped Darcy. 'In fact, Mr

Rainfleury, please help yourself to another head of hair just to see if it's satisfactory. Whom shall you be having next?'

Now Ida too erupted into tears. 'Will I not be getting a doll at all? But doll men will be getting *me*? I don't understand! And will the gentleman be putting nits in the dolls so they are really Swineys?'

Darcy clapped one hand over Ida's mouth, and slapped her rump hard with the other. 'Just Ida's idea of a joke,' Darcy guffawed. 'You'll find nothing living above the neck here.'

'That's a lie of you!' Ida struggled free.

'Do not speak of the nits,' whispered Berenice. 'It will just remind them to come back. There is nothing a nit likes better than to be spoke of.'

'An unfortunate plague upon decent girls,' burbled Mr Rainfleury, 'and no doubt provoked by the low company you've been obliged to keep while your talents have been so underexploited. Small blame to you on that score, of course. One does not hear of nits and worms in genteel, prosperous circumstances in Dublin Town. Such as you shall soon – with my help – be among.'

Darcy muttered, 'Company does not get lower than the Eileen O'Reilly.'

Dublin Town. I thought of the freckled muzzle of the butcher's runt pressed against our window. Mr Rainfleury's plans would remove us from her view, perhaps without my ever having a chance to forgive her and be forgiven.

'Dublin Town itself!' breathed Oona.

'To be dolls so,' said Ida sadly.

My face was reddening and my fists were clenching because I knew Mr Rainfleury should never dare to ask a decent girl to be a doll. Would Mr Rainfleury bring his shiny case and his contract up the grand steps of Harristown House to ask the ladies there for their likenesses in bisque? Would he be so tranquilly sure of carrying all before him?

No, at Harristown House he'd be slung out on his porky ear for insulting the ladies so.

But we Swineys were his for the asking.

Part Two
DUBLIN

13

No matter how much he winked and gargoyled at Darcy with his tufty head on one side, Mr Rainfleury got no more than one sister to handle at a time until the doll contracts were signed.

We were presently following a season of Fleadh Cheoils around the country, learning the old Gaelic songs for our own turns on the stage. Mr Rainfleury and his avid mouth were there as often as they ever could be. Having myself limp-fingered by Mr Flittergoblin felt worse to me than exposing my hair onstage, but I dared not say against it. To my relief, although I had been his first choice, Mr Rainfleury soon made a firm favourite of Berenice, who indeed began to show a precocious liking for his breathy attentions. Whenever I ballyragged her about Mr Rainfleury's near-baldness, she reproved me, 'And be quiet yourself, Manticory. The mighty brain on him has worn out the poor hair roots. You know what they say: "Grass does not grow on a busy street." '

Berenice's defence attracted Enda's suspicion, and then her jealousy until she too declared that Mr Rainfleury might have his way with her hair at any time, even offering to take the places of less willing sisters like myself. Guiltily, I permitted Enda's sacrifice. And this had the predictable result of rousing Berenice's ire, to the extent that she plaited dried strands of goose doings into Enda's hair one night while her twin lay sleeping, a thing that ended very badly with pulled ears and eyes near scrabbed out all round.

Once the contracts were signed, Mr Rainfleury was given the run of us. Oblivious to the twins' feud, or perhaps secretly feeding on its drama, Mr Rainfleury took delight in sitting on a stool behind them so he could weave their hair together into a single plait as thick and muscular as an anaconda. Then he would unravel it slowly. From behind them, of course, he could see neither the grotesque faces his 'poppets' pulled at one another nor the eloquent gestures of their fingers.

Darcy, being of age, insisted on signing the contract on our behalf. Each doll would have its own debut night, for which Mr Rainfleury would be obliged to subsidise new costumes all round, and stand a hot rum punch for the customers.

Mr Rainfleury put forward an advance sum, enough for Darcy to pay a year's rent on a Dublin townhouse of five lofty storeys, from where the Swiney Godivas would take the town's many theatres by storm. She came back from Dublin full of our new home, which, she told us, was furnished, stuccoed, wallpapered, fanlighted and hung with swarthy oil paintings. It stood in Pembroke Street on the corner of rose-bricked Fitzwilliam Square. 'It's entirely grand and cosy at the same time,' she boasted, 'and but a quick trot from the La Touches' Dublin mansion!'

We were to remove there on Midsummer's Eve, leaving the slow crows and the Eileen O'Reilly far, far behind.

The thought of that separation drove me to seek out the Eileen O'Reilly. I did not want to leave with her hating me, and counting me no better than Darcy.

I followed her home from school, a respectful three yards behind her.

She stiffened her back, never once looking behind.

When she reached the butcher's shop, she turned to fix me with her eyes.

'It's too late,' she said. 'I know ye're taking your great selves off to Dublin Town. That's nothing to me and less than nothing. But I'll not be the poor little country mouse ye left behind to be sorry for and think of jest occasionally from time to time.'

'It would not be like that,' I protested.

'And why wouldn't it be? Are ye not Darcy Swiney's true sister?'

Her voice tore on the last word.

She walked into the shop and slammed the door behind her so hard that it lifted the bloodied clumps of sawdust on the path and closed my eyes with pain.

Annora refused to come to Dublin with us. She had tried her pallid utmost to dissuade us from the enterprise.

She had never been to Dublin, and insisted that it was a city rife with evil ways and that she would not be exposed to its sin and stinks. 'Indeed, I'm asking myself why should you girls be wanting to leave Harristown at all when we're snug as in God's pocket here? My feet are wet with tears that you are even thinking of it, Darcy. Not that it would stop you.'

'It would not,' agreed Darcy.

But Annora, her eyes more sunken and her teeth more prominent than ever, showed a rare spirit in refusing to countenance a move for herself. 'I'll be stopping peaceable here at home. I'll be grand with a bit of griddle bread of an evening and Mrs Godlin to visit, awaiting on when you have a mind to come away home.'

I saw Ida open her mouth to say, 'I'll stay too,' and Berenice putting her hand over it to spare Ida a slap.

'What about us?' Darcy turned on Annora. 'What if we never come back?'

Never come back, I thought. Was it not what I had wanted all this time? Yet when I had dreamed of leaving Harristown, it was not to leave Annora and be put under the protection of an oyster-mouthed Mr Rainfleury and reproduced in bisque-faced miniature.

Darcy demanded, 'How will it look, seven young girls unchaperoned in Dublin while their heartless mother amuses herself at her country residence? And what will you do with yourself without us to tend to?'

Annora plunged her hands into a tubful of laundry and shook her head. 'I'll not be sleeping at night over you every day you're gone, God love you.'

Darcy crooned, 'Isn't it the proud woman you'd be, strutting down Dame Street in silk with your seven daughters behind you?'

This last argument did not weigh greatly with Annora. She muttered stubbornly, 'It's myself wishes that none of you would ever go away.'

I stood beside her mutely, taking in her smell of soap and sadness. As it had when I was tiny, my hand crept towards hers, finding it in the warm water of the tub.

The tongue in Darcy's mouth flickered. 'Don't be so soft, Manticory! If there's a worse mother in Ireland, I won't know where to look or ask for her.'

Fashionable magazines began to arrive for Darcy. She studied them by the light of the seashell lamp, practising gracious phrases. She turned down the corners of fat catalogues. Her black books were stacked in a fine new trunk.

On the day of our departure, with the carriage waiting outside, Darcy staged one last attempt on Annora's resolve. 'So you're still content for your poor innocent daughters to wade barefoot and alone through the swirling rivers of Dublin sins and stinks, is it?' asked Darcy, adding cruelly, 'With our guardian angels weeping for our souls outside every evil door we motherless innocents might enter? You're perfectly sure about that now?'

While wincing at Darcy's crude blackmail, I hoped it might yet sway Annora to come with us.

Annora's uncomprehending silence annoyed Darcy into a great cruelty. She hissed, 'Not to mention that our friend Sin has made at least six visitations to Harristown, and indeed overnighted on each occasion at this very cottage.'

This was the first time Darcy had ever mentioned our supposedly various paternal provenance, and the reason for the whispers in the street behind us all our Harristown years.

'So,' Darcy continued, 'sure it *is* better you stay here in Harristown and let *us* escape your moral contagion. And do not trouble your old conscience as to the practical matters. Rainfleury's hired us a cook-housekeeper.' She waved a dog-eared letter. 'Mrs Hartigan's character here says she is known for exercising a wholesome influence on those in her sphere.

She shall mother us to perfection, and so much the worse for you.'

Far from being goaded by Darcy's insults or the prospect of a maternal rival, Annora was defeated by both. She hung her head and stammered for a few moments without ever framing an actual word. Then she went to the ironing basket behind the kitchen table and handed Darcy seven new white pillowcases, each embroidered with one of our names in the red thread she used for mending petticoats. At the finality of this gift, I began to cry.

Darcy stopped her goings-on immediately. She reached into her reticule, pulling out a lozenge of impacted banknotes. She thrust them into Annora's apron pocket. I thought she looked a tint sorry as she did it. She seemed to hesitate. For a scant moment it seemed she might even embrace our mother.

The moment was lost when a thin goose sighed loudly under the window and Ida piped up, 'Sin and stinks! Sin and stinks! Dirty girls in Dublin! We'll be famished for a bar of soap so! Don't be worrying, Mam, we'll do like St Ita and keep a stag beetle on our bellies to keep the men from ravening us! Except' – she began to sob – 'I mightn't be fit.'

Darcy was required to resume full gladiatorial ferocity, pinning Ida to the table. Before any of us could intervene, she was yanking Ida's plaits violently, shouting a word for each hard tug, 'Why is all the sense on the outside of your head, girl?'

The seashell lamp above the table swung to and fro, set aquiver by Darcy's hot breath. Pertilly lumbered between Darcy and Ida, and took Ida into her arms.

We filed outside, me wiping my eyes and Ida snivelling into Pertilly's armpit and clutching the hearthbrush made of the latest Phiala's wings. I glimpsed the Eileen O'Reilly hiding behind the woodpile, with something shining on her face. If Darcy had not been behind me, I would have waved to her.

Instead, I rushed back into the kitchen and swarmed all over Annora with a feverish hug to every limb. 'I really didn't think we'd go without you.'

She stroked my hair with her soap-rough hand and whispered, 'Be gone with you, girl. Darcy's right. I'm no good to you in your coming grandness. And 'tis you – of all of us – who needs to get away from Harristown, do you not? You'll not be happy here again, Manticory.'

What does she know? I wondered. *Did Darcy tell the troll against me to her too?*

Annora tipped my chin up to look at me, and wiped away my tears with her apron. 'I have a great job of work for you, Manticory. Write to me, will you? Will you do that same? Mrs Godlin will come read to me. A letter every now and sometimes would be a fine thing, and better than butter, may God ease me. A letter in my hand, that will be something to have a hold of. And I'll know you were thinking of me when you wrote it and that will be a gift in itself.'

The Eileen O'Reilly threw stones after our departing carriage. She cried, 'The curse of the crows upon Darcy Swiney! My heavy hathred on ye too!'

Darcy poked her head out of the window to retort, 'The back of my hand and the sole of my foot to you, runt! I am better and far better than you shall ever be.'

I heard the sob in the Eileen O'Reilly's parting shout. She blamed Darcy, I understood, for taking me away without our ever healing the hurts between us.

I would not humiliate her by witnessing her distress. I kept my eyes on the slow crows, wet with rain and glittering on the grass like the spilled beads of a rosary. But at the last minute, as the carriage passed her by, I turned and raised the little finger of my left hand at her, and she did the same to me.

I took Darcy's slap almost with pleasure, because the Eileen O'Reilly saw that I took it for her.

When the carriage pulled up at Pembroke Street, Darcy had to bully us out of it into the lilac-scented air. We huddled with all the dignity of frightened chickens on the roadside until she hustled us up the steps of Number 1 and through the front door into a grand hallway. I was ashamed to put my foot on its flagstones, so clean were they in the bright sunlight. I caught sight of our stricken faces in a bevelled mirror. Annora's absence was visible there too. The smell of burning peat gave a breath of comfort – I sucked deeply on it. Darcy introduced us to Mrs Hartigan, 'our cook-housekeeper'. A middle-aged woman curtseyed primly, bewildering us into returning the courtesy, which caused her high, pale brow to furrow and Darcy's fists to tighten. Ida dropped her fiddle case and sent a vase of cut flowers crashing to the floor.

Our first instinct was to scuttle down into the forgiving gloom of the basement. In a tumbling mass, everyone except Darcy dived for the stairs, with Mrs Hartigan calling out, 'No, my ladies, you shall never need . . .'

We found ourselves in a kitchen bigger than our whole Harristown cottage, with a black range that seemed like a factory. Enda lifted up a wooden potato masher – even that was polished and patterned and carved from an expensive-looking wood. Pertilly sniffed inside the salt box. Ida touched the lid of something that resembled a copper coffin. 'Do they boil babies in Dublin?' she asked. 'The babies here must smell dreadful like fish, though.'

We hurtled out of the kitchen in different directions. Down there in those dim catacombs of the house we discovered a large bedroom with a single bed, a larder with a rat-rack attached to the whitewashed ceiling, and a rabbit hanging from a hook, a wine store and other mysterious doors with monumental locks.

'It's that gloomy down here,' said Ida dubiously. 'I think I'll go home now.'

Berenice shouted, 'I'm sleeping in the real bed. I saw it first!'

Enda sent the potato masher flying at her head.

By that time Mrs Hartigan was behind us. She laid a gentle hand on Berenice's shoulder, her face soft with understanding. 'This is *my* room, my dear. That is my bed, and that is my darning mushroom for mending your stockings, and my irons for smoothing your clothes. You young ladies are to be accommodated on the floors above the parlour. Mr Rainfleury has it all arranged just so.'

Silent and ashamed, we followed her back up to the hall where Darcy glowered and pinched each of us as we passed her. Mrs Hartigan showed us the ground-floor dining room, led us up the stairs to the parlour and an adjoining 'withdrawing' room with two thrillingly tall and full bookshelves. We trudged behind her up two more storeys arranged into seven separate bedrooms, each with a flounced counterpane on the bed and a flowered ewer on a mirrored stand. There was a music room with its own Julius Blüthner upright pianoforte on which rested a formidable rosewood metronome. Mrs Hartigan described as our 'bathroom' a shiny white shrine populated by unfamiliar objects. Darcy muttered, 'I'll explain later,' when Mrs Hartigan showed us the commode chairs and the mahogany bidet boxes by every bed. From each window there were glimpses of the rose-brick canyons of Fitzwilliam Square or the mews behind it, and our own vegetable garden and a coach house at the end. From the top floor, the Dublin Mountains could be seen hovering in the pale distance, not far from the clouds.

Mrs Hartigan ushered us back down to the parlour. 'So, what do you think, my dears?' she asked. 'Isn't this something like, now? You are powerfully quiet for such famous little singers of songs.'

'But there's a fireplace in every room so!' breathed Ida. Finally, she let loose her grip on the goose-wing hearthbrush and laid it on the hearth. 'We'll be out all day in that square there collecting firewood! For there's not a bit of turf to be dug down there in those gardens. And then we'll get drove over by a carriage every time we cross that murdering road and turned into red rashers lying there!'

Mrs Hartigan pointed wordlessly to the pot-bellied brass scuttles brimming with peat and coal.

What did we think? Only that morning, we had woken up with the thin geese and a mother in a Harristown hovel. That night we'd be sleeping on goose down in Dublin, mothered by someone paid to do it. The hedges and copses that had delineated our world were gone – instead we were penned by red brick and slate with the sky available only in glimpses. Even the rain that now commenced to fall seemed more sophisticated than in Harristown: the grey shreds of it barely dampened the noisy confidence of the carriage-rattling city. The very geese in Dublin would be fat and prosperous, I guessed, and seen only on the roasting plate, and not just at Michaelmas. I suddenly felt a sharp longing for the keening of the slow crows and the sight of them rising from the sodden branches to perform their lovely dances over the pea-green fields of Harristown.

Worst of all, we were in the land of Rainfleury. Mrs Hartigan mentioned him in every second sentence. He had already been all over the house and even in our bedrooms. His very smell clung to the air of the parlour – cloying flowery cologne sullied the sweet notes of peat.

The coachman was carrying our possessions upstairs, directed by Darcy, who had already decided who would sleep where.

Enda and Berenice were safely separated by a floor. Naturally, Oona and I had rooms adjacent to that of our tribeswoman Enda, while Berenice's party of Pertilly and Ida were to sleep either side of their heroine. Darcy and her black books occupied the grandest room on my own floor.

Before we could go and jump on the beds, we were introduced to the rest of the household: it was not just Mrs Hartigan to keep us fed and clean. Living out, but attending daily, were a maid to empty the chamber pots, dress the beds and scrub the steps, and an elderly houseboy, with a scut of a pipe hanging on his lip, to run the turf and coal. We had our own coachman to attend to our horse and carriage, both glinting with polished brass and accommodated in a stone pavilion at the end of the garden, and at our disposal for every excursion, complete with a carriage-warmer of hot coals kept ready at all times for our use. A sewing-woman, Darcy announced, was to call on us three times a week, to make clothes for our acts, reproducing them in miniature for our as-yet-unseen dolls. An accompanist would be paid by the hour to rehearse us. And there would be daily elocution lessons to deSwiney our tongues and make our vowels lie flat upon them.

When I asked, 'What about schooling?' Darcy replied, 'Why are you asking and you almost fifteen, Manticory? The whole of Dublin is your school now, and haven't Pertilly and Oona all their wise older sisters to ask any questions of so? Ida's not going to be learning anything more anyway. Now watch this!' She reached towards a wide, stiff ribbon of embroidered braid hanging from the ceiling and yanked it as if it were one of Ida's plaits.

Mrs Hartigan came scurrying up from below, the keys jangling at her waist.

Ida rushed to hug her and was detached with difficulty.

'Do you lock us up at night?' Ida asked, fingering the keys.

'Oh no, my dear, you are the mistresses here. These are the keys for the spice box, the tea chest, the wine locker, the silver press and the drawer with the accounts ledger.'

Darcy announced, 'For supper, we shall want a pair of boiled fowl, sweetbreads, haddock and salmon patties and plum pudding with jelly.'

I stared at Darcy. Supper? How had she even heard of that kind of food? Then I remembered the magazines delivered to Harristown.

'Thank you, madam,' replied Mrs Hartigan. 'Shall it be convenient for me to serve dinner at eight?'

'What would prevent you?' said Darcy carelessly, as if dining at that distant hour was her habit.

'Eight?' squealed Ida. 'We shall starve to death in Dublin. We'll have perished before then.'

'No more you shall,' smiled Mrs Hartigan, 'for in the intervening time there's to be a fine tea.'

And there was time for me to inspect the bookshelves. I found them full of dull agricultural affairs – not a single novel or volume of poetry. I guessed that the books had been bought for their handsome bindings.

Mr Rainfleury appeared at teatime to refresh the house with his scent. He frowned at Ida scraping broken pieces of cake and toast into her handkerchief 'for later'.

'You must bring her up,' he told Darcy, 'to put those starveling ways behind her.'

But Ida would not be brought up.

'This,' she declared, holding up a portion of Mrs Hartigan's raised and ruched veal pie, 'is food good enough to be kissed. But it is too good to be eaten.'

With each successive meal, Ida secreted more choice bits of food into her pockets and hoarded them inside her fireplace or under her bed. Pertilly crammed bread and meat into her mouth as if every supper was her last. Berenice and Enda competed for whatever was deemed the finest item on the table. I found myself reaching for cherries and plums I did not want, just because they were there. Only Darcy seemed to have shed the skin of poverty with ease and discarded it with easy pleasure.

Three breakfasts, two luncheons, two teas and two suppers later, Mr Rainfleury escorted Darcy to a grand bank in Dame Street, where our affairs were put in order with the clerks and lawyers. That evening I watched Darcy hide a large document, with plentiful stigmata of red wax, under the blotter of her desk. As a final touch, the 'Swiney Godiva Corporation' was furnished with stationery headed with our new address in flouncing copperplate. I started a letter to Annora on it, but soon put it on the fire, and asked Mrs Hartigan for some of the plain paper she used for kitchen orders.

I wondered about writing a small note to the Eileen O'Reilly, to say my overdue sorries to her about Darcy's last insults, but feared to humiliate her with our new grandeur.

Perhaps, I thought, I'd find a way to send her a doll, secretly. Not a 'Miss Manticory', but a 'Miss Darcy', to do with as she wished, and as hard as she wished.

I pictured her forcing a greasy crubeen into the doll's hard lips, smashing the bisque face in the process.

The design of the dolls was a drawn-out affair, entailing much conferencing and clashing between Darcy and Mr Rainfleury, particularly as to the fullness of the lips and the hardness of the jawline of her own doll's bisque maquettes. The 'Miss Darcy' doll would be the first launched. Its original made sure that it cost Mr Rainfleury the most trouble. Meanwhile, the rest of us were shown our doll selves in various separate stages of their evolution: a glass eye was held up against our own in a strong light; a hair sample plaited into ours to see if it disappeared in a perfect match. Strangest of all, a pair of wet clay lips was briefly pressed on our own to trap the tender shape.

Whenever not needed at the factory, Mr Rainfleury pronounced himself incapable of renouncing the pleasure of our company. He was a regular fixture at Pembroke Street for suppers and luncheons. His smell was never out of the house. I tried without success to superimpose Annora's face over his when he took the seat I thought of as hers at the head of the table, facing Darcy.

While Mr Rainfleury agonised pleasurably over our bisque features, we Swineys taught ourselves how to live in a house. At first we constantly roamed the floors, looking for our tribal sisters: we were not accustomed to being out of sight of one another. It was only after several weeks that I could sleep easily without Enda's breaths to lull me. With much shrieking, we learned the uses of the commode chairs and mahogany bidets and grew to trust that the claw-footed bath would not walk away on those nimble-looking feet with our nakedness inside.

Enda loved to trail her delicate fingers down the mahogany banisters. Berenice took to waiting on the stairs for Mr Rainfleury's visits.

Mrs Hartigan coaxed and coached us into corsets and crinoline cages, encouraging us to sleep in our stays with the promise that we could reduce our Famine-tidy waists to fairylike proportions in a year. Oona admitted to loving the breathless faintness brought on by each heart-stopping new constriction. I hated my corset for its uncomfortable intrusion on my thoughts. No longer was I able to read for hours: I had to rise from my chair, stretch and walk to avoid weals and worse.

Annora had laundered our clothes to thin threads, but we'd not known the luxury of multiplication. Ida never tired of counting that she had seven of everything. There were rainbows of flannel, taffeta, rep and quilted silk in our wardrobes. Every evening Mrs Hartigan laid out on our beds freshly laundered longcloth drawers with lace pointwork crisp and snowy as beaten egg white. We learned to remember to check in the petticoat mirror under the hall stand for incriminating glimpses of white, scarlet or violet.

We began to work, engaged to perform at the Antient Concert Rooms in Brunswick Street. The Royal Dublin Society requested us for a show at the Botanic Gardens at Glasnevin. I wrote our new scripts on Superfine Cream Laid, using a newfangled pen with its own reservoir of ink and an iridium-tipped gold nib, the only gift for which I would ever thank Mr Rainfleury with actual sincerity, even though suspecting that it was the new Swiney Godiva Corporation that had paid for it.

We set ourselves to learn Society as it was done in Dublin. The volume of our new skirts fortified us against the world, keeping its terrors an arm's length away. We found ways to cross the roads, at first in an arrow formation of seven with Darcy at its tip, and later in our billowing tribes of three. We took tea and cakes at Mitchell's in Grafton Street, alongside great ladies of the capital, who appeared unable to detect the stench of former poverty on the Swineys of Harristown, perhaps because so many of them were bent over the port cunningly concealed in their teacups. We made excursions further afield. While Darcy forced Ida, Pertilly and Berenice to accompany her to the races, Enda, Oona and I rode the wooden horses at Donnybrook Fair and strolled arm-in-arm past the caravans of Shakespearean players murdering the saddest scenes of *Othello*. We took carriage rides among the undulating acres of Phoenix Park and promenades around the pond in St Stephen's Green, where Ida could not be stopped from picking up choice pieces of kindling and where Berenice and Enda threw stones at one another's reflections in the water.

I made myself at ease in the bookshops. I attended literary readings on nights when we did not perform. I listened with an absorbent ear, taking in what functioned upon the audience's wits and what did not. A trickle of warm courage stole into my heart. Dublin was an ants' nest of writers and performers. Some were even in Society. Some were even women. I dared to think that it was in my own gift to tell my stories more finely than Darcy told me to.

She'd never be noticing, for it'd not appear on a ledger. Like Adam, I would name things in my garden and have power over them. The commercial imperatives of the Swiney Godiva routines need not rule my vocabulary. The rite of writing could be celebrated in other ways. Via incessant narratives of my own, I vowed – for was I not as Irish as any wordster – I'd write myself better and far better than I had been. One day the Eileen O'Reilly would hear of me not as Darcy Swiney's sister, but as a writer.

Perhaps she would read me, and remember me with fondness and forgiveness, because reading was the one sole gift she'd had of me to keep.

We attended Mass at St Teresa's Church of the Discalced Carmelites in Clarendon Street, a church chosen by Ida 'because it has seven arches at the bottom like Harristown Bridge, so we can make our confessions here'. I looked at her sharply then. Had she too met with a gentleman on that bridge? She smiled glassily back at me, and I knew I'd never have the truth of her.

For Darcy, the better argument for St Teresa's was that the church was near her favourite watering-spot, Mitchell's.

St Teresa's was an old granite brute of a building. Each of its plump stones seemed to thrust out its grey breast in the stubborn service of God. Iron railings protected it from the constant and irrational Dublin traffic. Inside, the painted green arches reminded me of Harristown's close-knit hills.

We Swineys were a much pointed-out feature of the congregation and a picture of fashionable propriety in our new bonnets; that is, until Ida made a spectacle of us. I'll not deny that we were all deeply fascinated by the life-size statue of Dead Christ lying under the altar in front of six gingerbread-coloured columns. I myself had certainly noticed the friendly shape of him, and the fact that there was nothing missing from the catalogue of masculine beauty in his face, limbs and naked torso. Our hymns seemed like love songs when we sang them to the beautiful Him under that altar, and no more so than to me, whose faith had been shattered by Father Maglinn's siding against me and with the troll on Harristown Bridge. So I looked at Dead Christ with more frank pleasure than any of my sisters – except Ida.

On our second Sunday Ida interrupted our singing with a cry. 'He moved! Something twitched under that loincloth there!'

The worshippers around us drew in their breath and expelled it in a hiss of disapproval.

'You should not have been staring at that part of him!' said Darcy, who rarely lifted her eyes from it. 'And you not yet twelve, you scrattock.'

Ida was hurried out by two tutting nuns. We followed, our heads cast down, trying not to hear the whispers of the women in the congregation. Even the priest stopped in his sermon to stare us out of the nave.

It was some weeks before we dared to show our faces at St Teresa's again.

Instead, we enjoyed some pagan Sabbaths for ourselves. Our carriage took us to Black Rock south of Dublin Bay where we made squealing use of the bathing machines. We visited the museums in Leinster House. At the Hibernian Museum we inspected the entire Fossil Elk found in County Limerick half a century past.

Dublin's map imprinted itself on our minds, though it was never possible, for a solitary minute, to conceive that the stern Liffey pulsing greyly through the heart of Dublin was the same dappled stream that flowed under Harristown Bridge. We tried to get used to the equestrian statue of William, and not to be intimidated by the porticoed grandeur of the post office or the mêlée that was Carlisle Bridge.

There was no respite from grandeur at home either. We struggled to accustom ourselves to the high ceilings of the rooms at Pembroke Street, and to the white tiles in the bathroom with the black grouting glowering between their shiny purities. The chortling of the water pipes brought on a fit in Ida, as did the wet tumbling of the water closet.

After reading accounts of Society suppers in the papers, Darcy tortured Mrs Hartigan with demands for mutton cutlets with macaroni, roast turkey, barnacle goose and seakale, boiled rumps of beef, snipe, apple puddings, orange jelly and pigeon pie. She ordered raisins and almonds, which were kept locked in a box in our withdrawing room to, which only Darcy had the key.

We tried not to look frightened whenever our doorbell chimed with a new delivery: we were now accomplished shoppers, Darcy the most acquisitive of all. In our first month at Pembroke Street she acquired fourteen pairs of pointed boots and a terrifying new crocodile-skin reticule with the traces of a grinning reptilian jaw and a hooded eye on each side.

'I was exceptionally astute in a certain private business this week,' she told us, demonstrating the fearsome object. 'I deserved a little something extra. With all I put up with, all I do to make sure the rest of you are swimming in luxuries . . .'

'What private business?' asked Oona.

Ida commenced to gallop around the room beating her thigh like a jockey on a horse, until Darcy caught her and slapped her ear, sputtering, 'Be sitting down for yourself, you bold-behaved torment!'

She turned to the rest of us. 'Ida is really not up to herself today.'

A day rarely passed without my taking a book down to leafy Fitzwilliam Square to read. I was homesick for my hiding places in Harristown, the sweet clover where I used to lie full-length in front of a volume of poems. Perching decorously on a cold bench, I could never arrange my limbs with that same happy abandonment. I missed dipping my mouth in the stream for the taste of living liquid. In Dublin, our water was delivered to a great coffin of a tank and piped into the house. I missed the solid blackness of the Harristown night – in Fitzwilliam Square, even a moonless midnight was muddied by gaslight. I missed Annora's low voice keening for the goose Phiala in the softness of the evening. The Eileen O'Reilly's face floated into my mind often. I pictured her grimy finger on the page of the primer, and I wondered if she had continued with her studies. Perhaps, now that she could read, her father had taken her out of school to work in his shop, as he had sometimes threatened. I imagined her there, standing in the blood-soaked sawdust, frowning over an account. I never stopped missing the slow crows. Neither did Ida, I realised, when I saw her gazing sadly at a dusty blackbird as she practised on her fiddle by the window. Instead we had to make do with the wheeling, screaming Dublin gulls, their beaks dripping with pink and grey intestines they had ripped from some living creature. There was no sad music to those birds – only the sound of murder and the strident stinks of fish and salt.

I wrote of these things to Annora, on brown kitchen paper, by way of telling her that I missed her too.

It was a great day when the first entire dolls finally appeared. The time was set at just before tea on a rainy afternoon in December, with the house already got up in its Christmas finery and a pile of wrapped and ribboned gifts under the tree.

Mr Rainfleury had announced that he would make a cere-mony of delivering each doll in person to her original. He also insisted that each sister should meet her own doll privately.

'And you should each have a little minute or two alone with the creature, to get used to her,' he explained. 'Then you may present her to your sisters. Trust me, this will be the best manner of proceeding.'

Now that each of us had our own bedroom, Darcy saw no problem with indulging Mr Rainfleury on this point. 'Let the old man have his way,' she said dismissively.

'Not an old man!' protested Berenice and Enda in one voice, and then glared at each other.

When we heard the doorbell chime at five, we obediently repaired to our separate rooms, as arranged. As we paced silently up the stairs in time to the beating rain, there was a febrile atmosphere churning, as if a wild game of hide-and-seek was in progress, with breathless ghosts concealed in every wardrobe and under the armpit of each gable. The smell of luncheon's boiled tongue and greens hung heavily in the air. I noted all my sisters' smiling, eager faces. Dolls, my sisters seemed to think, were light-hearted creatures and there must be merriment in their first coming among us. It appeared that I was the only one to nurse any apprehensions about Mr Rainfleury's creations.

I listened at my keyhole as our patron was admitted by Mrs Hartigan. She exclaimed loudly at the sizes of the packages he had brought. She knew about the ceremony, of course. The dolls were to be presented in order of our ages, oldest first. Soon I heard the housekeeper conducting Mr Rainfleury up the stairs towards Darcy's room next to mine on the second floor.

That was never going to be an entirely pleasant encounter. Darcy's displeasure grumbled through the walls in fragments of 'Never!' and 'So much the worse for you . . .' and 'I'll break your head for you if you—' 'Black book—'

Then it was the third floor – Berenice's turn, and back down the steps for a lingering visit to Enda's room across the corridor from my own. Listening at the wall, I heard a sound that resembled the purring of a cat. With everyone except Berenice, I thought anxiously, sweet Enda was too kind for her own good. I worried about how kind she was being to Mr Rainfleury, for I guessed he would lap up any amount of kindness, and then ask for some more in that tranquil steely way of his.

At last came Mr Rainfleury's tap on my own door. As ever, it was too light, too tentative.

It should not have made me start or shiver or blanch, or screw up my face. But it did all those things, and more.

14

My little likeness arrived in a pink cardboard box, fastened with a black ribbon, which Mr Rainfleury untied for me, kneeling at my feet. He cautioned me to stay in my chair as, 'The excitement of meeting "Miss Manticory" may be too much for you, my dear.'

'Doubtless,' I scowled. 'How my heart beats!'

'Sarcasm does not become a young lady,' he told me indulgently.

He pulled the doll gently from her box and set her on an occasional table in front of me. Her red hair almost covered her face, cascading over her shoulders past her waist and down towards her boots. The hair was burnished like Sicilian citrus where the light found it. A burnt purple brooded in the shadows of its curls.

'It is my hair,' I admitted. 'I mean, very like.'

Mr Rainfleury reached through the canopy of curls and waggled her right hand at me in a coy wave. Then he rustled in the box and placed a miniature comb and hair-receiver in my unwilling lap.

'You may touch!' he urged. 'Do!'

I parted the curls that curtained her face and peered into her eyes. Her hair thrummed silkily in the pinch of my fingers. I wondered how much of it was human, how much horse, but Darcy had forbidden me to raise that question any more. Mr Rainfleury would not retract his account of 'artificial hair of spun silk and the essences of rare plants'.

Miss Manticory was undeniably like me, just shrunk to thirty inches tall, thereby refining every detail of my own appearance. I had no reason to be surprised by the doll's accuracy. I had sat for her portrait in a series of photographs showing every angle of my face. I had submitted to the dyers, offering four separate samples before Mr Rainfleury judged that the doll hair conformed to my colour. 'Miss Manticory' carried a mesh purse like the one I favoured. Her complexion had been painted and refired until it was an exact match to my own.

Her dress, like the hideous stage one also just made for me, was in silk trimmed with lace and muslin. The bodice in solferino crimson was lined with cotton, again with a lace trim. She wore a diaphanous pinafore, three silk petticoats, circular-striped wool stockings and Balmoral boots. A bow sat at a jaunty angle in her hair, sewed right into her scalp. To complete her rig-out, around her neck hung a tiny silver locket on a velvet ribbon, just like mine.

The green glass eyes were also mine in shape and angle, though exaggerated in size in proportion to the face and placed centrally, like a child's. Mr Rainfleury confided that the eyelashes were the only items of real hair. I imagined young girls, screaming, being held down, while their eyelashes were plucked from their lids with long tweezers.

'Such a beautiful, rich red,' he crooned, lifting one of Miss Manticory's curls. 'Royal red. Did you know that peasants were once forbidden to wear it? It was too good for them! Too fierce, perhaps. The colour is sacred to Mars, god of war. A colour so potent that our ancestors believed that it could ward off illness and witches—'

I was not listening, instead wondering what stories Mr Rainfleury had prepared for my sisters, to ease their acquaintance with their dolls, with what legends he'd flatter them, how he'd assure them of their primacy, soothe them with pretty anecdotes, whatever was needed to force them to accommodate these glass-eyed graven images without screaming. Although 'Miss Manticory' stood still as a stone in front of me, I myself felt as if I had been run at by a mad bull. My breath came faster. Mr Rainfleury noticed.

'This is another effect of the power of red. It makes the pupils dilate too.'

'It is not the red,' I said slowly. 'It is the theft.'

'No, no, no, no, no,' he protested, understanding me perfectly.

Mr Rainfleury had stolen more than my likeness. The idea of me was presently to be put for sale, in a pink cardboard box with a black bow. Darcy had sold us Swineys into a dirty kind of trade. She had whored us – Darcy, who tongue-scourged poor Annora for her fleshly sins. Annora had compromised only her own soul and reputation in the eyes of Harristown. Darcy had prostituted seven virgins. Anyone might put their money down and have a handle of us, with nothing to fetter their pretty-fingering or their imaginings. Anyone – even gentlemen collectors! – might tip up our skirts and examine our pantalets, or sleep with us in their beds.

When he saw the glitter in my eyes, Mr Rainfleury chose to believe that I still worried for the poor girls shorn to bedeck 'Miss Manticory's' bisque pate. He'd heard enough of my fulminations on the hair trade on his various visits. He soothed, 'There, there, my dear, it's fine as fine. You *know* I would not dabble in the human hair trade. How often must I tell you? This is my patent silk and gum *imitation* hair. But, my dear, really it does not do to be so intemperate about the hair trade, a transaction that does not harm the . . . er . . . donors. Those girls in Paris are queuing up to sell their hair – they do it for the relief of the thing, I assure you. For it's well known that in the weaker-minded a head of heavy hair can actually lead to madness or debauchery. It's a great ease to those unfortunate girls to shed it.'

'The Swiney Godivas are all finely suited as to wits,' I retorted. 'Yet you'll seldom see heavier heads of hair.'

Even as I said it, however, I thought of Ida, who was not quite what she should be. But was that because of her hair? She was the last born, and after her it seemed that Annora's fertility had finally been extinguished. Perhaps, by the time Ida was conceived, Annora had not had within her all that was needed to produce one more entire and intellectually wholesome infant. Then I

121

remembered the grave in the clover field at Harristown – the death of *PS* was the most likely reason for the lack of any further sisters.

Mr Rainfleury rose, consulting his fob-watch. 'I have other stork duties to perform. I must not keep your dear sisters waiting too long, particularly Ida, who's as giddy as a water sheerie.'

So he too had been thinking of her, when he spoke of madness.

Then, perversely, I did not want him to leave. Not because I craved his company but because I did not wish to be left alone with 'Miss Manticory'. I moved a step away from her, but that took me closer to Mr Rainfleury, dangerously within reach of his fluttering hand. So I bid him a tense good afternoon. Confused and ashamed, I even thanked him with a doll-like curtsey.

'There's a good poppet,' he said approvingly. 'A gentleman always enjoys a curtsey and a dipped head. Enda and Berenice have learned that to a nicety.'

I did not see him leave. I was already in the grip of 'Miss Manticory's' glass eyes. I noticed that the real eyelashes were supplemented by long painted lashes all around the lids, giving 'Miss Manticory' an extremely alert and alluring look.

I stood her on my desk and made myself sit in front of her. I ran my finger along her feather eyebrows. The doll seemed to possess an inner confidence I'd never own. It was provocative. Provoked, I stripped her, unlacing the eyelet holes of her fitted stays, and unbuttoning each of her petticoats, her pantalets and her chemisette, right down to her lumpen composition body, clad in kid. I manipulated her ball-jointed limbs in a graceless gallop of a dance. I unclipped her tiny jade earrings. I unfastened the locket. As I unpeeled her, I was amazed afresh at Mr Rainfleury's attention to detail. On every item I removed – from her bodice to her Balmoral boots – was sewed or glued a tiny label announcing: *'Miss Manticory'* – *the latest sensation from the Swiney Godiva Corporation*. Even inside the locket, Mr Rainfleury had managed to insert a tiny handbill, folded a dozen times, illustrating all seven dolls in the collection. The mesh purse contained seven tiny coins with Swiney Godiva profiles where Her Majesty's should have been.

There was a light footstep outside my door. What if someone were to catch me in the obscene contemplation of the naked 'Miss Manticory'? Hurriedly, I re-dressed her, forgetting one of the petticoats, and sat her on an armchair. I kicked the stray petticoat under my bed and continued my visual negotiations, searching for a way to accommodate her in my thoughts.

The footsteps passed on. I immediately started to hate 'Miss Manticory'. Her hands were stiff claws. And her bisque skin was repellently hard to the touch. Her mouth was half open in a fly-inviting pout. I suspected her composition body of being horridly like Mr Rainfleury's in texture. If she were to come to life, 'Miss Manticory' would be a cold minx with a cavity where her brain should be, and another for her heart. She would walk like a shuffling ghost. I reached a threatening hand towards her. After all, it was dolly-bashing I'd been bred to. But then I snatched it back, remembering how little I liked the feel of her under my fingers.

When the bell rang for tea, I grasped 'Miss Manticory' by the neck and took her down to introduce her to my sisters and their dolls.

For this auspicious occasion Mrs Hartigan had supplied a spread that would make you lick your lips to look at it. Towering sponges rubbed shoulders with seedless raspberry jellies and ziggurats of tender-fleshed scones and buttery potato cakes well peppered and studded with caraway seeds. I was suddenly sorely homesick for stirabout of Indian meal spooned up by Annora under the swinging seashell lamp in Harristown. I was surprised to discover that my sisters, even with the jam bloodying the corners of their mouths, seemed to be in the same black mood as myself, and were letting loose a bellyful of laments.

Darcy complained that her doll looked 'iron-hard' and 'overly animal', though she was also certain it would be the greatest earner. Pertilly feared hers appeared simple, yet she was relieved to find under the skirt as pretty an ankle as you'd find in Dublin. Oona worried that hers was too babylike. Enda thought

123

Berenice's unfairly pretty and vice versa, though in truth both dolls mimicked perfectly the twins' slightly elfin ears and the shadows under their eyes and their smooth oat-coloured complexions.

Ida disliked the low brow of her doll, which reproduced her heart-shaped face and upthrusting chin. Its eyebrows sloped downwards, capturing her look of permanent anxiety. The lips, like hers, were wide and slightly parted. A miniature fiddle dangled from one hand and a bow from the other. To complete the resemblance, Ida had already wound around the doll's wrists bracelets made from hair freshly pulled from her own head.

She whined, 'The problem is that "Miss Idolatry" copies me *too much*! It is very very wicked that she should be so exactly like me.'

'Why wicked?' asked Berenice. 'She is *supposed* to look like you. She is a great success!' She smiled ingratiatingly at Mr Rainfleury. Enda's shoulders tensed.

'I cannot explain,' wept Ida. 'But "Miss Idolatry" is a demon. And she is a very rude bad girl too.'

My troubled sisters gazed into their demon-doubles' eyes, searching for evidence of what Ida had said. From their faces, they sensed the corruption too, and yet they knew it was too late to forfend.

Mr Rainfleury, in contrast, was in seven separate raptures about his creations. He could not be stopped from fondling their hair, and waltzing them along the top of the mantelpiece, and pretending to feed them morsels of cake. He paid not the slightest attention to our complaints. I flinched at the steel that lined his emollient manners.

He shows us great respect – but only from the teeth out, I thought. *In the end, he will not let our feelings get in the way of his empire.*

He had 'Miss Manticory' clapping her hands in front of the Christmas tree.

'Ah!' he exclaimed, 'I had quite forgot.'

He produced from various pockets seven tiny gifts extravagantly wrapped. He laid them under the tree, next to our full-sized presents.

Darcy failed entirely to be charmed. 'Christmas presents for dolls?' she asked him. 'I hope that they are little rolls of string? So you can operate the dolls as marionettes,' she suggested to him sourly. 'As you already do with their originals.'

None of us sisters wanted the consequences of reminding Darcy that it was she who had signed the contract, and she who had agreed to sell us. Meanwhile, Mr Rainfleury's jubilations continued at industrial strength. Darcy could not dent them, not even with her spiky tongue and iron tone.

He gloated, 'Jumeau shall die seven deaths from jealousy whenever he sees these darlings!' he rejoiced. 'I've taken out an advertisement in the *Gazette de la Poupée*, just to make sure he does!'

Then he told us how the great Parisian doll-maker had caused a sensation with his long-haired beauties, and kept whole streets of seamstresses busy sewing miniature dresses. There were entire shops that sold nothing but trousseaux for Jumeau's creations.

'And so it shall be in Dublin and with the "Miss Swineys",' Mr Rainfleury assured us. 'So it shall be.'

15

It was not yet a street, like Mr Jumeau's enterprise, but the Swiney Godiva Corporation kept a large brick building fully populated with employees. A few days after a brief Harristown Christmas, we were driven – in two carriages to accommodate our skirts – to Mr Rainfleury's factory. The unheated building hummed and rustled with the sawing, sewing and nailing of 'Miss Swineys' and their accessories. Shabby Dubliners of both sexes were bent over trays of eyes or sat stitching small clothes, nightgowns, skating costumes, dressing gowns and riding habits. *Posticheurs* were marrying clumps of hair to incised bisque pates. A few older women were seated at baroque-looking treadles that stabbed roads of black stitches into miles of cloth. Girls barely older than Ida sat fashioning miniature baskets, fiddles, umbrellas and photograph albums. Everyone's fingers were white with cold, and their breath ghosted the air around them.

Mr Rainfleury purred, 'Each item will be monogrammed, of course, and can be collected separately by the public.'

Of course the 'Miss Swineys' were a tint discounted in this mass manufacture. Their statures were shrunk from the magnificent thirty inches of our own dolls to an economical eighteen. The heads were still bisque, but cloth replaced the kid covering the composition bodies. Our own dolls' silk petticoats were reproduced in cheap gauze. And the hair seethed in seven frighteningly familiar colours in great cotton bins suspended from girders in the ceiling. When I asked to see the apparatus that spun artificial hair from silk and plant extracts, Mr Rainfleury hushed me and drew me aside. 'The room where *that* alchemy is performed must be kept locked. We cannot have our competitors spying on us! One of you girls, in your innocence, might let drop a word that could lead them to our secret formula.'

I thought his tongue should smoke from that burning lie. He, for his part, looked at me with frank dislike. All attraction for my long hair was gone: he did not like the brain that worked beneath it.

In silence, we watched the seamstresses, gluers and wig-makers. I looked under the table at their shoes, saw them thin and holed, and was sorry. Their eyes travelled over us nervously. They did not allow their faces to express any comment, but I was convinced that they must hate us for their poor wages and the cold in which they were forced to work. I was relieved when Ida said, 'I believe we should go home directly, isn't it?'

She meant to Annora, and Harristown, I was sure.

We had a real reason for not lingering: we had very little time. Like the newest recruits in any brothel, we were exceptionally busy. 'Madam Rainfleury', my latest name for him, had us working at a breathless pace.

Now he'd invested his money in us, Mr Rainfleury took a keen interest in making us more famous. The greater the legend of the Swiney Godivas, the better their dolls would sell, and the higher the prices they and their miniature accessories could command. And I believe it also swelled the private pleasure in Mr Rainfleury's merchant heart to imagine his pets the objects of general and commercial admiration.

Darcy might have suspected how things would turn out, but she had been uncharacteristically disposed to reticence on the subject. So we younger sisters entered into this new chapter of our fame like kittens venturing out of the basket for the first time – unsure, fearful and always keeping an eye on where we might bolt back to.

But I knew there was no safe place.

After we visited the factory I crept down in the night to the desk in the drawing room. I wanted to read the grand Corporation contract Darcy had signed on our behalf. By the light of my candle, the words were plain and ugly for all the glowing wax, the black copperplate and the flourishes. The contract provided for no return, no change of heart on our side. We were bound to the Swiney Godiva Corporation without waiver.

The only person who might withdraw without penalty was Mr Rainfleury himself.

In fact – and to my surprise – 'Miss Manticory' made it easier for me on the stage. Although I was almost insane with my aversion to the little idol, she gave me something to cling to. According to our new Corporation contract, Mr Rainfleury's dolls were to sell on the back of our shows, being displayed in the lobby where the audience passed the intermission. The dolls featured prominently in our act: just before the interval we all backed onto the stage, and held up our dolls above us with their bisque heads facing our customers. We made them talk in our voices – an animated conversation. Then slowly we ourselves turned round and took the dolls in our arms like babies and kissed them tenderly on their unyielding cheeks, making them seem like the most precious objects in the world.

Exactly as Mr Rainfleury had calculated, this part of our act certainly cultivated desire for the dolls in our patrons. Their sales soon accounted for far more of our takings than our admission tickets did.

The dolls had their own reviews: *'Miss Enda' surpasses anything we have ever seen, both in design and taste.*

One fanciful lady correspondent wrote:

It is possible to believe that these enchanting miniature beauties are capable of exercising sympathetic magic – surely tending to their magnificent locks will make their adoring owner's grow!

'Think of that now!' breathed Oona.

Mrs Godlin from the Kilcullen dispensary wrote that gossip had it that the two daughters of the Master of Harristown had requested a whole set of 'Miss Swineys' for under their Christmas tree. She also told us that the Eileen O'Reilly had been seen with two black eyes glowering under her fringe and that her butcher father had passed a night in a stupor in the cells.

'Shame he didn't take the whole head off her,' observed Darcy.

Sales of the dolls doubled and then tripled. So it seemed perfectly natural that Mr Rainfleury should take charge of the Swiney Godiva show bookings as well as the dolls. For this purpose, he bought an enormous ledger with columns for travel expenses, costume costs, beauty preparations such as Cheltenham Salts, eau de Cologne, Elder Flower Water, stage properties, set painting and teas, all of which were deducted from the takings before the rest was committed to the bank account in Dame Street, to which Darcy alone had access, and from which she doled out weekly allowances with grudging hands, dropping six coins by each of our plates every Sunday evening supper.

After a few weeks, Ida threw hers back at Darcy.

'Want to *see* my money,' she insisted. 'The big money in the bank.'

'That you would not,' retorted Darcy, scooping up the coins and pocketing them. 'It's not a decent girl who'd ask such a thing. Think of your money in the bank like the geese doing the deed in the bushes and making more geese. You'd not be wanting to look at it. But you'll be happy of the additional geese by and by.'

'I always looked,' admitted Ida. 'I want to go back to Harristown.'

Darcy replied, 'That sounds like an excuse for slapping some cheek to me.'

At which point, Mr Rainfleury entered the fray with one of his amiable sentences. 'And, Darcy, I have been meaning to speak to you about this matter of slapping. And pinching, and boxing of ears. In Society, ladies do not vent their grievances with acts of violence. They leash their tempers, Darcy. Like ladies, Darcy. Some incidents have come to my attention via third parties. We cannot have the public thinking that there's any brutal behaviour in this nest of goddesses.'

'Perhaps Society ladies do not have as much to put up with as I do,' retorted Darcy.

'I merely put the matter to you,' said Mr Rainfleury, 'and the thought that you would not want the "Miss Darcy" doll to be known as the virago of the Godivas.'

Leaving Darcy for a rarity speechless, he bowed to the rest of us, and assured us that he had many good things to address on our behalf and must be off to do so.

As well as our accounts, Mr Rainfleury had taken it on himself to enrich the content of our show, constantly suggesting refinements and additions, though he was no one's Shakespeare and always concluded, 'So, Manticory, you'll write up the new piece that way, dear?'

Mr Rainfleury rewon Darcy's friendship by introducing a coffin into the act. The coffin came equipped with a gormless and infinitely flexible stuffed black cat which Darcy held up triumphantly before consigning it to the underworld along with all her other worldly treasures. The cat was laid in the coffin with its paws in the air. I wrote a special song about the grave-goods that Darcy's corpse would take with her. As she sang, Darcy dropped her ribbons and crucifixes, one by one, into the silk-lined lacquered box – avoiding the cat – along with plentiful tears squirted from a perfume bottle concealed behind her left ear, with a tube running to a pump under her armpit.

Darcy also made play with a death's head puppet, a bleached monkey's skull sewn on a glove of white. She had Enda, in a black dress printed with a skeleton, perform a dance of death with Berenice, in red silk, accompanied by Ida playing the fiddle with the unearthly grace and the hollow eyes of one who had sold her soul to the Devil.

'Good evening to my seven queens.' Mr Rainfleury arrived for dinner in the indulgent mood that meant he had something new to sell us. Sure enough, out it came. 'And speaking of that, my queens must have their attendants. Settle down, my dears, for I have lovely news.'

Having reddened the fire with the bellows, he consigned his bulk to his favourite armchair, his soft rolls settling in increments like goose feathers in a pillow. He announced, 'I have engaged a professional hairdresser to put a little cultivation in your admirable animal growths.'

'A little less of the animal from you, sir,' growled Darcy in her most scalding tone. 'And for the hairdressing we have Pertilly – who does not require to be paid extra.'

'Our programme is intensifying,' said Mr Rainfleury with the mild but unequivocal tranquillity of a folded blanket. 'Remember, I have new activities planned for you – in department-store windows and lecture halls. We shall presently need your hair dressed twice a day, with suitable styles for morning and evening engagements.'

'What's wrong with our hair?' Darcy's brows knitted. 'No one has ever complained about the hair.'

'Except the Eileen O'Reilly,' piped up Ida.

'Even a flowered bower must be attended to,' burbled Mr Rainfleury persuasively. 'Art and craft are both employed in the garden, and upon the flowers themselves. And so art and craft must also attend the lady's toilette table.'

Ida stared at him. 'We are getting a gardener, is it? For our hairs so?'

'Imbecile!' barked Darcy, so I knew she didn't understand either.

Mr Rainfleury laughed delicately. 'Let me use language you will comprehend, my poppets. Hair in its natural state is like a raw potato or a plain boiled one. But hair may have aspirations. Hair may leave Nature and become Culture, may express Civilisation. Whenever we want the humble potato to be its best possible self, to be fit for a duchess's table, we employ a chef to deal with it. And that chef will dignify and beautify the potato, creating such masterpieces as *pommes de terre sautées*, and *pommes de terre dauphinoise* and *pommes de terre gratinées*. Now Pertilly has a natural aptitude, to be sure, and her labours have served you well—'

Pertilly's face pinkened with happiness to find her work recognised for once.

'But you need someone working *in the back room*, my dears, so that you can flourish better in the front room and on the stage. *My* candidate has studied at the leading hair academy in Holborn, London, where the students practise for months on wefts of hair glued to board until they are perfectly accomplished in every fashionable style. Tastefully arranged hair adds elegance and finish to the features of the human face. I'll mention no specific names but there are faces in this room that might be glad and grateful for those things.'

Pertilly frowned, understanding herself insulted. She looked to Berenice for defence, but Mr Rainfleury was still talking a torrent.

'Moreover, my Miss Craughn – who has reached the elegance of middle age in her profession – has acquired the art of incorporating false hair invisibly into the natural growth. No!' He held up his hand. 'Sit down, Manticory. You ladies shall not object to resting your own hard-working hair in gentle nets and using hairpieces from a reputable source – and no, of course not every day, or often – only for some theatrical exigencies, of course. Yes, you too shall have your scalpettes and frisettes and single curls cunningly gummed to your foreheads; your torsades, your two-ended braids, all gardened and landscaped into your own hair so subtly that no one shall know what is home-grown and what is not.'

'You mean,' I asked slowly, 'you want us to wear false hair, just when we are selling *your* dolls on the back of our supposedly natural hair?'

Again, I received that look of unqualified dislike. 'Of course you shall own it, Manticory, for you shall pay for the hair out of *your* dolls' earnings. And the more hair you show, the more dolls *you* shall sell, and the more money you'll get, and the more hair you can buy,' he chortled. 'Show some imagination, dear!'

The *Hairdressers' Chronicle and Trade Journal*, Pertilly's favourite reading matter, lay open on a pertinent page. I seized it and waved it under Mr Rainfleury's nose.

'Hair you can buy! See this!' I told Mr Rainfleury. 'Black straight hair is these days imported via Marseilles from India, China and Japan. It says here that they boil it up in nitric acid to take out the black, which ruins the health of the poor hairworkers. And then they recolour it to fashionable reds and blonds with poisonous dyes! And frizzle it with tongs into curls, so it stinks—'

'And even *African hair* comes into Marseilles.' Darcy had read the article too. She spluttered, 'And its wool can be disguised. You ask us to put that on our heads?'

'Oh no!' flourished Mr Rainfleury. 'Far from it! How many times must I say it? It is not *human* hair I ask you to nestle among your own. It is my own invention, hygienic and safe. For my sweet poppets, nothing but silk and rare-plant extracts. It's that naughty Manticory feeding your heads with nonsense again – the *Hairdressers' Chronicle* is *bound* to tell lies about hair; they make money out of sensation.' He dropped his voice to a wheedling tone. 'Miss Craughn brings with her a treasure chest of tortoiseshell combs, amber pins and diamanté combs. Why, she even has a portable nitting machine to deal with your own little . . .'

Seeing our blanched faces, he stopped tactfully.

Was it my own Enda, I wondered, or was it Berenice who had confided to him that the lice still sometimes made themselves at home on us, even in Dublin?

Mr Rainfleury had not puffed the hairdresser beyond her abilities. Miss Craughn was a true professional, who gave performances in her own right. She made a theatre out of the sewing room where she conducted her business with the tongs and frisettes, her crimping irons. We all assembled to watch her whenever we could, relishing the chance to be part of a hair audience for once. Small, mouse-haired and with a tight little mouth, she sat on a stool to work on us. Miss Craughn loved our hair – she acted as if it were hers and not ours. She insisted upon it being just so. But the desiccated little lady wished no intimacies with us Swineys, quietly giving it to be understood

133

that she had worked with better blood and breeding than ours. I overheard her exclaiming to Mrs Hartigan, 'To think a grand house like this would hear native accents like the ones on those girls in its very dining room! And that Darcy creature makes it the home of all the profanity in Ireland.'

While she worked on our heads, Miss Craughn spoke only to herself, muttering about necessary pins and technicalities of combs and lotions with terrifying names. I liked the prissy woman's skills well enough, but I never accustomed myself to the smells of the liquids she painted on my scalp. And I hated the false hair, for I never stopped picturing the girls obliged to be shorn so that I, already luxuriating in hair, might greedily have yet more. In fact, the more Mr Rainfleury spoke of his silk curls, the less I believed in him.

Miss Craughn very promptly found her way into Darcy's black books. In front of the hairdresser, Darcy assumed her most lordly airs. She gave peremptory orders for her own styling. Miss Craughn ignored both the order and the tone. Darcy did not scruple to administer a slap or a curse to a recalcitrant sister in Miss Craughn's presence, until she found that the hairdresser faithfully informed Mr Rainfleury of every act of violence.

A month after the hairdresser arrived, Ida was alone in the sewing room with Miss Craughn after the latter had exchanged some bitter words with Darcy. Poor Ida took the brunt of it. The hairdresser brushed her frustrations into her scalp, knotted her anger into curling rags and roasted her impotence with hot tongs. Finally, Miss Craughn's comb made a too-swift and merciless progress though Ida's curls. Ida lost the run of herself and threw a fit. She turned her head and bit Miss Craughn's hand.

In a moment both Ida and the hairdresser were screaming heroically.

The noise had us all running into the room. At the sight of Darcy, Ida bolted out.

'That Miss Ida is a mad girl!' cried Miss Craughn, showing us a bleeding finger. 'I'll not stay among bastard madwomen!'

'How do you dare?' demanded Darcy, advancing on her.

Oona placed herself between them. 'Do not be so harsh on Ida, oh please. You know it's an affliction just to be the youngest. There's a want in her, Miss Craughn honey,' she cajoled. Oona had rather taken to the hairdresser, who had found a way to make her hair glitter with a subtle gold powder under the stage lights. 'There's a want there but no real harm. Don't take any notice so.'

But Miss Craughn was already packing up her frisettes and scalpettes and her hackle for carding our combings, and her nitting machine. All the while she crammed her valise and offered bitter remarks such as 'The obscenity of it! Just a hedgerow harem for that curdy goat Rainfleury.'

Darcy towered over her. 'I'll take no tongue from you, you old bitch! It's better you're gone. You're nothing but a slippery-fingered spy.'

Miss Craughn retorted, 'May your own black tongue wither to its dark root, Darcy Swiney. You do not use it for anything but nasty, is what you don't do. I'm sorry for your sisters, frankly. The things I've seen and heard here! And you, with your hand in the accounts . . . and all those brown envelopes for the groom, coming back empty besides!' She stared meaningfully at Darcy.

'That is a look I take from no woman!' Darcy shook her fist. 'Be gone from this establishment.'

'As quickly as I can,' Miss Craughn assured her.

Ida reappeared, holding one of Darcy's black books.

'Miss Craughn! See here!' she said. 'Darcy has language on you! You must do better than this! These are not good words. "Trollop". "Bacon-fed whore". And she says that while you were visiting the haberdasher on Tuesday she dipped your hat feathers in her chamber pot.'

Miss Craughn pointed a quivering finger, still dripping with blood.

She told Darcy, 'You are cursed. It may take time, but my curse will catch up with you. And if I can do anything to hasten it on its way, you can be sure I shall.'

'Why are you still here, you besom?' asked Darcy. 'I don't give a whooping cough for your old curses.'

'Would it kill you to bid the woman a courteous farewell?' asked Oona reproachfully.

'It would,' said Darcy.

From the doorstep, Miss Craughn turned and cried up to the windows, 'This will get out, mark my words.'

I silently agreed with the hairdresser's opinions on both Darcy's tongue and our patron's proclivities. The more Mr Rainfleury insinuated himself into the tight knot between Enda and Berenice, the less easy I felt. The twins were engaged in an increasingly painful competition for his approval. Both had now achieved exactly six feet of hair, but they spent hours stretching it around the banisters to try to extract an extra quarter-inch. Mr Rainfleury goaded them on, measuring their hair with a soft tape every week, taking his time over it too.

There was something faraway in Enda's manner when Oona and I brushed her hair at night; something absent-minded in her hugs, which were far less frequent than they had been. We both missed her attention, and I hated the reason for her distraction.

Pertilly resumed her role as hairdresser with a smile of satisfaction playing about her mouth.

It was a small victory over Mr Rainfleury, who worried not at all about the accusation of a harem – I believed he loved that. But he was badly frightened by the thought that the hairdresser might go abroad with stories that the Swiney Godivas were not all quite as sane and sensible as you might want them or that their business manager's words were not all they should be, or that our hair was a creation of glue, pins and chemical artifice. The extraordinary superfluity of our hair, as we had known from childhood, made us vulnerable to name-calling, to intimations of freakishness. We could not afford to be painted as eccentrics, sensualists or frauds.

With Mr Rainfleury's money resting on our hair-heavy heads, we could not afford to be anything but perfect.

16

At the rate of one a month, the dolls had made their debuts. Each was celebrated with a new song in which her special qualities were laid out. As far as possible, I matched their virtues to those of my sisters, and I made up some for Darcy.

Over those months, we grew somewhat reconciled to the dolls or at least had come to an outward accommodation in our different ways. 'Miss Idolatry' had to be recoiffed several times when her eponymous heroine pulled out all her hair. I myself always placed 'Miss Manticory' facing the corner of my bedroom and was not above giving her a kick. She'd already needed a new head after mysteriously falling down the stairs. Although we gave out that we slept with our dolls in our beds, Darcy rejected the nocturnal comforts of hers and had a miniature coffin constructed for it to sleep in. 'Miss Darcy' acquired a stack of miniature black books in which were recorded the crimes of her sister dolls. Berenice and Enda, in a rare moment of unity, had swapped their twin dolls, and each claimed herself happy with the new version. Oona liked to croon to her doll whenever practising her new songs. Pertilly rehearsed hairstyles on hers.

'Now our sweet Godivas are fourteen in number,' Mr Rainfleury liked to say.

And he sent all fourteen of us on the road, or, that is, on the railway tracks.

In those days, very few Irish people travelled. They waited for the world to come to them. Strange worlds did – circuses, pedlars, sometimes foreign soldiers, all reinforcing a general opinion that the world outside our own county was surely a queer and dangerous place and better left where it was. The Swiney Godivas joined the picturesque itinerants, offering new worlds of hairy strangeness and extremity. We were always invited back.

From Dublin, we could be in Cork or Killarney in just over four hours. We journeyed in comfort and style, never missing a refreshment room at one of the grand stations, and travelling with an abundance of tea baskets, pillows and plaid rugs, courtesy of the Great Southern and Western Railway. We often overnighted in the railway hotels, where dignity and luxury were properly tempered by economy. And nor did we let the railway company limit our journeys, for at the end of branch lines there was always a painted private omnibus to transport us to the stately Royal Marine Hotel at Kilkee or the grand Lake Hotel at Killarney. We jerked along on the hard banquettes watching horses make dark bridges of their bodies on the tops of hills, rehearsing under our breaths, Darcy scribbling in her black book, me working on new scripts, Ida counting geese in barnyards, Pertilly studying new styles in the *Hairdressers' Chronicle and Trade Journal*.

It was to be Oona's misfortune that her doll outsold all the others and by a considerable margin. She was the public's darling on stage too, for the public ever loves a bushel of golden hair and a willowy figure. And the men were intrigued by Oona's unusually deep voice and her eyebrows, which were straight and darker than her curls and angled in a way that increased the sweetness of her expression.

Oona's getting all the love going from the audience did not go down well with Darcy.

So it was with an intention of menace that Darcy introduced into our repertoire a performance of the old ballad, 'The Cruel Sister', which I reworked to suit. Despite Darcy's dark intentions, *The Cruel Sister* was my joy and privilege. I wrote it mindful and heartful of my sisters' outer and inner lives. We sang and acted it as an operetta.

There are a good three dozen different versions of this

song, but they all agree on the following account of events, as did my Swiney Godiva rendition: a beautiful blonde maiden is preferred over her dark-haired sister by a handsome suitor they both covet. Oona being my tribeswoman, I wrote her lines yielding and irresistible. In her love song with the suitor (played by Enda, pert and inimitably stylish in breeches), Oona's deep voice plumbed hitherto forbidden depths of passion.

After overhearing the duet, the dark-haired sister, played by Darcy, invites her blonde rival for a walk along the cliffs – cardboard, painted – and pushes her into the sea, the splashes being generated backstage by a ladle in a bucket. Sinking beneath the waves, the fair one pleads for help, offering everything she has, including, finally, her lover.

'I'll have him anyway!' laughs the ink-haired murderess. 'You shall never come ashore!' Darcy made these lines intensely credible.

And the blonde girl drowns. Her white body floats as a dead swan on the waves, her hair rippling from her scalp like wheat stalks devastated by a tempest, an effect movingly achieved by use of a long flat trolley on ropes and some blue gauzes flapped from the wings by myself and Enda.

On another shore, on the other side of the stage, two minstrels, played by Berenice and Pertilly, find the sodden corpse. In an act of mixed poetry, butchery and carpentry, they fashion a harp from her breastbone. They string it with filaments of the dead girl's golden hair. Ida, playing her fiddle backstage, makes the harp sob sounds to melt a heart of stone.

Presently the minstrels are summoned to a grand wedding. It is the nuptials of the dark-haired sister. She is marrying the suitor won by her treachery.

But when the minstrel lifts his harp, the music that comes forth tells the tale of the sistercide, and points a bony finger at the murderess.

The rivalry between Darcy and Oona was so tangible on stage that I feared for my fair sister. Each night Enda was ready with the arnica for there was genuine malice in Darcy's push that sent Oona tumbling off the cardboard cliff. The audience felt it too. When Oona, backstage, voiced the deep-toned song of the breastbone harp, there was always whimpering in the front rows.

After the show – but only after they were reluctantly persuaded that the Swiney Godivas had absolutely no encores left in them – the public rushed to the doll stall and bought more 'Miss Oonas', now equipped with a miniature breastbone harp made from vulcanised rubber.

I wondered that Darcy chose such a story for me to Swiney Godiva, and that she herself elected to impersonate the villainess, until I realised that in this tale the dark-haired sister was the winner, and the one who remained the centre of attention when the blonde sister was reduced to a memory and a plaintive melody. For the wedding scene, Darcy's black curls were stiffly dressed in impressive battlements and crenellations – her hair was the queen of the stage. Of course Darcy, as if knowing that her hard features and her height made her femininity debatable, never took a male part in our productions.

The rest of us played the chorus. At the final scene, we all held up our hair as we chanted, the motes dancing in the dusty luminescence above our heads:

> ' 'Twas the hair, the hair, the hair that sang.
> 'Twas the hair that told the tale.
> 'Tis the hair, the hair, the hair that speaks
> On the hair this tale shall hang.
> On the hair shall hang the murderess,
> And on the hair shall this tale hang.'

The Cruel Sister was a sensational success. One critic wrote: *It is enough to knock the heart across you.*

More operettas were devised by Darcy – and scripted by myself – and the tale always hung on the hair.

As you might imagine, I never sought a starring role in any of these productions. But Darcy chose me to play the poor Goose

Girl – her comment on my pretensions to intellect. Perhaps Darcy also went for the story out of some unconscious nostalgia for the thin geese and slow crows of Harristown, though such a notion may have attributed too much heart to her.

A princess travels to her wedding to a great prince. But on the way she is betrayed by her maid (performed by Pertilly of the spacious hips and peasant ankles), who steals her rich dowry, her amiable talking horse and her fine clothes. The maid compels the princess to take a vow of silence, and to become a Goose Girl. Arriving at Court, the maid marries the gullible prince, played by Oona of the deep voice. The wedding cake, iced, piped and ornamented with cornucopias and horseshoes, is wheeled in, taller than Ida. The wedding guests dance round it.

Out in the countryside, the Goose Girl's radiant red hair attracts the attention of a Goose Boy, voiced by Ida in a sack cap. He tries to pluck some of the glowing treasure from her head. The Goose Girl will have none of it, preserving her hair as she would her virtue. The rejected Goose Boy takes his laments to Court. He reports on the Goose Girl's arrogant behaviour to the king, whose suspicions have already been aroused by the thick ankles of his son's new bride.

The king himself (Oona doubling up as *père* and *fils*) comes to spy on the Goose Girl, and immediately realises that such glorious tresses can be the perquisite, symptom and crown of true nobility alone. The impostor is debunked and dismissed, and the Goose Girl takes her rightful place as princess. My goose-beak-coloured hair tumbled about under my wedding veil in the last scene. The guests toasted us: 'Long life to you, a wet mouth, and death in Ireland!'

As I played my part and accepted Oona's – the prince's – soft hand in marriage, I wondered how the Goose Girl would feel, bedding down with a man who had happily lain with her betraying maid. Did she not care about where those princely hands and loins had been?

The Goose Girl was popular but *The Cruel Sister* remained the true highlight of our repertoire, and was requested universally.

141

And perhaps it was a good and useful thing to let Darcy murder Oona night after night.

It seemed to make her gentler, afterwards.

17

Eventually Mr Rainfleury wanted to touch more than our hair.

By that time, all of us had come to womanly maturity – signified by a growth of hair where there had been none, and a consequent sobering and constraining of our heads' hair into neat, if bulbous, snooded chignons to denote that our newly unleashed feminine hankerings were firmly under control. Of course, I understood that the putting-up of our hair immediately conjured the reversal – pinned up, it had the potential to be let loose, just as it was in our shows.

Both twins had fixed on Mr Rainfleury as their object, but it was Enda whom he chose to wed, making a formal request in writing to Annora for her daughter's hand. The transaction included a cash settlement, and a field of bitter cabbages besides, with a fee for Joe the seaweed boy to tend them. Given these blandishments, and Enda's utter willingness, Annora gave her permission, despite a difference of a quarter-century between the groom and his nineteen-year-old bride.

It was not Enda but Mr Rainfleury who broke the news over a specially monumental cake constructed by Mrs Hartigan, who was in on the engagement, and whose views upon it, I suspect, had been softened by a new hat. As Mr Rainfleury spoke and gestured with a tender fork, Enda grinned like Darcy's crocodile reticule. The rest of us sat frozen in mid-mastication of the four-layered sponge. I suddenly felt as if I was eating a light, sugary tombstone spread with a thickened blood of raspberry jam. I felt for Enda's soft hand under the table, and found a hard band of metal interrupting her fourth finger. She smiled emptily. My eyes stung with tears. Enda had been privy to all these negotiations but she had kept them secret from me and Oona. For the first time, I felt betrayed by her.

Of course, I worried, Enda's greatest betrayal was of herself.

I tried to fasten my anger on a more suitable object. Mr Rainfleury had taken my favourite. *Him*, I would never forgive. Indeed I would add this at the top of the list of things for which I would never forgive him. Oona was staring at Enda with horror. Ida shook her fist at Mr Rainfleury, saying, 'Oh no you don't!'

Berenice's mouth stretched in a silent, agonised '*Why?*' meaning, 'Why not *me?*'

I myself was wondering how exactly the choice had been made between the twins when Darcy observed, 'Cabbages, Mr Rainfleury? You bought Enda for cabbages, is it?'

Still Enda smiled, the hard, dumb smile of 'Miss Enda', a smile of manufacture, not nature. I wanted to take her head between my hands, to shake out whatever madness had made her accept this obscenity of a marriage. Was it simply to spite Berenice? Had all my scripted rivalry led to this?

Mr Rainfleury said, 'Cabbages, with a pretty plantation of vetches, turnips, rape and mangolds besides. And do you see Enda looking sorry? No, my bride comes to me joyfully on her own lovely tiny feet.' He rose and went to kiss Enda's nose. My fingers itched to slap his detestable mouth away. The tears dripped from Berenice's eyes, down her nose and upon her abandoned slice of cake. She moaned quietly. Mr Rainfleury carefully averted his gaze.

I murmured, 'Rapunzel was sold to a witch for a handful of bitter green herbs.'

Ida whimpered, 'Are you meaning that Mr Rainfleury is a witch?'

'More an old goat,' replied Darcy.

But her words were drowned by Berenice flinging herself around the walls and knocking any picture of Enda off the mantelpiece. Oona and I scuttled behind her, trying to save the broken frames from Berenice's trampling feet. Enda continued to sit quietly, as if tied to the chair, the smile on her face seeming fixed in bisque. Mr Rainfleury made a hasty departure, citing an urgent meeting at the doll factory. He did not kiss his bride again, though her eyes followed him.

Berenice's 'Why not *me?*' finally made itself heard in a shriek that fell upon the window panes and rattled them.

A black mouth was what Berenice had thereafter, whenever it came to describing Enda's way of getting Mr Rainfleury, accusing her of everything from naked seduction to opium and blackmail. Not being chosen by a suitor of as little blatant appeal as Mr Rainfleury – now that carried a special kind of ignominy. Berenice bore it badly. She swore she'd not attend the Christmastide wedding and we were obliged to put it about that she was indisposed with a throat. Mrs Hartigan kept Enda's Spitalfields satin dress locked in the wine-pantry for safety, for Berenice never went near the clothes press but that she carried a pair of scissors with her.

Berenice took to wearing a long white dress around Number 1 Pembroke Street at all times, and decorating her hair with flowers and bits of net. If Mr Rainfleury came to visit, she would take every possible opportunity to swoon into his arms.

'Save it for the stage, you mimsy mare,' Darcy told her tartly.

'Yes,' said Enda disdainfully, 'spare us.'

On the night before the wedding, Oona and I stole into Enda's bed, where we lay compressed like three 'Miss Swineys' in a single box. I cried into Enda's neck, hating to imagine, but unable to prevent myself from doing so, that the next night it would be Mr Rainfleury lying against her, smelling the lavender on her skin.

The wedding breakfast was a small affair in a private room at the Shelbourne, attended by a few business associates of the bridegroom. On the Swiney side, there were most of the sisters of the bride along with the Harristown priest, Father Maglinn, who had been persuaded to take the branch line to Dublin for the first time in his middle-aged life. Annora would not leave

Harristown. It was the priest who gave Enda away. You could tell he wished he hadn't.

Outside the snow fell in thick threads. I wondered what Berenice was breaking at home, apart from her own heart.

Over the fish course, Mr Rainfleury told his new sisters-in-law that we must henceforward call him 'Augustus'. None of us – except Berenice – would ever manage it, and not just because Mr Rainfleury could not fulfil the lineaments of an 'Augustus', which should of course properly include height, thick tawny hair and something awake and leonine about the eyes. My new brother-in-law could barely rise to a 'Jerome', in my opinion. That day even Enda referred to her husband as 'Mr Rainfleury', at least in our presence, to my relief. That way I could pretend that she was not now subject to his private empire as well as his business one.

When the time came to leave Enda to her bridegroom, she embraced me and Oona last of all. 'Oh, look at your faces. It will not change anything between us. Come here!' And she drew us to her breast, and away from the others.

'It has already changed everything between us,' I murmured, 'that you will lie with Mr Rainfleury, and that you don't seem to be sick on the thought of it, as I am.'

We Swineys considered ourselves very up on all the matters of animal generation as we'd seen the geese and the slow crows and the Harristown goats at their courtships and wedding nights.

'But a man has a very different idea of the thing to a goat, Manticory,' Enda insisted. I thought her voice lacking in conviction. She hugged me more tightly and kissed the top of Oona's head.

Mr Rainfleury consummated his love of Enda's hair in the bridal suite of the Shelbourne Hotel. The next afternoon, Enda dragged me and Oona down to a bench in Fitzwilliam Square. We were safe from Darcy's scrutiny: she was signing something at the bank again. Enda described to us breathlessly how her bridegroom laid out her hair in seven points of a star on the bed before lifting his own nightshirt. And he himself, she giggled, turned out to be hairy in hitherto unsuspected parts of his anatomy, including, but not exclusively so, his back and his chest.

For all her laughter, I thought Enda looked pale. And she could not stop me imagining the coarse shadow of a billy at his labours on her bedroom wall by moonlight.

A special bridal incarnation of the Enda doll – in a veil of real Honiton lace and a white Spitalfields satin train – was put about in selected stores, selling almost as well as 'Miss Oona-the-fairy and her breastbone harp'. To accompany the bride, there was a limited edition made of a somewhat idealised doll of Mr Rainfleury: tall, slim and shapely, and therefore recognisable chiefly from the droop of his moustache.

There was no exotic honeymooning, for the Swiney Godivas' bookings were solid. Whenever Enda murmured about the postponed wedding journey, Mr Rainfleury kissed her nose and chuckled, 'In God's good time, my poppet.'

And Berenice glowered near by, clenching and unclenching her fists.

Enda and Mr Rainfleury were immediately set up in their new Dublin townhouse, in all possible cosiness and convenience because it was the twin of our own, and adjoined it. Mrs Hartigan was persuaded to housekeep the two establishments, with an extra parlour maid provided on both sides of the dividing wall. At the Rainfleury residence, the drawing room was occupied by his extensive gentlemen's collection of long-haired dolls in glass cabinets to which even Enda was not permitted a key.

'You have made it lovely, so,' breathed Ida, walking around Number 2 Pembroke Street. It was hardly necessary to get to know the place, being that it was a mirror of Number 1.

With Mrs Hartigan ruling both households, Enda's duties were few. She devoted herself to collecting white Belleek porcelain writhing with seashells and coral, provoking Berenice to set up a rival collection of Killarney-work boxes in bog-oak and arbutus, with motifs of harps, round towers and wolfhounds.

Enda matched her twin's purchases, item for item, with rigour.

In fact Enda kept her old room with us, because her new husband was very frequently absent on Swiney Godiva Corporation business, sometimes for a week at a time. Mrs Hartigan declared that it would be madness to run up the expenses on two houses when one was nearly empty, and wouldn't it be best for Mrs Enda to hie herself back to Number 1 and her sisters when her husband was away?

Enda confessed that she did not like to sleep alone at Number 2 with the gentlemen's collection of long-haired dolls in the study below her bedroom: 'All those eyes that never close. They glitter in the dark, you know!'

Enda was with us so much that it was sometimes possible to forget the awkward ceremony that had unSwineyed her and made her the unlikely Mrs Rainfleury.

Yet as winter mellowed into spring, the marriage imposed itself more. Enda took to referring to 'Mr Husband', no matter how pompous it sounded in the context of an informal family visit. As often as possible, and particularly whenever Berenice was listening, Enda reported him an ardent consort, even when Darcy cautioned her for a 'midden mouth' or Ida wept and covered her ears or I took notes with a warning look on my face. There seemed to be a matrimonial conspiracy afoot, for Mr Rainfleury also took every opportunity – when Berenice was not present – to speak approvingly of his own uxorious nature.

The Rainfleurys' domestic felicity was embodied in the frequent exchange of hair keepsakes, though naturally most of the giving was on Enda's side: his sparser locks necessitated materially smaller gifts. Mr Rainfleury's monocle hung on a chain made of Enda's hair and his watchband was plaited too. Enda was inordinately proud of a filament of 'Mr Husband's' moustache set in glass on a gold ring. The flimsy morsel floated like a primeval mosquito fossilised in amber. Enda never tired of telling how she shaved 'Mr Husband' each morning, though such events were likely unproductive on the whole – his growth of beard was less pronounced than Darcy's. Enda boasted constantly of her spouse's unfailing chivalry.

'He will not let me pick up a handkerchief if I drop it!' she marvelled. 'And have you seen how he hands me into the carriage as if I were a queen?'

Mr Rainfleury, if present, kept his eyes modestly downcast whenever Enda delivered her praises.

As well he might, for the sister he really craved, now that he should not have her, was Berenice.

The love affair between husband and sister-in-law must have commenced, I calculated, almost immediately after the marriage. It would appear that it was accomplished in carriages and in back rooms of theatres where Mr Rainfleury was on indulgent terms with the management, or in hotel rooms rented by the hour.

It became clear to me, if not to my sisters, that many of Mr Rainfleury's business trips – allegedly to Ulster for his doll-dress fabrics – in fact took him only as far as the other side of Dublin. Whenever Enda was lodging with us, Berenice was often strangely absent, having developed an unlikely passion for studying French and Italian at the Royal Irish Academy in Dawson Street. Three months after the wedding, through the handsome iron railings, I glimpsed Berenice and Mr Rainfleury promenading the gravel outside St Stephen's Green. Berenice clung to his arm with wifely decorum, looking up into his moustache with a meek sweetness I was unaccustomed to seeing on her face. I hid behind a bush until they passed, watched them arrive at the Shelbourne, and tried to let my imaginings leave them at the door.

Mr Rainfleury, I thought, *you are half a husband and a whole goat.*

My next thought was, *Berenice, how could you?*

And then, *How do they* dare *so in public?*

Then I realised that no one but a Swiney – or a Mr Rainfleury – could tell Enda and Berenice apart. The adulterous couple was outrageously, uniquely and perfectly safe from gossip.

They were safe from me too. I would not add to Enda's miseries by publicising them. So I told no one, not even my tribeswoman Oona, that Mr Rainfleury was buttering his bap on both sides.

Yet Mrs Hartigan knew. I was certain that she knew – because the afternoon after I saw the adulterers in the park, I observed the housekeeper tucking something that rustled into the pocket of Mr Rainfleury's second-best brown coat that hung permanently in our hall press. She did so furtively, even though she was unaware of my watching from behind the dining-room door. As soon as Mrs Hartigan began her descent to the kitchen, I was out in the hall with my hand in the coat pocket. I drew out a packet labelled: *Vulcanised Rubber Gentlemen's Prophylactics, E. Lambert and Son, Dalston, London.* In the other pocket was a note from Berenice, suggesting a meeting at four the next day *in the usual place.*

The brown coat was the lovers' post office, I realised.

I rattled the packet of vulcanised rubber with appalling images studding the backs of my eyelids. I dared not break it open. Such devices were forbidden in Ireland, though they were to be had. Mrs Hartigan would have needed to procure them personally, of course, as it was in those days even illegal to order 'obscenities' through the post. I imagined her holding out her hand for them at Mr O'Mealy's pharmacy. Then Standish O'Mealy must know too. And he in turn must send a boy to England – to Dalston – to obtain his supplies. My heart contracted with compassion for my beloved Enda. So many conspirators against her marriage!

If Enda knew, she kept very quiet about it. And if Mr Rainfleury felt uncomfortable or anxious, well, it did not manifest itself in any diminishing of his girth or in less sparkle in his small eyes. Only once, I saw him overcome by sentiment, when the two sisters exchanged a hard word about an oversalted *boeuf en daube.*

We were dining *en famille*, that is, with all our hair let down, and Mr Rainfleury nestled in perfect happiness among us in a flowered silk dressing gown with a purple velvet cap on one side of his head. We were disposed along tribal lines around the elegant walnut table of the Rainfleury household. 'Mr Husband' sat opposite Enda, our hostess and so the notional purveyor of the beef. Berenice sat beside her lover. Waiting for a moment's lull in the clattering of cutlery, Berenice spat out a mouthful of *daube* onto her sister's white damask tablecloth.

'Vilely salty, it is. Morbidly salty. How can anyone dine off such sour meat? That thing you call a wife serves you ill, *Augustus*. Have you noticed she's left the *luncheon* cruet on the table? At *dinner*time?' Berenice looked disparagingly at Enda's reddening skin. Then she reached across the table with a grotesque slowness to overturn Enda's beloved Belleek salt-holder, smashing two of the delicate seashells that decorated it.

'There's a sweet sister for you, Mr Husband,' Enda smirked at Berenice. 'Mrs Hartigan will be hours whitening that cloth next door. As they say, it is a lonely wash that has no man's shirt in it.'

That is one for Enda, I thought.

Mr Rainfleury choked on his wine, coughing till the tears spilled out from under his lids. He rose and stumbled over to his wife. He reached for a hank of Enda's hair to wipe his eyes, allowing a sudden shocking insight into their matrimonial intimacy. At the sight of it, Berenice upended her chair and ran downstairs. We heard a door slam, and boots battering the cobbles abroad. When we came home, Berenice was locked in her room and would talk to none of us for two days.

But she was eloquent about her feelings in the note I intercepted in the post office coat, which smelled of lies in its armpits and pain in the pocket where Berenice had left a letter and a shredded rose. The tear-stained page throbbed with:

This killing, killing betrayal, the worst yet in a line of betrayals! Why must you live within an ass's roar of us, so that Enda can flaunt you at me every day?

Mr Rainfleury replied with due tenderness, and promises of a special treat. He concluded:

If only the toss of the coin had gone the other way, my darling. But it did not, and here we are. There were always three figures in the Garden of Eden, poppet. We must manage as best we can.

I thought, *And who is the corrupting serpent?*

So Berenice's happiness and Enda's marriage had been murdered by the toss of a coin. I resolved to write such a scenario into our next show, and began the sketch immediately. I took a hate upon that coat of his that knew too much. The next time he took tea with us, I asked, 'Mr Rainfleury, did you know that you have forgotten your brown coat in our hall press? With the summer coming in so early this year and the evenings so light, perhaps you'd like to take it to your own home?'

Berenice whispered, 'It does no harm here,' and Mrs Hartigan dropped the teapot. In the wet mess and exclamations that followed, the coat was no more mentioned. But it never again held any secrets. The guilty couple and Mrs Hartigan must have found themselves a new post office, one I never discovered, despite industrious investigations.

The marriage between Mr Rainfleury and Enda proved barren for more months than one might expect, at least to listen to Enda's many and indelicate hints about their mutual sensual felicity, each one of them sending Ida and Oona into fits of wriggling and grimacing. Berenice's face was taut with keeping in her fury.

I saw the doctor arriving next door every few weeks and noted Enda's anxious face at certain times of the month. Enda admitted to Oona and myself, 'Just a little baby, is all I want. Do you not want to be favourite aunts yourselves?'

Perhaps to deflect attention from the lack of an interesting event, Enda regaled us with stories of Mr Rainfleury's collection of portable moustache-curlers with heating devices, and the protector he wore at night to keep its supple walrus droop. The masterpiece was the German-made *Schnurbartbinde*, a device confected of silk, two leather straps and soft twin webs, which kept the precious taches in a state that King Wilhelm himself would not have despised, despite his well-known facility for sneering. We could also see for ourselves that whenever he must imbibe, Mr Rainfleury produced his moustache cup, which prevented any liquid from running down his whiskers.

On the last Sunday in August, Mr and Mrs Rainfleury arrived at Number 1 for a family dinner, with Enda looking happier than usual. Leaving Mr Rainfleury to his post-prandial cigar, we were scarcely out of the room before his wife was yawning theatrically. 'Didn't get a wink last night.' She taunted Berenice with sundry sunny observations of married intimacy and its blessings. I knew she would die rather than hurt anyone else that way. With Berenice alone, Enda lacked decency or mercy. 'Do you know what he says? He says he climbs up my hair to my narrow tower, just like a prince. He says it is because of my hair that he can ascend. My hair gives him *potency*!'

Berenice shot back, 'The prince who climbed up the tower and had doings with Rapunzel left her with child. Manticory wrote it, remember? So when the witch cast her out in the wilderness, Rapunzel gave birth to twins. If Augustus is so potent with you, why is it that you beget *bother-all*, Enda?'

Berenice had fallen into a trap.

'Actually,' said Enda, showing all her teeth as she did only when talking to her twin, 'the doctor has just confirmed it. And my baby will grow up to hurt you better than I ever could, brown bitch heifer.'

Berenice sat down sharply, her mouth working but nothing coming out.

'Enda!' said Oona. 'That is surely no way to introduce a dear little baby there!'

Darcy mused, 'I reckon you can still dance until the sixth month, Enda. Then Manticory will write you sitting-down parts. With cloaks. We needn't lose any bookings at all before your confinement.'

I protested, 'But what if Enda does not feel so well in herself?'

'You can write death scenes for her. We'll put her in a bed under a quilt. She can groan to her heart's content.'

Berenice clutched her own belly and vomited. In fact, for the next two months, it was she who exhibited all the heinous signs of morning sickness: the faintness and disembowelling nausea. Enda prospered, fattened and bloomed on her triumph, carrying her belly like a precious vessel in front of her.

18

T he baby died inside Enda in the fourth month.

Enda curled herself up in a cocoon of unbound hair and wept.

Her husband and her twin disappeared for long hours. I cursed Mr Rainfleury and Berenice even more. Where were they? It was not a time to steal a triumph.

And, I wanted to tell Berenice, *this triumph is tawdry, screwed out of a dead baby.*

But Berenice suffered too, every time Mr Rainfleury left her at the door to Number 1. And of course I could not utter a word of my bitterness to Enda, who was still bravely pretending not to know what was going on between her husband and her twin. Enda lost the next baby, and the one after, and every other child conceived inside the marriage. Those babies who might have been conceived on Berenice were prevented by Mr Rainfleury's vulcanised rubber.

In the interweaving of Swiney hair and Swiney destiny, that first foetus and all the other dead babies who followed it were other strands in the plait of hatred and intimacy that bound Enda and Berenice.

And my writing weaves it too, of course. Women are forever weaving their own narratives out of the growings of their own bodies, fashioning their own accounts, knitting new characters into their own stories. Even a tongueless woman – even a creature of regrets and impotence like me, Manticory – may embroider messages and stories with self-grown filaments of truth.

And one more strand, back in our Harristown cottage, was our mother, Annora, still pounding the threads of the laundry she took in, for she could never bring herself to spend the money that we sent her, even refusing when I offered to take her to Lourdes to see the Virgin lately glimpsed there.

Our visits to Harristown were increasingly rare, and it was perhaps kinder that way. Our aggrandised corporeality seemed to frighten our mother – we were plumper as well as taller than we had been when in her care. In our fine, voluminous dresses, we were too big for the cottage. We could not fit around her table. Our hats grazed the roof. Our elbows sent jugs flying. No, we did not in any way fit now. Our senses of ourselves were too vast as well.

The La Touches had diverted the railway line to run through their estate. But somehow, our landlord and his family never did happen upon us, no matter how much we made ourselves worth the seeing in our finery. We disembarked unseen and trudged unseen by them the short distance to Annora's cottage. I sometimes thought I saw the Eileen O'Reilly flitting through the trees beside us, but she'd grown too cunning and lithe to let Darcy catch sight of her. And she still, it seemed, did not want to be seen by me. We carried with us Mrs Hartigan's sponge cake in a basket. Our tastes had been flattered by the delicacies our housekeeper prepared for us. Once we had craved Annora's oat scones but now we regarded them with disdain. She'd never lost the habit of stretching the batter with stale breadcrumbs.

In the beginning, I had kept my promise to Annora. I wrote letters for Mrs Godlin to read aloud to our mother, to keep her apprised of our own great doings, of the crowds in Dame Street, of the latest fashions of our dolls, the trinkets we bought, the Frangipani soaps with which we washed our hands, the Domecq Manzanilla sherry we sipped, the grand dinners we ate. Sadly but baldly, I recorded the deaths of each of Enda's babies.

Mrs Godlin was a willing scribe, but Annora rarely replied. Although she herself had begged for them, perhaps she dreaded my missives – so I think now – for she wished to live alone with her memories of seven little daughters who had briefly lived only because she had birthed and fed them, and who'd not been devoured from the head downwards only because she saved them from the nits with the combs she had carved herself.

I tried to weave our mother into one of our shows, as a wise old lady who sews spells and proverbs onto finest silk under the light of a candle in a seashell. But the image would not fly. I could not write Annora wise or magical. And none of my sisters would want to play her, anyway. When my mind strayed to our mother, I thought of myself as one of the spiders who wove their stories in the rafters, watching her at her lonely work. It was no comfort to be that spider, so I gradually stopped visiting Annora in my thoughts.

All writers are spiders, knitting patterned tissues of life out of what grows inside themselves. Their webs also knit together diverse entities. Did you never see a tree married to a lamp-post by an industrious spider? Such miscegenations does a writer also create, as I did, first by writing the humble Swiney sisters into myth and legend for our stage shows, weaving a wild tribe of Irish starvelings into Lady Godivas who were not real ladies, and then weaving impossible desires for hair like ours into the hopeful hearts of the women who came to watch us.

'Clever girl, Manticory,' Mr Rainfleury told me. 'Keep working out those happy endings.'

Happy? I looked at Mr Rainfleury with despair that even my contempt could not enliven.

Is it any wonder that writers, and spiders, are disliked?

As Madame Defarge at her knitting was disliked?

But everyone loves a poet.

Do they not?

19

I was not the only industrious spider among the Swineys. Ida, though never shining in brains, had hands that were a credit to her. Using the combings we laid nightly in our hair-receivers, she embroidered a large picture on white velvet. It was of a tree with seven branches, each one sewn from real Swiney Godiva hair. A daguerreotype in a locket nodded at the end of every branch. The trunk was sketched with a pencil. It should, of course, have been made of Annora's hair, of which precious little was to be spared. It was too brittle for sewing, anyway, and its greyness was discouraging. The hair of Phelan Swiney, Mariner, had never been available to us.

The picture was framed behind glass and displayed on a cherry-wood easel beside the ticket desk wherever we were to perform. It built up the excitement nicely.

It was after our first show at the newly opened Gaiety Theatre in South King Street that we witnessed a young man unabashedly tracing the stitches of Ida's picture with a dancing light in his eye and a stagey tremor in his hands. We were waiting for our carriage in a corridor concealed by a curtain. We liked listening to the audience talking after the show. In this way we heard many pleasant things about the wonders of our hair and I was able to calculate adjustments to my scripts.

The large-eyed handsome young man, whose own curls were notable, appeared to be not quite exactly singing our praises.

'Looks so innocent, so soft,' he was telling a small group of bystanders, 'but this silky extrusion is a deadly danger. Hair! The thrilling, killing human instrument – the half animal, half stuff – that plays men's hearts more sweetly than a harp.'

His audience – who had just been ours – drew closer to him.

'Beware these hirsute *projections*' – the man described a ring-let with a twirling finger – 'of midnight black, of seething red, of primeval brown – they have been the death of a power of young men. Hair like this will wrap itself around your heart, your eyes, your soul, until you are choking to death on its delicious spun-silk witchery.'

Darcy bristled, 'Oho, he'll be asking for money next, you'll see. The Devil boil him a black pudding!'

It took six pairs of arms to restrain her from rushing out of our hiding place. Oona pleaded, 'Let us hear him, Darcy honey. He is a grand talker. And is he not a romantic figure of a man there?'

'I don't want to marry him, fool,' Darcy retorted. 'I just want to stop him from frightening the audience. Some of them are repeaters. Choking to death indeed!'

But I had been observing the audience closely, as was my habit. I tugged Darcy's sleeve. 'I don't believe he's in the way of hurting us.'

The young man intoned, 'It began with Homer's sirens, swooping down on sailors' ears with songs that told of their long locks. Were those sailors' hearts as hard as Ballyknocken granite, they'd not be resisting that siren hair. These young ladies should be called the Swiney *Sirens*!'

The crowd, rapidly swelling, shivered pleasurably. Our speaker leaned towards a pair of men confidentially, saying, 'Sixpence a ticket? A shilling? What a negligible amount to buy the chance to flirt with your very lives!'

Darcy jerked forward. 'Hoy! That's going too far. He's talking manure at them. I'll have his liver—'

But now Oona laid a hand on Darcy's shoulder. 'Look at that queue by the ticket desk there.'

Even as the crowd deserted him for the ticket desk, the young man bowed, kissed his hands to his admirers and slipped away – in our direction. Boldly, he parted the curtain and wove past it, right into our corridor, where he bowed theatrically. He'd clearly known all along that we were part of his audience.

'If I may, my Sweet Sirens, I'll make you famous,' he said. 'And rich.'

'Is that so? We're already famous, and fairly rich,' snapped Darcy. 'Without your help.'

'But Darcy honey, did you see what the gentleman just did to those people there?' asked Oona. 'He put an enchantment on them!'

'Like a cannibal witch doctor in Africa. Frightening them into worshipping us?' I mused. 'People love to be frightened. You should know that, Darcy.'

'I suppose not entirely unlike,' the man replied. 'Indeed those primitives in Africa will fashion a goddess out of wood to adorn their savage altars. Then they *make themselves forget* that they made that object with their own mortal hands. By means of the clever urgings of their witch doctor, they start to believe in the wooden idol as if she were a divine creature who dropped down from the moon or rose up from the sea. They bring her tribute – precious stones, essences, gold. Essences, liquid essences, in the name of the goddess, that's what I have in mind. Highly marketable essences. A little drop of liquid goddess that everyone can afford. Are you perhaps getting my drift, ladies?'

'A divine creature who dropped down from the moon? Sounds expensive,' smiled Darcy.

'Be thinking of rolls of money and piles of coins,' he answered, 'and the ledgers filling up with long lyrical lines of profit.'

And that was how we Swineys got ourselves a poet.

20

Tristan Stoker declared that he would offer his services for free, almost.

'Just a taste, I'll take. Nothing more. For isn't it an honour to myself to help the scintillating Swiney Sirens along their way?'

He stood us dinner in the Railway Hotel, a small investment on his part, as it turned out – unlike a recent excursion into charity when he had self-published a volume of his verses, a special free edition for the poor. The ungrateful poor had refrained from taking up his offer, leaving him a thousand copies that Relief Committees across Ireland had returned to him, postage paid on delivery, he told us indignantly.

'Perhaps *you* will appreciate my *oeuvre*, however, Miss Manticory.' He handed a slim volume across the table to me, while my sisters – always ravenous as gulls after a show – applied themselves to diamond-bone sirloins that spread themselves out all over the plate, not neglecting to hang over the edges. All of them, that is, except Oona, who looked from the meat to Tristan Stoker and back again continuously and seemed to have forgotten the use of a fork.

Pushing my plate aside, I applied myself to the book, eager to discover what kind of poet Mr Stoker was. He continued with his autobiographical account, revealing how he had selflessly devoted himself to his family business, pursuing his true passion – poetry – only in his fleeting moments of leisure. After skimming through 'An Ardour Unabated in the Arbour' and 'A Tress Too Far Away', I was certain he had made a correct division of his labours, though I nodded sympathetically when he sighed, 'Duty first!'

'Oh yes,' breathed Oona, 'duty first.'

Even if the poetry was lacking from his poetry, Tristan Stoker was a fine poetical figure of a young man with shapely hands, lustrous hair and a melting look to match the lilt of his voice. He was a different proposition entirely from Mr Rainfleury. I watched my sisters one by one putting down their knives to devote themselves to staring frankly, and with no small pleasure, at our host. Had he offered us a new line in cats' meat to endorse, my sisters would have considered it.

So intense was their excitement that they could not manage even apple pie with custard. Darcy's mouth tightened as our poet threw sheep's eyes at Oona over his brandy. Oona's neck was mottled with a flush.

'Enough about my tedious self,' our poet opined, finally. 'Let us talk about the Swiney Godivas. My diagnosis is that you ladies are not making the most of your gifts. You poor innocent girls have no way of understanding the true and terrible power of your hair,' he told us. 'Rainfleury & Masslethwaite have sheltered you from it, keeping you among childish things. Dolls are the mere infantile exposition of your potential. Dolls are bought from doll-purses, from the impulse that buys a gift, and does so only on a special occasion, or but rarely. I want to see you tapping the quotidian pockets of the real engines of economy, the gentlemen and their wives. But first the gentlemen . . .'

'The gentlemen doll collectors?' Darcy asked harshly. 'That is but a small pocket.'

'No, no, no,' laughed Tristan Stoker. 'I refer to a deeper, richer vein that is throbbing for a tapping. For there is a brotherhood of us, the susceptible men who nurse a strange and disturbing passion for long hair. We rarely speak our love explicitly in public, unless under the mask of poetry, for it is too passionate and wild a thing to contain in mere prose. You have seen the scandals brought down on my brothers-in-art Rossetti and Millais by their daring to expose it. But we Brothers of the Hair know one another, and we silently pray at the temple that could, with a little skilful massaging of the public's perception, become

162

any place where the Swiney Godivas lay their delicate feet and let loose their torrents of rampant, excessive, killing curls.'

I stared at him with hatred: that handsome young face hid another troll.

'Killing again, is it?' Darcy was showing all the signs of being about to dispense with her temper – the shallow breathing, the jerked gestures and the drawing in of her black brows. She began to gather up her reticule and caught our eyes in a sweep of the table so that we automatically half rose to leave.

'Ah, stay, Miss Darcy. Killing is the greatest compliment. Killing is power. Power is money. You can turn a fine fortune on said killing curls. I am about to explain how.'

Darcy put her reticule down on the floor again.

'I have watched the faces of my brothers in the audience. They imagine themselves smothered in your hair, choking on it, such sweet deaths as the poets, ahem, such as myself—'

'So we heard already,' interrupted Darcy. 'You'll have to do better than that. Where's the working part? Where does Tristan Stoker his great poetic self come in? The men pay their shillings anyway to get an eyeful of us. And the women and the girls buy the dolls.'

'But what if there were even more shillings and doll sales to be got?'

'Explain.' Darcy chopped her wrist on the dining table. 'But no more poetry! Understood?'

Oona whimpered quietly.

But Tristan Stoker nodded. 'Very well, to business, unadorned. With a heart and a half. Here is the nub of it. Do you think the *women* are unaware of what thoughts are in their menfolk's heads whenever they look at the Swiney Godivas' hair?'

'When was a woman ever unaware of anything?' agreed Darcy, albeit grudgingly.

'It has recently occurred to the great minds of industry that it is *women* who undertake most of the domestic shopping. Such small decisions as to the choice of soap or buttons may be safely left to feminine judgement. Now it is generally agreed that the way to a woman's purse – I speak of a woman of an economically interesting class – merchant and above – is through the craving in her breast for the admiration *of her own person*. That craving far outstrips her desire to appease the hunger in her husband's belly with wholesome dinners. She'd far rather have her husband's passionate adoration than his bloodless compliments on her faultless housekeeping. After a year of matrimony, passionate adoration naturally expires in the hearts of husbands. However, it can be nursed back to life by cunning means and at a certain cost.'

Enda leaned forward, intent. 'So how is the poor wife to buy it back?' she asked.

The poet smiled. 'Isn't it the wish of the feminine world to have hair cascading in torrents like yours? Don't you think a woman might be wishing her own hair was as flowy and showy and seductive as a Swiney Godiva's, to bind her man's thoughts solely to her? And that some portions of the housekeeping funds might well find themselves diverted to that purpose?'

'Mmm, so? Some men like the dolls themselves, but a doll won't make a man adore his wife. You still haven't interested me,' Darcy informed him flatly.

'Let us put the "Miss Swiney" dolls aside for a moment, though I have no intention of denting their graceful profits. Let us imagine that the wives want not just to own your likenesses, but *to be like you? With hair like yours?* What if there was a patent Swiney Godiva Hair Essence and a Swiney Godiva Scalp Food for sale at a folding table by the door as your entranced audience left your performance? Or better still, what if the ladies had already found on their theatre seats a piece of paper that might be tucked into their pockets for later consideration? A discreet piece of paper with an address to which they might write in order to be supplied with such a product. Such a letter they might write at their own snug correspondence desk, away from the vulgar observation of their neighbours and the general public.'

An equivocal noise escaped from my mouth. Oona looked at me reproachfully. 'Are you misdoubting Mr Stoker there, Manticory honey?'

'Devil a hair I care if she is,' quipped Darcy heavily.

'Of the present generation of young ladies in Ireland, surely your Miss Manticory is the most misdoubting of all.' Although Mr Stoker's teeth sparkled, his tone was abrasive.

How does he know that of me? My suspicions tightened.

'Let him go on,' Darcy decreed. 'Until I say.'

'Sweet Sirens,' Mr Stoker resumed, 'we are living in the era of improved home plumbing, where a power of women even have bathrooms, where they may use such products in complete privacy, and hide them away in presses with keys. But most importantly – what if this product was said to be the very same magical detersive used by the Swiney Godivas themselves, which causes them to be so marvellously endowed with hair? There is a commercial atmosphere abroad – ladies are in a mood to pay for what they did not receive from their good Maker. Let us disqualify Nature – who lets so many ladies down – and give them Swiney instead.'

Oona interrupted, 'We don't use an essence, Mr Stoker. We always used the soapy water left over from our mother's laundering, and we do the same now. Mrs Hartigan saves it for us. When we were young we never had the money for the bottled things they sold in the dispensary. Our mother even made her own soap from things you wouldn't want to talk of.' She blushed.

'Who'd buy her suds?' asked Pertilly.

'Frankly, my dear, the women would buy pressed dung beetles in a bottle, so long as it bore a Swiney Godiva label. Because it would be the wish and the promise of Swiney Godiva hair that they'd be buying. And the genius of it is that we shall have them needing *two* products, one being no use without the other, thus doubling the purchase.'

'I still don't understand what exactly *we* are purchasing from *you*, Mister Poet?' Darcy rapped.

Tristan Stoker offered me his card. I read aloud for my sisters:

'Stoker Vitreous Manufacture
Fine Glass Bottles &
Discreet Sanitary Necessities for Discriminating Ladies'

'I'll supply the essence for washing the hair and the scalp food, the bottles, the labels and the handbills for the advertising. And perform the miracle of having it distributed to every dispensary and general store in Ireland.'

'And we?'

'Must sit for some photographs at my direction, my lovely Medusas, to be printed on the labels and the handbills. And—'

'And?'

'A merest nothing. Sing some new songs with a mere slight mention of the product at judicious intervals. Wash a dolly's hair in Swiney Godiva Hair Essence on stage, perhaps. Sit in a shop window or two surrounded by my – your – bottles, just to reinforce the connection in the public's mind between Swiney Godiva Hair Essence and Swiney Godiva hair.'

'What do you put in scalp food, your honour?' asked Pertilly, licking her lips.

'A little nothing, bay rum-based, put together by a respectable pharmacist named O'Mealy. It will not harm the ladies, or aggravate their credulous scalps at all. Only because they'll not be putting it on their heads.'

O'Mealy, I thought. *Standish O'Mealy, no doubt! The same one who supplies Mr Rainfleury's vulcanised rubbers. Tristan Stoker and Mr Rainfleury . . . do they –?*

Ida was asking, 'Where shall they put that scalp food then?'

'Down their throats. And the more they drink of it, the better they shall feel for it. And the more easily they shall be pleased with their hair.'

'And the more they shall be craving it?' Darcy raised pleased eyebrows.

'Exactly. And the better their hair shall look to them, especially when washed in Swiney Godiva Hair Essence.'

While my sisters were digesting the Mr Stoker's idea – and apparently finding it palatable, from their grins – I was growing concerned for the literary aspect. I asked, 'Mr Stoker, being as you are a poet, will *you* be writing these new songs with the mere slight mentions of the essence and the scalp food? All I was thinking—'

166

Tristan Stoker smiled reassuringly. 'In my capacity as poet, I would venture to compose *some* material, but in close collaboration with the resident Shakespearess of the Swiney Godivas, of course, who occupies no mean place among songsters.'

'She could do with some help,' observed Darcy. 'Manticory's hardly good at all.'

'But she writes all our shows, Darcy honey,' protested Oona. 'And don't they clap them in the halls?'

Darcy paused for five beats of my heart. Then she replied, 'Just because a chicken has wings doesn't mean it can fly.'

She turned back to the poet. 'But even if, even *if* the Swiney Godivas agree to help you out with this project, you must share your snack of the new profits, Mr Stoker. We already have a business partner. The Corporation is managed—'

'That it is, by Mr Rainfleury of the dolls. As it happens, I took the liberty of discussing this matter with him before I came to you with it.'

'How dare you?' demanded Darcy, for once voicing my own thoughts. 'Going over our heads like that?'

'But Mr Rainfleury is also family, is he not? I spoke to him as your protector, the moral head of your household. He wanted me to present the idea to you myself—'

'I wonder why,' drawled Darcy, glaring at Oona.

'You will find Mr Rainfleury a staunch supporter of this proposal. In fact, we have agreed to produce miniature bottles of the essence to put in the boxes with the dolls. And the dolls shall be put in every shop window that makes a display of your essence and scalp food. It is a masterpiece.'

'A darling idea!' Oona clapped her hands and gazed on Tristan Stoker with eyes aglow with adoration.

Enda tried to look wise, as if her husband had already informed her of this new development. Berenice laughed at her twin's obvious failure to be confided in. 'Didn't *Augustus* tell you?'

From the shame in her eye, he'd clearly omitted to tell Berenice as well.

Tristan Stoker was busy returning Oona's moist gaze. 'Of course Mr Rainfleury wants the Swiney Godivas to ascend to a higher echelon of admiration and fame! Out of *love* for you, he could not turn me away – even if he had wanted to, which he patently does not. He too desires to have your names and your stories on everyone's lips.'

'Everyone's lips,' mouthed Oona.

Darcy pulled a wing of blonde hair aside and whispered in Oona's naked ear, 'You are setting yourself up for a staring-mad fool. It's long sorry you'll be for letting your heart go at the first sight of a big-eyed man.'

After that, things moved so fast that I suspected the pharmaceutical arm of the Swiney Godiva Corporation had been set in motion some time before it was presented to the Swiney Godivas themselves.

The first handbills showed our likenesses from behind: cascades of hair, with just a hint of our profiles. Immediately below was a decorative text:

SWINEY GODIVA HAIR ESSENCE
An invigorating, healthful restorative for all those who long for
BEAUTIFUL HAIR
like that of the sensational Swiney sisters from Old Ireland
SWINEY GODIVA HAIR ESSENCE
will cause your hair to grow to extravagant lengths.
It will impart the natural vigour of youth and the freshness of
dew, communicating a brilliant lustre and delicate softness.
Meanwhile, dandruff and scurf will not survive a single dose of
SWINEY GODIVA SCALP FOOD
which also cures weak and thin eyelashes on the instant.
REFINED AS THE SISTERS THEMSELVES
this Secret Irish Formula is captured in a bottle for the first time.
Used strictly in combination, these products are
positively the finest hair dressings available –
unrivalled in agreeableness, surpassing all pomades and greases,
so efficacious that they will make hair grow on bald heads.

168

Demonstrating just how imaginative his poetry could be, Tristan Stoker had added in small print at the bottom:

Supplied by direct command to HM the Queen of Romania,
HRH Princess Victoria of Schaumburg-Lippe,
HRH Princess Hohenlohe
1s, 2s 6d and (triple 2s 6d size) 4s 6d per bottle

We were bemused by these extravagant prices.

'No one will buy it!' fretted Pertilly.

But Tristan Stoker soothed us. 'The more expensive it is, the better the ladies will imagine it to be. That is the poetry of the thing.'

Of course Tristan Stoker himself wrote poems the way Mr Swinburne ploughed cabbage fields – not at all. He was the consummate poet in his velveteen waistcoat, in his lacquered curls and in the magnificent droop of his moustache, in his long-lashed brown eyes and in his fluid gestures. He was a poet in the way he loped into a room, and in his lingering glance. He was a poet in the way he lifted a soup spoon, and most of all in the way he ran an elegant finger down the column of his account book.

We were Tristan Stoker's creatures now, so we were poets too. Like literature, he assured us, we Swiney Godivas transcended social barriers. 'Never forget that by the poetry of your hair, you are transforming yourselves directly from peasant girls into goddesses. The stench of your childhood poverty shall be finally extirpated, for you shall have that precious quality of celebrity to sterilise your humble origins.'

'Away with your stench and humble!' snapped Darcy and she kicked Oona who was mouthing the poet's words after him.

We would earn 10,000 guineas in the first year of Tristan's essence and 'perfectly innoxious' scalp food. We earned it hard, performing four nights a week, travelling constantly, and posing in shop windows for face-tightening hours on end.

Tristan Stoker rejoiced. 'Your hair is becoming a metaphor for Empire and Industry.'

We bought outright our townhouse in Dublin, hired an extra maid, and began to call 'Tristan' by his Christian name.

More money flowed from the essence and the scalp food than even Tristan's poetic mind could have dreamed of. And the popularity of Tristan's products had a stimulating effect on the dolls' sales. And that in turn sold more tickets to our shows.

I now purchased any book I so much as fancied for cash money, without even glancing at the price. I could never quite get over myself in a bookshop, spending and spending. We were all in a fever of retail, Enda with her Belleek, Darcy with her glacé-button calf-galoshed hand-sewn kid boots and Baretta court shoes, Berenice with her carved boxes, Oona with her quack preparations for lightening the voice, Pertilly with her baroque tortoiseshell combs, and myself with the books. Ida's purchases were more eccentric and less consistent. She might come home with anything from a horrid grinning fox stole to a cone of fried fish and potatoes from one of the Italian street stalls. She insisted that we send Joe the seaweed boy a water-proof driving cape and found a vulcanised India rubber hot-water pillow for Annora.

In fact, we were so busy spending what the essence and the scalp food earned that we never saw the danger to Ida, who, as we would discover too late, had taken to swallowing a drop of scalp food whenever she was affected in her faculties. The drop soon escalated to a spoonful, and the spoonful to a long swig direct from the neck of the bottle. And after drinking it, she would take to her fiddle, filling Pembroke Street with melodious howls to break your heart and send it out of your body in pieces.

21

Tristan would go ahead to each town, posting signs. As promised, he'd give the local stores a sample and a doll – almost always 'Miss Oona' – to decorate the window and associate the shop with the Swiney Godiva sensation, of which the most sensational part remained Oona's white-blonde hair.

On the nights we performed he'd stand in the lobby too, uttering his familiar thrilling warnings that married hair to bodily love and love to death.

As well as a fixture onstage and in the railway carriage returning from our shows, Tristan became a regular inhabitant of our parlour. Mrs Hartigan automatically set a place for him at supper, beside Oona. He appropriated a desk by the withdrawing-room window for his literary labours, claiming our company for his muse. But the desk opened out from a cabinet with mirrored doors to its upper part, and I noticed that Tristan took his most visible inspiration from his hand-some face reflected in them. Oona was never far away from him, and her eyes were never off him. She was allowed to accompany Tristan on quite frequent excursions to buy pen-nibs and blotters. I would have been amazed that Darcy permitted this, except that I was growing to believe that Tristan had chosen Oona for his bride.

He was taking an unconscionable time to mention it, however.

'Why does he not . . . speak?' Oona searched my face in the mirror. I was brushing her hair before bed. Even in the grandeur of Pembroke Street, we continued to perform this service for one another as we had always done back in Harristown.

'Tristan?' I paused mid-stroke. 'He does nothing but speak. I'm exhausted at the words gushing out of the man.'

'Why doesn't he speak up for *me*? That's what I mean. I am certain that he, so. I mean, I have had certain . . . proofs . . . of his *affection* for me.'

I dropped the brush, upsetting Oona's green bottle of Breidenbach's Eau de Cologne. Leaving the puddle to infuse the rug, I gently turned her face round so that I could look into her eyes. 'You're just *seventeen*, Oona! Does he not know that? And is he as prudent in his *proofs* as he should be? Has he sent away for the . . . necessary?'

Oona nodded, her blush whitening into tense misery. She turned away from me.

I resumed punishing her head in silence with the brush until she moaned, 'What do you think, Manticory honey? Have I ruined it so?'

'I think,' I said carefully, 'that what you have done was not clever of you.'

'I read in the *Freeman's Journal* on Tuesday that if you want to marry within a year then you must hop barefoot round the Shipwreck Tower at Tramore.'

'Oona, please do not utter that thought to anyone but me. Tristan does not want *you* doing anything poetic. Don't be giving up yet. Perhaps he's just distracted by his poem.'

Tristan claimed to be working on a grand hairy epic of his own. But Tristan was a covetous, lamenting kind of poet, and continually distracted by Mr Rossetti's and Mr Browning's productions. He claimed that they stole his best lines, forcing him to waste months of work.

'*This*,' he declared in the parlour, waving Mr Browning's *Pauline*, '*this* is grand larceny from my own canon! Alas, as yet unpublished and now already thwarted.'

He flung *Pauline* across the room.

I picked it up and read aloud the passage he had scored through with an untidy pen:

172

'*Pauline, mine own, bend o'er me – thy soft breast*
Shall pant to mine – bend o'er me – thy sweet eyes,
And loosened hair, and breathing lips, arms
Drawing me to thee – these build up a screen
To shut me in with thee, and from all fear . . .'

Immediately the troll on Harristown Bridge sauntered into my mind, his designs on me a perfect illustration of this verse. I dropped the book. Tristan nodded in misconceived appreciation of my gesture. 'Quite right, Manticory! A shocking theft!'

It was Darcy who answered him, pelting words from the corner where she presided over the *Hairdressers' Chronicle and Trade Journal*. 'If there is any theft that has gone on here, it is of virtue. We all know it, Tristan, you've been making hair bowers and grottoes and screens and tents with Oona for months now. And if *real* poets like Browning make such fantasies revoltingly explicit, then who is it you are – you posing poodle – to object?'

This was the first time Darcy had treated Tristan to the full length of her tongue. This unexpected assault instantly fossilised him. The rest of us forgot about breathing; Tristan sat with his pen raised in one hand and his mouth open. Oona began to speak, but Darcy silenced her with a cutting gesture, saying, 'We'll come to you in a minute. I have not finished with our poet yet.

'Oh yes,' continued Darcy, 'I am sure it is dim and hushed inside Oona's hair tent. I am sure the tousle-haired poet nourishes his muse in the private weather in there. But does he actually write poetry when he is sighing so close to Oona's breathing lips and counting the heartbeats pumping out between her two breasts? Is it any wonder we've had nothing more than a slim volume from you yet, Stoker? Did it never occur to your poetic brain that a marriage proposal – in writing – would be briefer and more manageable and more to the point?'

Tristan made a glowering exit, refusing to meet Oona's pleading eyes. She fixed on his shapely back with desperate regret.

'How do you like that coward?' demanded Darcy. 'He has put the fool on you, Oona. It had to be said.'

'It did not at all have to be said,' I told her.

I was heartsick in the days that followed to see that Darcy's intervention had done nothing but harm. Tristan did not look straight at Oona any more. The excursions for pen-nibs and blotters continued but Oona now had to beg Tristan to allow her to accompany him. Then he came to announce his departure to pursue poetical business in the glass factories of Blackfriars and visit 'a place of interest' in London.

Oona stared at Tristan as if memorising him, as well she might. He had still not made any move in a matrimonial direction, and the life-blood was dripping out of her. She cared not a whisker that the audience loved her best every night. She only wanted Tristan to love her. As I brushed her hair, she confided to me that she had imagined romantic evenings dandering arm-in-arm along the Thames with Tristan. Our eyes met sadly in the mirror.

Mr Rainfleury had also deserted us for a 'hair fair' in Paris, and proclaimed a passion for viewing the same 'walls of a certain private drawing room in London as Tristan'. Mr Rainfleury left both his wives at home, rather than take Enda with him. I guessed that he could not but disappoint one of them, so he had decided to disappoint them both.

When Tristan did speak again, it was not of marriage but of golden hair.

Hotfoot back from London, he had us assemble in the dining room, with Mr Rainfleury hovering supportively in the background. Tristan held a pile of books in his arms. He placed them solemnly on the table and asked us to sit.

'Ladies,' he announced, with the lyrical jut of his chin that always prefigured a commercial speech, 'there is something that you shall need to understand for the sake of our continued collaborations. Ladies, let us think on the richness and fineness of golden hair. Such as Mr Rainfleury and myself have just been privileged to see in the home of Frederick Leyland, a collector of certain works of art, and a Brother of the Hair—'

174

'Ahem, whether he knows it or not,' mentioned Mr Rainfleury.

'A Brother, if there ever was one,' pronounced Tristan. 'And a lover of yellow hair. Yellow hair: the colour of light; the colour of gold. Gold is a precious rarity; men will kill and die for it; gold is power.' He waved the *Freeman's Journal*. 'Look here. The Gold Rush in California has caused eggs to sell at $10 a dozen. A pinch of gold dust buys a man a glass of tawny yellow whisky.'

'And no doubt,' interrupted Darcy, 'pays the purchase of a good-time girl with golden hair.'

Tristan was not to be deflected. 'What I was about to say, is that *good* girls are "as good as gold". Think of spun gold and spinning wheels; faithful wives at abandoned hearths; spider women at their lures. Golden hairs are glinting fishing lines, catching men. "Reel him in, the Golden Youth, devour him," whispers the lady spider, dispatching pale gold silk from her fertile thorax.'

'Spiders?' mourned Oona. 'You'd have us spiders, Tristan?'

'Weavers, combers,' he answered hastily. 'Gold for gold, shuttle and comb, in and out, in the sister arts of weaving and hair-combing. I see rolled gold ringlets on napes of necks! The longer, the thicker, the more golden the hair – the more vigorous the bliss promised. Golden labyrinths of hair for men to make their way through or get lost in.'

Darcy glared at Oona as if she had personally generated this obscenity.

Tristan cleared his throat. '*Now*, ladies, now gold has graduated. As you Swiney Godivas have been taking your place in the golden footlights, literature and art have lately decreed that blonde women can, ahem, go either way. For golden hair is fairy hair, sacred and wicked at the same time. A blonde may be a delightful, passive, pure child of a woman, knitting nests of domestic bliss in her fair tresses. Her fair hair might shelter the man who is vulnerable to darkness. Or our blonde might tarnish like brass, and show its same shameful, cheap venality.'

A tear started in Oona's left eye. She raised a hand but dropped it again. Tristan did not look at her.

How could he ignore her? Onstage, we all knew, the greatest applause was still reserved for Oona. People wanted blonde. Our dolls' sales sang it. The notorious hair trade confirmed it: the *Hairdressers' Chronicle and Trade Journal* observed that false hair was a guinea and a half for blonde, even if indifferent quality, while best brown and black hair struggled to raise a guinea.

'And hair,' Tristan said sternly, 'be it ever so palely soft, is like a hard-hearted woman, for it feels no pain.'

'Now, wrap your long eyes around this!' He held up a hand-coloured daguerreotype of a painted woman. 'It is this lady I have been to London to see! She about whom all Brothers of the Hair are gasping. Here is gold for you!'

The woman's rich curled hair filled and seemed fit to burst out of the confinement of the frame. The corsetless nymph semi-reclined in an available manner, her diaphanous gown slipping from a shoulder. A poppy drowsed in a glass beside her. Her eyes were cast down to her mirror, but the effect of those lowered lids was not to exclude but to beckon.

'Trollop,' said Darcy.

'Sensational,' countered Tristan. 'The word they use for her is "stunner". As in "stunning, sensational success" – which might also, dear ladies, be ours. This is Mr Rossetti's painting of Lady Lilith, which we saw in Mr Leyland's house at Prince's Gate. And this lady's hair, the artist tells us, was "the first gold". *Gold*,' he repeated, meaningfully.

'Who?' Darcy demanded. 'Do we know a Lilith?'

'Lilith-the-fair' – Tristan lowered his voice dramatically – 'was created from the same handful of dust, and was Adam's first, wilful wife. Discarded by him, she consorted with devils, with whom she bred still-born babies, while dining on the infants born of innocent humans. She never died, they say, but returns to earth nightly to seduce mortal men in their dreams.'

'Trollop,' insisted Darcy.

On Oona's face I saw the dawning of apprehension. In front of my eyes I saw the words of the Corporation contract and I knew I would not be able to help her. In my bitterness, I asked,

'So you have forgiven the poets then, Mr Browning and Mr Rossetti and such gentlemen?'

'Mr Rossetti has done us the favour of writing an explicit sonnet about Lilith's talent for drawing men into the bright web she wore and wove round the heart of her chosen youth. And he translated a sliver of dear old *Faust* that is quoted in Mr Swinburne's essay here.' He opened a marked page in a volume entitled *Notes on the Royal Academy Exhibition 1868*, and read aloud:

> *'Hold though thy heart against her shining hair,*
> *If, by thy fate she spread it once for thee;*
> *For when she nets a young man in that snare,*
> *So twines she him he never may be free.'*

'Oh really?' drawled Darcy, looking from Tristan to Oona.

Tristan was not to be deflated. 'Not only have I forgiven Mr Rossetti and his friends, but I have decided to parley with them, for the greater glory of the Swiney Godivas. Manticory, you and I shall henceforth anthologise a little, associate with the other poetical Brothers of the Hair. I'll help,' he smiled. He pointed to the pile of books he had brought with him. I consulted the spines: *German Fairy Tales*, *The Rape of the Lock*, and *Paradise Lost*. There were already slivers of paper inserted at several pages.

'It's certain Tristan knows what is best,' murmured Oona disconsolately.

But you stand to lose the most, I wanted to warn her.

'The ledger agrees with you.' Darcy accepted Oona's primacy in that spirit, for with the essence and the scalp food she'd made sure from the start that we all profited equally from Oona's sales.

Tristan started Oona gently with a soberly clad Portia, whose hair was *a golden mesh t'entrap the hearts of men/Faster than gnats in cobwebs*.

He had Pertilly sprinkle Oona with silver dust for her role as Frau Holda of the fairy tales, a white witch of the spinning wheel who teaches good girls to comb their hair so that pearls and rubies drop into their virtuous laps.

Next Oona's hair was piled in a towering style and she was dressed in a dusty panniered confection to be Belinda of Mr Pope's poem. The audiences loved the strange contrast between Oona's deep voice reciting her lines and the moonlight hair that massed around her face, 'insnaring' men to rape her locks.

She also received a standing ovation for Eve in Milton's *Paradise Lost*, though I could not be sure whether this was for the poetry or the tight pink costume she'd been sewn into, and its three anxiously large fig leaves. Oona did her best to look wanton as she spoke of ringlets that curled like the tendrils of a vine.

Tristan set up a 'Floral Tributes' stall so men could throw flowers when Oona played a loosely robed Circe of the glorious hair, another weaver. Here again her hair rippled loose – not neatly braided or pinned, but cascading down in a way that was only suitable in the privacy of the married bedroom.

I carped, 'Won't the public be sick of seeing Oona's hair always on full display?'

'True,' said Tristan. 'Let's have a plait for a change.'

As Rapunzel, Oona's hair made a ladder for both a prince with a virile sword, played by Tristan, who had taken to joining her on the stage, and the diabolic witch, played by Ida, the possessor of the Swineys' most harrowing laugh.

Oona's short tableau of the blonde demon in *Lady Audley's Secret* was such a success that Tristan devised a whole show in which, via quick changes of costume and hairstyle, she portrayed a series of fair horrors from the latest sensation novels – libidinous, yellow-haired calculating machines for meshing money with sensual gratification. Tender-hearted men were their fuel. Ruined men, hollowed and exsanguinated, were the debris they left behind them.

Oona was never able to conjure enough ancient evil to do justice to these roles. So Tristan reconfigured the cast, with Berenice or Darcy narrating while Oona did her straining utmost to *look* the part.

And from prose Tristan moved easily into publicity. Oona was dazzlingly perfect in a Swiney Godiva Scalp Food newspaper advertisement that cleverly alluded to Mr Rossetti's *Lady Lilith* without being so derivative as to get us into trouble. Oona was required to perform the feat of impersonating an ensorcelling lady cannibal and, at the same time, communicating our scalp food's healthful properties to our customers.

It was small wonder to me that she cried so hard after her day in the photographer's studio.

Tristan was not going to put himself in the way of Darcy's tongue again if he could help it. So he took care to have me include a series of poetic effusions for night-haired, death-loving heroines in our shows.

The lights would dim and he would whisper offstage, 'Hair! Women's hair! It lies against their throats like a lover. A dying lover. Hair lives beyond death . . . Is it not the lure of the grave itself that gives raven-winged hair its irresistible, supernatural lustre?'

The lights rose to show Darcy glowering over a pomegranate as Mr Rossetti's *Proserpine*, the shades of Hell darkening her eyes and the serpentine gyre of her neck and hair showing all her power. She was Mr Sandys' *Medea*, clutching a blood-red necklace, and also his *Rosamund*, her murderous hair as black and tumultuous as her soul. In a shadowy background, a prone Tristan played the husband she had just slain, while I, in the wings, sent a skull spilling wine spinning across the stage. Darcy's most celebrated role was as Medusa, using an ingenious device adapted from an egg-beater to raise wiggling snakes in her hair.

In the Pembroke Street drawing room, Tristan constantly pestered me to darken my songs for Darcy. 'Threats of hair violence,' he advised, 'bring on fear and fear opens purses. Never let them forget that hair is a frontier, a precarious place of danger. Our bodies are contained in their skin-clad lineaments, except where the hair gushes forth,' he declaimed. 'The only other things that spill out of our bodies are the liquids of excretion or exertion—'

Ida began to cry.

'That is enough right there, Tristan Stoker,' said Darcy. 'If that is not an outrage, get me one! Step along with yourself! Go! And take your excreting with you! Look at Ida crying fit to fall in pieces from your botherations.'

Tristan's smile never faded. 'Ida's tears merely prove what can be done by way of stimulation of the imagination. I am sorry I let the poetry take me a bit beyond myself there. It is for Corporation reasons that we must remind your audiences that hair is a risky object. We must alert them to the consequences of not dealing with it! We want them to hate their own hair! Then they will buy the liquid solution for the destruction of what they hate and fear about it.'

He gestured to a sketch on his desk, showing a wife with tangled lank locks watching helplessly while her husband leered at a luxuriantly tressed beauty. The caption was simple: *Will he dispense with your services?*

When his sketch was turned into a photograph, Tristan was perceptive and cruel enough to have the spurned wife modelled by Enda and the coveted mistress by Berenice.

Having exhausted every moral shade of blonde and black, Tristan turned his attention to red hair, and to me. He had seen what I wished not to see – that red might sell and that I might sell red.

Red hair had been licensed for popularity by the disorderly young men of the Pre-Raphaelite Brotherhood. I suppose Millais started it, even painting the young Christ himself as a redhead, but Mr Rossetti was mostly to blame with his lubricious flame-haired heroines. Until then redheads had been decried as rare and unfortunate 'carrots'.

Once we were endowed with licentiousness, redheads became irresistible. This prompted the novelists to turn us evil. Mr Collins created Lydia Gwilt, the wicked, bigamous, rotten, bloody, heart-shattering redhead in *Armadale*. Within a year of her appearance, flaming heroines were ubiquitous in novels. So of course, I was Lydia Gwilt's impersonator, uttering terrifying monologues of her letters, in which she joked of how she craved a child to beat and loved to watch summer insects killing themselves in the candle flame.

And, just as I had always feared, Tristan had me 'do' Lizzie Siddal. In 1869, Lizzie, Mr Rossetti's late wife and model, had been exhumed at her husband's request. He had buried a book of his poems with her. But the poet had changed his mind and wanted his valuable work back.

'As poetic as Tristan then,' I muttered when I heard this.

There had arisen a rumour that Lizzie's opened coffin had overspilled with luxuriant curls that kept growing at a furious pace even as the corpse decomposed. One copper curl had twined itself around the book of poems. The creeping curl was cut off and lifted from the grave along with the book.

Tristan decreed that I must re-enact Lizzie's posthumous part using the coffin that Darcy carried around on all our tours. The coffin was too large for me, adding to the pathos of the sight of me inside it, clutching my husband's poems jealously to my breast. The mahogany box was mounted on a gurney that slowly raised it upright while my sisters chanted funereal hymns. I kept my eyes shut until the last moment, when I opened them on a terrified audience, and recited a Rossetti love poem, as if I were the artist's plundered wife lamenting in her grave.

The women screamed dutifully. The men gaped greedily at my hair as if they longed to stuff it into their open mouths.

There was no one to tug their sleeves and tell them not to. According to Tristan's handbills, every look they bestowed on our hair was an education for their minds, even if they *felt* us with their bodies. It was not the Swiney Godivas' fault if evil passions were aroused in men who thereby rendered themselves self-evidently unworthy to be present at such an exclusive and culturally irreproachable event as a Swiney Godiva performance.

With Tristan back from a second private view he'd finagled of Mr Leyland's 'stunners', I was set to impersonating the woman in Mr Rossetti's *La Pia de Tolomei*, the russet-haired wife left to die in staring melancholy in the malarial swamps of Maremma while the slow crows wheeled around her and the sundial's shadow chased an eternity of trapped torment.

But I knew that no one cared a handkerchief for the Pia's or my own suffering. They just wanted my hair, eyefuls of it, and if their eyes could have performed the feat, they would have torn my red hair out of my head.

Mr Rainfleury never protested on our behalf. Just once, I asked him to intervene – when Tristan deemed it necessary for me to lie in a bath with my hair flowing over the edges, like Lizzie Siddal posing for Mr Millais' *Ophelia*.

I stayed as close as possible to the door to his study to put my case.

'But you wear your chemise and are entirely hidden by the bath! Apart from your head and one arm, that is. You show nothing, or show it in a Christian manner.' Mr Rainfleury's tone was even. 'And do you know what it costs to warm the water?'

'I do not wish the rest of me to be *imagined* lying in my own bath, naked,' I explained. 'You know that is what they are thinking down there in the audience. Your dolls have stolen our identities, and now our whole bodies have been appropriated by Tristan for his advertising.'

Those words had looked so eloquent in my notebook but had come out prissily.

'What piffle, my dear,' Mr Rainfleury said tranquilly. 'You're a great girl for the suspiciousness, Manticory. I believe it has worn a furrow between your brows that is not at all flattering to one of your colouring. I think I see the permanence of a wrinkle in that shadow. I would not like you to be forgetting that the bit of talent that you have would scarcely be enough to live on, were you to grow ugly. Remember your contractual obligations to the Corporation.'

'The contract does not say anywhere *Denature yourselves*,' I muttered. 'Or *Sell yourselves for money like whores*.'

182

'Manticory,' Mr Rainfleury sighed. 'You are losing the run of yourself. Surely *you* would not be the mad creature who would put the Corporation in ruins with scruples you certainly weren't born with? What do you think pays for your home, the steaming platters of food, your books that pile up like ingots of gold all over the house?'

This spiteful tongue, I thought, *is what we see in Mr Rainfleury's mouth when one of his dolls deviates from the game he wants to play with them. What will he do to win that game?*

He smiled again. 'Don't you see that the Swiney Godivas *cannot* stop doing what they do? There must be seven Swiney Godivas or none at all. *You* may be able to earn yourself a pittance as a governess with the great literary genius on you, if only you can keep your stage past a secret – but what of your sisters? Do you think any of them capable of survival without the Corporation to pay their dress accounts? Would you abandon them to destitution? What would they do with themselves back in Harristown, penniless? Would you really leave them to that?'

I was dismissed. I stood outside the door, hating myself and Mr Rainfleury in equal measure.

I marched back in. 'I will not wear the hairpieces onstage. And neither will my sisters.'

He laughed, as well he might, at the reduced scale of my protest. 'We'll see what Darcy says, shall we?' A shadow fell over the threshold and Darcy slithered into the doorway.

'Ah, Darcy,' said Mr Rainfleury, 'we were just speaking of you. Please to come in.'

He explained what I had said, making it sound like a childish tantrum.

Darcy frowned. 'Rebellion, is it? A touch of the old foxy red-haired rebel?'

And she swished her hand in front of her, to Mr Rainfleury's bemusement.

'Do you think it makes any difference whether we wear Rainfleury's hair or not?' she asked me. 'Do you think that is your problem? Do you think throwing the hairpiece on the ground and stamping on it will make you a girl who never wore a hairpiece? Who never danced on the stage? Who never sold a bottle of scalp food? You're as moonstruck as Ida if you think that.'

'I say poor Manticory is not herself,' said Mr Rainfleury. 'Indeed it may be a touch of Ida's malady that she has, spreading between sisters? The blood of the old mad King Swiney himself in your veins? I'll have Standish O'Mealy mix her a powder.'

Bitter, it was, the powder, and I suspect that its purpose was punishment rather than cure. But I took it, to punish myself, for not having succeeded in my little revolution. Mr Rainfleury and Darcy had found its weak points in a moment.

Ida was not herself most of the time now. At home in Pembroke Street, Mrs Hartigan tied a copper flask to Ida's middle and kept it filled with hot water. If you asked Ida what ailed her, she would take a hank of hair into her mouth and weep, 'It is the cold creeping in my bones. Yet I burn.'

'And look at the face on you as long and green as a thin reed!' complained Darcy. 'And a red nose you could see from the Matterhorn! Who'll pay to see that miserable muzzle on the stage? Couldn't you pretend, just for our sakes, to be happy? What is it you are golloping down your throat there?'

She wrested the bottle of scalp food out of Ida's hands.

'You're drinking *this*? For your *unhappiness*?'

Ida keened, 'Yet I must have been happy at one time because presently I know that I am not. I think I was happy with Mam in Harristown. Perhaps we should—'

'Don't even think about it! Who says you have a right to be happy?' grumbled Darcy. 'All anyone's got a *right* to is mixed middling at best.'

She cast her black eyes over Enda and Berenice wretchedly rehearsing a duet, at Oona staring sadly at Tristan, at Pertilly grimacing as she forced her ankles into cruelly tight boots for her next solo. Finally, Darcy's eyes came to rest with satisfaction on me, disconsolately scripting my own next humiliations on the stage. In front of me were Tristan's

184

scribbled instructions. Below my sheet of paper was the blotter and below that the wax-smeared contract that bore Darcy's signature in crow-black ink, indelible as a dose of her contempt.

22

T ristan insisted there was something missing from the wallpapered, swagged, ruched first-floor parlour, crowded with
brutal-looking mahogany furniture and seven different tastes in
knick-knacks competing for every polished surface. It was here
that Mr Rainfleury and Tristan held meetings with important
clients from the big pharmacies and grand shops. The room was
also a place where we Swiney Godivas delivered short, colourful public lectures on the art and science of the hair to a select
paying audience.

'Can you imagine anything more appropriate here than a
dignified portrait in oils of the Swiney Godivas in their glory?'
Tristan pointed to the mirror above the fireplace. The glass
showed our faces arranged in characteristic expressions of worry
and doubt. As with any new idea that was not her own, Darcy
began to cavil. 'What's wrong with a photograph? We have
plenty of those!'

Tristan smiled. 'Art, by virtue of its engagement with the soul,
confers respectability, reality and luxury, whereas photography
is considered by many to be a cheap, shallow record or a mere
meretricious tool.'

'Oh and indeed,' I muttered. I had hated to be photographed
ever since the first time we'd been surprised by an explosion of
magnesium at the Poulaphouca Falls.

'You're talking to us, Tristan, not your precious general
public,' Darcy reminded him. 'Away with your meretricious
tool and tell me what you mean to be saying.'

Our male muse now explained in simple terms that he
and Mr Rainfleury deemed an oil painting more conducive to

profitable negotiations than the commercial kind of photograph we used to promote our show and the Swiney pharmaceuticals. That jade-green parlour, Tristan declared, was not a place to put individual bottles into trembling, confiding hands. 'It is a place to situate, perpetuate and congratulate the Swiney Godiva *phenomenon* – and to sign agreements for shipments of *a thousand bottles at a time.*'

Darcy nodded thoughtfully.

'And it will be helpful to the people who come to hear you speak. In that the vision of your miraculous hair shall be supplied twice over, in your seven persons and on the wall as well. It shall be as if the painting endorses and reinforces the reality of the seven living sisters.'

'So as to ensure they don't think that we are faking the hair?' I asked pointedly.

There had been some murmurs against us in the press about hairpieces and supplementary plaits recently, which had us nonplussed and helpless, until Mr Rainfleury had explained that such rigmaroling was merely confirmation of our success. 'The secret of my spun-silk artificial hair still eludes my competitors. So naturally they spread these clumsy lies that the Swineys are using hair from the human trade. Think nothing more about it, my dears.'

Exchanging a hard glance with Mr Rainfleury, Tristan said, 'Indeed. We must act fast to undermine any slander that would contaminate our sales. And there is also the all-important element of entertainment, for which the general public is so greedy. Of course, your little lectures impart knowledge without excessive fatigue to the brain, but a portrait would give the audience something to look at if their attention wanders.'

Darcy sniffed. Tristan frowned, realising he had made a rare wrong move in implying that we Swineys might fail to fascinate. He swiftly changed the subject and expatiated on how important it was to commission a 'properly foreign' artist to paint us: 'No native Irish dauber will do!'

He had one in mind, a Mr Alexander Sardou.

'You are going too fast,' Darcy cried.

But at dinner and luncheon the next day Tristan was still masticating on the portrait and its boons.

Darcy continued to raise every possible objection – from the expense to the wasting of valuable Swiney Godiva time in protracted sittings. I realised that she was afraid of this portrait. She dreaded seeing her true likeness up there on the wall. She'd assumed control over all photographs commissioned since Poulaphouca Falls, ordering the destruction of any plates that did not please her. She could not very well have an expensive original oil painting ripped in half. Art, as Tristan had pointed out, was different from photography. Where photography could conceal, art might discover Darcy's harsh looks. I understood that Darcy feared this foreign painter, this Alexander Sardou, would fall into the grip of some extravagant artistic *estro*, and forget to soften her hard jawline or might emphasise the hooding of her eyes for the sake of drama. He could even fail to understand her pre-eminence among us and place her in the background as a shadowy foil to Oona's blonde beauty or Enda's natural elegance.

I, on the contrary, was interested in this new way of telling our story – and in subverting Darcy's desires too. The quiet month of January stretched out in front of us. The snow always slowed our bookings. I suggested, 'At least let us meet Mr Sardou. An interview will soon show if he is biddable, no matter how foreign. If he's headstrong, away with him!'

'How foreign is he?' Darcy began. She was beginning to feel the portrait slide into her grasp.

Berenice mused, '"Sardou" sounds French.'

I said, 'It could also be Italian. But "Alexander"? At all events, shouldn't we find out more before dismissing the idea entirely?'

'I'll have him fetched directly to account for himself personally.' Tristan threw me a confused but grateful glance, and hurried off to arrange the thing.

Because he was foreign and artistic both, we had expected something swarthy and voluble from Alexander Sardou. But Mr Sardou was blond in Oona's style – that pure fairness without any dirtying of tawn. He was tall enough to eat his supper off the top of Tristan's curly head. His kite-shaped torso was even shapelier than the poet's. There was an attractive shadowing under his eyes; the brows were a soft smudge above them. I noted the unusual intensity of the gaze emitted by eyes as pale as a wolf's; my eye lingered on the delicate cleft in his chin. The velvet of his jacket became him, clinging to his slender form. His leather case was as perfectly groomed as he was, as if it had not lived at all, despite all his travels. He seemed shy, quite failing to raise those lupine eyes when he dipped his head in the Continental style to acknowledge us. I saw unmelted snowflakes glittering in his hair. I had become accustomed to Tristan's performative romancing. By virtue of the contrast, the painter seemed quite dazzlingly and authentically gallant.

Tristan fluttered around, introducing us and quite unnecessarily extolling the individual beauties of our hair.

'An honour,' Mr Sardou repeated each time quietly, with an accent that darted north, south and east in three syllables. In response to a series of questions, he let it be known, with a maximum economy of words, that his father had been Venetian, his mother was French but that he'd been educated in Geneva and London.

'It is St Teresa's Dead Christ come to life!' exclaimed Ida. 'Have him lie down,' she cried, 'and lay his head on a stone, with the clothes taken off him, and you shall see the twin of Him at chapel!'

'Listen to her!' Darcy tried to joke. 'Two ruches short of a curtain swag! Ida left her senses under a bush in Harristown, and we're still looking for them.'

In fact, now that Darcy had removed all bottles of scalp food from the house, Ida's senses were keener than they had been for some time.

Tristan told us, 'Mr Sardou has brought some reproductions of earlier portraits for your approval.'

The artist rummaged delicately in his leather case, causing a paintbrush and a book to fall out. I lunged for the book to pass it to him, but in truth my purpose was to discover its title:

189

Rhoda Broughton's latest, *As Red as a Rose Is She*, which I had recently skimmed myself. It did not seem like a foreign gentleman's book. Discreetly, I showed it to my sisters. Darcy made a face that said, as clearly as if it spoke the words, *a man who reads romantic novels is a piffler*.

The artist flushed, which made him seem even younger – so young that it was hard to believe that he'd put in the years required to execute his long list of important commissions, not to mention his training in four Continental academies of note.

The sample portraits were unimpeachable. Women of uniform prettiness and demureness stared at me from the sheaf of hand-coloured prints. I· was momentarily disappointed by their blandness, but Darcy was reassured. Even she could not object to Mr Sardou's remote, courtly manners or his air of humble compliance. The artist was hired for a sum undisclosed to us by Tristan.

He arrived in the green parlour and set up his easel three days later.

In fact, it seemed to me that Alexander Sardou was no more compliant than a sewing-machine stand. He simply avoided the trap into which people often fell. It was easy to think that if you wanted to have your way with the Swiney Godivas, the friendship of Darcy would be more profitable than the love of any two angels and an apostle beside. But Darcy didn't really go in for friendship – more for temporary, dedicated, strategic alliances. People who tried to flatter or ingratiate were given the rough of her tongue more quickly than those who, like Alexander Sardou, simply showed an unadorned kind of respect.

Somehow, from that first meeting, Mr Sardou had also divined that if he showed favour to Berenice then Enda would hate him. So he divided any words to the twins into strictly equal rations. He also seemed to know instinctively that it was better not to ask a question of Ida, and that both Oona and Pertilly were inclined to stammer pitifully if put on the spot. As for myself – he contrived ways to barely look at me at all.

The young man of apparently very few words arranged us according to the palette of our hair, from light Oona to dark

Darcy, left to right. He'd had Tristan ask us to wear black, and to explain that this uniformity would both confer dignity and emphasise the lively variety of our facial features. Without our being conscious of his gaze, the artist had also worked out a skilful disposition of our heads and shoulders. As we filed into the green parlour on the morning of our first sitting, Mr Sardou was to be seen with his back to us, busy stretching a large canvas over boards. But Tristan held up a captioned sketch explaining how and where we should sit. Mr Sardou's hand-writing was subtle, yet fascinatingly foreign, with tiny extra cross-hatches on some of the consonants. Those of us with the neatest profiles – myself, Oona and Ida – were presented in three-quarter view, while the sisters with slightly larger noses – Enda, Berenice and Darcy – were to sit facing the viewer's gaze, in a gentle, obliterating light. Pertilly's double chin was concealed by her being requested to sit on a low stool and gaze upwards.

Even Darcy could not quibble with the illustrated instruc-tions, though she sniffed, 'Why can't the man just tell us himself? Is he too grand for that?'

Tristan replied smoothly, 'It would be a brave man who tried to tell *you* what to do, Darcy. Indeed, even the sketch may be viewed as a suggestion, I understand.'

Mr Sardou nodded with lowered eyes, and of course we hurried to execute his design in all perfection, Darcy most of all: the light, she quickly saw, would flood her dark curls with rich blue and violet highlights. A quick glance in the mirror showed her that the shadow of her brow, so disposed, length-ened her lashes.

All through the sketching and then the painting sessions, Mr Sardou spoke only if asked a direct question. If he wanted one of us to move, he quickly sketched the desired position, with arrows, and held it up to us. We were, however, allowed to speak among ourselves unless he was working on our own face – indi-cated with a discreet pointed brush. From slight twitches of his eyes and mouth, I deduced that our conversations were feeding Mr Sardou's painting with details of our personalities that would enliven our likenesses and lend them the truth of conviction.

As for me, it was pleasantly and shockingly indecent to have so close a view of a man at his profession. We never really saw what Tristan or Mr Rainfleury did: their business was largely transacted in offices we were not invited to visit, or behind the closed doors of this very room. Mr Sardou worked in front of us, much as a performing bear might labour for an audience. I wondered if he resented this exposure. Perhaps his absorption in his task blotted out any subsidiary discomforts. It occurred to me that even Mr Sardou's quietness was a performance of sorts. He performed his silent rituals with his subtle tools. Yet his very silence was compelling. It put him very much in the room because it made a body ponder on his unspoken thoughts. I breathed in the woody smell each time he opened one of his collapsible tubes of oil, noted the delicacy with which he replaced it in its japanned tin box.

I watched his long fingers restless at the canvas; I followed his eyes measuring my sisters' features; I gazed at his profile when he consulted the sun's progress through the window. I watched him all the time, only dropping my own eyes whenever it was my turn to be observed.

In his positional sketch, Mr Sardou had shown my eyes downcast: a feathering of pencil. But, when it came to painting them, he asked me to raise them. It was as if he knew that this must be achieved discreetly, for the request was transacted silently, without the pointed brush, but merely by looking at me and drawing my lids up with an almost perceptible nod.

Mr Sardou painted our hair with polished walnut brushes wigged in sable. I imagined the sensation of his brush on my face; it made my nose twitch. Sitting by sitting, something unaccountably pleasurable was taking a stake in me, without my allowing it to happen. I was grateful that Darcy was positioned where she could not see its traces on my face; she would have killed it instantly.

I was exquisitely sensitive to every nuance in the artist's own features. His eyelids twitched if we ruptured our pose. His brow furrowed minutely the moment the sun shifted. From a slight flare of the nostril, I noticed that Mr Sardou did not relish Tristan's frequent visits and smug pronouncements. 'So how is our masterpiece of sisterly love coming along then? Ah, good, good.'

The end of a session was announced by Mr Sardou covering his work with a sheet and bowing before leaving the room as quietly as he had occupied it. We sisters were not privy to the artist's progress. When Darcy strode over to the easel during a pause, he quickly swivelled it away from her, murmuring, 'It is better not to observe the initial and transitional stages as early impressions may contaminate the impact of the finished work by casting a memory over it.'

This was a speech of unprecedented length from him, uttered with assurance and authority.

Darcy said crisply, 'Be at ease with yourself on that score, so. We would not dream of it.'

I dreamed of it. I wanted to see what his fingers had made of my face. I longed for it, and feared it too.

Too quickly – in a matter of three weeks – Mr Sardou's work was done, and the painter was bending again over our hands, this time murmuring his thanks for our patience. Then he was picking up his strangely neat leather case for the last time. He had covered up his work, as usual, with a sheet, and seemed about to make the most casual of departures. A shivery, shaky heat ran down my spine. I could not simply ease myself into thought of his disappearance from our lives.

Darcy could. 'Before you go, aren't you going to be showing us what you've kept us locked up in here all these weeks to do, cricking our necks and ruining our backs?'

I thought I saw him smile momentarily. To Darcy, he said, 'But of course, Miss Swiney.'

He drew the cover from his work and presented it to us, retreating back behind the easel.

Even Darcy was stunned to silence on the first view – and for Darcy to be silenced was a phenomenon that almost ran up to a miracle. Tristan rushed forward to pump Mr Sardou's hand.

But the artist cast his eyes to the floor and had no response for Tristan's poetical effusions about the number of bottles this portrait would sell.

It was indeed the most commercial of portraits. Mr Sardou had not neglected his role as flatterer. Darcy's Medusan brows were feathered to softness and her hips were as sinuous as a snake's in her tight black dress; Enda and Berenice's differences were brought to light; Pertilly's face glowed with a wisdom simple and pure as soap; Ida's bald patches were hidden. My red hair, centrally placed, fell in demure coils into my lap, leading the gaze of the beholder down to the floor and back up to my face. The red he had chosen was a single blazing shade of russet. My green eyes were the speaking heart of the portrait. Darcy shot me an accusing look.

'How did *that* happen?'

'I don't know,' I mumbled. I desperately hoped none of my sisters would read the story in my painted eyes.

I could not keep it from Ida, however. Quietly, she came into my room that night and sat on the end of my bed, hugging her knees.

'You are took sad, Manticory. But it is a pretty sadness.'

I nodded.

'How bad is it you are about the Mr Sardou? Do you want to get going with him?'

'Like a goose, do you mean? Ida!'

'But you are a great grown girl of twenty now, so if the heart of you is set on him, and you have such a wonderful wish for him, then you should have him.'

I shook my head, but I lied in that.

'Don't be dying just to have one kiss off him.'

'I will not be dying. You'll not tell, will you, Ida?'

'I'll not even remember it,' she said honestly. 'It came on me like an airy fit, and it will go again. But I wish you happy, you know that.'

I kissed her cheek and she wandered uncertainly out of my room. When I saw her the next morning, her face was blank again.

*

Hung over the mantelpiece, the portrait soon began to work for us. Tristan and Mr Rainfleury emerged from meetings well pleased with the results. We succumbed to public demand to print miniatures of the painting on souvenir tickets for our lectures. The rendering of Darcy's hair was particularly admired. My green eyes were also spoken of.

'Did you say Mr Sardou is also a sculptor?' I asked Tristan, so that Darcy could hear.

'I did. Indeed he is quite fêted for his bronze of St Molaise from the island of Inishmurray,' smiled Tristan.

And so, without my needing to say anything more, it was decided that the Swiney Godiva Corporation would commission a series of seven bronze busts from the fascinating Mr Sardou. Unfortunately, my discreetly closed mouth had no influence over the style of the sculptures. Commerce and poetry dictated that the busts would be placed on faux-marble columns of papier mâché, with our bronze hair cascading to the ground. These bodiless monsters would travel with us to our performances and stand in the lobby for people to admire, and even touch, before and after our shows. The project seemed to me inescapably vulgar. Was it only myself who pictured how ridiculous they would be, those severed seven heads held up on long hairy stalks? Surely Mr Sardou possessed too refined a sensibility to agree to such a thing? I told myself that I would think the less of him if he accepted, but the truth was that I could not countenance the idea of his refusing.

I took myself to Marsh's Library in St Patrick's Close and read about bronze casting until I could imagine Mr Sardou's hand forming the clay of my cheek, and laying his thumb in the shadow of my eyelid before pouring hot metal into my mould, which would be utterly different from the clay cases that defined each of my sisters.

I was rudely surprised to hear from Tristan that Mr Sardou had professed himself too busy to execute this exciting new commission immediately. He had two countesses and a mayor waiting for his quiet presence in their grand houses.

'Poor creature himself. Trout-ugly countesses and some hog of a mayor!' Darcy exclaimed.

'And of course, he is generally paid as much to do one head as he was to paint your seven,' Tristan pointed out. 'We drove a bargain for that group portrait.'

Darcy asserted, 'He must have wanted to do us, or he wouldn't have taken the lower stipend. So for the bronze busts, we'll pay him more. How much will it take to get him back?'

I smiled to see how quickly Darcy had become an addict of her own crafted image.

Tristan returned with the news that Alexander Sardou had consented to sculpt the busts but on two conditions.

'Conditions!' sniffed Darcy. 'Has it come to that?'

'Let us hear them at least,' I urged. Suddenly it was very important to me that we should be able to meet whatever conditions Mr Sardou demanded. I glanced around at my sisters, hoping that no one had observed my discomposure.

They were entirely occupied in gazing lovingly at their painted faces above the mantelpiece, seeming just as covetous as myself of a new engagement with Mr Sardou. Pertilly's eyes looked more focused than normal. Was she guilty of any feeling more visceral than vanity? Mr Sardou's portrait kindly flattered her more than any of us. Was she too feeling a squirming of her heart when she thought of him? Pertilly's submissiveness might attract a man, I thought. And Mr Sardou did not seem to place much value on conversation.

Mr Sardou's conditions were that he could work on the busts only when other commissions allowed and that he must not be placed under any pressure for delivery. The other was that for a sculpture, unlike a painting, he had need to observe us performing, 'to see how the hair flows and to record the features in the round'. So he requested permission to be allowed backstage to sketch us at any show he might be able to catch between his other commitments.

These conditions were acceptable to all the Swiney Godivas, particularly myself. After that, I hoped for his quiet presence every night. I hoped it would be my side of the stage where he'd be standing with his drawing block. I hoped he'd look up as I rustled back into the curtains. Very often, he did all these things. But he *said* no more to me than an enclosed nun.

Yet there he would be, from time to time, leaning his long kite-shaped back against a wall with a foot hooked around a curtain, the paper prettily dirtying under his pencil and the habitual look of concentration on his face.

Even excitable Ida got used to Mr Sardou's appearing there; I was relieved to see that Pertilly seemed impervious to the scratch of his pencil near by her now. Oona, fully taken up with admiring Tristan, barely noticed Mr Sardou capturing her likeness. Enda and Berenice were there only for one another and Mr Rainfleury, and Darcy's nerves had been anaesthetised to the artist's presence by the satisfactory portrait he had produced.

So it seemed to be only myself who was tinglingly sensitive to the appearance of Mr Sardou in close proximity.

That was all before he ever addressed a word to me personally.

And then he did.

23

I was last coming off the stage that night. My sisters filed behind the curtains, letting their shoulders drop and their faces fall into tired crumples the moment they became invisible to our greedy audience, who could not get enough, it seemed, of Darcy's blackbird-wing sheen, Oona's frolic fair curls, my tigerish pelt, Pertilly's auburn fronds, Berenice's and Enda's Madonna locks and Ida's chocolate flow.

It was exhausting work to love the sinister little dolls with enough visible passion to stir the customers to buy. I was not the only Swiney who found our unsubtle means of selling the essence and scalp food wearing to the soul and a violent crime against self-respect. After a show, we were desperate to wash as much sweat-crusty powder off our skin as was decently permitted by the ablution arrangements in the dressing rooms. Also, given that we still found it hard to eat before going on stage, the famine in our bellies needed urgent attention. Mr Rainfleury always ensured that a substantial spread awaited us on a checked cloth the moment the applause died out. There was a not quite jocular competition to reach it first, given that there was rarely seven of everything and that some things were generally better than others. Indeed I suspected Mr Rainfleury of orchestrating our rivalrous appetites for his own pleasure, for we always arrived at supper with our hair still down and our eyes afire.

That night I trudged through the velvet corridor, last in the line. Mr Sardou's slender presence was suddenly available to me, mere and tiny inches away, just as Pertilly's hair was disappearing round the corner, dragging in the dust.

Despite practising in the mirror for such an opportunity, I had not yet learned to smile at Mr Sardou without a corner of my mouth flittering. Now I was encased in thick powder, so a real smile would have cracked my face like that of a dropped doll. Rather than show the artist my incontinent features, I resisted the urge to linger where I might feel his breath on me. Miserably, I tucked my head down and made to follow Pertilly.

But as I passed him, he murmured, 'No, wait. Manticory—'

My name in his mouth: that was something I had imagined, along with his fingers on my cheek. And not 'Miss Swiney' either. It was my own individual name that he had uttered and it sounded like something fine on his tongue.

Not quite meeting my eye, but with his gaze hovering near it, he asked, 'So what is in that scalp food that you sold so heavily tonight? Will the ladies who buy it be made ill by it?'

These were more words than I had ever heard Mr Sardou put together consecutively. I had imagined his conversation to be hesitant, something to be drawn out of him by inches, only, perhaps only in confidential circumstances. But if he wished to banter, then I would banter. Our words might dance a light-hearted jig together while behind the scenes I got myself used to the private act of communication with him. From the tight-fisting of my heart and the tremble in my wrists, it seemed that my mind would become habituated to Mr Sardou's near presence faster than my body could.

'Well, if they overdo the thing, our scalp food clients shan't be feeling so well afterwards.' I succeeded in matching his faintly sarcastic tone, while thinking sadly of the scalp food's effect on Ida. 'O'Mealy the pharmacist swears it cannot kill, except in killing doses – and we make sure it's too costly for those. Otherwise, it does nothing much, good or bad.'

I was rewarded by an even longer sentence than before.

'So the Swiney Godivas are nothing more than a gang of lady quacks, who should really be called the Swindling Godivas?' he asked gravely. 'Of course your sister Darcy is an easy woman to please so long as the money comes in as fast as she can spend it. And it seems to me that the rest of you have no more courage than is in a mouse's heart to oppose her bullying. Why do you stand for it?'

The easy twists of his phrasing astonished me. He had absorbed the inflections of Irishness and made them his own. English was his third or fourth language – how might he speak in his milk tongue? Was it in the warmth of his native Italian where the real Mr Sardou was situated, lived and breathed?

The baffling language aside, there was blunt accusation in his words, with no arched eyebrow or smile to make me think he teased. All the banter left me.

'I am pained that you think it.' I dipped my head. 'Though perhaps you are right about the mouse hearts. As to *why* we stand for it, you can ask that only because you yourself have never tried to oppose Darcy. Only one person I know ever stood up to her, a butcher's daughter called Eileen O'Reilly, and it went very sore for her—'

'I don't blame you.' His mouth curved into something that was not quite a smile. 'Or at least I give you one seventh of the blame. It is a well-known fact that a person loses his or her individual moral identity when in a large group. The first things to be let go in a mob are empathy and insight – the qualities that prevent us all behaving like criminals.'

'Seven,' I said with dignity, 'hardly constitutes a mob. And we are every bit separate individuals. You have clearly noticed the differences between us. You painted them.' He bowed in acknowledgement. 'But are we the criminals? We have Mr Rainfleury for the dolls, and Mr Stoker and Mr O'Mealy for the liquids—'

'So you plead to being mere puppet dolls? Does your long hair make you strangers to intellectual rigour and loving friends to inane pastimes, vanity and superficiality?'

Suddenly I was crestfallen. It was obvious why Mr Sardou had never spoken like this in front of Darcy. But did this sudden and dazzling, too-candid eloquence reflect any admiration for my own powers of intellect? Perhaps, in my role as writer, he simply assessed me as the only adequate receptacle for his refrigerating disgust? Did his words, scintillating as sharpened knives, constitute frank disapproval or a piquant form of flirt-ing? It was beginning to hurt, extremely. I wanted to beg, *May we not presently desist from this clever game, and speak frankly and simply to one another, with gentleness?*

But I was afraid to presume on a chiming desire for kindness in him. So I played on. I forced myself to do what Darcy did, for it never failed: I attacked, borrowing something of her intona-tion for courage.

'I am disappointed to hear you endorse the vulgar proverb that women are cerebrally useless in proportion to the length of our hair. You philosophise quite freely on your clients, but what of your own profession? Does it never occur to you that *an artist* in these troubled times is about as much use as a silver tea-set in a bog? What do you believe in, Mr Sardou? Where is your own use?'

He surprised me yet more then by responding, 'I have practi-cal uses. I have beliefs. I fought alongside the Irish in Spoleto in 1860. And the siege of Ancona.'

'Our mother Annora would have loved you for it. Poor as we were, she gave her tithe to the Church for the Pope's Army.'

My mind's eye saw him splendid, willowy and elegant in uniform. Relieved at the change of subject, I told him how, during my own childhood, Harristown had been drained of young men gone off to save the Pope and his temporal powers from the nationalists. All the while I was thinking that if Mr Sardou had fought in the Risorgimento, he must have had a bare twenty years at the time. So he was perhaps twelve years older than my twenty.

It is the least of the distances between us, I thought. *And they are growing longer not shorter by the minute, that's the pity of it.*

I had not calculated aloud, and yet he corrected me, 'I was seventeen, and had run away from . . . home. There are not so many years between you and me.'

The distances suddenly shortened as if viewed from the wrong end of the telescope. Both of us caught our breaths. Then Mr Sardou was talking about the scalp food again, but with a slight flush staining his white throat.

Our argument over quackery spilled into another about Mr Dickens's golden-haired 'Fairy' and 'Angel' heroines – so sugared, so ignorant, so passive, in his view. Mr Sardou, it appeared, was a great reader of novels. He spoke dismissively of 'Girls like cows, who let cleverer people milk their hair! How can they do it? Sideshow hair – worse! Makes a sideshow out of women! Is this art? No, it is farming and manufacture. And if we look at the moral dimension, the use of the female body, well—'

His face flooded with dark colour.

He spoke up for Mr Dickens's witches and Medusas, even for women like Madame Defarge: 'Free to roam the streets and have adventures of their own devising,' he said approvingly.

Mr Sardou had read and thought about long feminine hair at least as much as I had. In what way, I wanted to ask him, was his thinking higher than mine?

I challenged, 'But do not strictly commercial sculptures like these ridiculous busts make you a stranger to great art? A hair-farmer yourself? A sideshow ring-master?'

'Yes, indeed. But that is not why I accepted the frightful commission, Manticory.'

Again he had said it, my name, my private label, the thing that made me not one of my sisters, 'Manticory'. His hand reached towards mine.

Darcy's voice boomed from the corridor, 'Manticory! Where are you?'

Mr Sardou added quietly, 'And nor is it why I am so often in the wings, watching you. Your Darcy makes the running, but it is *you* who makes the weather in the room. Yet—'

Darcy's heavy foot was audible on the stairs. 'Manticory! What is it you are about?'

When I turned to excuse myself, Mr Sardou was already gone.

24

Darcy mocked me for missing the best of the supper and informed me that there was not a crumb left of the cherry cake, which 'was the best thing you could imagine'.

'I'm too tired to be hungry,' I told her. I forced out a theatrical yawn.

I could not wait to go to bed and be alone with Mr Sardou's words.

His disparagements had not pleased me. I preferred to linger on the individual mouthfuls rather than the too-bitter general flavour of the conversation. I had never before met someone who spoke the way I would have loved to write, with the sinuous byways to his phrases and satire aflame between the syllables. I'd learned to blunt my instruments when writing material for our shows. But I still felt pain at every large and beautiful word I sacrificed to popular taste, and every literary allusion that was snapped off at the stalk before it could flower into a telling analogy.

Mr Sardou could make good words without my putting them into his mouth. The fact that he wrote his own script meant of course that he had said things I did not wish to hear. Why had he sought to diminish me in my own estimation? And so lightly, as if my shame were a pleasant subject for his wit? Yet his diagnosis of my moral state matched my own. I could not fight for a better view of myself. This line of thought being sadly uncomfortable, I preferred to dwell on his final comments.

And nor is it why I am so often in the wings, watching you.

The obvious construction was that he was watching me because he liked to do so. But there were undercurrents to those words, pitfalls in his final *Yet*—. The negative of my fears was not easily dragged into an uncompromised positive. But, as I lay sleepless hours in my bed, my own desire began to fashion certainties out of obscurity. I grew vain on what I imagined.

And there was no gainsaying *It is you who makes the weather in the room.*

None.

After that, Mr Sardou was even more often in the wings. Darcy was watching me, and I could not linger to talk to him after the shows. But I could steal looks. And so could he. He had a way of looking at me with an expression my imagination interpreted as frank longing and a tint of irony too, at his own unconditional surrender.

I never knew when I would see him. Sometimes it was once a week, sometimes a month passed without him. I longed for him so much that I was capable of imagining him there in pale corporality when he was known to be in Galway doing a coal heiress in marble.

Once I had imagined that he entertained warm thoughts towards me, my imagination became greedy and shockingly sensual. Contaminated by my own scripts, I grew Gothic in my imaginings. I craved a lock of his babyfine hair, which was quite unlike what a man usually has. I saw him waking up with my hair in his mouth. I dreamed of my hair growing from the floorboards beneath his feet.

Mr Sardou gave me not a filament's more substance with which to nourish my imaginings. After those words behind the curtains, our encounters had not stretched to another conversation. I was still feeding on the memories of the first one.

And the looks he still gave me, when Darcy wasn't watching.

After we'd done a hard nine months on the road with the essence and the scalp food, Tristan judged it time to birth a new Swiney Godiva hair preparation.

He summoned us to the green parlour, placing two objects on the table, each covered by a snowy handkerchief. He whipped the handkerchief off the first object, revealing a familiar pot: Rowland's Macassar Oil.

'First made in 1793,' he announced, 'and the happy owner of a distinguished literary and royal pedigree. According to its makers, Rowland's has been used by the Empress of Russia, the Emperor of China and the King and Queen of France. It was mentioned by Lord Byron in his *Don Juan*. After that, the oil developed even more literary pretensions – it advertised in the first edition of Thackeray's *The Virginians*, and has been seen in every possible newspaper or periodical since. Now!'

He lifted the handkerchief off the second object and turned it round to face us. A green glass pot bore the label: *Swiney Godiva Stimulation Oil to Ensure Vigorous Roots.*

Tristan bowed. 'It does everything that Rowland's does, but it will do it for the Swiney Godiva Corporation.'

The back of each bottle was illustrated with a personal testimony by one of us sisters, drawn in black-and-white ink. Reclining among our locks, our likenesses held up a box of the preparation with a smile. We were captioned: *I find Swiney Godiva Stimulation Oil exceedingly beneficial and I make a point of using it always.*

The launch of our new product exposed us to the point where we became what Tristan proudly described as 'eponymical'. Words were coined from our name . . . 'to Swiney' your hair meant to have it grow very long. In Ireland, to 'do a Godiva' no longer meant to ride a horse naked through Coventry but to let down your hair in public, an event that became as common in the rowdy public houses as dancing on the tables had once been.

Tristan told me, as if I would be pleased, 'And they're saying "as red as Manticory" instead of "as red as blood" these days.'

Alexander Sardou waited in the wings that same night. He showed me one of the advertisements, dragging it out of his leather case as if it were a dead fish.

'Did you know about this?' he asked me. 'Is this how you see yourself?'

205

It was so easy to please Mr Rainfleury and Tristan. All I had to do was be a doll, act like a doll, speak as little as a doll, open and close my eyes when they wished it. To please Mr Sardou seemed almost impossible, and yet it was the one thing I now craved to do.

25

I did not wish for my blood to be circulated by the mouse's heart Mr Sardou attributed to me: I made a stand.

'I am out of inspiration for new ways to sell ourselves,' I told Tristan and Darcy. 'It is not a decent way to go on. We are selling more than—'

By the next day, Darcy had made a convenience of my squeamishness. She herself devised a crude horror of a show whereby each Swiney impersonated one of the Seven Deadly Sins. She reserved Lust for herself. I was forced into Envy. But Pertilly as Greed attracted too much ribald attention. So that act was swiftly disinvented in favour of Tristan's idea of striking a series of 'mute attitudes' such as had been performed by Emma Hamilton, mistress of the hero of Trafalgar. Our 'attitudes', of course, were always to do with hair: the original Berenice lining the temple with her hair, Ariadne spinning her web, Lorelei luring men to their death, Medusa striking a man to petrifaction. An ingenious lantern swung across the stage, illuminating one Swiney sister at a time and plunging the others into darkness.

As long as we did not move, Tristan insisted that we could dare some quite provocative material, though only of course during shows staged in the later evening. Oona posed as Botticelli's Venus on a papier mâché scallop shell. In the same pink costume, with flowers in her hair, she impersonated the goddess Flora. Berenice took on Mary Magdalene washing Christ's feet, Jesus being played by Tristan. She dipped her hair in a large-labelled bottle of Swiney Godiva Hair Essence before approaching Tristan's shapely bare foot. Enda was Delilah cutting the hair of the sleeping Samson, also played by Tristan, while smiling at the Philistine soldiers waiting in the shadows, an effect executed with shadow puppets. Pertilly was Charlotte Corday having her long hair cut off before she faced our home-made guillotine, glinting in tin foil and fresh cranberry sauce.

When the 'attitudes' grew stale and the audiences took to muttering behind their hands, Darcy began to torment me with finely serrated barbs.

'I thought you wanted to be a writer, Manticory,' she taunted me. 'When was ever a backwoods girl given such a chance as this? Still, if you haven't the ambition, or the talent—'

To tempt me back to work, Tristan made me the gift of a new Hansen Writing Ball, a metallic hedgehog of a machine invented by a Danish priest. It shot out words in response to violent batterings of tiny circular keys. Once I got used to the dreadful massacre of the quiet, I loved the spiny creature, and would not be parted from it. It was pitifully easy to tempt me. I had missed writing; I missed writing for an audience who applauded and offered attentive silences in expectation of what I delivered. I missed the triumphs of inserting some good phrases and fine words that escaped Darcy's brutal edits. And I hated to see what Darcy and Tristan were doing to decent behaviour. They'd have the Swiney Godivas out there fully naked, I feared, if they thought it would sell more tickets. And soon enough that was exactly what they dreamed up. Tristan began to speak of acquiring seven wooden horses from a circus and the Swiney Godivas mounting them in nothing but our hair and discreet pink costumes, very tight around the limbs. When I saw his letter to Duffy's Circus lying in the silver tray in the hall at Pembroke Street, I finally broke, and consented to write, if only we could be spared the indecency of Lady Godiva-ing for the public.

Thinking to borrow some dignity, I consented to recast short sketches from respectable plays. I also rescripted hair-prone incidents from admired novels. So many writers of our time deployed female hair in fiction: it had got so that a hairless novel would have been greeted with disdain. A good head of hair was as necessary to a heroine as a stainless character and one interesting personality flaw for her hero to save her from. My brutal robberies were conscientiously listed in the programme as 'tributes' to the geniuses of Mr Dickens, Mr Thackeray and their colleagues.

When Mr Sardou reproached me backstage for returning to my Swiney scripts, I was ready with a reply. I told him that I was seeking out stories in which women who happened to be gifted with hair also had cerebral powers of their own – rather than dramas in which we Swineys deployed our bodies to sell hair products. I also pointed out how, in my new works, hair revealed murders, like Mrs Manston's in *Desperate Remedies* or how it acquired its own formidable identity, as did Arabella French's chignon in Mr Trollope's *He Knew He Was Right*.

Mr Sardou looked up into the dust motes above the stage, and shook his head.

I noticed a small tear in the shoulder of his velvet jacket.

'It is deft,' he said, 'and it is clever. You have words to burn, Manticory. But is this what you always hoped for yourself?'

I blushed and looked down.

When I looked up, Mr Sardou's eyes were on Ida, and his luminous forehead was creased with concern. Pertilly and Oona were also staring helplessly at the spectacle Ida was making of herself. She had stopped speaking her English lines and had disintegrated into gibberish while pulling her hair convulsively and feeding it into her mouth. Darcy dispatched Enda and Berenice to perform one of their duets in front of Ida. Oona and I tiptoed out behind the twins and gently pulled Ida into the wings. Mr Sardou picked her up, covered her mouth with one hand, and carried her off to the dressing room where Darcy was ready with hard words and sal volatile.

Ida struggled out of his arms, shrieking, 'Go away, you Sardou!'

Outside the dressing-room door, I apologised for Ida's words. He made a dismissive gesture. 'There is something I've meant to ask you. Did Ida always suck her hair? And did Darcy always hurt her for it?'

I sighed, 'As a child, she would do it unconsciously. Once we had detected her tendency, she would pull her hair only whenever she was out of Darcy's sight. But it has become so ingrained in Ida now that she does it in her sleep, I fear. And when she is upset she does it anyway. And I'm afraid she still drinks the scalp food too, if she can obtain it. Mr Sardou, I am grateful—'

'No, do not thank me.'

I wanted to thank him for the look of concern on his face, for speaking to me at all.

Then Darcy slammed out of the dressing room and Mr Sardou held up his sketching block like a shield. He threw a few supple lines on the page that caught her profile. She snorted and ordered me inside 'to help with Ida'.

I heard her say to Mr Sardou, 'I cannot imagine why you think you should get a second advance on the busts when you've barely started them.'

Inside the dressing room, I looked down sadly on Ida's contorted face.

'I don't want to do this any more,' she pleaded. 'Manticory, can we not stop and go back to Harristown?'

I stroked her forehead and shook my head. To allow Ida to retire and rest would dismantle the Swiney Godivas. Darcy had signed us up indefinitely.

Darcy's argument would be, as it always was, that it would not help Ida to desist from her work. Even more than her fiddle playing, her roles were a relief to her – they took her from her painful self. She was knitted to her stage parts, flesh and bone. In our shows, Ida did not so much impersonate her historical characters as invade them, and inhabit their bodies. Tristan swore that Ida *smelled* of each new role. Her portraits of famous women were homicidal: people came to watch Ida destroy and devour Cleopatra, and to wear her pelt. Of course Ida did not always win these skirmishes with her characters. And those struggles were what made Ida's face grow hot and churned her language into a witch's brew of English and Irish, of terrible sense and childlike nonsense, and forced us to drag her off the stage with increasing frequency. Darcy refused to understand the reasons for these episodes, called Ida 'wilfully mad'.

Mr Sardou was gone away to Paris before I could devise a way to show my proper appreciation for his concern. I resolved to write a poem for him, a nicely judged piece of praise with all my real sentiments tucked up neatly between the syllables. But when I set myself to the task, I found I was not equal to it. I wrote doggerel, fit for dogs to bark at. Even my handwriting sloped and meandered, as if the dowdy words were looking for an escape from the page, so unwilling were they to be seen.

I stared at my production, heavy and yet empty at the same time, a miracle of bathos, a neat piece of cunning, a painted whore of a poem. Yet I had once been able to write. *The Cruel Sister* was mine, and it was beautiful. Everyone had said so. I remembered what the critic had written: *It is enough to knock the heart across you.*

Tristan, I thought, *I hate you. You have murdered the writing in me. Just when I needed it to breathe.*

26

While I was making my despairing translations of bad poetry into good money, our mother Annora was failing. She had fallen to no particular illness. She was simply worn out from living most of her life a potato skin above starvation. In the last year, her own skin had shrivelled on her face, delineating the skull's presence beneath. We'd rarely seen her in months, being mostly on the road with our shows. We paid duty visits on some Sundays, if we happened to be within an easy train or carriage ride of Harristown.

That Christmas, Ida had showed more interest in the thin geese than in our mother. I suspected that the truth was that she was frightened by Annora's cadaverous appearance. After spending a visit on the floor with her arms around a pair of geese, she insisted on bringing one back to Pembroke Street.

'Do not take Phiala!' begged our mother. 'Do not take my Phiala away to Dublin, the creature.'

Ida selected an anonymous bird from the flock. In the train carriage, its head quested out of a grey stuff bag between her knees.

'It is to drop down the chimney, to clean it, you know,' she explained to Mrs Hartigan, who took the bird admiringly.

'It might so,' said the housekeeper. 'The finest figure of a goose in Dublin, dearie! And how did you find your dear mother?'

'Going on as usual,' said Darcy disapprovingly.

The coal man was dispatched to the roof with the goose tucked under his arm. The bird's beating wings scoured every lump of ash as it plummeted down to the kitchen fireplace. We did not need to wait till the next Michaelmas for roast goose, though as ever I refused it and Ida wept to see it turning on the clockwork roasting jack.

'This is not what I meant for it,' she moaned at supper.

'There's still a drumstick wants eating.' Darcy offered the sleek brown baton to her.

Annora's own final descent seemed to come on almost as swiftly as the goose's. Her mind had begun to wander and to fail. We knew things had worsened, for Mrs Godlin from the Kilcullen dispensary had written to tell us so, in a letter as full of sniffs as spelling mistakes. Our mother had been seen abroad at night *in her nightdress*, driving the geese over Harristown Bridge with a hawthorn switch, as if she were a young Goose Girl, with the slow crows wheeling overhead. And some mornings she was to be seen on the step rocking her favourite goose, Phiala, in her arms, like a baby.

She has a great trouble on her, the creature, wrote Mrs Godlin. *If it were not for Eileen and myself, she'd perish of loneliness, you know.*

Eileen? I thought. *The same Eileen?*

Annora denied all knowledge of the nightdress incident when we arrived to investigate.

'Sure that Mrs Godlin has been having herself some odd dreams, may I never die in sin. She's failing in her wits, you know. They say she takes herself a taste of the chloroform under the counter, God rest her.' Annora tried to laugh.

Despite Darcy's threats, Annora still refused to move to Dublin. She demanded, 'And how would your father find me when he comes back?'

I held her hand and looked into her eyes, afraid of what I'd see. But she looked back at me steadily.

Despite the funds we sent her, despite Darcy's rage, Annora kept a thin goose and laundered to the last.

'I cannot stop, it would kill me, the idleness,' she protested, when Darcy told her what would happen if the hacks of the popular press found out how she lived.

'They would say that rich and famous as the Swiney sisters are, they don't keep their old mother as they should. It would be a festival for the slimy newspapermen. They'd slither all over it! The Eileen O'Reilly would love to talk to a reporter about it, if one were to find his way to this place. She says so loudly on every occasion. I've had letters from Mrs Godlin informing me.'

'You've such a great spite for that O'Reilly girl, Darcy,' murmured Annora. 'Yet she's very pleasant in herself, if you give her a smile and half a small hour. She takes it hard that you've risen so high above her. You know, she comes to visit me still, and brings a bit of lard or a crubeen from time to time. Last Tuesday she brought me three rashers tied in brown paper, curled up like three blind mice in there and sweet as love to taste they were later with a bit of bread.'

'You let her in my house?' shouted Darcy. 'That knacky little monkey? For bacon? When we send you enough money to buy your own hog?'

'I do not leave the girl outside the door, and she so lonely and alone, and young-seeming. For all she's filled out, she's still so small that the crows wouldn't bother themselves to pick her bones. Peace, she cannot touch you. All she ever wanted was to be about the place. But with the contrary way you have on you, you'd never let her near you except to beat her. For shame. An only child like that, with the parents on her that unfeeling and so much drink taken besides, so much left to her own devices in the woods and lanes. She might have been—'

Yes, I thought, *she might have been*. I remembered the kindness of her smock to blow my nose on. It was only Darcy that the Eileen O'Reilly made war on – until I myself turned my back on her, when all she'd tried to do was be in Enda's tribe against Berenice.

Annora kept her hands in the tub, even as Darcy bellowed, 'That filthy get of a girl, she'll not disoblige a Swiney again!'

Our mother did not reply or move. It was as if she had become amphibious, breathing only through her hands in the cold water.

*

Annora died that way. She was found by Joe the seaweed boy, slumped against the tub, her head in the cooled water of a pillowcase wash, her hair swirling in the expiring suds, and the thin geese in a consternation outside the window.

We arrived at the cottage to find that Mrs Godlin and Father Maglinn had already made all the usual Harristown arrangements. Annora was laid out on a deal board and covered by a white sheet, with her feet aligned to the east and her head to the west. Her form barely raised the linen above the table, at the head of which burned three candles sprigged with rosemary for the Trinity. The clock had been stopped at the hour of her presumed death, and the one small mirror was swagged with black crape.

I lifted the sheet to kiss Annora's face. I stroked her brow, smooth now it had been released from its corrugations of worry. Mrs Godlin had seen to it that Annora's hands were clasped together, wound with a rosary and holding a cross. Her fingers were still wrinkled from their final long immersion. Her skin smelled of soap and salt. She was wearing a white robe with a ruffle at the neck and frilled cuffs.

Mrs Godlin sobbed, 'She prepared it for herself, the creature. She told me where to find it just a week ago, and she said, "Let my girls see me in this at the last." She must have known she was failing.'

'Did she confess?' I asked quietly.

'Not at all, it came on so sudden,' replied Mrs Godlin. 'And she with so much to tell.'

'And what manner of thing are you meaning by that?' Darcy's voice was low with menace.

Mrs Godlin backed away, blushing.

Annora had already commissioned her own coffin and her tombstone, to save us troubling ourselves over them. The coffin awaited her under the deal table. Mrs Godlin showed us the granite tablet leaning against the wall by the water butt. Annora, who refused to spend money on herself, had spent a fortune having all our long and wild names carved into the stone. *Mother of Darcy, Berenice, Enda, Manticory, Pertilly, Oona*

215

and Idolatry. She had not dared to have herself carved in the usual formula of *Beloved & Sorely Missed*. She would not presume so. But she wanted it recorded that she had borne us. In very small letters underneath were the words: *Wife of Phelan Swiney, Mariner*.

'Should we keen? And tear our hair?' asked Ida as we followed Joe's cart bearing the coffin along the sodden crow-haunted track to the ruined chapel at Harristown.

'Absolutely not,' hissed Darcy. 'It is a vulgar habit.'

Mrs Godlin was the only other mourner, apart from some shadows that flitted through the trees behind us and hovered by the back of the chapel. One of them, I assumed, was the Eileen O'Reilly, though she did not trouble us with her tongue on that day. I was ready, despite my sadness, to parley with her, and to tell her I was grateful for the times and the bacon she had shared with Annora in their mutual loneliness. Yet she did not come close. I could not guess the other figure, a large man from the glimpse I had. Darcy did not miss the furtive figures and shook her fist at them.

Mrs Godlin wept quietly through the service and disappeared before the end, when Ida fiddled a funereal melody of her own composing, full of dissonance and heart-hurting cadences. We put Annora to rest in a field outside the derelict chapel, for Catholics were still not permitted a decent burial. In the carriage on the way to Harristown, I had suggested the clover field near the house, but Darcy, as I'd quite expected, erupted in incoherent fury at the suggestion.

'Why not?' I dared. 'It is a lovely spot, if haunted with the souls of a thousand rabbits you killed there.'

If I expected Darcy to break then, and tell me the story of *PS* and his grave, I was wrong. She insisted that Father Maglinn already had Joe digging the chosen spot, and would I waste the seaweed boy's labours for one of my Shakespearean whims?

The moment Annora was laid in the hole he'd dug, Joe fled to hide his tears, with Father Maglinn screeching at him in unchristian terms. We left the priest heaping the sodden earth over our mother, muttering prayers under his breath.

Back at the cottage, we found Mrs Godlin wiping her eyes on the tea towel. A Harristown meal of bread and lard was laid out on the table vacated by Annora's corpse. We stood in silence looking at the food and at one another, and at a jar of salt-crusted pennies Mrs Godlin had placed in the middle of the meagre spread.

'Your mother asked me to do this,' Mrs Godlin said. 'It was her last wish.'

I reached out for the jar but Darcy, out of habit, pocketed it.

Darcy sold the lease on the Harristown cottage, including all Annora's basins, moulds, drips and crocks and pans.

We made one final visit to Harristown. Darcy personally killed the thin geese, saving Phiala for last. She burned Annora's threadbare fringed shawls. She emptied every drawer, over-turned each mouldy mattress. I knew she was searching for the money that Annora had never spent, and from a cry of triumph in the bedroom, I knew she had found it. My sisters quietly took up their old shoe dollies. I was able to salvage only the seashell lamp from Darcy's Viking progress through the place. I whipped it down and secreted it under my coat when Darcy was applying her fingers to the neck of the goose.

With Phiala's throat tendons, our last connection with Harristown was severed. We Swineys were extinct there now. We were Dubliners; we had no way back. There was no retreat now from the empire of Tristan and Rainfleury. I no longer had the right to the comfort of my image of home, of our cottage wrapped in autumn mist so it glittered like a fairy lantern in the dark, or of dawn's dew trails on the window next to Annora's crucifix, or the smell of warm straw from inside my mattress ticking. I would never again bury my head in Annora's apron, or stir the seaweed soup while reading Bible verses to her. All the missing I should have done in Dublin now arrived in a concen-tration of grief. Ida felt it too: I saw it in the glooming of her face and heard it in the keening of her violin.

Another ending had come too. With Harristown drummed out of us, we would no longer have to do with the Eileen

O'Reilly. She had not presented herself for any final farewell. This was a matter of triumph for Darcy, but I felt it as a loss, for the Eileen O'Reilly's unswerving attentions to the Swiney sisters had been the closest thing to friendship I'd known. Not even Mr Rainfleury looked at us with such intensity. I wished I'd had a chance to make it up with her. Our little feud seemed so sad now, so lacking in real outrage, being based only on a thing I myself had planted in the girl's brain.

Back in Dublin, with our past expunged, Darcy set herself to making new acquaintances. To have friends, you must have leisure and a home to invite them into. At the dim Harristown cottage, we'd never have dared subject ourselves to the pity or scorn of our schoolfellows, and there was barely enough food for ourselves. Offering hospitality would have been almost suicidal. Now we began to pay terrifying calls in Fitzwilliam Square and to receive stiff reciprocations. But these were not friendships either: we were like street cats carving out territory in which sleek pedigrees predominated.

There was one being, however, whom I was beginning to call 'friend'.

In the months since our first encounter behind the stage, I saw Mr Sardou nine times, and spoke to him on two more occasions. The total number of new words uttered between us was four hundred and forty-six. But he said his portion so well and looked at me with such penetrating attention as to nourish my imagination for the intervening weeks.

He was often away on other commissions, but he continued his sketches for the unlikely busts. So some nights he was mine, invariably on my side of the wings, his sketchbook like a shield balanced on his hip. We renewed our glances. Just once he started to speak but then Pertilly blundered in, looking for a cardboard sword, and he fled. The next day he was gone back to Brussels to make a portrait of a lawyer.

It almost did not matter. My grief for Annora was being translated into a different feeling, a swooping, searing feeling that replicated and reversed grief as if it were a laundered chemise turned inside out. I was picturesquely melancholic and, at the same time, I was deliriously, wantonly happy, and I knew it, because it was a condition completely unlike any I had ever known before.

Any time Mr Sardou left, I told my stung and throbbing heart he would soon be back. I was not even impatient for his return for I had my fantasies to live out, hour by dreaming hour.

What had formerly been periods of intolerable waiting to go onstage or to finish a rehearsal had become luxurious minutes for thinking of Mr Sardou's last look or sentence, for re-examining each nuance and scouring it for affection and regard. I counted up the few facts on him I had. I realised that I knew almost nothing except that I wanted him with desperation.

On the day before my twenty-first birthday, at the Gaiety Theatre, with the twins singing on the stage, I felt the thrum of his breath on my neck. I knew its softness by heart by then.

As my gift to myself, I spoke to him without turning to face him. 'Will you meet me for tea at Mitchell's as if by accident at three tomorrow? Darcy has a dress fitting in Rathgar.'

I felt him take a step backwards, dangerously close to the stage, where Enda and Berenice were sharing a ballad of love I'd written with Mr Sardou himself in every word and look. An inch more and he'd be in the stage's blazing light, in full view of those privileged people in the boxes with red velvet curtains and the horseshoe of the balcony with its cushioned rail. With the golden dome above him, and the theatre's gold-and-white-stuccoed balconies behind, Mr Sardou looked every inch the hero, not just of the song I had written for him, but as if he were the object of the love of the whole world.

Yet he was silent.

'It is not convenient, Mitchell's tomorrow? No matter,' I faltered.

Then, unable to resist the sight of his face, I turned to him and I threw my fate in the air.

'Mr Sardou,' I said, meeting and holding his eyes, 'it is no use. I love you.'

'Do you?' said he in a quiet voice. 'Dear heart, you don't love me more than I love you. And probably less.'

And his lips hovered on mine so that I felt the imprint of every delicate, moist fold.

Into my mouth, he murmured, 'But I am married.'

Part Three
BEYOND

27

It had been an expectation dating from childhood that he would marry his second cousin Elisabetta.

'How I hate even to say her name!' he declared, endlessly stirring the sugar in his cup. Through my shoulders, I felt the curious glances of the fashionable ladies of Mitchell's on his tragic countenance, and their reproving looks at me for making the pale hero so very miserable.

The deed of marriage had been 'inflicted' on him when he returned from his precocious soldiering. They had lived 'as children live together' for a few years, but the relations had soured, 'without ever flowering'. There had been no offspring and never would be, he assured me.

'So you never loved her?'

'I am full of you.'

'And you do not see her?'

'Of course every penny I earn goes to her. It is a matter of pride. And her expectation of tribute.'

'Have you ever thought of parting . . . officially?'

'That is something she would never do.'

'Because of her religion?'

'Because of pride. Marriages, in her class, are never finished. Form must be observed in Venice, after all. While I believe she entertains an admirer of her own, she maintains a fiction that she joins me on my travels sometimes and so leaves for Paris for a few weeks several times a year, in the secret company of her lover.'

I paid for the coffee and we left Mitchell's to continue the conversation on a secluded bench in St Stephen's Green. A great cruelty of bright sun had both of us lowering our heads.

This is surely a day for rain, I thought. *Rain and mist and the dirges of slow crows.*

'Do you hope for a reconciliation?' I asked, finally.

'There is nothing between us to reconcile. And anyway, now there is you. And yet, we cannot—'

'We cannot be together,' I agreed, and I offered him my mouth.

The first sensible thing he said afterwards was, 'What can I be to you? I cannot even advance you the role of established mistress.'

I flushed at his assumption that this would be acceptable to me and that only practical considerations stood in the way of it.

But he continued, 'I have no home. I live from commission to commission, with money constantly demanded by Elisabetta. She . . . well, you've seen the shabbiness of my clothes.'

In fact, Alexander was always turned out with the utmost elegance. But men's vanity, I understood fondly, was always to be humoured and they always wished better for themselves.

He continued, 'Here in Dublin, I have been ashamed to tell you, I lodge with cousins of hers, in a room they give me for little rent. Because Elisabetta—'

'Let us not hear any more about her now,' I suggested.

'Not that I would live on *your* income,' he continued, 'but I am guessing that you are currently bound to the Swiney Godivas by the purse-strings. Darcy, I'll assume, controls all your money? Your true part of those takings is not distributed to you personally?'

I nodded. 'Just an allowance. But let us not talk of that either.'

'And the full takings are enormous?'

'Vast,' I told him. 'But—'

'So I thought. And anyway – how can I take you from the Swiney Godivas? Without you to write the words, the girls would be entirely scripted by Tristan Stoker and it would all descend to farce and obscenity.'

In his opinion, as I knew, it hovered at the point already.

'And they'd not find your equivalent in red hair anywhere in the world, would they? If I were to take you, I'd dismember the Swiney Godivas?' he said in a speculative tone.

224

'Six doesn't have the ring of seven,' I agreed. Shame stopped me short of telling him about the contract that could be dissolved only at the whim of Mr Rainfleury, and I was too afraid of Mr Sardou's disapproving words if I did.

Of course there were endless ways to prolong this discussion about why we could not be together, all the while being together.

We were together for at least a few minutes of every day in the next weeks, the transparent hairs along our wrists aligned, sharing the same Dublin air, close as two reeds in a pond. We walked along the quays, passing alternating benches cupping drunks or lovers drunk on one another. We met on Ha'penny Bridge, watching the sun swim the full length of the Liffey towards us. We met among the solemn, dusty students in the dim galleries at Marsh's Library in St Patrick's Close, where we might not speak, but only look, and compose letters to one another as we sat side by side, solemnly exchanging them as we parted on the street. When the Black Wind jostled Dublin, we hired a carriage for 1s 3d an hour, with the second hour being 8d, and asked the driver to take us to wherever he fancied, until the horse was tired. We saw nothing of what we passed by. And when I paid the driver, Alexander looked away, too sensitive to bear the reckoning of our time together in coins.

One month into our discussions of why we might not be together, Mr Rainfleury bustled in with a letter exotically stamped and travel-worn. 'Girls, I believe this is an opportunity that might appeal. Tristan is all in favour.'

He tapped the envelope smartly on a cherry-wood table. A page of fine handwriting spilled out, along with a note from Tristan, which Oona eyed hungrily.

The letter was from a Brother of the Hair, though not of the usual variety. He was a photographer in Venice, who concerned himself with albumen portraits of stone, water and human forms. One of our photographic trade cards had reached Signor Saverio Bon, and he was proposing to take photographs of the Swiney Godivas and their miraculous hair in various Venetian settings.

225

Even Darcy could find nothing to object to in the fee offered by Signor Bon, although that did not forfend a great deal of grumbling on her part about the cheek and lunacy of the proposition and the certain prospect of catching or falling to our deaths in a swamp city deprived of carriages.

Ida said, '*I'd* like to try my chance and see what sort of place Venice might be at all.'

'Well you would not,' declared Darcy, who had recently seen a stage version of Mr Disraeli's novel *Venetia*. 'It is a louche place where they are too busy loosening their moral elastic to replace a fallen brick or paint a peeling wall.'

'As for moral elastic, I'll be coming with you, of course,' said Mr Rainfleury, 'at least to settle you in and make sure this Bon character is all he should be. And arrange for a confessor to hear you in English, and other sundry matters. Your dear departed mother would not forgive me if I did not.'

Mr Rainfleury smiled, first at Enda, then at Berenice, mouthing, 'The most romantic city in the world!'

Oona whispered, 'And Tristan there? Will he come too?'

He'd been a good six weeks in London, and Oona had received precious few messages from him.

Mr Rainfleury consulted Tristan's accompanying note and shook his head. 'He writes of fees, and of use of light on the hair . . . and, oh yes, some technical aspects of the photography for label reproduction. No, nothing about coming to Venice. With business so delightfully pressing in London . . .'

He avoided looking at Oona, and at me, plunging deeper into the letter.

'Ah,' he rejoiced, 'regarding the *Venetian* Swiney Godivas, Tristan has some ideas for this Signor Saverio Bon. Oh, such delicious ideas, my poppets! You have no conception how delicious.'

28

Alexander was less enchanted than I'd expected at the prospect of my visiting the city of his birth. He said little but I read his disapproval in the way he stood arms folded to watch me in the new 'attitudes' of women combing their hair. Mr Rainfleury and Tristan were keen to mine the possibilities of 'Venetian' Swiney Godivas. We were set to performing tableaux of Titian's and Tintoretto's ladies. Tristan thought it an excellent idea for Alexander to repaint some vignettes of those nymphs and saints with our faces.

Alexander declined. Indignantly, he told me, 'They told me you would wear tight pink chemises for these portraits. I said that the *suggestion* of nudity was more suggestive than nudity itself. I explained – in small words – that I, as an *artist*, could look at all the Swiney Godivas naked without an impure thought, but I would not collude in such sensational exploitation for the benefit of men's impure desires.'

For a moment I let myself laugh silently at Alexander. Did I sound so prudish, so pompous when I railed against these things? Did he realise how it sounded coming from the married mouth that spoke so desirously to me? But I loved the show of jealousy.

I asked, 'How did Tristan respond?'

'I didn't wait to hear. If the man were worth an explanation, I would have also told him that I will not paint gratuitous references to the Bible or myth! Any excuse to have the artist paint a woman in the act of touching her hair, drawing a comb through it. And if she can be naked, apart from the hair, all the better. The raised arm lifts the breast invitingly, offering it to view.'

I too was in possession of a breast and I coloured to think of it that way. He continued, 'Thus the narcissism and essential indolence of women is satisfyingly exposed.'

'All women?' I asked.

But Alexander had mounted the platform of his polemics, and he disregarded my questions just as Tristan and Mr Rainfleury did. I did not blame him: it seemed that there was something about my opinions that made them easy to overlook. I wished that were not so; most particularly I wished it in Alexander's case. And I could see that he was offended by his financial servitude to Tristan, and that I was in the way of this butting of male horns.

He continued, 'And have you noticed how the artists often present these paintings from a keyhole point of view?'

I had. A keyhole point of view – that was myself and Alexander, snatching minutes in public places, dining on food that was not food, because I might not be absent for any family meals and also because he had told me that he could not afford to treat me as I deserved. He paid only when we went to the squalid coffee shops by the river.

'A tea and a scone stretches my funds,' he admitted, looking down. 'And you deserve all the finest things, the very finest, Manticory. It is as well that you Swineys earn enough to buy them for yourselves.'

He looked at me for reassurance, and I gave it. 'Yes, there is so much money floating about we hardly know what to do with it.'

His mouth twisted for a moment, though whether with irony or pain I could not tell. Then he began to talk to me of Paris, and the 'coming men', Monet, Cézanne, Renoir, Pissarro, who were painting not what the eye sees, as he explained it, but as the eye sees. 'To understand it properly, I'd need to show you the way they debate the shadows to capture light, movement,' he told me. 'Of course, I can never dare to innovate like that. With Elisabetta always wanting—'

You have to paint the way I have to write, I wanted to say, *all banality and commerce.* But I dared not risk the wound to his pride.

And if it often turned out that he had forgotten to recharge his pockets with coins at all before our excursions, I was determined not to notice it. And it did not matter at all, in any case, because my own purse was always full.

There were three weeks and then two weeks and then days left before the Swiney Godivas departed on their Venetian adventure. Darcy was entrusted with our new passports and the first-class tickets that cost nearly £8 each. She kept on her lap at all times a new velvet purse full of the gold Napoleons that Mr Rainfleury told us were currency everywhere in Europe.

I put myself through an intensive course of Italian study. I even stole some official time with Alexander under the pretext of Italian lessons. Alexander left five days ahead of us, having fortuitously remembered a long-postponed commission to render the portrait of a French aristocrat transplanted and living languidly in his native town.

I longed to ask, 'Where do you stay in Venice?' but did not, because I feared the answer.

'Do not worry about what you are worrying about,' Alexander urged me.

But he had still not said, even once, that he was happy I would see his home.

The Swiney Godivas, the 'Miss Swineys' and my Italian grammars and art books were transported to Paris via a brief sojourn in London. The day was stormy and the Dover steamer made us suffer every one of the twenty-one miles of the Channel. At Calais an elegant train was waiting to take us to Paris, our breath steaming the windows all the way. The London breakfasts we'd lost on the steamer were replenished eleven and a half hours later at the Hôtel Meurice in the rue de Rivoli, where we had our own fine drawing room looking over the gardens of the Tuileries and three large bed-chambers, where we slept in tribal alignments, with Darcy having a room to herself. Darcy did not permit us outside our gilded and flounced lodgings except to be Marcelled from head to foot with Monsieur Grateau's famous steam *ondulations*. Titled ladies jostled genteelly for appointments but Marcel Grateau had sent his card to our hotel, scenting an opportunity for mutual publicity. We Swineys posed for a photograph in his salon, fully 'ondulated' by a cunningly simple device that he and his assistants heated on a gas stove. I made one secret excursion to the sensational show of the Société anonyme coopérative des artistes peintres, sculpteurs, graveurs, so that I could tell Alexander that I had seen the work of the 'coming men' of whom he'd spoken with such fervour. When I returned, dazzled with captured light, Darcy told me that she was on the point of calling the police. I had to promise Enda that I would not leave her at the mercy of Darcy's temper by further disappearances.

From Paris, we came by train to Nice and over the Alps to Italy, shimmering with spring. While my sisters congregated in the dining car, I sat in the finely cushioned first-class carriage and fed on my books, making sense of where we were to go and what we were to be when we got there.

From the colour plates and the captions I began to learn things about hair that Tristan would never master. The paintings pleased me more than photographs, for I felt in constant dialogue with Alexander as I examined each colour plate. Moreover, I felt that I knew intimately what was depicted by Titian and Giovanni Bellini. As if they had worn Swiney hair on their own heads, they knew all the places hair can fall: where the bare arm meets the bare shoulder, along the elbow, rustling into the well of the clavicle, dividing itself at the breast. And if it can fall as a light, porous, penetrable veil, why then all the better, for the veiled woman is an object of more erotic speculation and desire than a naked one.

While we rattled comfortably through France towards Italy, I was learning how the Venetians loved the colour red. My books taught me new names and shades of red – *scarlatto, cremesino, rosso, marrone*.

And in Venice, it seemed, there was nowhere they liked those reds better than on a lady's head, and cascading down her back. In their churches, Titian had provided the Venetians with redheads to gaze at even while they prayed. Perhaps the illiterate – or the imaginative – among them thought that they were hymning the red hair of the ladies instead of God? Or even thanking Him for furnishing their native city with such a luxuriance of red hair.

Now I was about to arrive in Venice with more red hair than the Venetians had ever seen, wishing it to be seen by only one Venetian, Alexander Sardou.

It was a mild silky night draped with organza wisps of cloud. An egg yolk of a moon, which I felt that I knew, hung over the water dripping runnels of yellow light as our train muscled over the narrow causeway into town. Venice glowed russet where the lamps lit it, glowered mossy black elsewhere.

I knew that Alexander could not be at the station. He had telegrammed us in Paris regretting an 'unavoidable commitment'. I would not truly have arrived in Venice until I had seen him. Instead, we were met by Signor Bon himself, a lanky, quiet man in his thirties with expressive green eyes under a generous brow and a crown of crisp chestnut hair. An agreeable scent of sweet leather and milky coffee lingered about his person. His English was excellent, his voice low and pleasing.

After the introductions, Ida remarked, 'This is a good creature. Do you see what a good creature it is? And the legs are shapely too. Darcy, remember Mr Rainfleury says that you may not pinch me in public. Please wait till we get home.'

It was, I thought, a shame that Darcy seemed to have fixed on treating Signor Bon as if she were his landlord and he her recalcitrant tenant. He seemed to accept her disdain without resentment – in fact I thought I saw the corners of his lips twitch upwards once or twice. He gallantly tolerated my attempts at Italian without laughing at them.

Guided by Signor Bon, we handed over our tickets to the station gate-keeper, ran the gauntlet of the passport inspections with speed and jocularity, and suffered our luggage to be opened by the customs men, who promptly confiscated Mr Rainfleury's cigars.

231

Outside the station, the water winked at us slyly, urging us to forget our reticules and our tiredness. Signor Bon helped us into two gondolas with respectfully gentle hands. We set off through moon-sequinned waves.

To my surprise, nothing surprised me. My first journey through Venice was like combing my own hair – slowly, with the teeth of the comb buried deep in the bed of the hair, a little hair-breath raised by the action, and a tint of hair-scent too – and finding something new, and mysterious, among its familiar textures and smells.

The *palazzi* and churches let their fretted stones hang down into our faces like beautiful, insistent ghosts. Beckoning lanterns hung at arched water-gates. Inside their houses, exquisitely dressed Venetians displayed themselves in glowing tableaux so that each palace seemed to host a puppet theatre performing just for us. The city was mystical and barbaric all at once, a floating fortress so delicate that the fairies would hesitate to place the weight of their wings on it. I never saw a place that wanted loving so desperately. My sisters were silenced by the sight; even Darcy forbore to carp.

It is a taste of our own Swiney medicine, I thought, *to be dazzled by an unnatural plenty of beauty.*

We passed the smiling mouths of side canals; more palaces shied away coquettishly or loomed down with faintly patronising friendliness. I felt not immaterial to the intensity of their engagement.

This, I thought, *this is for me.*

I smiled as we passed a Gothic window lit up by a chandelier. I thought of the seashell lamp that used to hang in the Harristown cottage, whispering of the ocean, or so I'd believed. *No, it was telling me of Venice, it was whispering of this all the way over the sea to Ireland. Perhaps the creature of the shell once patrolled the Adriatic floor on a slimy foot, and found this place, and ever after boasted of it.*

My sisters remained uncharacteristically silent, except Ida, who whispered to me, 'It is like the perfume counter at Clery's, when you try too many scents at once. It makes you happy and confused. It makes me want to play my fiddle at it.'

'It is like that,' I told her.

Mr Rainfleury sat between Enda and Berenice, not daring to hold the hand of either, though you could see his very ears convulsed with romance. I was almost sorry for him, craving Alexander's presence as I did, with extreme impatience. Soon I would see Alexander and I would not share him with anyone, not even a Venetian mosquito, and certainly not with Elisabetta, I thought defiantly. I felt Signor Bon's eyes on me. I smiled at him, offering silent compensation for Darcy's loud sniffs.

He smiled back, his face pleasantly creased.

Ida was right, I thought. *It is a good creature.*

But my thoughts were taken up with a different one, my paler, pale-eyed Alexander. We'd been separated just days but I struggled to superimpose his image on the rich backdrop of Venice. Signor Bon, with his chestnut hair and green eyes, and that voice you could build a nest in, seemed to personify the city more perfectly.

A mist set in during a gondola journey that was longer than any of us expected. At first Signor Bon tried to put us up at the Hotel Vittoria in the Frezzaria where the rooms were 6 lire a night, but Darcy objected to its humbleness, notwithstanding the photographer's plea, 'But your Lord Byron stayed near by when he first came to Venezia. I thought—'

'Don't you be trying to get round me. The cheek of you! Somewhere better,' said Darcy, marching stiff-legged back to the gondola and settling herself into it. Again, Signor Bon's eyes searched out mine. I shrugged, hoping to save him the trouble of arguing with Darcy, and the inevitable humiliation that would follow the unpleasantness.

As our gondolas loped like long black wolves from palace to palace, the mist began to coat everything with an uncertainty that seemed thrillingly spiritual, as if a thousand delicate lamps were uttering ectoplasm like the famous lady mediums back in London. The water seemed to smoke and boil beneath us. The buildings steamed, dripping with this strange false cold heat, as if Venice were a Gothic Atlantis pulled suddenly from the freezing-hot depths. Gulls wavered in the thickened air. The mist chewed at painted walls, darkening the pale ones, bleaching the vivid.

The boat-bound Venetians made friends with the mist, singing crooning lullabies to it and holding aloft lanterns that made but tiny incursions of happiness into the gloom.

'What is that caterwauling?' demanded Darcy. 'Is someone slaughtering a goat?'

'We have our special fog songs,' explained Signor Bon.

The photographer pointed out Ca' d'Oro, which hosted a private well of fog inside its fretted coffer of a courtyard. The side canals were abysses of darkness, with just a few white ghosts of walls to bear witness to the finiteness of things. The Grand Canal was transformed into a tunnel. Even the prows of our own gondolas were blunted by the mist. And the empty palaces, which seemed to dominate the city, grinned like rows of skulls, their eyeballs dark on the brain.

By the time we had been rowed to another three establishments, we were creatures of the mist, our minds clouded with it, our lungs soaked with it, our hair darkly stained by it, our imaginations rife with it. Darcy was finally placated by a brocaded, balconied apartment at 90 lire in the Albergo Reale Danieli. Signor Bon's face showed a mixture of amusement and pain. I commanded my own features to remain bland when he said, 'I shall advise Signor Sardou of your final lodgement here.'

He waved up at the elegant staircase. Like Annora's, his fingers were pallid – from constant immersion in the liquids of his trade, I guessed. I noticed that he stooped a tint, perhaps from habitually accommodating low doorways in Venice, or from passing so much time under the black-velvet hood of his photographic apparatus. I wanted to ask if I might see his studio, but he quickly bade us goodnight – addressing me alone in Italian. From the safe privacy of the Italian tongue, I longed to ask him how well he knew Alexander.

Instead, I asked, 'How you come to speak such excellent English, Signor Bon?'

Making sure that I could follow him, he told me in simple slow words that he had learned my tongue from a priest who served the expatriate Church of England community. He had refined it by many conversations with the '*anglosassone*' tourists who came to him as clients.

'They want to be married to Venice for ever, in an image, so I suppose I am a priest myself,' he smiled.

In English or Italian, his voice was never static. The words came out like the shine brushed into hair, a roughness shed at the point of delivery yet that still gave a sense of energy to the quiescence. There was a trapped hilarity inside it, even when he spoke gravely. Now, without changing his expression, he told me confidentially, 'But I never had such a subject as your sister Darcy before. She makes one long for the tender manners of Attila the Hun. I would not like to watch her eating meat.'

Up in our private parlour, Oona remonstrated gently, 'That seemed a rather hard introduction for Signor Bon, Darcy. He must think we are very spoiled, the way you carried on there.'

Mr Rainfleury added reproachfully, 'I hope he does not reconsider his offer. It has put the Corporation to considerable expense to get you all here.'

'In fact, the first place was acceptable,' said Darcy, 'but it was important to show this Bon-Bon how we are to be treated before he starts pointing that nasty black thing at us and blowing our heads off with its explosions.'

Alexander arrived within half an hour. His mouth was bent all out of shape, and even the sight of me did not bring a smile to it. No wonder he looked out of sorts, I reasoned indulgently. He must have longed to be the one to introduce me to the Grand Canal. Meanwhile I longed to tell him my polished impressions of Monet, Cézanne, Renoir and their debates with light and shade.

He listened coolly to my sisters' laborious descriptions of his own city. He escorted us to a restaurant, making sure to brush his hands against my own at every possible opportunity, sending ripples of pins and needles up my arms which, surprisingly, did not spend themselves until they reached my breasts. He knew. He truly knew. I saw it in the beckoning shapes of his smiles. He suppered with us, ordering simple dishes in a sumptuous Italian. In his native tongue, his voice was elegant; the movements of his head subtly adjusted to accommodate its inflections.

Alexander and I exchanged a telegraph office full of communications under the cover of the drawing block he set on the supper table. Silently, I forgave him for not meeting me at the station. Silently, he told me that he would make it up to me.

'What do you think of the Swiney Godivas in Venice, Mr Sardou?' chortled Mr Rainfleury, his poor creature of a moustache lurid with tomato sauce.

'It suits them beautifully,' smiled Alexander. 'I see possibilities for them here.'

He slid his eyes over mine. His smile went trickling down my body, inside my clothes. And all parts south of my waist lurched and churned like water cleaved by a gondola.

There was little time for sightseeing – or Alexander's possibilities – as Signor Bon desired to put us to work immediately the next day.

'Wants to recoup all his old expenses at the Danieli,' Darcy observed acidly, counting the gold Napoleons in her purse.

'More likely,' said Mr Rainfleury, 'Bon doesn't want the public glimpsing for free what he hopes soon to sell them printed in albumen on board.'

Nevertheless, we squeezed in a few hours of Venice early in the morning and late at night. Our hair tightly coiled in snoods, and our heads covered with hats, we were whisked by our *laquais de place* around Piazza San Marco and led over the Rialto Bridge to the squabbling market. Ida squealed at the fish still flailing on the stalls and crabs curling their red fists at her. The Doges' Palace was fit for just half an hour of our time, and we covered the Accademia Gallery at a trot. As for more gondola trips, we were told 'later', in a mysterious voice by Signor Bon, who had succeeded in a negotiation with Mr Rainfleury, that Alexander might *not* be permitted to sketch while the photographer did his work.

236

Mr Rainfleury told us, 'It seems the photography fellow has taken a dislike to Sardou's portrait. He says he does not sell girls like Mr Sardou does, whatever that means.'

'I'm sure—' I commenced indignantly, and then stopped myself before Darcy could see my blush.

In the end, I was relieved that sketching was forbidden, for the work – the part dictated by Tristan and Mr Rainfleury, that is – would have made Alexander pity me, or despise me. Signor Bon's own compositions were, however, a welcome revelation.

The first photograph was at the Ca' d'Oro, the palace we had seen on the night of our arrival. By day it seemed to consist mostly of air laced together with slender ribbons of pink and grey stone. We sisters were posed in profile on its monumental first-floor balconies. Then we let our hair down, side-saddle, as it were, so it streamed off the parapets like medieval pennants.

The city might have been designed as a showcase for long hair, which, we now discovered, never looked so soft as when juxtaposed against marble, nor so liquid as when lolling above jade-green waves.

The next day we were made to climb the dusty bell tower of San Vidal, an idea that little pleased my sisters. I volunteered to go to the topmost floor, for the joy of the view over the back-bone of Dorsoduro – as Signor Bon explained – to the lagoon and its islands. I was to push my hair out of the belfry, and below me was Darcy, feeding her hair from an arched window, and below her Oona and so on until there were seven Venetian-Irish Rapunzels with their hair hanging down one tower in one multicoloured rope.

Signor Bon ferried us in his own green boat to and from our lodgings at the Danieli, his apparatus nestling among us like an eighth dark sister. He brought us the first prints that evening. I had to concede a quiet admiration for his way of telling stories with our hair. He was a better poet than Tristan, because he understood the feel of things, of the sensations to be gleaned at the conjunctures of stone and water and hair. He was sensitive to the potency of the imagery he created, and he was afire with the possibility of creation. For him, our hair had its own things to declare – and they were nuanced, natural, thought-provoking things – not just something hot and vulgar, staged to strike primal fear or envy, rousing all those passions only to sell something else. And then there was his voice. Even talking of a broken hinge on one of his many monstrous pieces of machinery, Mr Bon's voice told a story that kept your ear pleasurably inclined towards him.

The photographer's mood darkened the next evening, when it was time to execute the first of Tristan's 'delicious ideas'. He had hired seven gondolas and fourteen gondoliers, each more handsome than the last. We were stationed in front of the Corte del Duca, where Signor Bon had set up his apparatus. One Swiney sister was made to stand in the steadying embrace of a gondolier at the bow of every gondola, her hair flowing into the next boat, and so on until there was a procession of seven gondolas going down the Grand Canal, all linked by hair. A skull illuminated by a candle burned at every pair of Swiney feet. The photographs were taken at dusk, each of us holding a ceremonial torch to illuminate our faces and the ends of the hair of the sister we followed.

Signor Bon worked rapidly on two devices, two boys assisting him with the plates. He fired magnesium at us endlessly, until my eyes were afire with stars and dust.

The technique 'chiaro di luna' he explained, required two photographs of each image, one to capture the light of the background and the other for the buildings. He would combine the images in the studio, one bathed in light, the other dark, on pale blue paper.

The photographer executed his work with his mouth drawn down. This much I already knew from Mr Rainfleury's comments: Signor Bon loved the aesthetic qualities of our hair, but he did not like us flaunting the sexual allure of it, or hinting at looseness in our characters. He had flinched at the skulls, protesting to Mr Rainfleury. 'Why must there be death? What is lacking with beauty alone? It is not respect. For love *or* death, to make them be so . . . intimate.'

Signor Bon was no happier with Mr Rainfleury's order that a second set of gondola photographs be taken in the same way, but by daylight, in which each of us cradled our own 'Miss Swiney' as we reclined on a velvet banquette. He regarded the dolls with ill-disguised disgust. We were required to point with pleasure at certain buildings, as if showing our dollies the great beauties of Venice, while, of course, surpassing all of them with our own hirsute kind of loveliness. For the occasion, the dolls were dressed in pinafores embroidered with Celtic crosses by the nuns of the Poor Clares Convent in Kenmare.

'Make sure you get the detail,' urged Mr Rainfleury, by which I guessed a private financial connection with the convent that would not appear in the Swiney Corporation books.

And Signor Bon's expression was positively thunderous when Mr Rainfleury put us Swineys to work in the Sala Orientale at Caffè Florian in San Marco. The room hosted seven exotic painted beauties framed in golden arches. One, a Negress, was scandalously clothed only from the waist down. We Swineys undressed our hair, and draped it from the frames of the paintings and nestled back in it, so all that was visible to Signor Bon's lens was our faces, the lovely features of the painted harem, and a web of variegated curls. The crowd pressing its noses against the window roared with delight. Signor Bon muttered, '*Poverine: che insulto!*' I longed to tell him that he was not the only one who regretted that we Swineys had filled that elegant space with our hair, where Mr Goldoni, Lord Byron and Herr Goethe had filled it with their intellects.

Unlike other photographers and unlike our patrons, Signor Bon always asked permission if he wished to touch our hair, to lift it or drape it. His fingers never lingered, but their movements were agreeably quick and firm. Only his pleasant scent of leather and coffee lingered.

More gondoliers were hired for scenes in which each sister lassoed her cavalier with her hair, wrapping it round his pale neck and drawing him to her. I tried not to meet the hot toffee eyes of my all-too-willing gondolier, and was again extremely grateful for the absence of Alexander.

Poor Oona was also required to act out Mr Browning's poem 'Porphyria's Lover' in which the narrator, currently lodging in a madhouse cell, tells how he ended the girl's life:

> *. . . and all her hair*
> *In one long yellow string I wound*
> *Three times her little throat around,*
> *And strangled her . . .*

People gathered to watch the photography, but were shooed away by the barefoot boys specially hired by Signor Bon. I was sorry whenever the boys succeeded, for I loved to look at the Venetians, particularly the females. The working women adopted a fetching hairstyle: their dark hair was fanned to fullness around their faces before being gently drawn back and fastened in a high topknot. Curls and tendrils were freely allowed to escape. Whether they were young girls lithe as ferrets or squat barrels of grandmothers, the women all dressed the same way. Their skirts were often a dirty cream colour, made to look dirtier by contrast with the grey-white of their stockings underneath. The men looked dashing as matadors in their knee-length dark capes and their felt hats.

I was fascinated by the Venetian ladies' ways with their long-fringed shawls. A few wore red, fewer white; black was overwhelmingly chosen. Some of them wrapped their fabric tightly round their torsos in shapely figures of eight. Others draped their shawls loose around their shoulders and let them fall to their knees, with the extravagant fringes undulating like waves in night canals. The women's hands were always at work on those shawls, sometimes lifting them to cover their heads, other times tucking a stray curl into the hood.

Catching my eye on one woman's hands, Signor Bon smiled. 'Graceful, yes? The shawl is called a "*sial*" in our dialect.'

The next morning he brought me one as a gift. 'Just do not ask me to find one for that horrible doll of yours,' he muttered.

I answered, 'No. I'd rather get her a shroud.'

*

The Venetians loved their city – their ferocious affection for it was contagious. Each seagull, it seemed, had its own bit of Venice that it defended with beak and claw.

I too was forced to defend the place.

Darcy's staunch position, asserted every time something beautiful appeared by way of reflections under a mossy bridge or a tumble of geraniums on a balcony, was that Venice was not notably different from Manchester.

'It's also black inconvenient with the canals all over waiting to be fallen into,' she observed. 'Dirty as a dirty girl's bathwater.'

Venice did not charm Enda and Berenice, who saw very little beyond Mr Rainfleury's moustache. Oona pined palely for Tristan. If she might not share Venice with him, she could barely experience the place. Pertilly was dizzied by the dancing light of the water and clung to every balustrade. Ida fell into peals of laughter at the sight of the Basilica of San Marco. 'That is not a church!' she cried with glee, 'that is a fairground tent!'

'No, more of a reliquary,' I told her. I dragged her in and choked her on the bones of more saints than even Annora would have been able to believe in. The phial of Virgin's Milk in the crypt made me gladder than ever that Tristan was not with us, as it might have bred untenable ideas in him.

For all the briefness of the glimpses I'd been allowed of it, I alone among the Swineys had formed a hot love of Venice inside me by the end of our first week. I was greedy for it, and woke before dawn, stealing away from the Danieli. Some mornings, Alexander met me at pre-assigned places. We had precious minutes murmuring our lovely nonsense together in quiet alleys – not so much streets as mere fissures in the marble – or we stood close together on bridges to gaze at towers whose leprous feet paddled in the green water and whose bony spires disappeared into opalescent skies.

'How could you ever leave it?' I asked, hoping he would reply, 'Because Elisabetta is here.'

But he just smiled and held the rationed finger of my hand more tightly.

In Venice, we started again. We were learning to touch, just a few fingers at a time and our shoulders aligned or my hand tucked up under his arm. We hovered around one another's faces with our lips. We would, by mutual but silent agreement, eke out more of this churning, uncertain time before we took to anything more than these Venetian almost-kisses. At the Antico Panada, Florian, the Orientale, we kept on at not kissing, devotedly. We always left separately. When he left first, I nursed the dregs of his coffee, sipping them till the last grains embittered my tongue.

He still had not told me where he lived or if he saw his wife, so I needed something to withhold too. By a carefully casual question to Signor Bon, I found out where Elisabetta Sardou dwelled – a tall and pretty *palazzo* on the Corte de la Vida near San Samuele. I had found many reasons to walk down the street that passed through it, and once I caught sight of a woman I believed to be Elisabetta herself, a small robust figure with strong features and a taste for bright colours. She wore that expression of magisterial discontent that only married women are allowed to show on their faces.

I did not ask Alexander for confirmation as that would have necessitated a confession of my shameful spying.

Even when he could not meet me, I still rose before dawn to see more of the city. I loved the chimneys that looked like ice-cream papers rolled for a scoop, the wooden buckets clustering around the sculpted well-heads in each square, the loose-lipped onion girls, the diminutive stone kings at the entrance to the Doges' Palace, the way each gull interviewed the water with the shadow of its wings before deciding to slide its yellow feet into it. And how magical in the mist were those marriage-breaking snores emitted by steam ferries on the Grand Canal in the last shreds of the night.

And the colours: the scalding pinks, the skin-warm terracottas, the angelica greens – at first I could understand them only as the opposite of the colours I had grown up with. Harristown colours – I remembered them all in sepia, even the forty Irish shades of green were tinged with muddiness. Now they appeared in my mind's eye as if someone had spilled coffee on a dimming watercolour and then wept over the damage for a long time.

I used the *traghetti*, standing up in the gondolas like a Venetian. I loved to be afloat the little golden fists of waves shaking hands with one another while knees of blue and elbows of vivid emerald poked up between them. And how different it felt to have the water coming up beneath instead of constantly falling on top of me as in Ireland. When no one was looking, I could not refrain from wriggling my shoulders luxuriously in the unaccustomed sun.

The morning after the doll photographs Signor Bon passed me at the San Tomà *traghetto*. He turned his green boat in a graceful arc, raising a serpent ridge of water in his wake. He beckoned me over, smiling frankly.

'It is very early, Miss Manticory! I suspect you of coming out to drown your doll, perhaps.'

'And I suppose,' I smiled, 'you have a perfectly rational reason for being out so early, some errand, perhaps?'

'You have caught me, Miss Manticory. I confess to wanting to see the sunrise from the water before I bury my head under the black velvet. Would you care to join me?'

Signor Bon seated me in front of him so that my view was unimpeded. He rowed, as he explained, '*alla Veneziana*', standing behind me, stooping rhythmically over a pair of oars. On the back of my neck, I felt the warm air disturbed by his efforts.

It was worth all Darcy's anger, all Mr Rainfleury's clucking and even worth keeping a secret from Alexander, the hour I was late for breakfast, the hour I spent as the sun rose above the city being rowed by the photographer around the back canals of Venice, dipping under trailing vines, being enveloped in the sudden shadows of bell towers, following the sugar-scented bakers' boats. The ferry stops snapped their crisp striped awnings at us. I watched the women throwing ropes into the water to teach their young children to swim. I listened to the happy chatter of the bead-stringers of Castello sorting the treasures in the wide wooden trugs on their laps.

I never once saw Alexander, no matter how hard I looked.

By a mutual understanding, Signor Bon and I did not talk, but at times the pleasure was so great that it needed to be shared. Then I could not refrain from twisting round so that our eyes met. When I did so, he nodded with a solemn smile like a benign priest who has made a convert of an unlikely sinner.

I loved Venice so much that I probably should have confessed to idolatry at the moonlight-white church of San Tomà, where the priest was said by Mr Rainfleury to speak English, and indeed did so, richly and baroquely. His penances were far lighter than those the priests at St Teresa's in Dublin had thought to give us – and he did not need to hold my hair through the grate like Father Maglinn in Harristown.

I did not tell him, *I am on fire for a married man of this town, and I pass tranced hours in desirous memories of him, and bitter minutes of knowing I may not have him for my own. This is the cost I knowingly pay for loving Alexander Sardou, and I had not realised that it would be beyond even my Swiney-fattened means. Meanwhile I take morning boat trips with another man, who may well be married. I am so wanton these days that I have neglected even to ask him. His intelligence and kindness come free of cost, and so I do not value them properly. Even that is a sin in itself.*

Instead, I excavated an older sin, a Harristown sin: I confessed to the Venetian priest that once, on a bridge in Ireland, a man had touched me.

He asked, 'And did you allow it because you loved him? Or was it for sensuality alone? Or was he an evildoer who wished to hurt you, my poor child? And did this foul thing against your will? If so then he is damned to Hell without my intervention, and your own innocence is unstained.'

He added, 'And anyone who tells you otherwise is the one who carries the stain.'

Outside, in Campo San Tomà, I looked straight up at the sun, dazzled by my new freedom. And in that moment I wished I might never, ever go back to Ireland.

I even wondered if I should now confess for Darcy, that she had quite possibly murdered our father. I trusted this priest. Would he express the right outrage and comfort me for my loss, and tell me how to set my feelings in order about those crossed spoons over the secret grave in Harristown that my mind kept ever green and tended?

I was still thinking about it the next day when Signor Bon announced that he had discharged his commission in its entirety. Darcy ordered our trunks brought up to our rooms.

Signor Bon took me for one last dawn boat trip around Venice. This time my mood was tragic. The photographer told me, as if he guessed how it hurt me to be leaving, 'Let the tears out, Miss Manticory. If you rinse your eyes, you shall see more clearly.'

In front of him, I was not ashamed to weep, though it felt wrong that he did not know all my reasons for not wanting to depart.

Two days later we were aboard the train at Santa Lucia Station, with Alexander staring up at me from the platform, getting smaller and smaller.

We travelled back to Dublin first class, stopping in Paris for new gowns and hats, as if born to shopping in glass arcades and dining on *cœurs de filet Rachel* among the better types of American and English travellers behind the impeccable lace curtains at Voisin's in the rue Saint-Honoré or drinking tea among the crushed-strawberry upholstery, carpets and tapestries of the Ritz in the Place Vendôme.

Signor Bon's photographs earned us a fee per random dozen – this was the rate agreed with Mr Rainfleury, who had learned the hard way from the dolls that it was better not to let us know when the public chose its favourites. The pictures went to press immediately and were in the Venetian shops in days. Every tourist wanted to take a piece of Venice away with them, despite the tax on photographs – charged by the pound of weight – and now they also took a piece of Swiney Godiva. Signor Bon reported wonderful earnings, especially after Mr Rainfleury set

245

up a discreet mail-order business for Continental gentlemen collectors.

But a problem emerged. With fulsome apologies, Signor Bon revealed that a new convulsion of fiscal law meant that he could not send the money out of Italy. It was safely deposited in the Cassa di Risparmio di Venezia, which, Signor Bon reported, sternly refused to be so unpatriotic as to empty its coffers of Italian currency and send it in the direction of Dublin.

Back in Pembroke Street, Darcy fulminated, 'I knew he would rob us, the slimy Italian! Too mean to give us a fright! I'll make him scratch where he doesn't itch.'

'It's not his fault about the money,' protested Ida. 'Did you know his first name is "Saverio"? It is like sageness and good savour altogether. And maybe even "saviour". And he was so sweetly partial to Manticory.'

'It was only because I tried to speak Italian,' I protested hastily, for Darcy had turned to fix a black eye on me. 'And as for the money, why don't we go back to Venice and spend it there, staying a while?' I suggested quietly.

A letter from Alexander – sent to a secret post office box I'd rented – had informed me he'd been hired as the painting tutor to a noble Venetian youth, whose brains left him unfitted to other activity. It did not tell me where Alexander was living. If the work came with lodgings, surely he'd have told me? He offered only a *poste restante* address for my replies.

Darcy mimicked my voice, '*Why don't we go back to Venice?* For Manticory to moon over the old photo man? Or the bleached-looking Sardou? Because I don't care two rows of pins if I never see that dirty place again. *Why don't we go back to Venice?* Because it's humid and inconvenient,' she snapped, 'and because I don't wish it. I suppose the money's safe enough there until we can work out a way of getting at it. It's not as if we're not earning in the meantime, anyway.'

It was true. The dolls were still a resounding success. The sales of the hair essence, slackening slightly during our absence

246

in Venice, had tripled again when we returned to Dublin. We had regular slots in shop windows in Grafton Street, where we arranged ourselves in 'attitudes', or drank tea, advertising the latest china service from Mr Wedgwood as well as our own hair. We still gave our lectures on the history of hair, and we sang and danced, even at the Theatre Royal in Hawkins Street.

There was plenty of money, but the twins still made it a fighting contention for, every time a penny was spent on something Enda wanted, Berenice would take revenge, and vice versa. Finally came a day when Berenice discovered her pillow smouldering with a puddle of carbolic liquid, because she had demanded a new counterpane for her bed. And Darcy threw up her hands, and went to the bank, dragging Mr Rainfleury with her.

She came back with seven booklets, each bearing our names and a starting balance of 100 guineas. She announced, 'Your share of the takings will be deposited in there. After expenses. An allowance of £5 a week.'

'Is not £5 a week a trifling outrage compared with our great earnings?' I asked.

'Then you shall receive the £5 just once a month so you'll be less outraged less often, you scrattock,' Darcy replied.

My sisters stared at me with resentment. My tongue had cost them £15 a month. I acknowledged my stupidity with a muttered 'Sorry'.

I wondered how I might mitigate what I'd done. I took my candle down to Darcy's desk again. I found her bank book to contain some £154,000, a figure I tucked in my memory for whenever it would be needed, for it surely would. Very little new money appeared in our own bank books after that, in spite of the promised allowance. If any of us raised the matter, Darcy waved a sheaf of household accounts at us.

'So do you want to be taking care of the dressmaker's account and the butcher's notes yourselves then?'

'And who will give the groom his brown envelopes?' asked Ida. 'To take to the betting shop?'

'She's talking swill again,' snorted Darcy. 'Ida, you are so funny I can hardly stand it.'

She let such a laugh out of herself that I could see the tonsils dangling in her throat.

29

We were rich, even if only Darcy saw the real money. Our muskrat coats were almost too heavy to walk in. Mrs Sims, dubbed the Worth of Dublin, condescended to make our dresses. The Lord Lieutenant's wife was the owner of a 'Miss Berenice' doll. Mr Parnell himself was rumoured to have been seen at one of our shows. We attended the Lord Lieutenant's reception that began the Dublin Castle Season, and the assorted levees that followed, performing at the St Patrick's Day Ball that ended it. Lady Nithervilles invited us to a Drawing Room; Lady King offered us tea. We now saluted the great personages of Fitzwilliam Square with ease and elegance, or a good semblance of it. We attended the Irish Grand National at Fairyhouse Racecourse, with Darcy openly sending our groom to lay a 'small' bet.

People stopped dead if they saw us walking down the street. The bolder ones besieged us for our signatures on their paper bags, shirt-cuffs, library books, even their bare skin. We kept a small printer in business, stamping out our trade cards, placards, billboards and setting the type for the advertisements in newspapers. We had three display carriages with glass frames on the outside for our latest posters.

Each 'Miss Swiney' doll had her own stack of miniature trade cards. Every sister had her personalised cards too. These were eagerly collected by our most loyal followers, especially after Mr Rainfleury hit upon the pleasant idea of dipping our trade cards in perfume.

There was a cartoon about us in *The Nation*. In a restaurant, a man pointed to a bowl occupied by a great nest that had pushed all the liquid out onto the tablecloth. He cried, 'Waiter, there's a Swiney hair in my soup!'

We received love letters and offers of marriage, and even a badly spelled page from some pretender who styled himself 'Phelan Swiney, Mariner', and claimed to be our father:

Having read of your great doings in the Kildare Observer, *I have the honour to ask for an interview with my long-lost daughters. I hasten to add that the losing of you was my own fault entirely. I was a sad disappointment to your poor mother* [he wrote in a clear, large script]. *When I joined the Fenians I was obliged to take up a secret existence, and could visit her only in the dead of night.*

'Dead of night! That's what Mam always said!' cried Enda. 'It must be true!'

'Only a weak mind would think it true!' retorted Berenice, and the matter instantly became grounds for new warfare between them.

Darcy picked up the letter with tongs and fed it into the blue belly of the fire.

Of course, I thought, Darcy was the one person who could be completely sure that this man was a pretender, as she was the only one who knew if our real father lay under crossed spoons in a clover field in Harristown.

The man was persistent. The next letter from 'Phelan Swiney, Mariner', brought Enda and Berenice to blows, and suffered the same fiery end.

After the first two letters, Darcy no longer even read them aloud to us before destroying them.

When Enda protested, she jeered, 'What is the likelihood that this man has heard of our success and chases our money? He does not mention anywhere that he wishes to return to the bosom of his family and settle his fortune on us. And that must be because he has none. There is no address, even!'

'If he is a Fenian then it would not be safe to supply one,' Enda pointed out.

'If he is a Fenian then let him go explode himself, as they are so talented in that direction. And don't tell Tristan or Rainfleury about this. They'd not like us to be associated with charlatans or Fenians or pretending long-lost daddies.'

We had so many requests for locks of our hair, often enclosing guineas, that Mr Rainfleury formed a separate department in his doll factory to supply them. He had a former convent girl working cruel hours to compose tender replies from the Swiney Godivas. The missives were wrapped around the so-called silk hair that gave me so many misgivings.

Mr Rainfleury reassured me, 'Absolutely no human hair! You know I would not damage your reputations for the world.'

In America, Tristan placed advertisements for Swiney Godiva Hair Essence in the *Pictorial Review, Ladies' Home Journal* and *Good Housekeeping*. The Swiney Godivas were reinvented as *'gently born ladies of delicate breeding'*. Tristan did not hesitate to add the usual endorsements from various princesses from obscure royal houses of small Continental states. When I drew Darcy's attention to this travesty and the trouble that might come from it, she shrugged, 'I don't give a lash of a whip.'

We were so rich, I understood from this, that we didn't have to care about the truth or fear that it would one day catch up with us.

The Swiney sisters, who had once been the recipients of Relief Committee alms, now performed charity benefits at the Rotunda of the New Lying-In Hospital, and for the Richmond Institution for the Industrious Blind at the Gaiety Theatre near St Stephen's Green. But St Teresa's rejected our offer of a benefit concert. The nun muttered to Enda and myself, 'Young Ida is too come-at-able. It will not do. Your hair . . .' – the nun gestured at my snood – 'there is something ungodly and unwomanly about its . . . exaggeration and . . . fecundity, God forgive me for saying so.'

I wanted to tell her that I understood and agreed.

'We have had a man here,' the nun added. 'A Phelan Swiney making enquiries about you.'

'What did he look like?' Enda asked eagerly. 'Was he a man with a fine figure of hair?'

The nun's face closed up. 'We do not look at men.'

'And we do not let conniving, lying men look at *us*,' said Darcy when we reported the conversation. 'And Enda, there is no real Phelan Swiney, don't you understand?'

Thereafter Darcy insisted that we shun St Teresa's again. We took up promiscuously with other Catholic churches on different Sundays, never observing more than one Sabbath a month in the same establishment.

Mr Rainfleury was happy with this division of our favours, for it gave us more opportunities to show ourselves to more members of the public, and to have them remark on the splendours of our hair.

We were so rich that Pertilly confected rich women's hairstyles for us – the ornate, theatrical kind that were so time-consuming to create that we could do nothing but submit to her hands for hours on end; the kind that were so cumbrous and uncomfortable that we were fit for no useful work when got up in our capillary fortresses and weighed down with combs, feathers, jewels. Our heads became the compendium of our wealth – as if we carried rich houses, priceless galleries and whole department stores on our heads.

'And what a waste it is,' lamented Ida, her cheekbones stretched and her eyes narrowed by a heavy new creation, 'when people love us best when the hair on us falls down.'

30

'Phelan Swiney, Mariner' still sent the occasional letter. His mistake was addressing his missives to Darcy, who waved them at us before throwing them into the fire unopened.

But Darcy could not always be there. While she was off on one of her mysterious errands, I filched an envelope from the salver in the hall. I managed to read a few paragraphs aloud to Enda before Darcy caught us.

He pleaded:

I can well imagine the reason for your everlasting silence, dear daughters. To be sure, you're black offended with me. But please be assured I do not pursue you for your money. In fact, my own ship has come in to a rather wonderful extent and I wish only to share the bounty. I have long since desisted from my political activities, and indeed repent my pursuit of them, because they took me from my family. It shames me to think how I did not do well by your mother.

And for nothing it was too.

I was no more than a hot-head with a long hot tongue; I never committed any act of violence, but between voyages to and from America, I ran with the Irish tribes in Dublin and New York, our safe place – coward that I am – and talked the talk of the armchair revolutionary, speechifying in cafés and swearing all kinds of self-important oaths. I gave what money I had to the cause, and drank the rest, God forgive me. The Fenians' ridiculous attack on Canada made me doubt. One long sea voyage and a near shipwreck cleared my head.

I apprenticed myself to a Philadelphian shipwright on dry land, and began to work in the hope of sending more money to the family I had abandoned, though I dared not show my face publicly in Harristown for fear of bringing down trouble on your mother. I will admit this much too – by then I had an American wife, no, two. But every quarter I put money in the La Touche Bank for the daughters I hoped to see grown one day. I prospered in the business and in the affections of my employer. I was made the shipwright's heir. Now I—

I had reached this point when Darcy snatched the letter out of my hand. 'His handwriting does not improve,' she sniffed. 'And lately he has changed tack and now he's using his so-called fortune as bait to trap us, a well-known ploy in the swindling classes. He plans to win our confidence with this tall story, this mock-confession! Even your old Mr Dickens could not make up such a maudlin tale. We'd not have him in the house five minutes before all the silver would disappear. Though of course it's hardly likely to be the same man all this time, but no doubt a whole tribe of thieves taking turns to try to have a bite of our purses with this sentimental claptrap.'

'But the writing on the envelope is always the same,' Enda pointed out. 'Does he ever mention a seashell lamp? Or our names? Mam said he chose our names.'

'I've no idea,' snapped Darcy, 'and even less interest. What do we need a father for, with Tristan and Rainfleury providing and providing?'

'But they're taking too,' I said. 'And the things they make us do—'

'Would you have us stop being rich?' Darcy rapped.

'How rich are we?' I asked, thinking of the difference between her bank book and ours. 'The Swiney Godivas, all of us, I mean.'

'I don't believe I said.' Darcy was pulling on her outdoors boots.

Two days later, I took myself to the La Touche Bank, braving its grandeur to enquire about a Phelan Swiney's account, or one in the name of Annora.

254

'There was such a thing,' the clerk confirmed, his hands drumming with nerves on the counter. 'But it was cleared.'

'Cleared?' I asked.

'Emptied. Yesterday, it was. By a person of interest mentioned in the documents.'

'Would that be a Darcy Swiney then?' I asked.

'I couldn't possibly say, miss. And who is asking?'

I already had my answer. The clerk's face was imprinted with the unmistakable punched look of one who had suffered a recent encounter with Darcy, and the pallor of a man bitten by a venomous snake.

And when I saw my own face in the hall mirror at Pembroke Street it too bore an expression of fear and wondering.

If he was not our father, why would this so-called 'Phelan Swiney' give us money? And if he was our father, then Darcy had not killed and buried him. And if Darcy had not done it, then whose was the grave in the clover field that she had so hated me to enter?

31

I f Darcy had taken the money at the La Touche Bank, she made a mighty cover for her crime out of anger towards the robber-photographer Saverio Bon with his hands all over our rightful Venetian lire. Signor Bon had written to ask if we might like to donate some small percentages to the poor nuns in Venice, who'd been dispossessed of their grand convents by Napoleon and were still scratching for pittances decades later.

'The Church?' fumed Darcy. 'The Bon fellow's got the poor bowl out for Venetian nuns, I ask you! It's all your fault, Tristan,' she raged. 'You sent us there to Venice to be taken advantage of and fleeced.'

Oona said mildly, 'It's not as if we're in a pinch now, Darcy honey. We can wait.'

'Is it that you are smarting because of the Grand National?' asked Ida. She told us, 'Darcy had a power of money on a lamed nag there.'

'You took a big bet?' breathed Oona. 'No! Say you did no such thing!'

'A tiny flutter,' said Darcy firmly.

Gathering all my courage into an intake of breath, I voiced an idea that had flown into my head. I spoke quickly without giving the notion a chance to cower. 'Let's turn our Venetian money into a *palazzo*,' I said.

'What sorts of bushes are palaces growing on in Venice? With what Bon will pay us,' said Darcy, 'we shan't afford more than a doll's house or maybe a gondola. Or a straw hat for a gondolier, more likely. However, you are for a rarity right, Manticory. Stone and bricks are a good investment. And it wouldn't hurt to be away right now, somewhere that faking Phelan Swiney hasn't got our address to pester us with his lying letters.'

Mr Rainfleury and Tristan agreed with the idea of property in Venice. Tristan undertook to write to Signor Bon. In the meantime we agreed to a series of bookings in London.

I awaited Signor Bon's answer with increasing anxiety, daydreaming my way through the days, and thinking of Venice and Alexander half the night. The Swiney Godiva shows did not flourish in London. Irishness was out of fashion thanks to some Fenian threats much exaggerated in pungency by the press. We were turned out of the Alhambra Theatre in Leicester Square in favour of Marian the eight-foot-two-inch Giant Amazon Queen. On an outdoor stage in Hyde Park, we were booed and a man shouted, 'Female Fenians!'

I whispered to Darcy, 'Perhaps he's another one who thinks we are the daughters of one Phelan Swiney, Fenian Mariner . . .'

She couldn't answer me as she was taking her bouquet from management. Afterwards, however, I was treated to the full length of her tongue on the subject.

Unable to work, we fell into a lassitude that rendered even shopping a chore. Only Darcy absented herself, returning flushed and irritable.

It was not only myself who was relieved when Mr Rainfleury appeared at our London hotel with tickets for the boat trains and new passports. 'It is done. Your palace awaits you, my queens. Sadly, Tristan cannot attend you. But Mr Sardou has promised to assist. And I'll be there at the first.'

His endearments also fell emptily on Darcy. 'Away with your queens and more of the nuts and bolts. And bricks. What kind of hovel have we got? I want my own bedroom, I'll tell you now.'

'That will not be a problem,' smiled Mr Rainfleury. 'Signor Bon is proud as a dog with three tails.'

Alexander's letter caught up with me at the terrifyingly grand Élysée Palace to which we'd been promoted in Paris. He'd written mysteriously, 'You'll not be humiliated by your new lodgings, Manticory.'

*

257

When I saw what Saverio Bon had done for us, I kneeled and kissed his graceful hand while the sweating porters lifting our trunks up to our floor deplored our parsimony with the tips, operatically calling us 'Barbarian Dogs of the Virgin', quite unaware that I understood them.

Alexander appeared in their wake. 'What do you think, ladies?' he asked.

He was scrupulously careful to let his glance rest equally on our flushed faces.

He exchanged a glance with Signor Bon. I was surprised to see the animosity written on their faces. Of course Alexander was not happy to see me kneeling at the photographer's feet, but there was more to it than that. I promised myself to ask Alexander about it later, but was forcefully distracted by my desire to explore our new home.

We got a sight of *palazzo* for our lire: an entire vine-clad *piano nobile* in a Renaissance *palazzo* romantically situated on the Grand Canal.

When we bought our *piano nobile*, we bought the right to linger in the great hall, where we might sit on benches with black-boards painted in chiaroscuro with cupids in a water-stippled space, lit at night by a ship's lantern bulbous like the thorax of an ant and as large as two tall men stacked one on top of the other. We bought the right to enter the stairwell via marbled corniced doorways that the second man couldn't even reach with his fingertips. We bought the right to open inner gates of such intricate iron filigree that they should have been worn by rich giants as belt buckles. There were seeming splinters of ruby in the windows to our grand staircase frescoed with pastel porticoes on which lounged blonde ladies and liveried monkeys. We had bought the right to clasp our hands around the heads of green lions whose duties were to hold silken ropes in their mouths by way of banisters. And when you finished mounting the stairs, lion by lion, you looked up to a fresco of a painted sky, with nothing more to say than *Good morning, it's a beautiful day – see here's a hint of pink amid the azure to promise you a good heating-up later*. I think that empty fresco was my favourite thing of all.

We had bought gilded red damask that hung like flayed skins from the walls in a walnut library filled with books in Greek and Latin. A dense Austrian-looking crystal-drop chandelier gushed from the library ceiling. We bought a great *salotto* with yellowed painted beams and steps up to a pergola on which we might perch and own four bell towers with our eyes. And from which height the gondolas below were toy boats and the tourists were toy people, their eyes happily raised to the prospect of Rialto Bridge arching its back like a white cat in front of them.

We had bought twelve-foot architraves, and door hinges cast with delicate acorn tips. We had bought bronze rococo door handles. We were set up with an abundance of scrolled gilt candlesticks, armchairs fancy as iced biscuits (and as friable with the worm). Our gilded consoles rubbed up against diseased mirrors so tall that the spiders dangling from the cornices might admire themselves without descending an inch.

We'd bought acres of *terrazzo* flooring picked out in crests, and a mile at least of parquet stained with interesting formations.

Two small *palazzi* had recently been torn down simply to create the elegance of a walled garden with a pool of emerald grass in front of the jade-tinted blue of the Grand Canal.

We had bought an encrustation of amethyst wisteria in the garden and a view of water and marble through grates between nine stone columns.

It did not bypass my thoughts that all this magnificence was created at the beginning of the sixteenth century, when Swineys immemorial back in Ireland were living on oats and sleeping in windowless turf huts heated by roasted dried cow dung, only dreaming of the luxury of a thin goose at Michaelmas. And most of all, I realised that we sisters who had once owned nothing but the air we breathed had now bought air – air trapped in the gloomy heights of the ceilings, the length and breadth of the rooms that made us all look like small afterthoughts.

There was an enfilade of bright bedrooms along the garden side; on the inner linings lurked secret passageways for the servants where perpetual twilight reigned.

Back in Harristown our cottage had been so tight that you couldn't lift your arms without bruising someone. Those same Swiney Godivas – now a little older – who had slept on straw pallets by a turf stove would that night lay themselves down on beds of antique splendour rustling with velvet and silk, made up for them by two servants, after being fed by a cook and served with ceremony and silver plate.

Darcy of course took for herself the chamber on the Grand Canal with the oval ceiling fresco and the marble fireplace of dramatic zebra-striped marble, topped by a gilded mirror that rose up into the sky. Except where broken by gilded stucco work round the windows and doors, Darcy's room was entirely panelled with squares of pocked and plaintive mirror, which refused to offer any semblance of your reflection but threw a dull shine into your eyes.

Berenice demanded the next room, hung with gold-silk damask cutwork in which acanthus and flowers of dull red-gold floated in a gold glossy background. The ceiling was afrolic with satyrs and busy nymphs (one breast being fondled by a satyr, the other giving milk to a cupid), flowers, fat ears of wheat. The whole scene was thickly infested with cupids fluttering the wings of cabbage white butterflies. Curious and impossible architectural forms were rendered in a bilious green around the edges where the ceiling met the walls. But Berenice pronounced it 'perfect' for her. The remaining sisters were pushed through the door to the next room.

'This is mine!' I claimed it instantly. The room was warm as an apricot on an August branch, painted in sun-infused pastels and buttermilky golds. Chinoiserie panels showed impossible Oriental architectural forms rising out of limpid lakes and drooping with spindly trees and outsized convolvulus. Cone-hatted figures bearing delicate standards ran over bridges that led to nowhere, or they smoked hookahs on gnarled outcrops surrounded by water. Each panel was highly peopled, yet every individual was confined to his or her own tiny island, with no boats or rafts to carry them back and forth. The upper parts of painted pavilions were occupied by grand ladies with double pagoda umbrellas, but there were no stairs to convey them up there or down again. My ceiling was stucco strawberries and peaches beaten and ploughed roughly through thick yellowy cream, particularly rich food for the eyes in the vibrant afternoon light.

'Oh no!' cried Ida, pointing. Of course, it was Ida who detected a darker side to those frescoes of a floating world. A man in red stockings vigorously beat his dog with a reed switch. A bound servant raised the terrified whites of his eyes to a master who appeared to be ordering him to throw himself into the depths of the lake. Another dog was caught in the act of a suicidal leap into the infinite water. And who was that hunched man lying in wait for the beautiful lady ascending to the pavilion? How did those rotting branches hold up those towering pavilions? Into what mist-shrouded distance did those perspectives of tufted palms and misty cypresses disappear? Where, if anywhere, did the water end and true land begin?

Then I discovered the best thing about my room – a secret passage behind it that led to the lobby and the stairs, which set me pleasantly speculating until I heard Oona's chirrups and sighs of delight from next door.

Oona's room was so encrusted with stucco that it no longer had corners. It had undulating outcrops, like a bleached grotto. Mother-of-pearl glittered in the tiny tiles in the floor. Oona pronounced herself 'in heaven' with the white marble fireplace that was more ornate than mine, and with the arched anteroom where a bed was made up with brocade hangings. She admired herself in her two mirrored presses. Her ceiling cupids had doves' wings, and the little plump ones sported with the birds, whose feathers were as pillowy and luminous as Oona's own hair. Gilded eagles draped gold garlands of leaves and medallions of laurel-crowned poets.

After Oona's room came the bathroom we would all share and then, by default, Ida's chamber – once a family chapel, still equipped with a kind of altar and painting of a friar in rapture being crowned with white lilies by a nymph. It looked over the back garden that joined our *palazzo* to the teeming streets of San Polo.

'For me,' pronounced Ida.

From Ida's room, one reached a new wing at the back of the garden, tall chambers with painted ceilings looking down to the wisteria and the Grand Canal below. Enda and Mr Rainfleury took those rooms.

I was almost sick with the excitement of the *palazzo*. Within a day, I was already afraid of leaving it. I wanted somehow to make it part of our act, so that even when forced to leave it, I might inhabit it onstage. 'An image of it on canvas as our backdrop?' I mused over dinner served under the lucent gush of a chandelier, with the gondoliers singing beneath us.

But Mr Rainfleury ordered us to keep the palace a secret.

'It wouldn't do to boast, my darlings. A Venetian palace will attract envy. Envious people will want to hurt you. And if you are hurt, if they scent blood, that will excite the hack reporters and bring them swarming to you. Remember that you were not born respectable. You are raised to your current enviable position by my efforts and those of Tristan.' He gestured at the damasked walls with his crystal goblet. He looked shabby in that room; disreputably shabby in contrast to its graces.

'But even we cannot save you from the Grub Street hacks. Those men will bring down every good thing in this world with their busy black scribbles. They are the flies who feed on the wounded, simultaneously poisoning the weakened flesh by rubbing their filthy hands in it.'

He set down his goblet and rubbed his hands in imitation. I looked away. He had succeeded in disgusting and frightening me.

I felt hatred towards all journalists in that moment, that they might prevent me from taking joy in what I had earned.

It came into my mind then, a new Swiney Godiva script about a sordid Grub Street hack who follows seven blameless sisters to Venice, seeks to bring them down with scandal. It is his especial pleasure to destroy their lives and their dreams. Aroused by the story he has invented in the darkness of his brain and the dirty fork of his groin, he pollutes Venice with his own lechery, persecuting a young hotel maid with his unwanted attentions. And therein lies his downfall.

After supper, I sat on the balcony to sketch out the tale in ballad form, distracted from time to time by the waves that swarmed like rabbits in a field below me and the songs of the gondoliers that reminded me of the slow crows in Harristown.

On my candlelit page, my villain met the picturesque, protracted death he deserved.

As I knew from former perambulations with Alexander, every dawn a great whale of a laundry boat came to the dog-legged *calle* that fed foot traffic from the Grand Canal to the street door of the Hotel Squisito in Cannaregio. The laundry boat arrived at six, loaded with clean sheets in bales as rotund as sheep. We'd often dawdled to watch the men – their vigour seemed almost health-giving. They disappeared down the *calle* bearing two or three sheep on their shoulders.

Shortly after, they returned, bearing even fatter sheep of used sheets, which they threw into the hollow bowels of the boat, sheep after sheep, until the boat was piled higher than a man standing on another's shoulders. I remembered from the men's chatter that the end of their rounds took them to Mestre, where the boat was unloaded. There laundresses soaped and rinsed and mangled. The afternoon sun emptied the damp out of the sheets and the women ironed into the night. By five in the morning, the bales of clean sheets were ready to return to Venice.

In my ballad, I wrote of the women's strong arms and their lusty voices singing at their work. I wrote of one old laundress, called Annora, who crossed herself over every joyfully stained sheet. And I wrote of how the villainous journalist is asked by the hotel maid to meet him at dawn at the end of the *calle* where the men loaded the boat with heavy bales of soiled sheets. He arrives at the assignation, ready to pounce. But the canny Venetian girl lures him down to the mossy step. Slight as she is, there's a hammer in her pocket and she knows how to cling to the rusted rope-ring on the wall when her pursuer loses his footing on the slick green moss and falls into the boat. Her white shawl quickly covers the unconscious villain, and she is lightfoot down the street before the men return with the bales of sheets that will cover and suffocate the man, as if a building or a tower had collapsed on top of him, as if Nature herself had intervened in meting out the rightful end of his story, making sure he was smothered by the soft pages of the linen.

It was the most vigorous writing I'd done since *The Cruel Sister*. The words flowed out of me like honey. There was dark humour, wit and poetry in my poetry again, at last.

A few hours later Darcy found me asleep by the Hansen mechanical writing hedgehog, with eighteen verses beside me.

'What's this?' she demanded, casting her eye down the page.

'No, nothing, just another ballad, something maybe for our show, should we ever . . .'

'Oh really,' drawled Darcy, turning to the second page. Her face tightened with surprise. She saw what had happened to my writing. But she quickly masked her surprise with disparagement. 'The part for the dark-haired sister. How does it work? Where is it? Stop wasting paper. I'm sure it's a sight of a price in Venice.'

'And how are the lottery tickets?' I asked. 'Moderate in cost?'

In the middle of our second night Ida's painted friar dropped out of his frame with an apocalyptic clap.

'A small earthquake,' we were told by a servant. 'It happens in Venice.'

'Not enough that the dreadful place floats – but it also shakes!' growled Darcy.

Ida insisted the friar be covered with a nailed sheet thereafter, 'to stop him coming to get me'.

Mr Rainfleury was gone the next day. Venice did not agree with him, he said. The pleading eyes of Berenice, and Enda's searching looks, pleased him even less. We spent a month arranging our new, engorged doll's house to our satisfaction, spending every last penny of our Venetian earnings on damasked linens, vases and ostentatious glass trinkets. Under the gushing chandelier, we dined on veal stewed with cherries, a bittersweet blackened chicory, liver the Venetian way. We were on nodding terms with the waiters at Florian, where we soaked our rolls in chocolate. Despite Darcy's discouragement, I finished my script about the murderous bales of laundry, and smiled every time a boat laden with sheets passed us by.

I saw Alexander for whole quarter-hours at a time alone. He appeared at the *palazzo* regularly to sketch us for the bronze busts.

All too soon Mr Rainfleury called us home to Ireland. *The dolls need you back at work on their behalf. And there's a stack of letters here from some mad chap with very poor handwriting.*

'I'll contrive a way to get to Dublin,' Alexander promised me.

The last thing I packed away was my finished ballad, knowing that by writing a Venetian story, by doing what I did there, by doing it properly again, I had married the place in the only sense that marriage was possible for me.

In Dublin there awaited a frenetic programme of appearances in theatres, department stores and art exhibitions. Despite our tradeswomen's labours, our insistent presence on the edge of Fitzwilliam Square gradually elevated us; we were now on nodding terms with our local lords and ladies. Eminences of the medical and legal profession also surrounded us in the square, and did not shun us. One of the glamorous Butcher girls, who had modelled for an Academy painting, waved to us in the street.

'Don't look so humble when she gives you good morning, Manticory! How is what she did so different from what we did with Signor Bon?' demanded Darcy.

Do you really want me to tell you? I wondered. *Would you really like to have the difference between art and vulgar commerce laid out for you? Do you truly want to know the difference between a Butcher and a Swiney? Between a gentle education and Tristan's training academy? In short, between an aristocrat's artistic daughter and a Harristown girl who sells her body parts?*

Alexander wrote to say that he was detained in Venice by a lack of funds. *And it seems that in my efforts to be near you, I have foolishly painted Dublin Society to extinction. No one else needs a portrait.*

Darcy had refused to advance any more on the busts, and I had to acknowledge that there had been no progress of significance.

Oona sometimes spoke of having a ball, or a soirée, though we still lacked the outright confidence to pull it off. We played at being Quality, experimenting by giving alms to the beggars of Sackville Street, and buying sugar-candy and burnt almonds for the flower girls with their withered blooms, by being rude to the servants and condescending to tradesmen. And I, constantly reworking and refining my Venetian ballad, allowed myself to privately gloat about our secret palace in Venice, imagining the looks on people's faces if they only knew.

Those delusions were quickly and violently extinguished.

Even if Darcy didn't see the difference between Eleanor Butcher and a Swiney, the criminal classes of Dublin knew us surely for low-life dissemblers, and they did not wait long before launching an attack.

P ertilly was assaulted on her way home from the central post office. She was nearly at our door when a masked man threw vinegar in her eyes and hit her on the side of the head with a knobbed cudgel. Then, as she swayed, he used her hair as a handle to drag her to the mews at the back of our house, where he kneeled on her back while he shaved her scalp with a curved dry razor, none too carefully. Pertilly told us afterwards that she lay there a while, her eyes pressed to the cobbles, her faltering hands cradling the back of her blood-smeared, denuded head. Then she crawled out to Pembroke Street and collapsed again at the sight of our grand front door, for she did not feel she had the right of entrance any more.

An elderly gentleman of the Royal Irish Constabulary found the bald Pertilly sobbing in the gutter. He dragged her into the house, her weight being too considerable to permit him a more heroic entrance. He laid her on the sofa in the dining room and took off his small cap and fanned her with it.

No one had missed her, but we came to her now, running down the stairs from our various bedrooms, our hair undressed and streaming behind us, providing all the more contrast for Pertilly's naked poll. I smoothed her dress back down over the secret immensity of her knees, naked in a tumble of petticoats.

I let my sisters do the exclaiming and squealing while I called for Mrs Hartigan to bring hot water and clean rags and ran myself for the arnica and the smelling salts.

Poor Pertilly looks more like a nun than ever, I thought, attending to her cuts. *She has gone away from us. She is alone.* I began to weep at Pertilly's loneliness, and the thought of the violence she had just endured. *Would the man on Harristown Bridge have stolen my hair if he could?* I felt her fear, smelled it in the air. I tried to bury it by holding my arms around her and kissing her face as I wiped the blood from it.

The constable smiled indulgently at my sisters' cries of murder, and calls for the military, telling us that our sister had suffered 'a personal theft'.

'Theft, you call it?' Mr Rainfleury raised his voice too high. I had not known he was in the house. Then I realised that he had arrived on the scene with Berenice.

'It was a great unkindness the scoundrel did her. But nature will replace what he has robbed,' said the kindly constable, quite baffled at our hysteria. 'Pray control your nerves. The poor girl is not dead, my dear sir and ladies. Nor is she seriously injured.'

He adjusted a button on his black livery, and smiled, happy to deliver reassuring news. 'I suggest a drop of brandy for her, and maybe some laudanum.'

'But her hair is dead!' howled Ida. Oona and Enda joined her in all the luxurious abandon of fresh mourning.

'Come, come!' urged the policeman, giving Ida a worried look.

Mr Rainfleury added, 'Sir, you have no comprehension. The girl has taken a body blow. Her dignity and status are assassinated.'

You mean, I thought, *the Swiney Godiva Corporation has taken a body blow to one seventh of its profits. We'll hardly be selling a great many bald 'Miss Pertillys'.*

'But you ladies' – the policeman's eye flickered around the room – 'surely present an easy prey, so you do, with such a volume of hair to tempt one of them maddened hair-thieves. I must warn you that there are such men about. But . . . have I not seen you somewhere?'

Darcy suddenly collected her wits when the officer asked for our names to record the incident. 'The Misses Harris,' she told him. 'Just visiting your fair city from County Cork. Clearly, some violent fit has come over a person of weak wits and our sister was the accidental victim. I agree with you, sir. Our sister's in a fine way herself already, and will presently be up and dancing, I assure you. Let us not make a sorry incident into a tragedy. We'll not be pressing for any extra attention from your good self who must be having a great many awful crimes to be solving outside this house. At this minute.'

She gave us warning looks, and briskly ushered the officer out.

'If news gets out about Pertilly, the Swiney Godivas are dead,' she told us flatly when she returned. 'Now you see the secret object of that pretender, Phelan Swiney. Enda – I know you are still romancing about him. But my guess is he dangled father-hood and money in front of us, just to get close to our hair. And now you see the result.'

'Yes,' said Berenice, '*now* we see the result, Enda.'

'How can you say that Phelan Swiney did this?' asked Enda. 'How?'

Mr Rainfleury shook Darcy's hand. 'Admirable presence of mind in your statement to the constable! As for the so-called Phelan Swiney character, I had not thought him so danger-ous . . .' He strode out of the room muttering, 'And the bookings solid for six months.'

'But what about Pertilly?' I cried. 'She's—'

I was talking to a slammed door.

After the doctor left, having tranquillised her with lauda-num, we filed into Pertilly's bedroom. She sat upright, her eyes lustrous but blank. Her right hand constantly quested towards her phantom hair, recoiling at its lack. We clustered around the bed in silence. Her plain skull was unexpectedly beautiful and delicate. It was shapely. Yet there was something obscene about its baby nature. Without her hair to guard her, it was indecent for twenty-two-year-old Pertilly to display her naked originary self.

'Hide it!' said Darcy in disgust. And Berenice rattled in the drawers for a night-cap, which she crammed over Pertilly's dulled head. Pertilly smiled, swayed and fell back on the pillows with a sudden snore.

'What will Tristan say to this?' murmured Oona.

'Seeing as Tristan is no more poet than I am a lion-tamer, he will say that Pertilly has lost her value – her money-earning power to bewitch – and that it will take her at least a decade to reacquire it,' I replied.

Darcy put in, 'By which time she'll be a long-haired hag and no use to anyone. Without her hair, she will have no pull over the crowd. Do you think they've been coming to see Pertilly dance? Or sing? They might as well come to see a cow bawling and swatting at the flies in a field. They want rich, long hair – they want a woman who is gloriously fecund in the head. Not some old barren-headed, thick-ankled foozler of a baby.'

My hand flew into the air; for the first time in my life I wanted to strike Darcy so badly that my body obeyed my feelings. Enda caught and clasped my hand and shook her head.

Darcy jerked her thumb at the sleeping Pertilly. 'No,' she declared dramatically, 'she's no more use than a bunion presently.'

'We can wig Pertilly?' suggested Berenice.

Ida clapped her hands. 'Yes! Perhaps we can each give a bit of our own hair' – she yanked out a clump of her own – 'and make Pertilly a real Swiney wig, so she will still be a Swiney Godiva and . . .'

The rest of us touched our hair for solid comfort, instinctively unhappy at this idea, and relieved when Darcy snapped, 'Is that so? And what kind of piebald monster would she be with all our hair mixed? Striped like a tiger!'

'She could have a choice of different ones. *The Hairdressers' Chronicle and Trade Journal* says that Elizabeth I had eighty different wigs, but everyone knew it was her underneath,' suggested Berenice.

'Except Elizabeth had a brain and a title. There would be nothing under Pertilly's wig.' Darcy swept out of the room.

'She's very upset,' observed Oona. 'Even for her.'

I spent the night sitting beside Pertilly's bed, holding her hand. Ida and Berenice should have done it, but they were too distressed in themselves. Ida was locked in her room, keening on her fiddle.

The old tribal bonds are loosening, I thought. *Is this the way of things now?*

I picked up Pertilly's work basket. She had charmed fingers at her embroidery, which was as delicate as she was not. I burrowed through it until I found what I wanted: her shearing scissors.

If I cut my hair, there could be no more question of Swiney Godivas. Darcy might be able to somehow deal with one hairless sister, but not two.

I unpinned my chignon and let my hair cascade to the floor. As I had, after the man on the bridge, I held the beak of the scissors over a hank of it. The hair rustled around my throat and elbows. Did I wish to lose this shawl, this shelter I had grown for myself? Might I be as much of an infant in the world as Pertilly seemed, if I was without it? Would Alexander love me without the hair? He never mentioned it, but it was hair that had brought him to me.

I put the scissors down.

Mr Rainfleury's suppliers were secretly briefed with the mission of a wig, and he personally made sure that in colour it was indistinguishable from Pertilly's old hair. But the wig never rooted – in the sense that Pertilly's face never lost its shaved expression. She was no longer able to sing, except ghost songs, as if the phantom of her real hair flew about her, haunting her. And even then she sometimes forgot the words. Dancing was forbidden, lest it dislodge the fictitious hair.

'We must retire her and interview a new sister,' announced Darcy, on the disastrous night when Pertilly returned from the stage with the parting of her wig hanging over her left ear, exposing an inch of the stubbled right side of her head. Enda peered through the curtain and reported people in the audience exchanging looks and whispers, and pointing to their own heads.

271

The interviews for a new sister were conducted with the utmost discretion. Darcy ordered me to place advertisements in publications where maids looked for work.

'Maids?'

Darcy explained, 'We want her humble.'

'You mean we need her to feel inferior?'

'And it wouldn't scald either for her to have a guilty secret entrusted with us,' mused Darcy.

Long-haired, unmarried maids seeking an interesting new situation were invited to send photographs and hair measurements to the post office box. *Hair must fall below knees*, specified the advertisement, *and be of a genuine chestnut colour.* Surprisingly, the post office box filled up with replies, but few offered the vital details of their hair length, apparently believing that they could distract us with glowing characters from previous employers. Those few candidates who claimed the requisite hair length and colour were lured to the post office. There I, my own hair hidden in a bonnet, would accost them first, and draw them into apparently random pleasantries, while Darcy approached and listened. If she found the girl's answers and looks acceptable, she would push a note into her hand, requesting another meeting on a park bench at St Stephen's Green.

Those meetings proved unsuccessful, or so it seemed from Darcy's dark mood as she returned home. Anxious weeks of cancelled engagements passed. We advertised Pertilly as 'indisposed with the influenza' and other illnesses that seemed serious without being life-threatening.

The last girl I met in the post office had more than long hair of the perfect chestnut shade and a pleasant scent of Otto of Roses about her – she also had a swelling below her bodice. I hardly thought that Darcy would interest herself in a girl in such a contentious state. I was wrong. I saw the corners of Darcy's mouth seize up in one of her horrible smiles; the rare brutal highlights appeared in her eyes. She rushed forward and pushed the prepared note into the pregnant girl's hand, saying, 'Three p.m. sharp, mind!'

The next morning she announced, 'We have a new Pertilly. She will join us in four months. We must fend off the curious until then, and perhaps even have ourselves a small holiday.'

'But the girl is expecting a child,' I protested when I had Darcy alone in the music room later.

'And is therefore bound to us for ever. We shall see to the confinement and the little bastard will be placed properly. In exchange, we buy her infinite secrecy. And she has some months to become used to her new name, and to learn to sing. And to do the thing properly, or I'll eat her without salt.'

The desistering of Pertilly was as abrupt as her haircut.

The real Pertilly, Darcy announced, was to become our dresser and hairdresser.

'We shall give her a new name, Pudel, like an Austrian maid. And she must learn to speak with a German accent. Manticory, next time you are mooning around a bookshop, try doing something useful and buy her a German phrasebook.'

I did. And I coached her as best I could. But Pertilly's 'jawohl's were always 'yarvel's and her 'bitte schön's were always 'beetle shun's. The accent would never quite come off, but her new name suited Pertilly very well, perhaps because there had always been an element of Tyrolean milkmaid about her complexion and figure. 'Pudel' cut the front of her wig to create some nose-tickling frizzled bangs. In her case, the fringe did not travel with any baggage of beauty beneath, however. Darcy referred to it as 'the antimacassar' or 'the brothel lampshade', but only when Pertilly was out of the room.

Alexander's presence was requested to retouch Pertilly's face in a new likeness. Two weeks later he was back in Dublin, being sworn to secrecy by Darcy.

We all assembled to watch him repaint our sister's face, using a photograph of the new Pertilly supplied by Darcy.

'Are you sure?' was all he asked, with brush hovering over our sister's nose.

'I am not,' I whispered.

'Just get on with it,' said Darcy.

Later, at the library, he wrote to me: *It felt like killing.*

And I was only happy because at that time every act that bound him to the Swineys, even the murder of Pertilly's face, was one that kept him closer to me. He eked out the new features for as long as he dared, and then he was off again, taking my happiness with him.

33

B y the time the new Pertilly, nervous and pale, was installed in the house, it was hard to remember that Pudel was anything but a maid. If any of us called her 'Pertilly', she was the first to remind us not to do so. 'You have forgot yourself, ma'am. I believe you mean "Pudel", ma'am.'

She insisted on moving down to the lower ground floor. A storeroom next to Mrs Hartigan's quarters was set up as a bedroom and parlour for her. She looked perfectly the part in her white cap.

Pudel was happier than Pertilly had ever been.

I guessed Pertilly had ever thought herself inferior because of her ungainly figure, and it must have been a desperately painful thing for her to impersonate – as she felt it – a magnificent Swiney Godiva, without feeling worthy of being one, to faux-elevate herself from her own estimate of herself – regularly reinforced by Darcy – as bovine, graceless and uninteresting. As Pudel, though, she could lower herself comfortably into the humble role for which she secretly thought herself fit. As Pertilly, she had been a cumbrous nullity; as Pudel, she shone, and her plain looks were a neat emblem of her incontestable efficiency. If anything, her stock rose in the old tribal alignments. Berenice and Ida were proud of her, for the first time.

Pudel was especially attentive to the new Pertilly, grooming the girl's chestnut hair to a living simulacrum of her own former locks. When the new Pertilly developed the first of a series of head-colds, Pudel prepared scalteen for her, boiling a mixture of whisky, water, sugar, butter and caraway seeds in a pot. The new Pertilly was already a far better dancer than Pertilly had been, though some of her gestures were overly florid, and some of the movements of her lower body too frank. Darcy was forever shouting at her, 'Less harlot, more saint, girl!'

Pudel had by now become something of an asset to the Corporation, not just because of her hairdressing skills, but for her extreme formality in answering the door. No one could usher one of Mr Rainfleury's business associates into the parlour with more impeccable dignity.

Pertilly's assailant was arrested six months after the attack. When the constables broke into his home in Wicklow, he was found to have more than thirty switches of long hair in his wardrobe, each plaited and bound with satin ribbons of different colours. I asked to see the prison doctor's report, choosing not to share it with my sisters:

I see in the current subject one of the race of 'hair-despoilers' or 'plait-cutters', as they are known – men who infiltrate crowds of young lower-class women at fairs or horse races and use the dense crowd as cover when they cut and make away with the hair, which they then fondle and idolise in private to have and to hold for ever, unencumbered by a whole and possibly inconvenient woman. Some men merely steal ribbons, or hairpins, but there is a solid core of cutters.

The prisoner has confessed to obtaining intense pleasure from handling the disembodied female hair. His erotic malady is that touching a woman excites no urges in him; indeed it discourages them. Only if the hair is separated from its owner can he find delight in it. And the violent act of separating it from its owner is the height of his joy. As he shears off the hair, he experiences his climactic moment – so obliviating that he is often unable to recall the street or the day on which the crime was committed. When he pleasures himself with the hair at home, it is done by remembering the isolated moment of amputation.

The man had seen Pertilly leaving the ostentatious portals of the central post office. It so happened that a long brown curl had escaped when she paused to adjust her bonnet in the shadow of the pediment. *The statues of Hibernia, Mercury and Fidelity*, his confession said, *had seemed to wink at me, urging me to take a closer look at that young woman with a good five feet of hair. I recognised her for a Swiney Godiva, long objects of my erotic imagination, and her fate was sealed.*

His name was not Phelan Swiney, a fact that I paraded to Darcy.

But she said, 'And do you think that an arrant pretender would use his real name when he tried to tempt us into his clutches? Would he not borrow a name that would attract our attention? It is the same man who wrote those letters, and there is nothing more to be said about it.'

Pertilly's shearing proved we had crossed a dangerous line of celebrity. We had fallen into just that danger Mr Rainfleury had warned of back in Venice – of being overpraised, a thing guaranteed to attract envious anger, parasites and black hearts. Tristan railed to us, 'Money, in the quantities you have it, lives in the light, but it casts a dark shadow. Darkness brings on darkness. There stir low forms of life, who feed on darkness, even capturing what is good and dragging it down below to feast upon. These cannibals of human happiness devour what is wholesome, excreting only what is vile onto the pages of their newspapers. Newsprint is black for a reason.'

Our rivals, like the makers of Hall's Vegetable Sicilian Hair Renewer, had reasons to donate to such a carnivore, or steer his hunting in a certain direction. With every day of our increasing fame, the jealous fates were shaping for us a perfect enemy, a single man who had access to the eyes of many, and who knew how to make every one of them look crooked at seven sisters from Harristown, County Kildare.

34

We almost didn't take him seriously, the man with the shadowed jaw, reeking of cheap pomade, who turned up on a day when the first sharp wind of autumn was stripping the trees of Fitzwilliam Square. He had a leather briefcase and breath to inebriate or kill you. We were distracted, about to depart on a short tour of England with the new Pertilly and furiously rehearsing.

He told Pudel he was a journalist, come to puff our next show. She'd believed him.

'Yarvel,' she must have told him, 'Komm in.'

She ushered him into the green parlour so he might gaze at the retouched portrait of the Swiney Godivas while he waited. The paint had dried on the new Pertilly's face.

Even I would have done the same with the man, suspecting little. Such a call was not unusual. We bestowed rehearsed, formulaic interviews frequently. The Brotherhood of the Hair had lately expanded from the arts into the sciences. We'd had several bespectacled gentlemen come to study us. A Doctor Samuel had deployed our example in a learned article to explain why men could not vie with women in the production of hair. He elaborated on three theories: that the manufacture of manly beards extracted all the necessary hair-producing materials from the blood; that the intellectual labours of men disadvantaged them in the production of hair; that women's scalps were fattier, rendering the integument more agreeable to hair follicles. And he developed a theory of 'conjugal selection', explaining that bald or skimpily tressed women rarely found husbands to breed with (Annora being the exception that proved the rule) and so the long-haired subspecies prevailed. He added the surprising statistic that flaxen-haired women were at a slight discount on the matrimonial market. 'Poets have a preference for fair hair; no poem is complete without a flaxen-haired maid, but prosaic mortals in search of an actual wife seem, upon the whole, to prefer the brown or the black.'

Oona had flinched when Tristan murmured, 'Fascinating!'

Pudel climbed up to the music room to tell us of our latest inquisitive visitor. She handed over his card, which was poorly printed on cheap paper and smelled of a saloon bar.

'A newsman in the best parlour? The class of man you'd not want to meet in an alley! What is wrong with the hall? Or the front step? What is he at now?' demanded Darcy. 'Did you leave him loose among the silver, Pudel? Manticory, this one's for you.'

I was dispatched to give him a few brisk words and some photographs.

But when I entered the parlour, it was as if the air had been removed from the room. He was of no great stature, Mr Millwillis, with undistinguished features. I supposed him about forty years of age. The eyes on him were small and blue, vitreous as any doll's. He was the kind of man who instantly made you feel a poor kind of a thing. This was perhaps the intended result of his air of quiet yet penetrating and contagious cynicism, which assassinated every pleasant sentiment in the near vicinity. Before he'd uttered a word, I knew that the man was a black breaker of spells, a squelcher of dreams.

'Manticory Swiney, the redhead!' he said. 'St John Millwillis.'

Outside, the wind rifled and shook the trees, battering the roseate bricks of Number 1 Pembroke Street. The house felt barely safe. His lips parted and tugged upwards, showing greygreen teeth. He spoke confidentially. 'It was not in fact quite right, what I said to your maid. I am a newsman to my toenails, but I have conceived the idea of writing a book, and its heroines are to be none other than yourselves. And your hair. I thought you'd like to know. I've already done' – he laughed at 'done' –

'the Baboon Lady Julia Pastrana, the ugliest woman in the world on account of her hair, where hair should not have been, and coarse as wire, so it was like a swarming of private hair all over her public body. And yes, my book was a great success with the public, the public that is so moral and backward that it likes to show its own hair only in private!' He grinned. 'Now you Swineys have hair where it should be, but nothing else is quite – shall we say? – in order. A little digging has uncovered some things so dark you need to strike matches to see them. And *that's* just what I've been looking for in my advancing years – a story that will last longer than a column of newsprint.'

He paused for effusions and confusion on my part. Clearly, he was one of those men who believed my hair the most intelligent part of me. He thought that this gambit would frighten any silly Swiney Godiva into a useful revelation. The pause stretched uncomfortably and the grin tightened on his face. I was too afraid to say what I was thinking: that the Swiney Godivas were worth three Bibles in stories, but there were precious few we'd like aired, and none by his hand, on which the nails were bitten and black.

'Did you get the hang of what I'm saying there?' he rapped. 'Gaping at me like a cow who wouldn't know a farmer from a bull? I'm going to put you Swineys in a book.'

Words swam into my mouth. 'I must fetch my sister Darcy to meet you. Pray excuse me.'

His mocking tone followed me out of the room. 'Darcy Swiney? I thought Tristan Stoker and Augustus Rainfleury were the brains of the Swiney operation. Is it not they who direct the Corporation, and harvest all the profits from your hair, passing the money through the filter of their own pockets before you dumb girlies see a sixpence?'

I turned on my heel and marched back in. 'No, it is not like that. Someone has been keeping you going with lies. The Swiney Godiva Corporation is our affair. Mr Rainfleury and Mr Stoker are our respected colleagues, our *accessories* in business. And of course, Mr Rainfleury is *family*.'

How I hated to say that last.

Mr Millwillis grinned as if I had offered him not just a bottle of poteen but a whole still. 'Indeed,' said he. 'Mr Rainfleury is the consummate family man. I've heard how devoted he is to his Swiney girls. How he's thinning on top from wearing his head out on the bedstead with them. Well, it's one way to keep you hairy nymphs under control, I suppose.'

I retorted, 'Mr Rainfleury acts under our direction in all things.'

I do not know how that lie failed to scorch my teeth while passing through them. Mr Millwillis, meanwhile, pointed his dirty finger at me.

'Is it one of those New Women you are, then – aping the female savages of Africa with bits of stick and bone in your puffed-up hair? Reverting to primitive times with your monkey screeches for power! Or should I say that you don't need men, as you have grown your own huge snakes from your head to make up for what a man normally, shall we say, *supplies*.'

'I am not. We are not,' I said with an attempt at mildness. 'No snakes. And no monkeys. No bones. No sticks.'

'Well, *you* personally don't need them, do you? You know what they say about redheads, Miss Manticory?'

I did. So this was the direction he'd be taking. He'd be using our hair against us, feeding his public a savoury combination of old cliché with new imagery. It was a sensation like meeting my doll again, to glimpse Millwillis's 'Miss Manticory'. But the newsman would be selling a quite different version of me, while cleverly trading on the fame of my doll. Her sweetness would be revealed as corrupt. Her hair – I suddenly realised – would likely be unmasked as a traded human artefact. Her passivity would be exposed as a cover for her raging redhead lusts. I would be Lydia Gwilted and Lizzie Siddaled by someone less scrupled even than Mr Rainfleury and Tristan.

Who could protect me? Mr Rainfleury and Tristan? And Alexander, would he revert to the man of disapproving ice?

I nodded to the journalist. 'Pray excuse me. I shall be back presently. With Darcy.'

281

'Dark devilish Darcy,' he grinned. 'The Medusa who ejaculates poison from her snaky hair, not to mention her hot black mouth. Dark Darcy Swiney. The Cruellest Sister.'

I followed Darcy into the parlour as the camp followers must have entered villages in the wake of massacring the Roman legions. She was already demolishing Millwillis even as she trod the first Turkey rug. By the time she was jabbing his chest, she had summed up his idiocy and arrogance with remarkable succinctness. She concluded, 'So you can quench that ridiculous book idea straight away.'

The terrifying thing was that Millwillis remained quite calm. I'd never seen a man face off Darcy before. In fact, if anything, he seemed rather gratified at her rage. I realised with a cold pang that this was because it was exactly what he wanted – bullying drama, intemperance and verbal violence. Of what else are chapters about raven-haired Medusas made?

When Darcy finally took a breath, he said smugly, 'Well, it's of course refreshing to hear your point of view, and who could not revel in its robustness? To twist *the screw of pleasure*, so to speak, even tighter, you're everything I thought you'd be. Satisfying, indeed! But the fact is that there is nothing you can do to stop me. I don't even need your cooperation. I already have my title, *The Breastbone Harp*, and three different publishers agog for a glimpse of the manuscript.'

The full horror of the situation finally reached into Darcy's mind. Her wild eyes fell on me. She declared quickly, 'Well, you would be wasting your time because Manticory here is our resident writer, and she has *already finished* our genuine biography, *The Swiney Godivas, by one of their number! Intimate confidences and secrets revealed! Illustrated with private family pictures never before seen by the public!* Your sordid second-hand production shall wither in its shadow. And of course, our stage performances will combine with book sales most agreeably, as people always like to invest in a little something to take away with them, we find, after enjoying the *authentic* item, on the stage. Your offering, I assure you, shall not have these advantages. Who wants to read stories from a tainted source when they can have the truth from one of the Swiney Godivas herself? Beautifully written, too. Not some hack's scribbles! Manticory has been trained by a poet and writes like an angel.'

She shouldn't have said that. Until that moment, I had, with care, been able to keep the stupefied wonder from my face. But a compliment to me from Darcy – and such a compliment – caused my features to crash into one another as if passed through a mangle. And Mr Millwillis caught it all. He put on his hat and walked to the door, his face a wall but his shoulders shaking slightly with what must have been mirth. With his hand on the doorknob, he composed himself and turned back to address me.

'I shall race you to the publishers then, Miss Manticory. May the best man win. You may have *already finished* your magnificent tome, but I am far advanced in my research with a second draft already at the polishing stage.'

'Fiddle!' spluttered Darcy.

In answer, Mr Millwillis balanced on one leg, held his case up on his knee, opened it and pulled out a sheaf of typewritten papers, thick as a loaf. I thought, *There must be five hundred pages there of all the ills he's laying up for us.*

And I thought, *Does this man know of Pertilly's lost hair and Phelan Swiney, Mariner, and the dusty answers he's been given? Of my own dalliance with a married man? Of the* palazzo *in Venice, even?*

Darcy had no experience of a situation in which her foe was not at her mercy. Only the Eileen O'Reilly had ever presented a threat to her, and the butcher's runt too had been thoroughly vanquished.

'Oh put it away, you silly man!' She snapped her fingers at Millwillis and his sheaf. 'See him out, Manticory. And check the silver candlesticks and grape scissors first.'

She swept away up the stairs with her nose in the air.

He called out, 'I'd send your groom out with a brown envelope to lay a wager on my book coming out first.'

Darcy stopped short, visibly shaking. Then she continued up the stairs. Enda, Pertilly and Oona were peering through the banisters, vainly trying to see the man who'd uttered those words.

'Back to the music room!' shrieked Darcy.

At the street door, I attempted severity and authority with the journalist. 'You'd better not be doing it.'

I was no match for him. He was far beyond me in menace.

'I'd *better not be doing it*? Because it is Darcy Swiney ordered it, so it is not to be interfered with, at the risk of having my scrotum halved?'

Millwillis was his full self now. He was bullying me with everything inside him, the annihilating power of his cynicism, the force of his vulgarity. He was treating me as he would any bastard girl who grew up in shameful want and ignorance in Harristown.

'Why did you come here,' I asked, 'if you did not mean to negotiate with us?'

'Because in your foolishness, you let me into your lives, and now I can describe three of you from the life, and you can never deny that I saw you with my own eyes and heard you with my own ears.'

'Even if you lie about what you saw and heard?'

'Even so. Now hadn't you *better be* hurrying to your desk now, Miss Manticory, to put the final touches on those gilded pages of yours?'

A tumble of leaves wove around his departing feet, their colours disintegrating into rushing dust.

St John Millwillis pointed to them.

'The long summer of the Swiney Godivas is over,' he told me.

35

'He writes for the little people, phooey to him, that Millwilly,' muttered Darcy.

'For the fairies?' asked Ida. 'Is it fairy newspapers there are then?'

'Have you anything at all working inside your head, Ida? He writes for the nobodies, I mean. I've seen his pieces in *The Nation*. The stookawn! The gobdaw!'

'Your mouth!' protested Oona. 'Darcy honey!'

'*We* are the little people,' I reminded Darcy, just as Millwillis had reminded me. 'No one is littler than the Swineys of Harristown. We have no business in Fitzwilliam Square. We are impostors.'

By showing us as little dolls, I wanted to explain, *Mr Rainfleury has made us strangely larger in the public's imagination.*

'Seal those lips,' shrieked Darcy, 'before any more lunacy spills out of them. He's got you all unstuck, Manticory. That wasn't hard.'

How could I make her see what I meant – that we did not carry our heads lined with memories of nannies, ancestral turrets and miniature pony-carriages? We had in our heads the thin geese, the slow crows; in our noses, the smell of the turf stove and the smallest and gnarliest of potatoes draining in the basket. I could still remember thinking the Kilcullen post office a mansion because it had sash windows. Only our hair carried any natural nobility. Mr Millwillis could return us to our original state in one page, in one paragraph of a book printed a thousand, ten thousand times. And what if he found out about Pertilly? And what of our paternity? And what—

'I'll tear out his eye!' mouthed Darcy. 'I'll put it on a tooth-pick and watch it shrivel day by day!'

'But you cannot tear out the eyes of all the people who will read his stories, and you cannot stop their tongues from spreading his tales either,' I said. 'Why don't I . . . write that book you spoke of?'

I surprised myself with my audacity. I did not know if I was capable. I half hoped she'd destroy the idea, which she did.

'Because you are a fool and you'd never write it right.'

'You think Millwillis will write it better than me?' I asked. 'You've been content to act my scripts.'

'Well, there's the Tiger Girl on her back legs at last,' mocked Darcy. 'You know how to fill a page, anyway. Pray don't be stopping on the old scripts, Manticory. Or we'd have to rely on Tristan.'

Ida said, 'Has Manticory died that Darcy is talking so nicely of her?'

I was flattered into muttering, 'A book is a very different thing from an article. A book is for ever. A book would have Harristown in it, and Annora, and the truth about where we came from.'

It would separate us from Tristan's advertising, and Mr Rainfleury's pretensions for us.

Oona whispered, 'Tristan will save us from a scandal. You don't have to be writing a great big book there, Manticory honey.'

Berenice added, 'Augustus will not allow it.'

'No more he will.' Enda for once agreed with her.

But Tristan and Mr Rainfleury refused to pursue Millwillis with threats or writs, a thing I could not at first understand. Then, after supper when I went down to retrieve a book forgotten under my chair, I overheard them rumbling and tittering over their brandy in the dining room. I paused outside the door and inclined my ear towards the slight aperture.

'It could be the making of the dolls, you know,' said Mr Rainfleury *sotto voce*, 'this Millwillis business. The public enjoys a bad woman more than a good one. Subtle changes of costume, you know, more red, more black lace—'

All the blood in my heart ran up to my cheeks. I waited for Tristan to respond with all the rightful misgivings. Something in him had an affection for Oona, at least. Surely he'd show pity for Oona and her poor sisters whose reputations would be smashed, and whose private shame would become another line of doll advertising. Surely, even as a poet, he couldn't allow it.

A hearty guffaw was Tristan's response.

'And that could be the making of the essence and the scalp food!' he crowed. 'The newsman might be doing us a favour. Dirty rags to sumptuous riches always sells. The more the public's imagination is exercised about something, the more they'll lay out on it. Let's get another good Christmas out of them, at least.'

With the proceeds divided between Tristan, Mr Rainfleury and Mr Millwillis, I thought, *their new secret but far-from-silent partner.*

'Let's drink to that, old fellow,' said Mr Rainfleury. 'And how are you enjoying little Oona these days?'

I heard Tristan giggle, and Berenice's name was mentioned.

Glasses clinked.

To the gutter with us, is it? I raged silently. *One of us is your wife. And two of the others are your mistresses.*

I retreated to the green parlour, where my sisters were gathered at the window, looking at Mr Millwillis dawdling under a lamp-post below.

Darcy made a noise deep in her throat. 'Look at him, the old bosthoon.'

Millwillis waved gaily at us and took a stride in the direction of our door. Oona and Enda squealed, stepping backwards.

'If he so much as touches the doorbell,' Darcy shouted, 'the divil a bone in his body but I'll powder it and blow it up the chimney!'

Oona said, 'Tristan would never let him in.'

I thought sourly, *Tristan has already given him the key to the house.*

'Anyway, we're off to London next week,' Darcy said. 'He'll not follow us past Kingstown.'

But Millwillis pursued us on our new English tour. He staked out every hotel. He was to be seen strolling backwards and forwards outside our quarters in the early hours. In London, he followed the fake Pertilly on an excursion to Harrods and cornered her in the hat department. She came back to our rooms incoherent with fear.

Eventually, after Darcy slapped her face, and Oona administered the sal volatile, she stammered, 'He knows I am no Swiney. He told me my real name. He knows about . . . my little one. He's going to put it in the newspaper. By way of building an excitement for his book, he said.'

'Nonsense,' barked Darcy. 'He has no evidence.'

'He has the records of the lying-in hospital where I . . . He has spoken to a woman called Craughn, your old hairdresser. He showed her photographs. She confirmed that I am not the girl Pertilly whose hair she used to dress.'

'Miss Craughn was with us for all of four weeks. Her head is muddled with sniffing the frizzle tonic. Servants always bear a grudge. No one sensible will believe her.'

'He says you are but poor bastard girls from Harristown, born in abject poverty. Pieces of Irish nothing. All feathers and no hat. Not fit for life outside a swinish sty.'

'He'll be stopped,' retorted Darcy.

'He said to tell you that his breath will always be on the back of your swinish necks and that the click of every deathwatch beetle in the night will remind you of the sound of his pen scribbling.'

'Away with him and his deathwatch beetle,' scoffed Darcy. 'Grow a spine, girl.'

But the next morning, the new Pertilly's bed was empty. Her wardrobe, however, was full. She had left all her stage clothes. We cut short our tour and fled, myself with a secret copy of Millwillis's biography of Julia Pastrana wrapped in my nightdress. He had mutilated the poor Baboon Lady in death, as the press had in life. He had faithfully recorded every disgusted comment, every accusation of beastliness, every mocking cartoon ever published about her, and added a gloss of sneering and innuendo about her sexual appetites and her feeding habits.

Back in Dublin, we tried to find a third Pertilly, this time advertising with height and waist measurements to accommodate the costumes already made. We were forced to take on a girl with inadequate hair, which had to be supplemented with hanks of Mr Rainfleury's so-called silk. I feared she would not last – and she did not. Darcy tried to keep her indoors, but the girl was restless. Soon Millwillis was whispering in her ear in a tea shop, and she too was gone.

Mr Rainfleury reluctantly agreed to send the Swiney Godivas into *temporary reposeful retirement after an exhausting round of superbly successful engagements.*

While we reposefully retired, Tristan experimented with a male product, taking in all the competitors to see if we could create a more pleasing mixture than the ever-popular Pommade Hongroise. *For Fixing the Moustache or Beard in any Desired Position.* Mr Rainfleury was unhappy with the results, which hardened his own productions to an enamelled texture and caused the precious hairs to fall out. The project faded away.

Instead Tristan assaulted the press with a round of Swiney Godiva advertising.

'Are we not paying to put money in Millwillis's pocket, rather?' I asked. 'We are giving advance publicity to his book.'

He waved me aside. 'Leave the strategy of things to me, Manticory.'

Tristan set up a Swiney Godiva Marrow and Daffodil Pomade, which was advertised as *Perfumed with precious* extrait *distilled from the choicest flowers and steeped in that excellent transdermal carrier, alcohol.* This was followed by a Lotion for Setting Perfect Swiney Curls. *To be poured into a saucer and applied with a sponge to the roots of the hair before curling.* And a Swiney Godiva Dry Vegetable Shampoo Powder with its own patent sprinkler. *Frees the hair from grease and dirt as effectively as wet-wash.*

None of this feverish production assuaged my fears about the ways in which Tristan meant to capitalise on Millwillis's scandal. I waited tensely for the threatened red costumes, the black lace – but they were not imposed.

It was only gradually that I began to understand that the truth was that Tristan had lost the run of himself. He – and Mr Rainfleury too – far from being sanguine, were now in a white-knuckle panic about Millwillis. Both had longed for the newspaper inches of publicity; neither had feared for the polluting of the Swiney Godivas' reputations. But, in observing the newsman's greed for detail, and his guile, they had finally realised that Tristan's less than gallant behaviour towards Oona might be exposed alongside Mr Rainfleury's failings as a faithful husband. The rash of new products was to milk the Swiney hair for all its gold as quickly as possible: the source might yet be dried up by Millwillis's book. Tristan was too exercised to think clearly about the havoc to our funds and the damage we were doing to the original essence and scalp food. The new products entered a market that was already too crowded. Their very number and variety smacked of desperation, it seemed to me, of overselling.

Then Millwillis published his first article.

Oona came trembling to breakfast, with a bastinade of newsprint in her fist. 'Here is the paper; and 'tisn't much good for us you'll find in it. And you'll never guess who's big with Millwillis now.'

The headline across the centre pages read:

SWINEY GODIVA HAIR SHOCKER – LICE! WORMS!
MADNESS! LIES! COMPULSIVE GAMBLING!
HEAD-SHAVING!
THE SEVEN SISTERS' SECRETS REVEALED
A sensational discovery by St John Millwillis

'Compulsive gambling?' I asked.
'Any lie will do!' said Darcy.
We craned over the paper, flinching, groaning, exclaiming and eventually falling silent.

The worst of it was that most of his story was based on frank information gained by colloguing with the Eileen O'Reilly. Who'd have thought it ever back in our Harristown days that the butcher's runt would have been sent to a finishing school in Switzerland at a rich butchering uncle's bequest when he retired on the sale of his abattoirs in Howth. But I knew that was true – Mrs Godlin from the dispensary had written to tell us. And we'd heard from Mrs Godlin too that the newly finished Eileen O'Reilly had been employed in the uncle's salami and olive import business.

A reliable informant, a close companion of their schoolyard days, reports that far from being the possessors of preternaturally fertile and healthy scalps, the poor Swiney sisters were riddled with vermin, and often half bald with the ringworm.

'No one,' added Eileen O'Reilly, a young lady of business, 'wanted to sit next to a Swiney Nitster in the classroom. Not only were their lice bigger and more plentiful than anyone had ever seen, so they were, but the creatures were also great acrobats and could propel themselves halfway across the classroom, even into the hair of respectable girls like myself. It was something shocking, so it was. It was not their fault, the creatures. The oldest sister, Darcy, was too mean to spend on treatments in case it cost her the price of another frightful new hat for herself. And then of course everyone in Harristown knew that Darcy Swiney was mad as a bull with the staggers and twice as like to go at you. It is the wonder of the world to me that Darcy Swiney's not yet finished in an asylum or a prison. And then we all know the Swineys are descended from a mad king who was condemned to wander Ireland insane and naked till he was put an end to.'

READ MORE ABOUT THOSE FAKING BIGWIGS THE SWINEY GODIVAS AND THEIR PENCHANT FOR MENDACITY IN THE NEXT ISSUE!

[Promised a banner in red.]

IT'S NOT EVEN THEIR OWN HAIR!

And learn more about their lust for power and money, their scandalous birth! Seven sisters with seven different fathers, den

291

of vice in the depths of the Irish countryside. And a fake sister in their midst!

The red-haired temptress Manticory Swiney says, 'Men are just our accessories.'

36

'I'm going to mutilate him into a female,' sputtered Darcy.

'Nobody will want us now,' mourned Berenice. 'And when Augustus and Tristan read what Millwillis wrote, we'll have no one to manage us or make our bookings, or prepare our accommodation or sell the tickets. They'll find other sisters, other hair.'

Oona said, 'They would never abandon us. They are brothers to us.'

But her voice broke on the word 'brothers'.

Darcy snapped, 'Your tiny brains are running away with themselves. We must simply keep out of sight until we can make this go away. If we go on the stage again, there will be advertising and newspaper stories and Millwillis will find us in a goat's leap.'

Ida said, '*Everyone* will want to come see the evil Swineys. I am surprised that Tristan and Mr Rainfleury did not think of that. So if we earn a great heap of money, we could give some to Millwillis, to make him go away and stop writing any more.'

'You mean *offer* to be blackmailed?' Darcy scowled. 'We can't afford him. He'll never stop coming after us if he sees that blackmail works. No, he has stolen our earnings for a while. We must hide. We shall retrench somewhat, cut our firewood expenses, that kind of thing. One less maid. You girls can manage without your pocket money for a while. Pudel can cover for the second maid.'

Berenice said, 'But at least we can have Pertilly back now – she doesn't need to hide any more. Everyone knows what happened to her.'

'No, no,' said Pudel. 'I am happy as I am.'

I thought, *Yes, she is. And there is dignity in her labour, compared with the degradation of public Swineyness.*

Darcy allowed, 'We can call her Pertilly again, so long as she continues with her chores.'

I cleared my throat. 'Why don't I just write that book then?'

'You mean the story of us?' asked Oona. 'The real story?'

I nodded.

'I told you why not,' fumed Darcy. 'Is it that you are all a bit more stupid than you were last week?'

'If we cannot perform and I may not write the book,' I said stubbornly, 'then why don't we go to Venice?'

'Not Venice again,' drawled Darcy disparagingly. 'Always on about Venice, Manticory. You're like a stray cat when it comes to that place. As if you once had a good dinner there.'

I suspected that she alluded to Alexander – I could never be sure that Darcy had not detected or sensed what was between us, as Ida had. Still I managed to bring off a great feat of pretended incomprehension, answering, 'I don't know about dinners. But we do have a home in Venice, all paid for, that will not need a lump of coal burned till October. Thanks to Mr Rainfleury's sharp advice, no one knows about it, not even Mr Millwillis, it seems. The article hasn't mentioned it. We might as well go hide in the Catacombs, it is so secret. And Signor Bon's postcards are still selling so we have funds there too, waiting to be spent.'

'We could remove ourselves very quietly there,' said Oona thoughtfully. 'And maybe Tristan would want to come too, to keep out of the limelight a while.'

'Better still, let's print handbills for a tour of Russia!' said I. 'And say that we are going there. And then travel secretly to Venice.'

Everyone looked to Darcy.

'I suppose Manticory makes a point.' She held up another smudged letter. 'And it would remove us from the charlatan mariner who seems very much inspired by Mr Millwillis's outpourings. Three more of these today.'

She tossed a bundle of letters in the fire, unopened. 'I expect *he* wants to blackmail us too, the species of thing that he is.'

Ida, sucking on her hair, suddenly convulsed and rushed out of the room.

'We must deal with Ida first. She's not fit to travel,' said Pertilly tenderly. 'And the cold is drawing in, ever so fast now.'

'There are doctors in Venice,' answered Darcy. 'Less costly than Dublin ones too.'

Millwillis published another article the next morning: this time he had Mr Rainfleury in his sights. It did not name Mr Rainfleury: but what other Dublin manufacturer had married into a large family and had made himself a fortune that could not quite be fully accounted for in doll receipts? The real source of 'Mr R's' wealth, it emerged in the press, was not the dolls, who were but his pretty pastime.

No, the article revealed, 'Mr R' was deeply and profitably involved with the ill-esteemed hair trade – the obtaining, cutting, selling, bagging, transporting, refashioning and selling of real human hair, a commodity worth five times as much per ounce as real silver.

Until this day, thundered Millwillis, *only the do-gooders and the anti-vivisectionists have gone deeply into where the coveted hairpieces are sourced. Now the free press shall have its say.*

In sweatshops in Dublin, 'Mr R's' workers toil with sacks of hair, each containing the glories of six hundred poor women who have sacrificed it out of hunger, sickness or for vice.

What a Bluebeard 'Mr R' was painted by the article! And what a purveyor of sordidness, employing small boys with fine-toothed rakes to hook clots and tangles of pauper hair from gutters and sewers.

To swell 'Mr R's' coffers, rich women now wear poor women, incorporating them, swelling their natural attractions just as cannibals eat up the substance of weaker beings and fatten on them.

And this is not to mention the switches, plaits, curls and severed chignons 'Mr R' has – knowingly – provided to all the male hair fetishists of Europe; those men, who by a complex conjuring, project their sickening lusts onto dead hair, animate it with their desire and worship it.

Mr Rainfleury disappeared on an urgent trip to Ulster. But we acquired a new protector. A man signing himself *PS* threatened the hack with retribution for his slandering of those blameless Irish roses, the Swiney Godivas. *PS*'s letter, published in full beneath the next article, asserted in picturesque terms that Millwillis deserved a dark destiny for murdering seven reputations, and that *PS* himself was more than ready to serve justice personally.

Every drop of poison ink that he spills is one more danger in his path. He can watch out for himself!

'I like the style of the fellow,' said Darcy.

PS. My thoughts were inevitably pulled to the grave with the crossed spoons in Harristown. Of course our father would have wanted to defend us, were he alive. And the same conundrum defeated my speculations: if it was not our father lying in that clover-scented grave, who lay there?

'Did you notice,' I asked Darcy, 'that his initials are the same as Phelan Swiney's?'

'Did you notice,' she replied, 'that there are a thousand other names you can get out of those letters? If you wanted to waste your time that way.'

Millwillis deployed the letter for his own glory. The newsboys ran along our street shouting, 'Anonymous death threat to journalist!'

'How frightened is Millwillis by this *PS*? What do you think?' Enda asked Tristan.

For once, the master of publicity was silent, and would not meet our eyes.

*

To no one's surprise but Oona's, Tristan regretfully declined our invitation to join us in Venice.

'I shall just have to bear it here,' he sighed. 'Without you.'

By letter, Mr Rainfleury pronounced his presence indispensable in Ulster 'during this crucial period'.

He said, 'Mr Sardou has agreed to see to you.'

Alexander met us at the Élysée Palace in Paris – though he did not room there – and escorted us all the way back to Venice. Over coffee in the train's dining car, he told me, 'I am sorry to get you this way, but it is better than not at all. Is it a frightful thing to say? Is that what makes your lips set themselves so?' He touched my mouth. 'This smile of yours would be hard to paint.'

'It's not a smile. I am distressed that it has come to this, hunted across the Continent. And I am sad that you should find it amusing.'

'You should be angry. You should be furious. I am only sorry that you make me the object of your scorn. We both know it should be Darcy. And perhaps you should look to yourself as well, for allowing her to sell you, to run you and your sisters like dogs at a race, and for keeping all the money to herself. It should be Darcy who sees this outraged dignity, who hears your anger.'

'Money! You too! So if I had my money, could we be together? Is this what you mean?'

The air seemed to bristle around my tight eyes.

Alexander said, 'Don't waste your hate on me! Or is it that you can show anger to me because I am less frightening than Darcy? It is not *my* venality that is in question. Manticory, can you not see the clear path for yourself? You must free yourself. Whether you come to me—'

Clear path, I thought. Well, the contract Darcy had signed could not be unsigned. But was that really any obstruction in my path to Alexander's love?

In fact, I decided, *I shall be with him. He need not know about the contract. It is not relevant. There is no mention of love in that contract. Darcy sold the use of my body. My love is still mine to bestow as I wish.*

'So,' I said boldly, 'come and tell me that again after midnight. In my sleeping car. Oona is taking care of Ida tonight.'

'And you shall be alone?'

'I hope not,' I smiled, one corner of my mouth flittering.

Part Four
VENICE

37

It was as if the train did it.

It was the train, shuddering and screaming through the night, that jolted my naked body against his.

The anger that had driven me to the act still fuelled it until the moment I lifted my coverlet to welcome Alexander in and he lay down in my arms, having shed his clothes in the dark.

'Did you lock the door?' I whispered.

'Yes,' he told me. 'We are safe.'

Then I was afraid. I could not see his face. He had no scent. His mouth on mine had no taste of its own. As he deftly unlaced my nightdress and pulled it over my head, his voice quietly reassured me that I was doing this strange and sticky thing with the person I also loved in letters and looks and by my side in libraries. His hands and mouth were gentle as a hot flannel; he kissed my forehead and told me I was adorable before he turned me over, raised my haunches and pushed my head down into the pillow.

When he roughly unseamed the fabric of my body, put himself inside the tear he'd made, and commenced to move there, I knew he was doing with me what the paying-for men wanted to do to every Swiney Godiva; it was as blunt as the lechery of the beasts in the Harristown fields. I felt as if I was bedded on hot wet earth, rolled in the curses of the world like a newborn snake. Alexander's hands cupping my breasts were cold and brittle as scallop shells. While we grappled, my hair slipped from the confines of its braid and uncoiled around us, the tendrils weaving us together till we kneeled exhausted inside a cocoon of dark-washed red.

'You are thinking too much,' he whispered into the back of my neck. 'Stop thinking, that is half the pleasure of the thing – it defies thinking.'

And he started again, too hard where I was too tender now.

I should not have been thinking. Alexander was right. It was lovely to feel Alexander's body aligned with every inch of mine, to feel his skin, that was not pale and delicate in the dark. Without the light, it felt strong and full of the jungle's breed of darkness.

But it was not quite lovely. For whole seconds at a time it was delicious, and then my thoughts fell out of their clouds. But the constant quickening too quickly died away. The sensations were ticklish to the point of being sickening; Alexander's pitiless rhythm found no answer in them. So the pain of the impalement would not let itself be forgotten.

I wanted to see Alexander's face instead of the pillow into which I was being pounded. And that longing spoiled even my bits and pieces of pleasure, rendering them wistful, though we were doing the very thing that was supposed to bind men and women the very closest they could be.

How could I stop thinking? I thought of Eve eating her portion of God in the apple, and my biting down the Body of Christ in the chapel of Harristown after I lost my faith. Alexander had broken faith with his wife to do this with me. And I – who had condemned Tristan and Rainfleury for their lubricious marketing of our bodies – I had just broken faith with the moral creature I'd been in judging them. These fragmented faiths drove my thoughts to Annora. I wondered if she'd known any pleasure in the couplings that created her daughters. Even the first coupling? Was it as awkward as this one? Had Annora learned to stop thinking of God while our father or fathers seeded her with daughters? I then commenced to worry that I might have inherited my mother's fecundity.

My body made one more cry for completeness, but Alexander growled something in a language I did not know, and collapsed on top of me, pushing my nose into the wood of the bedhead. He wiped my back with the sheet.

I dared not weep, lest he took it personally. I felt nothing but the dumb agony of that collision for a while, and then the loneliness of not being built for the kind of love that Alexander seemed to wish on me.

By the time we arrived in Marseilles, a few hours after Alexander left me, I had abundant, vivid proof that our coupling would be without any tangible issue. I threw the stained sheet out of the window.

I gave him the news as we breakfasted on sweet shared air and newly shy long looks in the dining car. Alexander kissed my hand, spoiling my relief. Perversely, I wanted him to regret it.

My feelings about the act of love were equivocal but I had no doubts that I must have Alexander lying next to me again, stroking my forehead and kissing me. I would get used to the part he seemed to like best, the part where he turned me over. I promised myself that. A first time was bound to be awkward, I told myself.

I did not want him to think that I did not love the way he loved me.

The best way to achieve that was to tell him about the secret back stairs to my Venetian bedroom, and my thoughts on their use, and about the gates that were never locked at the *palazzo* and the apartment door that might be left slightly ajar last thing at night. His tired eyes widened. He smiled.

'And will you –?' I asked brazenly.

'I shall obtain what is needed, and we shall not worry again. When will you talk to Darcy about freeing yourself?'

But now my sisters began to appear in the dining car, tousled and lamenting the jolting night they'd passed in their travelling beds. Ida did not appear.

'Better she does not, the creature,' whispered Oona. 'She's in a bad way there.'

All through the night, Ida had suffered continual convulsions. Oona reported, 'In the end, I gave her from the laudanum bottle, and now she sleeps at last. I hope I did right.'

303

Saverio Bon was waiting at the station, with all the practical arrangements already made. As soon as he saw Ida, he called for two porters to improvise a stretcher.

He bowed stiffly to Alexander. On me, he unleashed a frank smile which, given the night's events, I found impossible to return without blushing.

'Welcome home to Venice, ladies,' he said, looking at me with concern.

'We'll see about that,' sniffed Darcy. 'It's only your Manticory that's happy as a cat in a tripe shop here. The rest of us come strictly on sufferance.'

Signor Bon was unable to contain his amusement.

'Why,' demanded Darcy, 'is the man grinning like a robber's dog?'

Oona nudged me. 'He's not laughing at Darcy,' she whispered. 'It's her calling you "his" Manticory that has his face split in half with joy.'

Alexander glowered beside me, his eyes little chips of ice.

My plans to demand my share of the money were set aside because of Ida's illness.

'*Temporarily* set aside,' I told Alexander that night. 'It would be heartless to provoke Darcy when Ida needs all our attention.'

Seeing the doubt tightening his eyes, I told him, 'Stop thinking.'

I myself was trying to stop thinking when we lay together. I did not care for my thoughts, especially those concerning my own hypocrisy, where Alexander would eventually lay his head and what would be said of me if this behaviour were found out. I put those unlovely images aside, and listened to Alexander whispering from behind me that I was a sweet creature. I heard myself telling him I loved him, and his answer of, 'Yes.'

The creaks and groans of the old *palazzo*, which were continual, masked our own noises. Again I found myself carried to the brink of not hearing anything – but then some movement of Alexander's, or some pause, returned me unwelcomely to sentience, and I felt him inside me as I had known the grinding of prayers in chapel and the fumbling of hunger in my belly as a child.

The nights continued so. The only difference was that sometimes the familiar Venetian earth tremors rocked us, releasing little showers of white stucco. And then we heard Ida weeping in her bedroom, and Oona soothing her with tender words soon afterwards.

Ida had taken immediately to her bed, rising only to rush to the water closet for mysterious and vociferous purgings, which she would allow no one to witness. The fiddle was strangely silent. Whatever she vomited up had a strange effect on the *palazzo*'s drains, which seized up. For several days, there was always a plumber in the place, disconsolately bent over a pipe or lifting the floor for a hopeless inspection.

We came in a convoy to demand an explanation from Ida.

'What is the matter with you?' demanded Darcy. 'The next plumber's account will come out of your postcard stipend.'

Oona pleaded, 'Ida honey, you are in the worst discomfort there. If you won't tell us, will you explain to a physician? Surely it is some wicked thing strangled inside you and there'll be a bottle of something that will soothe it on its way.'

Darcy mused, 'The photographer says the Scottish surgeon by the bridge is reasonable in his rates.'

Ida lay silently in the bed, sucking the end of her plait, until Darcy, as ever, yanked it out of her mouth.

The next morning, Ida locked herself in the water closet again. Oona and I stood outside pleading, while she retched for two hours and then fell silent. Darcy, who would have wrenched the lock out of the door with the strength of her fury, was engaged with fittings at the hat-maker's, so I sent for the plumber and he sent for two gondoliers, and they called in a carpenter, who summoned his apprentice boy, who – now properly supported by four other specimens of manliness – assaulted the door with an axe until the lock dangled on a pin. Ida was found collapsed with her head halfway down the aperture of the water closet and the wooden lid half closed on her head. She had stuffed the torn pages of three newspapers into the bowl. In the meantime, I had summoned the Scottish surgeon, who had her carried over to his nearby rooms on a litter.

'I must open her up,' he told Oona and myself half an hour later. Ida lay on a wheeled bed in the next room, convulsing, with the plait still in her mouth.

'A small incision,' he promised. 'I have located the source of the difficulty. I can feel a lump the size of an egg. It is probably undigested food of some kind, but it may be a malignant growth. I must have your permission, ladies.'

'Cut Ida?' said Oona faintly. 'In the middle of her?'

'Come, dear! I am no butcher. It will all be done with the utmost humanity and liberal amounts of chloroform, and a lady nurse in attendance. I would go as far as to say that if you do not permit me to do this, then I cannot answer for your sister still being alive by midnight.'

A particularly eloquent paroxysm twisted Ida's body at that moment, seeming to beg us to release her from the pain.

'We must let him do it, Manticory honey.' Oona tugged my sleeve. 'We cannot lose her, the honey. And if Ida dies before Darcy gets back, it will be our fault there. And haven't you the brains of the world in your head, and so you must know what to do.'

By the time Darcy returned from the hat-maker's the sun had set – and Darcy was, I noted, without any sign of a new hat and looking rueful. Hot on her heels were the surgeon and his apprentices with Ida on the stretcher and something in a glass jar. He settled Ida in her red room. Then we received him in the library. He set the glass jar on the table under the foaming chandelier.

Oona had to rush from the room, but the rest of us gathered round to peer inside the jar, where a neat brown sphere floated in a clear liquid. A small tail trailed underneath it, like the plume of a bedraggled hat.

'Ladies, I present a trichobezoar of sizeable proportions. In layman's terms, this is what you might term a "human hairball".

306

Your sister has Rapunzel syndrome,' announced the surgeon. 'This is an intestinal condition in humans that results from the eating of hair, a condition recently named as trichophagia. The eaten hair accumulates in the stomach, eventually causing distress. I was obliged to remove the main offender from her stomach, and extract its tail from her small bowel.'

Darcy pulled a handkerchief out of her sleeve and covered the jar. 'So that's the end of it,' she announced.

'I'm afraid not,' said the doctor. 'Trichophagia is sometimes associated with a known hair-pulling disorder. I took the liberty of examining your sister while she was under the chloroform, and I discovered that she is unusually hairless about the arms and legs, and in the private areas where hair is normally manifested. There were inflamed patches of skin that seemed to result from violent depilation. I must ask you, her closest and dearest, does your sister Ida pull her hair?'

'Darcy usually pulls it for her,' muttered Berenice. 'Her head hair, anyway. Ida also does it herself, when she's scalded in her feelings.'

'Which is quite a deal of the time,' I observed.

Enda added, 'And 'tisn't today or yesterday that it's been happening with her. It has been so since Ida had hair enough to pull. That's how long she's been pulling it there.'

'Aha,' said the surgeon. 'Then it is no wonder. Both conditions are a rarity, I must say. I have not personally come across either before.'

'This is not the kind of rarity we want to be!' Darcy snapped. Then her expression mellowed. 'But it might be useful, I suppose. Can we keep the hairball, Doctor? It could be described as a "Phenomenon Never Before Seen".' She muttered to herself, 'Perhaps we can present old Ida as the "Human Cat"?'

The doctor raised his grizzled brows. 'I feel that you are not quite grasping the seriousness of the thing. Your sister might easily have died. Trichobezoars are gravely hazardous since human hair cannot be digested. By which I mean that it will not pass through, and, ahem, be excreted from the human gastro-intestinal system. As your poor sister demonstrated, vomiting, while effective in cats, cannot remove a hair mass from the human stomach. If your sister continues with this, and another hairball forms, I cannot answer for her surviving it.'

'Can Ida be made to understand her habits are suicidal?' I worried.

'Self-inflicted!' raged Darcy. 'Sabotage! We would not survive losing another sister!'

Darcy seemed to believe that her aggression could keep the Swiney Godivas functioning. I wondered at what point she would give up conniving and contriving our continued existence. Pertilly's scalping had not deflected her. Millwillis had not dampened her belief. Anyone else would have long since given up. But then Darcy was not troubled by doubt.

Will she give up when I make my stand? I thought. *When I leave the Swiney Godivas?*

'More to the point, Miss Swiney,' the doctor reproved Darcy, 'we must think of the source of the problem, not how to exploit it! Your youngest sister is of a tender and excitable disposition,' he warned. 'This mania may be triggered by depression of the spirits or anxiety. Sufferers have recorded an increasing sense of tension before pulling the hair and gratification or relief in the act of ripping out the hairs. Your sister pulls and sucks on her hair, I've no doubt, as some small children suck their thumbs.'

'For which there are known and effective punishments,' mentioned Darcy.

'And punishments may be part of the syndrome for her. I would suggest that there is a strong tendency to masochism in your sister. I mean a desire to be hurt by others.'

'I always thought it was a solid comfort for her to curse her and yank on her hair,' said Darcy defensively. 'The worse, the more she likes it.'

'It may not be so easy to wean her from her disorder.'

Meanwhile, Darcy's eyes began to glimmer. She marched the doctor to the door, saying, 'I'm sure you'll not be feeing us for the privilege of being exposed to two marvellously rare conditions! I've an excellent idea for making sure this doesn't happen again.' Darcy walked downstairs with the doctor, fastening her bonnet on as if donning a helmet for war.

'Come with, Manticory,' she ordered. 'And bring the sewing basket with the lid that fastens. Oona, fetch some forcemeat from the kitchen. And a lantern.'

That night, we roamed the streets of Venice, looking for cats. Darcy strode resolutely, calling, '*Mici, mici!*' in an authoritative voice. 'Where are they?' she complained. 'The place is rotten with felines normally.'

It was mild and moonish. Oona and I walked behind Darcy, who undulated like a black snake through the narrow alleys. I was unsure as to whether to rejoice or worry about her newfound interest in the creatures, which she'd previously decried as 'perfumed rats', including the stuffed black cat that had supported her coffin act.

Eventually a few cats responded, though with an air of doubt. Even when Darcy spoke in a petting tone, the cats raised their tails and took to their four heels. Darcy was hunting something in particular. She rejected tabbies, marmalades and calicos before we found what she was after – a cat of monstrously long fur, sitting on the wall of the Palazzo Soranzo Cappello's beautiful garden. The cat was soon tempted to earth with the forcemeat, whereupon Darcy bundled it into the sewing basket. Its yowls had windows being thrown open above us.

'Run!' gasped Darcy, and we fled to a dark *sotoportego*, where the cat's cries echoed.

'But the creature belongs to someone!' Oona protested. 'It's no stray. It is loved and spoiled. Why, it even has a little paunch there. Someone's heart will be broken.'

'We have a need,' said Darcy. 'It's for Ida. It's her cure. Home!'

She set off resolutely in the wrong direction and it was no small thing to change her mind about the way.

At the *palazzo*, she performed her straight-legged walk through the garden, not noticing that I, having contrived to trail slightly behind, had left the gate off the latch. Upstairs, Darcy turned right from the main hall towards Ida's room, with the basket under her arm.

309

'Don't follow!' she warned.

'Should we go after her?' asked Oona.

'There's no harm in a cat. I'm so tired,' I told her impatiently. 'All that running about. An early night for me.'

A few minutes later, Alexander was climbing the stairs and slipping through the servants' corridor to my apricot room.

It took us a few days to see what Darcy intended with the cat. I doubted if the creature would be going home so in that interval I left a note at the Soranzo Cappello to say that I had found it dead and buried it in my garden. I hoped to save the cat's owners the pain of searching for it fruitlessly.

Darcy had delivered the cat to Ida's bed, where it settled quite happily, with no apparent nostalgia for its Venetian family. Like all long-haired cats, it groomed continuously, and within a few days, dosed with paraffin, it brought forth a spectacular furball directly upon Ida's counterpane.

'Clean it up, Ida!' ordered Darcy. 'Oh look, there's another one coming.'

I called the cat Caramella because of her toffee-coloured eyes. Berenice called her Brigid. Oona called her Columba. Darcy, of course, prevailed. The cat was finally named Kitty like every second cat in Ireland (the ones of the male persuasion being called Captain MacMorris). Despite her unreliable looks, the cat proved herself useful. She was particularly prone to hairballs, so that Ida had to be constantly clearing up the acid-sauced missiles that the creature ejected with so much drama and so many unpleasant vocalisations. When she was not engaged in her expectorations, the cat spread herself into seductive odalisque poses. She also dispatched two rats, bringing Ida the heads.

Ida was quickly cured of sucking her own plaits. I judged the moment right to approach Darcy with the speech I'd rehearsed with Alexander in whispers under the coverlet.

But then Kitty went missing and was found limp and strangely sodden under Ida's bed.

'How could she drown on the third floor?' wept Ida, cradling the cat.

There ensued a passionate argument about what to do with the corpse. It was Berenice who told us about the lime pit in the garden next door – she had always enjoyed gardens and spent hours daydreaming of Mr Rainfleury, I assumed, as she sat among the flowers with her Italian phrasebook.

'It's an old well, blocked at the bottom. Someone stole the well head. The neighbour's maid told me that for years the people in this neighbourhood have brought their dead animals there. There's even a dipper and a bucket of lime with a lid all ready.'

'In a pit?' Ida wept. 'Poor Kitty!'

She rocked the dead creature in her arms, sobbing.

I put in, 'Well, there's nowhere to bury a body in Venice. You can't dig a grave – it's all stone. They take the humans to San Michele island. And after a few years, the dry bones are taken away in boats.'

'Let's take Kitty to San Michele.' Ida clapped her hands. 'Let's have a grand funeral at midnight with candles and gondolas and flowers and a flautist and . . .'

'Let's not pretend to be any madder than we are, shall we?' Darcy snapped. 'The lime pit shall do very well.'

She picked up the cat by the tail, whisking it out of Ida's arms. Her casual handling reminded me that Kitty had accomplished her task some days ago and was in Darcy's eyes redundant and indeed had the day before committed the crime of chewing the expensive egret feathers off one of her most fearsome hats. I struggled not to suspect Darcy of harming Kitty but gave up. She was chivvying Berenice, 'Come, show me your vertical cemetery.'

Ida cried, 'Give her back! I haven't finished loving her! Let her lie in peace with me a while longer. There should be prayers at least, and hymns, and we should let our hair down, and I shall play a dirge—'

'I think you need a little drink from the old black bottle, and no, I don't mean the scalp food!' Darcy kept a small vial fastened at her waist for whenever Ida showed signs of embarrassing us.

The laudanum failed to dull her obsession with a cat funeral.

When Ida began to rave of a cortège of horses with ostrich plumes, Darcy took her to the island of San Servolo, where Venice kept her lunatics. Ida was admitted for observation. But the doctors made the mistake of taking away her much-thumbed copy of *Lady Audley's Secret*. Ida bit and scratched, drawing blood. When we came to visit, she admonished Darcy, 'There'll be many a dry eye whenever you're dead and gone, you white slaver!'

'We can do nothing for her,' the doctor told us. 'We could cut her hair, perhaps.'

'Darcy will cut your throat for you if you do,' remarked Ida.

The doctor shook his head. 'The weight of hair may be exerting an unhealthy pressure on her brain.'

'You will hand over our sister,' Darcy said icily, with me translating.

Released from San Servolo, Ida took to visiting the railway station.

'To be with the other sad people,' she told the policeman who found her the first time we reported her missing. The next time she disappeared, we went to the station and there she was. It became her daily excursion, and she was sometimes gone all day. We decided to let her have her way, so long as she bound and hid her hair under a bonnet before she left. The policeman promised to keep an eye on her, and stop any criminal from smuggling her onto a train. As I loved to walk around Venice, I took on the task of going to Santa Lucia to fetch her home for supper every day, walking from Santi Apostoli down to Santa Fosca, still raw with wounds from the new street recently smashed through the ancient clutter of the city.

I soon realised that Ida was just one of a tribe of women who attended the station every day, smartly dressed and armed with reticules and expectant expressions. They scoured the disembarking crowds for a face. These women were not prostitutes, but, like us, poor in menfolk, poor in diversions and poor in human affection. I guessed that they hoped to find someone who, even for a second, even if mistaking them for someone else, would be pleased to see them. Stations are the loneliest places in the world if you are alone, so these brave ladies went to the epicentre of loneliness to confront it and do battle with it. The one thing they did not do, however, was acknowledge one another. So Ida never waved goodbye to them as I escorted her out of the station, and they pretended not to watch her. Some of the older ladies had daughters or nephews of their own who came to take them home after a long day's longing.

Those with children were the fortunate ones. It seemed to me that ageing ladies gravitated to Venice in those days, probably because she delivered living proof that one may be decrepit and yet still seductive. The staled skin and bunchy lips of the old ladies were pleasantly set off by the peeling paint and fading colour of Venetian walls. But there was a difference. Life had devoured Venice with gusto. There were traces of the pleasure of consumption everywhere, in the tired leaning of the buildings and the exhausted state of the sheets hung out to dry. Unlike the ladies, Venice did not spoil as she rotted. She ripened, continually.

And sadly, not all the ageing ladies at the station had been devoured or even nibbled. Many, I guessed, were under-tasted and would die that way. Unfortunately it does not dull the sensibilities and the ego to become older and less lovely. The unadmired hour is longer and more painful by far than the youthful, flirting one. But even these dull, unadmired ladies, reeking of low esteem for themselves, of not being needed, even these women found their abbreviated, tight little joys in Venice, and I was happy for them.

Darcy did not agree with me that Ida's new occupation was harmless. When Ida started playing her fiddle at the station, and people began throwing coins into her case, Darcy commenced a voluminous correspondence with a 'private hospital' in Dorset. A month later, we were waving Darcy and Ida goodbye at Santa Lucia Station. Alexander accompanied us.

For some reason, Darcy wanted to take Ida all on her own.

She was leaving without giving me a chance to say what I needed to say about my money.

'She knows what you want,' Alexander said quietly to me, while waving and smiling at Ida, who perched happily inside the carriage. 'Your sister's malady is convenient for her. She's trying to avoid you till she calculates how to deal with you.'

'No,' I told him, forgetting to whisper in my panic. 'It is more likely that Ida's inconveniences have put her in Darcy's black books.'

Oona looked at me with horror; Berenice too.

'Hold tight to the rails on the boat,' I called up to Ida. 'Do not lean out of the window on the trains.'

Darcy appeared behind Ida, her ghastly black hat like a pirate ship on her head.

She saluted us without a smile and pulled down the blind.

38

Letters came from Darcy, who had taken rooms in a board-ing house next door to the private hospital that she now openly referred to as an asylum. I was shocked but also relieved. There could have been another outcome, the one that I had suddenly feared at the station.

Like the doctors at San Servolo, she wrote, the English physi-cians claimed that the heaviness of her hair was distressing Ida's poor brain and causing *an imbecility of the stomach*. Moreover, Ida's capillary system stood accused of *uttering secretions* that had *exposed her entire function to derangement*. Darcy fiddle-sticked and phooeyed these ideas with her usual bravura, but I thought her handwriting showed signs of lowered spirits in the uncertain rhythms of its descenders. Usually Darcy slashed at the paper like a swordsman.

The doctors at the asylum, Darcy reported, saw Ida's hair as a kind of excrement. *Her femininity is as a disease to her because of it, they say, dirty dogs themselves! And with what I'm laying out on the place, too!*

Hat money, I thought. The asylum is costing Darcy hats.

Darcy's next letter told us that the doctors had overruled her and shorn Ida's hair. *I came in this morning and found the thing done!* she wrote in angry strokes.

Done in the night. They did not ask my permission. They are sorry now. Oona, do not tell Tristan. I forbid it.

So off it came [she continued]. *Ida screaming like a piglet, you'll not be surprised to hear. It took four nurses to hold her down, they tell me. Now she looks like a gormless little boy in a nightshirt. And she wanted to send the whole lot to Mr Rainfleury for the dolls. Imagine! Now we are looking for some kind of useful employment for her, to stop her dwelling on the cutting.*

As Oona read out that letter, irrigating it with her sorrow, I imagined the sound of the shears at their work, the dark snakes winding themselves around Ida's feet. I wondered what it would feel like to be without the soft cloak we'd all worn since childhood. Pertilly did not need to imagine. She cried openly, remembering the attack on her in Dublin.

The shearing cure did not work as the doctors had promised. Inside Ida's clipped head, her brain continued to grind like old men's teeth. Darcy's next letter told us she would stay a while longer and extract some kind of compensation from the doctors.

'It's to avoid you she's doing this,' insisted Alexander. 'There's no reason for her to stay. It's clearly not out of tenderness for Ida. Darcy has bone where her heart should lie.'

Of course Oona could not resist whispering the tale of Ida's shorn head to Tristan, who was in Venice on a brief visit to collect our signatures for some banking documents: she would do anything that might loop an intimacy around him. It had the opposite effect. She came home alone from Caffè Florian with reddened eyes. Tristan would not speak civilly to any of us the next day. When we accompanied him to the station, he was still muttering darkly that the cutting of Ida's hair was but a re-enactment of evil Oriental practices.

'Ridiculous superstitions. Ida won't be any less mad without her hair. All she's lost is her womanliness and her modesty. They might as well throw away the key. The loss of her liberty is nothing compared to the castration of her hair! If this gets out, the essence sales will be castrated too.'

'Tristan honey,' began Oona. 'Let us not be having that language there.'

'I but evoke the ancients. In the sanctuary of Astarte in Byblas, the women were obliged to shave their heads annually, to mourn the beautiful murdered beloved Adonis. If they refused to give up their hair, they were forced to service the men –

strangers to them – who clustered at the temple at that time, and to sacrifice the earnings from these copulations to the goddess.'

'Copulations there?' said Oona faintly.

I pointed out, 'Darcy says there are only women patients there. There are no men clustering in the expectation of prostituting madwomen.'

But Ida found a man in the asylum: the butcher.

Darcy's letter arrived the day Tristan left. I read it out to my sisters. *'Ida has already acquired a dreadful reputation for being no end of a girl after the men about the place.'*

'I thought Darcy said there were no men there,' worried Oona.

I raised my eyebrows and kept reading:

'So when she started making sheep's eyes at the butcher – a great haunch of a fellow himself – I steeled myself for some painful discipline. But it turned out she was more interested in the meat. As we all know, she's good with her hands, and she has a talent for dressing veal and pork, trimming the fat, dicing the lamb for stews. The doctors regard Ida as a small risk with the old hatchet and she turns out to be quite a creditable bone-chopper. She spends her day among the dead pigs and sheep without a flinch. The only thing is that she will talk to the leg or the ribs as she cleaves them, saying, "Take that, sir!"'

Her way with a cutlet or a ribcage was astoundingly neat. The butcher, Darcy told us, regarded Ida as a prodigy and left her to these one-sided conversations.

'It is beyond vile!' squealed Berenice. 'Ida up to her armpits in dead animals there.'

No, I thought, *it makes sense. Ida is of the earth: she liked watching the geese getting married, she scented my animal attraction to Alexander. She is physically strong, too, and the exercise of it will help calm her.*

Darcy meanwhile sought to revive Ida's interest in a more decorous pursuit – her old talent for sewing with hair. At first,

Ida used her own shorn hair for these projects. Her early work consisted of simple braids in patterns, but soon she was embroidering. The hair was woven and stitched into an album. Darcy reported how when other inmates came to visit Ida, she would demand snippets of their hair, which she would incorporate into her work. Sometimes she would chop the hair to powder and glue it on like tinted pigment. Or she would lay colourless wax paper spread with glue over pulverised hair, and then cut the hairy page into mosaics with which to make patterns. She graduated to jewellery, embroidered cushions, tiaras woven from hair.

I imagined the hair in Ida's hands, taut with desires or grief. But I also nightmared of those hands, bloody from the butchery table, ripping the hair from other heads.

Darcy secured a continued supply of hair for Ida by putting an advertisement in *The Times* for 'hair-readings'. Innocents were invited to send a five-inch tress to a post office box to receive free character readings.

When Ida was set up with enough hair for a large repertoire of projects, Darcy came back to Venice. It was Alexander's suggestion that I should warn her that the longer she stayed around Ida, the more likely it was that Millwillis would snuffle her out.

'Darcy has a way of drawing attention to herself,' he said.

Meanwhile Millwillis was rising. He'd secured a job at the *Pall Mall Gazette*. He'd been distracted from the Swineys for a while by even more exotic assignments including a child slavery scandal and a society divorce.

But I was sure – and Darcy was surer – that it would be only a matter of time before the world dried up its supply of sensations and Millwillis returned to the lucrative Swineys and his book. Meanwhile, Darcy's insistence that all was now perfectly well with Ida was undermined by a parcel that arrived from the asylum.

Inside were four cuts of an indeterminable meat, being green and putrid from their fortnight's journey, but perfectly stripped from the bone. Beside them was a triangle made from drumsticks, with a little bone to play it.

Ida had embroidered a letter in hair to accompany it. Stippled with dried blood, it read: *Even the Eileen O'Reilly would think this fine work, no?*

'God help us if the Eileen O'Reilly ever found out about it,' said Enda.

'What makes Ida think of her?' I asked. 'And she so long out of our lives?'

'I hardly know,' Enda replied. 'Except that we must think of her with that Millwillis, slaughtering Swineys with all the terrible words in her, butcher's child that she is.'

39

I was ready with my much-refined speech about my share of the Swiney funds, but the morning after Darcy's return, I found her leaning over our *palazzo*'s balcony, busily shouting at the passing tourists in their gondolas. 'Yes, nice house? Very nice house! To be sure your *pensione* is sad and shabby compared to this! And then whenever you go back to your own homes, neither are they as nice as this palace, eh? Yes, gape away, it's very nice up here. Verrry verrry nice indeed.'

I tried to shush her, hanging back in the shadows of the room. She laughed. 'Here's a good one!'

She turned back upon her prey. 'You peasants! You Sunday trippers! Who cares what you see? Is your pleasure worth anything? Go away, you are cluttering up the canal.'

A pretty woman waved up at Darcy, confused. Darcy screamed, 'You are more ugly than the Hag of Helistree!'

I tried to warn Darcy that her exuberance might peel away our cover.

'We're supposed to be incognito. If you were shouting off the balcony in pure Italian, even then that would draw attention to us. But in English! With Irish curlicues! Do you want Millwillis to hear about this?'

'What do you suggest?' she snarled. 'From the deep well of the brilliant mind in you?'

The speed of panic upon me, I conceived another idea for our concealment, one that was actually an improvement on mere skulking and hiding ourselves. Darcy, I suggested, could wear a maid's uniform and mob cap like Pertilly's if she must sit on the balcony and scream. And so must I or Berenice or Oona if we wished to take the sun and the view there. And we were to appear no more than two at a time.

Pertilly, who hated Mr Millwillis more than anyone, because it was she who had first opened the door to him, saw the elegance of the plan and soon had us outfitted. With our hair bundled up in the caps, and in our black stuff dresses with aprons, all of us, and not just Darcy, felt a sense of freedom and naturalness.

I was gratified to see the bait quickly taken by 'Lady Abroad', one of the female scribblers who came regularly to Venice. In a column in *The Times*, which arrived in Venice a few days later, she wrote of the phenomenon of a pair of mad maids known to inhabit a certain *palazzo*, who, abandoned by their Venetian mistress, had taken to the balconies.

In the same issue, on a different page, it was reported that the famous Irish Swiney Godivas were on one of their frequent tours of Russia, where they were a great sensation. Tristan fed such stories to the press as often as possible.

'Lady Abroad' then offered us a nice free advertisement, for our Swiney Godiva Hair Essence, 'a universal favourite on the Continent', and for Mr Rainfleury's dolls, as 'highly prized as Irish cut glass by foreigners'.

I flung the newspaper in front of Darcy. 'Look – let us hope that Mr Millwillis is reading that! That's another month we're free of him.'

She gave it the barest glance. 'Look at the time!' she cried. 'The lottery draw is in half an hour. Come along, I'll need you to translate for me when I win.'

I was disturbed by the avidity on her face as she waited among the patient Venetians for the draw, and by the fury when her ticket was not chosen.

On the way home, she bought a sheaf of *cartelle* for the *tombola notturna* from the lady seated at the newspaper-lined table in the shadow of the Procuratie Vecchie.

And when I launched into the first words of my speech about our money, she simply held up her hand. 'Not now, Manticory.'

With her other hand she was scrabbling in her crocodile reticule, which was crowded to the brim with losing *cartelle*.

'Has Darcy cast a spell on you, Manticory?' Alexander asked me in the dark.

I had pulled my head from the pillow, having renounced the waves of wanting, and was contenting myself with adoring his profile and stroking his hair, having insinuated one of my legs across his thighs.

'All these months, and it is never the right moment, is it?' He brushed my caressing fingers aside. 'All I hear are Darcy's reasons why you should not speak – it's Ida, then it's Millwillis, then it's the lottery she's just about to win and must not be distracted from. Has she Medusaed your mind, turned your brain to stone?'

'There is a contract,' I answered at last. And finally, slowly and hesitantly, I told him about the document that bound me to the Swiney Godivas and the Corporation.

'A contract? Why can it not be undone?' He picked up one of my curls and pushed a finger down it, separating the strands in a smoothness of motion.

'Like this,' he said. 'Contracts are not stone. You're of age.'

'My sisters don't know about the contract. I came across it . . . by accident and I never told them. Which was cowardly, I know. But if I break up the Godivas . . . what would be the fate of my sisters if I left them to the tender mercies of Darcy and Mr Rainfleury and Tristan? I would not know where to start with—'

'You never know how to start, do you?'

Abruptly, Alexander disentangled himself from my limbs, rose and paced naked round the room, running his fingers around the faces in the violent paintings on my walls. The sun was beginning to rise. He picked up his clothes and thrust his limbs inside them angrily.

Wherever he lodged officially, he hardly ever slept there, rising from my bed early in the mornings to creep down the servants' stairs to the garden.

I'd made him a copy of the gate key by then.

He rifled in a pocket and handed it back to me now, saying, 'This is not as I pictured it should be between us, Manticory.'

'Why does it make such a difference, whether I have separate money or not?' I pleaded. 'There is nothing to stop us being together, really, is there?'

What I meant was that I accommodated every wrong thing, his unknown lodgings, the secrecy, the lack of a defined future. I accommodated even the act of love. At first I had made love with Alexander because it kept him coming up the stairs, and my bed was the only place we could be alone together. The parts I enjoyed best were still the tender preliminaries, which had become increasingly abbreviated before he turned me on my belly.

'Nothing to stop us,' he repeated bitterly. 'Nothing. If you but knew.'

'Well, tell me then, what I should know.'

He turned away from me.

'Where is it you are going? Home?'

I had kept Elisabetta's *palazzo* under surveillance many times but I never saw Alexander walk back into it or out of it. I had taught myself to believe that he slept in his studio, wherever that was. He never invited me there. Alexander, who owned and knew everything about me, did not answer questions about its whereabouts. I pictured a narrow divan and a shared water closet on the stairwell, with everything ordered as elegantly as his clothing and his hair, which never tousled even on our most vigorous nights.

Elisabetta looked prosperous in her clothes . . . so he stinted on himself, giving her all his earnings so that she might go about in every possible elegance? It made little sense, unless he did it from conscience – yet he seemed to feel no guilt towards her; only resentment.

Alexander's silence on where he lived made me sympathise with the shadow-wife Berenice had been all those years, the wife without rights either to recognition or information. Nor did I own Alexander; his presence in my life was as fragile as this, our first real difference of opinion.

In the dawn light, his fairness now took on the purity of ice, his hair white as a shroud, the shine of his eyes flat as glass. I remembered how the first time I met him in Dublin the snow-flakes had glittered unmelted in his hair.

'Where are you going?' I begged him again, holding up the key like a wand.

He did not answer.

I threw the key across the room and curled up in the bed, listening to his light footsteps on the stairs.

Was he on his way to Elisabetta's *palazzo*? I pictured a danger-ous journey for him. He did not quite reach her as he had left me. Along the way, he lost a leg to gangrene and an eye to an attacking gull. In my elaborate fantasy, he did not die, but he became less than he was, and needier. He could no longer paint or go about the world, so he needed the comfort of love. And he realised that the person he needed around him was myself.

The vivid strength of my fantasies only reminded me of my pallid impotence. And at the same time as I cursed Alexander, I was in dread of something happening to him.

Revenge is an imprecise tool, of course.

'. . . And my entire share of the money should be put in my own account. It is impossible that anyone could hold us legally to that contract. We can have a lawyer unpick it now I am of age myself. You see, I have read it . . . I shall stay in Venice – and—'

Until that moment Darcy had lain in her bed like a marble knight on a tomb. She had listened to my speech in silence, allowing my voice to falter and dwindle.

'You read it, did you? Poked your nose among my private papers, did you?' asked Darcy with quiet menace.

She surged up from under the bedlinen, striking the back of her head against the wooden bedstead. 'Oh you shall stay in Venice, shall you? And you made all these grand plans on your alonesome, is it? Or did you perhaps plan a romantic escapade for yourself? And that romantic escapade is functioning to a nicety for you, is it? That you came into my bedroom so early to disturb me with it?'

Her voice grew sweet and husky. 'Manticory, we have not had a sitting for those dainty bronze busts in how long? I have a fancy to sit for Mr Sardou this afternoon. I shall send for him. I believe it would calm me.'

Darcy has his address? I thought. *How is that, when I do not?*

I told myself, *She has Elisabetta's address. That is not where he lives.*

'I shall see you in the drawing room at four,' she told me, rising from her bed and thoughtfully consulting her image in the many mirrored panels of her room.

'But you did not answer me about the money,' I protested.

'No, I did not.'

Darcy left the house soon afterwards. She was gone all morning, and came back full of gaiety. I guessed she had collected on a ticket at the *tombola*, or bullied her tailor over his account.

As the hour for the sitting approached, Darcy sent Oona, Berenice and Pertilly on separate and extensive errands about the town.

Alexander arrived at our apartment as the sun was draining out of the afternoon, his eyes darting with questions. Darcy had detained me beside her for the previous hour so I could not intercept him at the gate or in the hall. I'd had no way to let him know that I had carried out the speech designed to engineer my independence – or to explain the attenuated result.

Darcy said, 'Ah Mr Sardou, how good to see you and your sketching block too. Today I think you should concentrate on Manticory and myself.'

She turned her head in profile.

'Draw!' she commanded. Alexander crouched on a footstool and began to weave grey lines on paper.

'You are a friend to this family, and I have decided to trust you,' she told him. 'Mr Sardou, I fear I must burden you with some painful revelations. Everyone gives out that Ida is the mad sister of the Swineys, but I must tell you that Manticory here is the one who gives me the greatest trouble. It is the old problem with the red hair, I suppose, the old whore-itch. She has tried to cover it with a veil of false modesty, but poor dear Manticory, well, she's a *broiler*. I regret, always fussed up and humid about some fellow or other.

'You flinch, Mr Sardou? I'm so sorry. I suppose she's been making love at you too? I feared as much. She *will* keep doing that to men. No matter what I do, I fail to put the shame on her entirely. Please don't let me stop you working, Mr Sardou.'

I could not read the thoughts concealed behind Alexander's expressionless face. Was it a mask of contempt for Darcy's manipulations? Was he remembering that it was I who had summoned him to my compartment on the train? Was he wondering what kind of decent woman would offer herself to a married man – or any man – so frankly? It was I who had given him the key to the *palazzo* gate and asked him to obtain the necessary items to ensure that our pleasures were fearless.

Could it be that he was even now asking himself, *Was I really the first for her?*

Darcy leaned towards him and took his hand. 'Pray do not think badly of our wild red Manticory, Mr Sardou. It is an *animal* thing in her. An abnormality of nature. She can't help it. Look, she cannot even speak.'

The fact that I could not seemed to confirm everything that Darcy said. Alexander's head was averted. I could not see if his pale eyes were stained by the images Darcy had painted for him.

Darcy leaned forward confidentially. 'I actually had to drag Manticory away from a man on a bridge when she was only thirteen years old!'

'It wasn't like that!' Even I was aware that my broken tones and my blush seemed more like guilt than any other thing.

'So she always says,' purred Darcy, 'whenever I've had to rescue her from a bridge or pull her from an adulterous bed at the last minute or even after it. Ah, yes, all this has come to pass. A great grief to me as her elder sister, I assure you.

'Oh, Mr Sardou, you've hardly done a thing on the bust today. Not even a proper sketch. Are you leaving already? Such a shame.'

326

Alexander bowed to Darcy. He opened the door. Then he shot me a single look from under his lashes, full of complicity and understanding. He told Darcy, 'I will not listen to such foul things about Manticory. It is not my business to hear them.'

My skin prickled with relief. He had not believed her. Of course he had not. And now he was leaving, out of loyalty, to stop her polluting the air with any more of her filth.

I rejoiced, *Darcy's intervention will bring us back together.*

'Watch his dust,' mocked Darcy. 'The long legs on him wishing to carry him so fast in the opposite direction of you, Manticory. No, stay, Mr Sardou. I have a few more things for you to hear, even though, of course, *you have somewhere else to go.*'

Alexander turned, visibly apprehensive.

Darcy rose and put her arm around me so that I smelled the acridness of her armpit. In tender tones she said, 'You're no great things yourself, Manticory, but at least you've shown a charming lack of interest in money until just this morning, as it happens. So you'll be sorely disappointed to hear that it turns out that our dear artist here is something of a fortune-hunter! Did you know that he made a point of marrying an heiress? I have been to call on the lady this morning, a pleasure I've delayed far, far too long.'

Alexander's pale face filled with dark-red blood.

'So charming and attractive she is! May I compliment you on your lady wife, Mr Sardou? You say nothing, but of course I can. A perfect Venetian *nymph*. She speaks excellent English, Manticory. In spite of the fact that people like myself are naturally retiring, the lady and I got along quite famously. Such a wonderful hostess, she is. Lucky Mr Sardou, *at home* he has the finest of eating and drinking.'

Darcy watched my face keenly for pain. I could not hide it. That Alexander was fed by Elisabetta was hurtful to me.

'The lovely Mrs Sardou wanted to know every detail about us! She told me she was quite convulsed with curiosity to see a Swiney Godiva show, and that somehow the pleasure had evaded her. When I told her about how her husband has shown such a passion for *drawing* you in particular, she was inspired to thank me for the information, the loving wife that she is. So understanding, so quick.

'Why that demented look, Manticory? Love! It's a class of feeling that men and women have for each other. Perhaps you've heard of it.

'And I'm sure you already know, with you and Mr Sardou being *such friends*, the happy news his wife told me this morning. She is expecting their first child! Starting to show a little under that lovely dress of hers. No? You had no idea, Manticory? It seems that our Mr Sardou is as full of secrets as a priest's ear. I had always thought him rather bleached-looking, like a man without bowels. But anyway, there was a baby in him the whole time,' she sniggered.

Alexander held tight to the door handle, looking as white as her description.

Darcy irrigated him with more of her venom. With an awful smile, she told me, 'Mrs Sardou informed me, in confidence of course, she now plans to keep him on a tighter leash. He's a light character – you could blow him off your hand, she says. She'll be cutting his living allowance now so as to stop him from floating too far. Keeping him short of the old folding – well, apparently it always works to keep him close to home. Only thing that does, apparently. There was an actress in Rome, you see . . . and a singing prodigy in Paris before her. He has a taste for showgirls, she says. Showgirls he can't afford. Naturally, he's never really earned from his art. Everything he makes he spends on his tailor. An eternal infant, she calls him. But so fondly! He'll have to be educated into being a father now, she says, and start behaving like a proper married man of their class.

'And, Mr Sardou, one last thing. For this thing is all of a piece. There's a contract, you see, that binds Manticory to the Swiney Godivas. Recent events have made me believe that you know of it. Why, even if I were to be so irresponsible as to wish to free Manticory to pursue her own perverse destiny, there's nothing I can do. Her behaviour since childhood dictates that I must keep her near to me, as she is not to be trusted in the world alone. There is something missing in her, something of decency, something of continence that binds a proper woman to her chastity . . . that I would hate to have to prove in a court of law on account of the embarrassment it would bring down on her – the man on the bridge, and all such and so forth. Indeed, even you your pale self might have to stand up and swear to how she has comported herself with you. I would hate to have to do it, and let it become a matter for the vulgar press, who already have a great interest in us. But I would, to protect Manticory, if I had to.'

She would. I saw that he knew it too, in the set of his lips and the way that his eyes travelled frantically around the room except in my direction.

'So, Mr Sardou, I must tell you to go hunt a fortune else-where, or reconcile yourself to a long marriage, for it's my belief you'll never get your hands on Manticory's money. The Swiney Godivas are not disbanding now or ever. The tide will go out on hair, which it will never do, before there is an end of us.'

Alexander did not say goodbye. He opened the door and left, stiff-necked as a fighting dog.

40

I heard the *portone* close downstairs. Alexander was no longer in the *palazzo*.

Darcy laughed. 'Don't you just hate the sound of a door slamming?'

It is not true, I told myself. *There is no baby.*

But Darcy had seen the belly. Alexander had not denied it.

'A baby?' I asked, stupidly.

'Would you like to keep up, Manticory? Yes, your Mr Sardou's wife is positively wide with child.'

Elisabetta must have tricked him into a baby, I told myself.

Probably it is not even his. She has a lover in Paris.

I could not look at Darcy. I could see only Alexander and myself, before Darcy said what she had just said, before he had walked out, to go home to his pregnant wife.

A fragment of anger, sharp and slender, broke free from my heart and then stabbed me. The baby was real. The marriage was real. Alexander and I, our being together, that was the thing that was not real.

And Alexander was a coward.

Darcy had done him a favour, telling me about his baby and about his financial dependence on his wife, supplying with malice the truth he'd lacked in courage to admit to me. Had he meant to break free of his wife, if I could supply the where-withal? He had returned the key to our gate when he heard about the contract that kept my teems of money in thrall to the Corporation. Returning the key was all the decency and honour he thought necessary in parting from me.

I had a sensation in my chest from the Harristown days when Darcy used to sit heavily upon my back to crush the poetry out of me.

'You seem out of sorts, Manticory. Why is it that I am always the one who brings bad news?' Darcy was musing. 'And the one blamed for it? Don't be looking knives at me, Manticory. Haven't I just done you a great favour myself? It is ironic, is it not, that the most suspicious sister, the one who always doubted our true patrons, should prove the most gullible of all? You accused Rainfleury and Tristan of making clowns of us. But who made a clown of your heart? You do not look as if you are appreciating the irony, Manticory.'

I would have found out about it, I thought, *and it would have broken me by whatever means the blow was delivered.*

'Perhaps you can make a ballad out of it?' she asked. 'Something about the poor abandoned backwoods girl from old Ireland? Who thought she'd ensnared her heart's eternal love? But finds he's just a great feckless fellow of an artist who had his eyes on her cash all the time.'

I felt it again, afresh, as if I had just heard.

I sank into one of the armchairs, clutching its damask arms, choking on dust.

'By the way, Manticory, have you heard from Mr Sardou?' Darcy asked at breakfast two days later. 'I cannot imagine why he shuns our company so, when he used to be so fond of it. Of course he has other old irons in the fire. I don't suppose we shall be seeing much more of him anyway. I have a feeling that he has fallen out of love with the idea of the busts.'

No, I had not heard from Alexander. Three more days passed. I was running mad with his silence. I craved an explanation from his mouth. Surely I was worth that, at least? I could not accommodate how bloodlessly he had abandoned me. I could not accept what that ease told of his feelings for me, all along.

Alexander's silence was tangible as ice, brutal as a blow that repeated and repeated, automated and heartless. It had more intensity to it than his presence, clouting me into silence of my own.

I settled into a gaunt misery in which hope refused to become utterly extinct; the wound was continually scraped of any healing closure. I told myself that two tiny minutes alone with him would undo the vicious lie that Darcy had stitched together out of several truths. All I needed to do was to find him. I wore my feet to blisters on circuits of the places where we used to meet, certain that his feelings for me would lead him to one or other of them, and that I'd find him there, a hopeful face raised every time the door opened. But Venice seemed empty of Alexander. Desperation devoured my dignity to the extent that I asked Signor Bon if he knew Mr Sardou's whereabouts.

He frowned, offering unwillingly, 'I saw him in Caffè Florian yesterday.'

Do you mean 'them'? No one goes to Florian alone, I thought.

'And I saw your sister Darcy coming out of a house where there is . . . forgive me, gaming, on a grand scale, where money is – ah, you do not wish to hear?'

I did not wish to hear about Darcy. I thought only of Alexander, whose absence filled my bedroom every night; his lost voice filled up my ears when my sisters chattered about our imminent return to Dublin for a month – there was certain intelligence that Millwillis had been successfully duped by our advertising and was looking for us in St Petersburg.

Enda came to me. 'Why do you want to be free of us? Is it for Mr Sardou? But Manticory, my dear, he is not for you. You know that, don't you? His wife is a noblewoman. Now that she knows he has dabbled with a Swiney, she will put a stop to it all. You will tell me that she does not love him. But she loves her social position and she won't want it known that her husband has been . . . with one of us. So why leave us, Manticory? Where would you go? What would you do? Don't leave us just for the sake of leaving Darcy behind you.'

Enda lowered her voice. 'I know you cannot hate him yet. That may take years. You cannot even believe that he is second-rate? You still think his love is just outside the door, don't you? My poor darling.'

I struggled out of her embrace. She looked at my face. 'Very well, I shall talk to Augustus for you. Surely we don't need to be bound by a contract after all that's happened . . . I shall work on his better nature.'

The fact that Enda still believed in Mr Rainfleury's better nature made me turn away from her, stiff with pity for the both of us. We were both women who were not loved, but she still pretended while I was already deep into a translation of myself as a woman unworthy of love.

Oona, also still pretending, shared my berth on the train. She was in a fever at the prospect of seeing Tristan again, full of wistful fantasies of a sweet reunion.

I was glad of her company, and the distraction of her happy prattling, for I was terrified of the pain of being in the sleeping berth on my own, and of the memories it would bring.

For once, I was glad to leave Venice. I was exhausted from false glimpses of Alexander, from trying to contrive ways to find him and turn myself back into the person he loved.

There is nothing so cruel, I thought in those days, as a beautiful city that is determined to hide your lover from you.

'It so hurts,' Oona whispered to me from under her sheets, 'doesn't it? Can all the hurt girls in the world add up to a single happy one?'

41

A meteor was seen in Dublin on the evening of 13 September 1876. The sky had faded to marine colours when it was pierced by a vivid light that pulsed more slowly than lightning. Then a streak of flame shot from the north-west to the south-east.

At Number 1 Pembroke Street, there was a different conflagration.

The gas pipe had failed out in the street and we were reduced to candles. Tristan had given Oona a brusque half-hour of his time in the withdrawing room, and left for an evening engagement. Mr Rainfleury was away on business – truly away and not just hiding with Berenice. Enda had returned to Number 1, as she always did.

Whenever Enda was with us at Pembroke Street, we observed the old rituals, one of which was a mutual washing of our hair. In those times, we mostly dry-washed it, massaging a cleansing agent through our scalps and then using a towel to extract the residue that emerged. But once a month we performed the full wet wash and applied Liquide Antiseptique, a hairdressers' solution of petroleum, to strip the grease. Darcy refused to remove her frizzled fringe hairpiece and washed it alongside her real hair.

If any Brother of the Hair had been privileged to glimpse us on those occasions of follicular déshabillé, he would have been convulsed with pleasure. After washing the hair, each of us, in our tribal alignments, combed the hair of our preferred sisters while it still dripped, squeezing the excess water into the claw-footed tub. And then we carried our damp hair in cotton turbans to the green parlour, where we unwound it and laid it out on stools and chairs to dry by the hearth.

We drank cocoa and talked while the fire – at a discreet distance – rendered the room cosy, and warmed the crisped the tendrils of our hair, from which the delicious petrol fumes rose, twisting up our noses like the spiked scent of lavender. Of course we knew better than to use the heated curling tongs on our hair until those vapours had evaporated. We had read of the risks in the *Hairdressers' Chronical and Trade Journal*. So we would slowly and gradually allow our hair to dry in the warm air. And when we were sleepy from the fire and the hot drinks, we would ascend the stairs to our bedrooms.

That night, as I have said, we were reduced to candles. By the uncertain light of those candles, Darcy, sitting awkwardly in her chair, had ordered us to sign some documents that were impossible to read.

'Just a formality. Why would you be needing to read them anyway?' Darcy chivvied. 'You wouldn't understand them.'

'But I'd really like to know more,' I said.

'Well, good,' said Darcy, handing me the pen and guiding my hand to the paper.

Alexander would hate to see me doing this, I thought as I signed. But Alexander had not manifested in person or in letter since Darcy's revelations. Whatever Alexander hated, now, that was what I would do. I felt too low to resist the rush of downward sensations in my ribcage as I passed the pen to Berenice.

The signing done, each of us held a stump of wax in a japanned candle-holder, shielded by a hand, as we took to the stairs for bed. Pertilly led the way, followed by Oona and then myself. Next came Enda, chattering about her latest gift from Mr Rainfleury – a sable stole. She did not notice who was coming behind her. If she had seen it was Berenice, who had received only a fox, then she might well, unconsciously and instinctively, have swept her petrol-vaporous hair over the shoulder furthest from her twin's flame.

But she did not.

'Enda!' Darcy's voice boomed from below. 'Stop right there!'

335

Then Darcy was galloping up the stairs towards her, pushing past Berenice, raging that Enda had forgotten to sign the document downstairs.

'Or maybe not forgotten! Just too high and mighty to bother, is it, Mrs Rainfleury? Of course you think you know all about contracts now, you interfering little . . .'

So Enda had broached the contract with Mr Rainfleury, as she'd promised. But he had betrayed her yet again, by telling Darcy. I threw her a grateful, compassionate look.

'Supposing I don't care to sign this particular contract?' Enda said over her shoulder. She kept climbing the stairs. Darcy charged after her. My heart beat fast for her. Darcy was not above administering a painful slap, even to a married woman.

Darcy pushed Berenice out of her way. Fugitive sparks from Berenice's candle flew upwards. The fire started in the middle register of Enda's hairfall, at the place where it covered her waist. It was simple but fatal misfortune, the inquest would be told later, that the moment the hair caught light, our maid opened the door to the coal man in the basement. The draught from the cellar door sent the ends of all our hair floating upwards. Having got vent, the fire travelled simultaneously along Enda's length both upwards to her head and downwards to her feet, snatching her nightdress up in a gyrating fin of flame.

It was too sudden for a scream. Enda's own lips were sealed with horror. But it was not the fire that killed Enda, though a look at her burn injuries afterwards would make you wish a speedy death upon her. It was the fall. For somehow Enda tumbled over the banister from the height of the thirtieth step. It all happened too quickly, and in such a thick web of malodorous smoke, the unforgettable stench of fire devouring Swiney hair, for any of us to see how Enda managed to surmount the banister on her own. Why she would have done it was another question, when she was just steps from our bathroom and its stout taps of life-saving water.

Although what led up to it had remained unclear, we would all have the image branded unforgettably on our eyes of Enda falling with her hair flaming above her, falling like a pale china angel, like a burning torch.

And it was like a pale china angel that she broke on the broad stone flags of the ground floor. She lay star-shaped on her back, her neck stretched to an unnatural angle. Her hair fell about her with the flames making dance, the only part of her that was still alive when I arrived down at her side.

'No!' I screamed. 'No!'

Water drenched me as I bent over Enda: Pertilly, at the head of that file up the stairs, had dashed into our room and was now pouring the contents of our ewers down onto Enda's burning hair. White columns of water wove down through the pulsing, stinking smoke.

I beat out the remains of the flames and lay full-length in the puddled water alongside Enda, holding her in my arms. Oona threw herself down on the other side, our arms meeting around Enda's unbreathing breast. Pertilly ran down and hovered in the outer circle of grief, her breath rasping. Mrs Hartigan was with us now, keening. Berenice was still up on the second floor, peering down the stairwell. Darcy stood next to her, motionless.

'I cannot spare you!' I wept into the ashes of Enda's hair. 'Not you too, not now.'

I raised my eyes to Berenice's stricken face hanging like a winter moon in the darkness at the top of the stairs.

'Smile!' I told her. 'Have you not at last got what you've always wanted – not to be a twin?'

'Hush, Manticory honey,' sobbed Oona. 'It does not help Enda.'

'Nothing will help Enda,' said Darcy crisply. 'If only she'd not flounced off without signing those documents. I am sure it was the flouncing that carried that current of air up the stairs.'

Alerted by telegram, Mr Rainfleury arrived back in Dublin the next morning, a destroyed creature.

He removed his hat and showed us a shaved head, obscene and pink. His eyebrows were gone too, and the moustache.

Pertilly rushed to inspect it. 'Not a hair and not a hair's friend, either!'

'So the Egyptians, the gods of death themselves, honoured their loved ones,' he moaned.

'Are you in drink?' asked Darcy.

Even now, I thought, *he aggrandises himself through Enda's hair*. His cranial growth had never been strong, more a suggestion of hair than an expression of it. I thought acidly that removing such a sparse growth as his made a disproportionately large claim of capillary bereavement.

My bitterness could not be contained. I must have said something aloud, for he ducked his head and looked away.

Berenice rushed to him, sobbing, but he had thrust her aside, demanding, 'Where is my poppet?'

'I am here,' insisted Berenice shrilly. She whispered, 'And I shall be here for you from now on, Augustus dearest.'

Darcy muttered, 'Better the leavings than nothing at all, is that it? You could show a drop of dignity yourself, Berenice.'

When Berenice put a hand on his sleeve, Mr Rainfleury shook it off.

'No,' he said coldly, as if she were a street hawker, 'I want my wife.'

'Is it that you're gone mad, dear Augustus?' pleaded Berenice.

'I am not. Grief has at last rendered me sane. Be gone from my sight, hussy!' He raised a shaking hand and struck Berenice a blow on the face.

The sweet foulness between the twins was what had kept him interested, I realised. One long-haired twin would be not half, but less than half, of what he had enjoyed before. He had loved the illicitness. Mr Rainfleury, that pallid, drooping man, had adored to creep around back staircases and to deceive. He loved to lie with Enda, knowing it would madden Berenice. And his trysts with Berenice were fuelled by Enda's humiliation.

A gentleman collector of female pain, that's what he is, I thought. *Alexander would* – but I stopped myself. I no longer knew what Alexander would think.

Blank with shock, Berenice swayed in front of Mr Rainfleury

for a moment before Pertilly hurried her away. Pertilly and I sat with Berenice in her room for an hour, in which she did not move and the imprint of Mr Rainfleury's hand slowly faded from her face.

The undertakers had arrived by then. Messrs Gerty and Rorke of Baggot Street were making Enda's as decent as a scorched body can be. A few hours later she was lying in a coffin on the dining table, her burned face covered with a lacy napkin and the remains of her hair fanned out around her. We sat vigil around her, in silence.

Much of Enda's hair had burned, but much remained – more than an ordinary woman would ever have. We were watching Pertilly perfecting the curls – one half was neatly ringleted, and the other still wild.

Mr Rainfleury burst into the room, sank to his knees and drew the ringlets over his own bare head. His incorrigible ears poked out through the rich brown hair, clammy and trembling.

'Dead!' he keened. 'Dead at twenty-eight. And me a widower at my age!'

He looks like a hog in a wig, I thought.

'Have a care!' Darcy ordered him. 'Do not rake at the hair. It comes off so easily now.'

Mr Rainfleury vowed thickly, 'I will make it live for ever.'

In sobs, he explained that he had already summoned Professor Sukolov of Moscow University, who had mummified the famous Mexican Baboon Lady, Julia Pastrana, along with her furry newborn baby, using a secret technique of injections over six months.

He enthused, 'Julia Pastrana still looks so alive you think she's about to break into one of her Highland Flings, and they say the embalming will keep her that way for ever. I've seen her myself at one of the travelling shows ... "The Embalmed Female Nondescript", they call her.'

'A dead woman performs in a circus?' I asked.

'Her keeper, I mean her widower, rents her body out to portable museums and the like,' explained Mr Rainfleury. 'Professor Sukolov is halfway to Dublin. Unfortunately our old friend

Millwillis is hotfoot behind him, for the news of my darling's death has somehow got out.'

'Is it witless you are?' said Darcy. 'Gerty and Rorke will do a perfectly adequate job of embalming her. We don't need Enda to last for ever. It took six months to do Julia Pastrana? We have not got such time at our disposal, not with Millwillis on our trail.'

'And nor,' I said bitterly, 'would we let you display Enda as another "Embalmed Female Nondescript". You have *finished* making money out of Enda and making a sad spectacle of her as a betrayed wife.'

For once, Darcy looked at me with something like respect. She jabbed at Mr Rainfleury's ear with her finger. 'Put him off at once, that Russian ghoul.'

Professor Sukolov was ordered home to his Anatomical Institute before he even arrived in Paris. Darcy urged Gerty and Rorke to make the funeral hasty and private so the depleted Swineys could scurry back to Venice.

But it appeared that our brother-in-law had no intention of promptly relinquishing the wife he had so thoroughly betrayed. Even when the undertaker's men departed, even when the smell of chemicals subsided to a dull ache in the nostril, Mr Rainfleury kept Enda's body by his side, now in a glass case designed to fit inside the oak coffin with its gilt mountings and carved shield. The glass case sat on a table beside the matrimonial bed. Meanwhile, the coffin itself stood upright like an Egyptian mummy down in the hall of Number 2 Pembroke Street.

It seemed that Mr Rainfleury found Enda's embalmed body a useful way of repelling Berenice, who would not enter the bedroom that contained it, though she continued to solicit uselessly for Mr Rainfleury's tender attention every time he appeared.

Oona was no more effective in squeezing affection out of Tristan. She confessed to me that she hoped that the pathos of her loss might arouse his compassion.

'He might write a poem for poor Enda,' she said. 'He might

mention her loving sisters. He might show his great heart and comfort me with it.'

'Do not hurt yourself with wishing for that,' I told her.

Mr Millwillis, we were relieved to read, had been detained in Paris by new developments in the story of child slavery unfolding every day more luridly.

Darcy would not be frustrated in access to Enda's hair. Eventually she went to Mr Rainfleury's room while he was bathing, and secretly extracted some strands of it from the glass case.

Ida was released from her asylum and appeared with a nurse escort for the funeral. She was more composed than I had ever seen her. Her hair had already regrown to reach her shoulders and was twice as thick as it had been before.

'They gave up trying to cut it,' she explained. 'It *would* have its way.'

Our mourning outfits were ready. The next morning we pulled on the black-bordered drawers and the heavy crape mantles. An angry wind raged around the cemetery, fraying the discreet veil of rain, tugging at the black-dipped feathers in our hats. Darcy's was as horrible a creation as I had seen in any of my nightmares.

Mrs Hartigan and Enda's sisters were her only mourners. I did not count Mr Rainfleury and Tristan, who looked over the tops of our heads while struggling to keep their hats on.

Tristan chose to walk as far from Oona as he could while still being of our doleful party stumbling through the grass to the place where the men were digging. He did not look at her, and he did not rush to help her up when a ferocious gust unbalanced her. It was my own arm she caught. I kept hers tucked under mine after that.

At the grave, Darcy was dry-eyed, angry as the wind, lost in her recalculations, I guessed. Berenice stood with Ida, her face contorted. Ida herself was composed, crying only a decent amount in the shelter of Mrs Hartigan's arm. I stood between Oona and Tristan, trying to shield her from the absence of his gaze, trying not to picture Enda sisterless in her coffin, going alone into that dark hole in the ground.

I thought of the crossed spoons over the wild grave in Harristown. Someone lay alone beneath them too.

From the corner of my eye, I caught a glimpse of a man hiding behind a tree. At first I feared it was Millwillis, come to gloat at our pain. I reminded myself that he could not yet have reached Dublin. Had he sent a minion to cover the story? A second glimpse of the man, peering around the tree, showed he was no journalist. He was elegantly dressed, with a long beard and luxuriant curls and sideburns. I could see dark shadows at his wrists and a fullness under his immaculate shirt front that argued for a thick pelting on his chest. Such a man was no Brother of the Hair: he had enough of his own not to covet any woman's. Anyway, the man who had assaulted Pertilly was in prison. It was Darcy's conviction, alone, that he was also the author of the letters to us.

The man appeared to be weeping. I saw his shoulders shake. For all that, he was a brave figure of a man in late middle age, with a grace to his bearing. My years of enforced sentimental banality, of the most vulgar operetta scripting, reduced me to a romantic theory.

Enda! I thought. *Did you keep a secret mature lover in revenge? If you did, you chose well, for that hair on his head and face utterly trounces Mr Rainfleury. My compliments!*

Suddenly my loss engulfed me, and I knew in a dizzy sweep of grief what I had lost in Enda, the queen of my tribe. And I allowed myself to be squeezed by dirty coils of guilt: if I had not intensified Berenice's hatred by my scripts, would Enda be dead? She had intervened on my behalf with Mr Rainfleury about the contract, raising Darcy's ire against her. She had sacrificed herself to Mr Rainfleury, and even at Berenice's worst betrayals she had protected all of us from the pain by refusing to share it. Then I remembered the lost babies. I forgot about the hirsute man behind the tree.

By the time the service was over, and Enda was below the ground, he was nowhere to be seen. One final gust of wind lifted

Darcy's hat into the air like a slow crow and flew it away above the treetops. Darcy lost her composure then, keening like an animal and clutching her frizzled fringe.

I had not known she had such pain in her.

Darcy wanted the hair she had stolen from Enda's coffin twisted into bracelets and braided into necklaces. Ida was set to making flowers and silhouettes and even small picture frames with Enda's likeness inside.

What Mr Rainfleury had done with the bulk of Enda's curls remained a mystery until Mrs Hartigan bustled in with his tea tray the morning after the funeral. She swooned at the fumes of opium and the sight of our brother-in-law deeply asleep inside a wig made from Enda's hair, topped by his usual jellybag tasselled night cap.

'From behind,' Mrs Hartigan gasped to me and Darcy, 'it looked as if Miss Enda was lying in the bed, still breathing, snoring, even. Then she turned and I saw Mr Rainfleury's ears sticking out of the hair. As you know, the ears on him are considerable, and they do *poke*. Oh ma'am, it was a horrible thing to see. It was as if he had eaten Miss Enda and was living in her skin, not just her hair.'

'I'll see to him,' muttered Darcy, and she was next door in a moment doing so. We could hear the roaring through the walls. She did not succeed, however, in wresting more than a few strands of Enda's hair from Mr Rainfleury.

Mr Rainfleury refused to accept the finality of Enda's death.

'Every night,' he declared, with his hand over his heart, 'love prises open the lid of my poppet's coffin, and I love her still and again.'

Darcy wrinkled her nose. 'You only ever loved Enda's hair; it was only public decency that made you marry the whole woman of her. And then you betrayed her day in and day out and every stolen afternoon you could.'

Yet Mr Rainfleury chivvied and whined until we agreed to attend a spiritualist meeting. We were ushered into a darkened room in a tumbledown house in Rathgar. Mr Rainfleury reverently laid a tress of Enda's hair on the table. A white hand reached out of the shadows and made a circle of the hair.

My eyes stung to see it there, soft and pliable as it had been when it still grew from Enda's head.

'This hair,' announced our guide into the spirit world, a cadaverous creature unconvincingly got up as a priest, 'was once a dead front on the living. Presently it shall reanimate the dead. This hair lives between two worlds, the living and the dead. Let it join us to our sister.'

'It is hair. It is not magic,' snapped Darcy, rising abruptly from the table and then groaning with some apparent pain in her hindquarters. I'd noticed she was very sensitive there lately.

'Be done with this witch-doctoring!' Berenice pleaded with Mr Rainfleury. 'Use your rationality. Enda has not taken up abode in this hair. She's gone for ever!'

Mr Rainfleury put a lace handkerchief to his eyes. 'There is an evil spirit abroad in this room,' he whispered. 'It frightens my poppet away.'

We left him there, with his money on the table. He barely noticed when we returned to Venice, two days before Millwillis was back in Dublin, on our trail.

Darcy arrived at Santa Lucia Station a few days later than the rest of us. She had insisted on escorting Ida to the asylum without our assistance.

Oona and I tried to raise the matter of Ida's illness that seemed not to exist at all any longer.

'Why do you need to take her back there, to that place?' I asked. 'The mind on her is ticking peacefully as a clock now.'

'I've paid the year in advance, for a favourable rate,' said Darcy. 'Food included, which it would not be in Venice.'

'Darcy honey,' said Oona. 'We have money for all the food in the world. Ida's not a greedy girl. Let her come with us.'

Darcy was not listening. She had a tattered air of worry about her and a slight tremble in her hands, which flew to her head very often to touch her frizzled fringe. She wore one of her monstrous black hats whenever possible, even in the house.

I hugged Ida farewell, whispering, 'We'll get you back to Venice.'

She said, 'I would like that greatly. How is Signor—?'

'Alexander does not visit us any longer,' I said quickly.

'No, I meant Signor Bon,' she said.

In all the time in Dublin I'd not heard from Alexander, who had failed to meet us at the station, failed to arrive in my bedroom via the secret steps, failed to send even the shortest note of condolence.

In his mind, it seemed, I had been neatly amputated by Darcy's slander and the news that my fortune might not be extracted. Without the appendage of me, he fitted into the life he'd been secretly leading and now planned to live in public, as the husband of Elisabetta and the father of their child.

But it was not like that for me, and returning to Venice brought back all the pain, renewed, violent, inconvenient. Despite our continual separations over the past four years, I had become used to sharing my thoughts with Alexander. It took effort and pain to cut a path for my lone brain. It felt as if I was dipping in my own flesh with a scalpel, trying to extract every second artery, the ones that flowed only for him. The hurt was so evil that I grew exhausted and silent with it.

Sometimes I was righteous. I tried to tell myself that I was just not entertained by this pantomime scripted to say that I was dead to him, when it was Alexander who was acting dead, impersonating a man without a heartbeat. He had always been a man without a scent of his own.

But I also told myself that he had been his best true self when he loved me, as I had been. And I believed, or tried to, that he would become bored with pretending not to love me.

And so I kept myself impaled on a fiery pitchfork of hopeless hope, my heart squirming without relief.

42

Darcy exchanged her frizzled fringe hairpiece for a more voluminous one. More packages than usual arrived for her from Dublin, but I assumed them part of her continuing retail campaign.

But as the sun rose on the morning of the Assumption festival she had Pertilly rouse me and escort me to her room. It was clear from her pale face that she'd passed a sleepless night, a thing she'd always claimed previously to be the province of hysterics and drunkards and those troubled by a guilty conscience.

'Manticory,' she asked, 'so is there something in your precious books that can explain this?'

She lifted her hairpiece. I took an unwilling step closer. At the top of her head, Darcy had grown two horns. They were not much more than half a finger long, a greyish yellow in colour. They curved to a tapering end, one in each direction, like a small antelope's. Above her black eyes and sallow face, their symmetry had a diabolic perfection to it.

The Eileen O'Reilly's voice came into my head after one of her beatings. *You doan frecken me, Darcy Swiney, great divil that you are. One on them horned witches of Slievenamon.*

'An extreme case of chignon fungus?' I whispered, racking my memory for conditions we claimed cured by Swiney Godiva Scalp Food in our extravagant advertising. '*Plica polonica?*'

'No, you fool,' she blustered. 'There is no such thing. Tristan made that up, to frighten women into buying the essence. No. I am horned. They just grew. I didn't put much consequence on it at first, but—'

When I recovered myself sufficiently, I asked, 'May I touch?'

The horns were hard, solid, dry and somewhat brittle. The surface was rough, like an old toenail.

I asked, 'Do they hurt?'

'Only whenever I try to knock them off,' she said wryly. 'And believe me, I've not woken in the morning these last months but that I've used brutality against them before night.' She pointed to a battery of bottles, knives and clippers on her dressing table. 'So has O'Mealy, by long distance. He's the only other person who knows, apart from Pertilly. He's sent me everything from Dublin.'

Pertilly had tried to soften the horns with a tincture of hydrochloric acid but they simply grew harder.

'So,' demanded Darcy, 'what are we going to do about it? As the so-called intellectual in the family, I'm assuming you'll have a brilliant idea.'

I spent the next few days in the medical sections of bookshops and libraries trying to discover sources and cures. My Italian had improved to the extent that I understood very well from the texts that Darcy's condition was a rarity and considered untreatable. But the tomes I found were aged and dusty. Darcy refused to consult a more modern, living resource – a doctor.

But one night she bent to inspect something floating in her consommé and her wig fell off in front of all of us. After the screaming was over, I insisted that she get a doctor in. This time I was reinforced by Oona, Pertilly and Berenice.

'Not from Venice, mind! No talk. No talk.'

The first doctor, from Treviso, turned pale and suggested that we call in a priest. A young man arrived in a cassock. His skin was moist and his beard as black as Darcy's hair. When he offered an exorcism, Darcy dismissed him in a most ungentle way.

Then the *Gazzetta* delivered a useful snippet. I translated for Darcy. 'There's a dermatological doctor from Austria presently in Venice. He works with the lunatics on San Servolo, on their skin maladies.'

'Well send for him, then.'

Doctor Morgolos was a dour old man, but his eyes lit up with a youthful flame when he saw Darcy's bare forehead.

'Quite the best specimen ever seen!' he declared with enthusiasm and in flawless English. 'May I touch?'

Darcy nodded. He ran his fingers along Darcy's horns, with an expression that reminded me of Mr Rainfleury's stare whenever his hands were amid Enda's hair.

'The best specimen of what?' I asked.

'*Cornu cutaneum!*' he pronounced triumphantly. 'A cutaneous horn! A pathology of aberrant female sensuality.'

'Aberrant!' shrilled Darcy. 'There's nothing aberrant about me. Or sensual! I am a respectable spinster. Away with your aberrant, man! I want hard fact, and plenty of it for your fee.'

He said, 'Technically, such a horn is a circumscribed hypertrophy of the epidermis, projecting an outgrowth of horny consistence. Closely agglutinated epidermic cells form small columns or rods. In the base, we find hypertrophic papillae and some blood vessels. They have their starting-point in the *rete mucosum*, either from that lying above the papillae or that lining the follicles and glands.'

'For the love of Jesus and Mary' – Darcy resorted to Annora's language – 'close his evil mouth.'

But Doctor Morgolos was not to be silenced. 'The lady is quite young – forty, is it?'

'Thirty!' screamed Darcy.

'Er – for such a pronounced growth. Horns are usually met with very late in life, and are mostly seated upon the face and scalp. Also, the pudenda. Do you . . . ?'

'Absolutely not, what a hideous and impertinent idea!' shouted Darcy. So we knew she had horns in the folds of her groin too. I flinched for her, remembering how awkwardly she had been sitting recently.

'*Why* does this happen?' I asked. 'I think *how* is too much for my sister.'

The doctor spoke cautiously. 'We do not yet know. Though some speak of the contamination lurking in foreign hairpieces, I see this growth is entirely indigenous.'

'Will they get bigger?' asked Berenice.

'I imagine these have taken quite a while to achieve this impressive size. Their growth is usually slow. But when they have finished growing, they will stop. They might even become loose and fall off.'

'Oh please!' breathed Pertilly.

'But in that case they almost inevitably grow back.'

Darcy slumped against her dressing table. 'Why?' she asked heavily. 'Simple words only.'

Simple words only? I thought. Ida would need to be here to say them. She would say, 'You have grown horns because you are a devil.' I would say, 'You have grown horns because of the lies you told Alexander that have turned him away from me, because of what you did to Enda, for the harm you did everywhere and for whoever is buried under the crossed spoons in Harristown.'

The doctor bowed. 'The cause is not known in the case of the head horns. Those that appear about the lower parts of the body usually develop from acuminate warts. As I mentioned, there are some who speak of excessive but unrequited libido manifesting in this way.' He added hastily, 'Obviously, not in this case. I presume you have tried to detach the base? Or break them off?'

Darcy's lowered head confirmed such an attempt and such a failure.

'An irresponsible physician would prescribe any of the well-known caustics, such as potash, chloride of zinc or even the galvano cautery. For your dear sister I would not advise such painful and unproven treatments. I literally beg you not to undertake them.'

Pertilly, laboriously writing it all down, crossed out the words.

'Another method is to amputate the base from the root, as it were. This necessitates,' he coughed, 'however, considerable loss of tissue. And blood. Obviously, I would not recommend it here.'

'So you are entirely useless to me,' Darcy mourned.

When Doctor Morgolos had gone, Darcy remounted her latest frizzled fringe and her ferocity. 'Stop staring at me like a calf in a field,' she snapped at me. 'Get out of my room.'

The trauma of her horns manifested perversely in her, as was to be expected. Darcy decided to rely on drama to distract the beholder. She began to trick herself out in the girlish ringlets of a bygone age – both hers and the decades' past. She rouged her cheeks to appley roundness. For me, there was something intensely sad about this masquerade of juvenile femininity, for if Darcy must mask, then there was something underneath of a different essence – of uncertain gender, of decrepitude, of death. Her looks became theatrical, increasingly borrowed from the rouge pot and the charcoal stick. This, I should have warned her, only drew closer looks and closer looks might reveal what was wrong under the wig.

I guessed that Darcy needed to masquerade because she was driven to even greater fury by her inability to control what grew out of her body. Whatever had been hard in Darcy hardened now.

Her barbs about Alexander grew more frequent and harsher.

Pertilly scuttled away to the kitchen at the sight of her. Oona lowered her eyes.

She certainly frightened the grave grey-haired man who came from Dublin to see her. He looked most unwilling when she cloistered him away in the dining room.

'What was the gentleman about at all?' I dared to ask after his gondola had taken him away in the direction of the station.

'A priest,' said Darcy, 'on God's own parish business.'

'He does not look like a priest,' said Oona. 'What business of what parish?'

'God doesn't please that you should know that,' Darcy said firmly.

Mr Rainfleury decided to come to Venice for a few weeks, being in no state to carry on his work.

He continued to droop over the wig of Enda's hair, claiming

350

that something of his poppet still clung to it. It was placed in the chair beside him at meals. I could not bear to look, and Oona refused to take her customary place as it was too close to Mr Rainfleury. None of us wanted to be near him. The Venetian heat brought him out in a swelter. He refrained from wearing toilet water or using perfumed soaps so as not to dilute the essence of olfactory Enda.

Berenice began to accept her demotion and no longer looked to him for any recognition. If she addressed him at all, Mr Rainfleury did not hesitate to make her understand, most forcefully, that she was the lesser twin, and it was she who should have died. Her lips, tormented with loneliness, had drawn downwards and no longer thought of kissing. I inspected myself in the mirror, fearing to see my own mouth in the same state. I practised smiles, even if they looked like death's head grins.

Mr Rainfleury was still trying to *feel* Enda's severed hair into feeling something back. His forefinger was red and swollen, because he had a tendril plaited into a ring that was too tight, so he could feel Enda on his skin at all times. He continued to exist in these two states of contradictory reality. I hated to have him in the *palazzo*. By night, when the windows were open, we could all hear him talking to Enda's wig. He took both sides of the conversation.

'Do not close your eyes, my precious poppet,' he pleaded.

Then the falsettoed Enda replied, 'But, dear husband, I close them only to keep out the sting of the smoke. Can you not smell it, dear? Is there a fire?'

'No, there's nothing burning. It's just a tint hotter than is altogether pleasant,' soothed Mr Rainfleury in his own voice. 'All the Swiney Godivas are safe in their satin beds. Do not shut your eyelids, dearest . . .'

'I'm burning,' wept Enda's voice from her husband's mouth. 'Quick, fetch your Wilson's Whiskerine and douse me!'

I practised smiles on Signor Bon when I was with him. But I failed to fool him entirely. He asked me if I was quite well. He had undertaken to improve my Italian with weekly lessons. My grasp of the language was faltering under the consciousness that Alexander surely now hated the sound of my voice.

'I do not see you in *ottima forma*,' the photographer told me sadly. 'And this grieves me. I can perhaps guess why, apart from the loss of your dear sister, but it would not be discreet to say. Can I offer you a dawn *giro* in my boat, perhaps? Would that cheer you? It used to make you . . . shine? Is that the word?'

It did not make me shine. I sat brooding in the prow. Whatever I saw that was beautiful only reminded me of what was not mine any longer, not even on loan.

Exhaustion made me feel like a lemon rind denatured in alcohol, nothing left of the flavourful essence, only the tedious crust of its former existence still evident. I wished I had been allowed to rot, disintegrate, disappear. But my doleful conscious-ness was like Enda's hair – it did not wither and it kept living after the death of Alexander's love.

'Do not thank me,' insisted Signor Bon as he helped me onto our jetty. 'It was not effective. Grief is a violent sickness. It breaks you apart, and complicatings set in where it is broken. I am so very sorry. I would love to have saved you from – no, that is not the right word. I do not pretend to be—'

'I do not need a prince or a knight,' I told him.

'I am pleased to hear you say those words, so pleased!' he smiled. 'Princes and knights are not reliable gentlemen even in the fairy stories. Very often and very easily a convenient nymph or a fairy will take this hero from the path of rightness, even if the knight looks bright as the sun in his silver suit and even if he *speaks* so very much of what is right to his lady with his pretty tongue.'

'Or a nymph *and* a fairy,' I muttered. 'And I don't want a prophet either.'

'Those prophetic gentlemen too are more speaking than doing. Even when they take the glitter out of the stars for you.'

'Particularly the false prophets. It's easier to wag your finger than to lift your finger,' I agreed. 'Telling you who not to be, as if you had a choice.'

Signor Bon hesitated. Then he said, 'Forgive me. But it is as if *this* prophet was food and drink to you. I see you diminishing without him. Were you so thirsty for love that you have become drunk on such an object? A man who lets his wife keep him, and trifles with vanity projects and the affections of . . . a person of ten times his value.'

I knew he spoke of Alexander, as I did. Signor Bon's animosity towards Alexander was these days barely concealed. I wanted to tell him that Alexander truly loved me but I knew the words would sound desperate, and shabby. I did not want to see the cynicism closing up Signor Bon's open face.

Signor Bon did not cease to call for me in the boat at dawn, or to row my silence and my misery around Venice. He took me to stand under the wall of wisteria at Ca' Foscari, and to listen to the eerie echo that poured out of the House of the Spirits in certain winds.

'Is it effective yet?' he sometimes asked hopefully. 'Does the shine start to come back?'

'No,' I would say. 'But can we try again tomorrow?'

He laughed quietly, and then looked at me gravely. 'Why, Miss Manticory, are you all over "no"?' he asked me. 'It seems to me that all you ever wanted was to say "no" to your sister Darcy, "no" to your hair and body being sold in crude ways, "no" to the losing of a man – forgive me – who has not loved you as you deserved. If your life is only about saying "no" – to what will you say "yes"? Is that not more important at this moment? Why must you put yourself in the thighs of the Gods with only the power of saying "no"?'

'The thighs of the Gods,' I snapped, 'are not as comfortable to the spirits as Venice on a misty dawn.'

'A woman no longer loved by one man, and such a poor specimen of a man, is not a woman who is unlovable. One should look at the blindness of the man, if he treats you like this, and see what else is wrong with him. And you will find a great deal. But you cannot hate him – that is my privilege. Instead you must think that he is not responsible for how much you chose to adore him.'

I was startled at Signor Bon's discovery of my thoughts. I should not have been. He so often guessed them.

'There is a proverb,' he told me. '"A true friend's eye is a good mirror."'

But I did not want a friend or a proverb; my griefs were too ugly for a mirror. They made me behave in an ugly way.

'I was not looking for philosophy today. Just a ride in a boat,' I said with quiet cruelty.

'You play words at me.' Signor Bon frowned. 'It cost me something of braveness to say these things to you.'

'It is kind,' I said, 'too kind. But I am a wild thing now, a hard thing, not absorbent of kindness at the moment.'

'If it is just a question of the moment,' replied Signor Bon, 'then Venice and I, we shall wait for you. If you are determined to be a wild thing, then the kindest thing is to let you hunt and kill your sadness for yourself.'

43

Tristan had for some months been baffling us with highly metaphorical references to collaterised bank loans, exceptionally venal and vulturine creditors, sudden swooping depredations of a tax inspector.

He drew our attention to a rival preparation born to an anonymous corporation trading somewhere west of Dublin. To illustrate their 'Growant', these shady makers used Titian's *Portrait of a Woman at her Toilet* from the Louvre, which we had visited, and upon which was based one of my own Venetian poses for Saverio Bon's postcards. The name of Growant's manufacturer was nowhere visible on the packaging, which we examined minutely when Tristan, who had not been to Venice for some months, sent a package of Growant handbills, labels and even a bottle of the product itself.

'*I've had it analysed and it's just soap and water with a drop of bay rum.*' Oona read Tristan's accompanying letter aloud.

'*The genius is all in the way that they sell it. They rely simply on advertising – no personal appearances by highly strung and problematic ladies, and so, sorry to say, no risks of exploded reputations or madness or dramatic deaths or disappearances to threaten the income, and no division of the profits: just a simple lyrical flow of money to the manufacturer.*

'*Despite its inefficacy, it pains me exceedingly to tell you that Growant has made grievous inroads into the Swiney Godiva Corporation profits. Therefore, I have been forced to make some adjustments to the partitioning of the accounts. No carrying on, please, my dears. The business has been kinder to you than a fairy godmother, and you'd be the ungratefulest of girls not to think of the luck that's befallen you, with very little effort on your own behalf, given how the hair storms out of your heads gratis.'*

'Adjustments?' Darcy began to pace the floor.

'For why is Tristan putting on the poor mouth?' asked Pertilly.

I could hear Tristan's poetic soul tapping on its pencil as it amended a row of figures to cut the Swiney Godivas out of the Swiney Godiva profits. Darcy's eyes looked far away, as if she too heard that busy tapping. 'The Divil choke him for that same,' she muttered. 'Dropping us like a hat.'

I extracted a final sheet of paper from the brown-paper package. The statement on Swiney Godiva products showed minus figures under our names. I wondered, 'But where has our money gone? The money that was earned *before* the Growant?'

Oona noticed, 'There's a postscript on the back of the letter there.'

Darcy snatched it up.

'It is something that must be faced, my dears, the fact that profits never go on rising for ever. There is a cycle, as with everything in our bounteous Goddess Nature. In the meanwhile I am in talks with certain parties to amortise our misfortunes by selling some of our manufactory equipment, at a vast loss, of course. And I must ask you to send us the deeds of the palazzo, as we shall need them for security.'

'Never!' I said. 'Send him the Dublin deeds.'

Darcy smashed Tristan's letter down on a fly.

'Why did he not warn us about the risks before?' she raged. 'We are down on the deal. Now he thinks he can just scoop out handfuls of *our* cash to save *his* skin.'

'He would have said it was poetical detail too sophisticated for us to understand,' I told her. 'That our complacency and stupid lack of curiosity allowed him to keep us in the dark. And the brutal amounts of money dazzled us.'

Darcy said, 'There's more!' She read:

356

'And I will leave it to you sisters to work out the most equitable way of sharing out what assets are left to you. Of course you have the nest-egg accumulated over the years. The house in Pembroke Street might be sold. I suggest that Ida be moved to a less expensive establishment, as her share should surely be less than anyone's, given her lack of contribution and her age.'

'No!' exclaimed Pertilly. 'That is fair in no way!'

'Ida should come home,' said Berenice. 'And have her share too.'

Darcy crooned, 'Of course I should have the largest share. I have put in the greatest number of years, ideas and strategy.'

'Strategy has brought us to this,' said Berenice quietly. 'And taken Ida away from us.'

'Anyway,' Darcy said quickly, 'when Tristan talks of the old nest-egg, I am sure I don't know what he means. And I sold Pembroke Street last year. The rent is paid by the month now. Barely, I might add. Not that any of you have ever worried your empty heads about how to manage on our income.'

Oona asked, 'You sold our home. You didn't tell Tristan?'

Berenice asked, 'So that was the bank man who came here from Ireland? Not a priest after all? If you sold the house for cash money, then have we not great grand reserves in the bank back in Dublin, Darcy?'

'And this place,' I asked. 'Have you staked our lease too? You have, haven't you?'

Oona mourned, 'We have no home in all the world.'

Darcy sputtered, 'Don't be harassing me, or it'll be the worse for you!'

'You mean you spent it all? Everything?' I asked. 'It must have been you who did it. Because you didn't share it with us.'

'Do you think you ate and dressed yourselves for nothing all these years? With your poor excuses for looks, did you think the cosmetic preparations were free? Do you think the railway clerks gave your first-class tickets for the pleasure of your company?' blustered Darcy. 'Do you—'

357

'We did not eat or dress or travel hundreds of thousands of pounds,' said Berenice. 'Where did it go, the money?'

'I invested it. But—'

I remembered Darcy's feverish looks when she bought the *cartelle* for the *tombola notturna* from the lady seated in the shadow of the Procuratie Vecchie. I saw her grasping the tickets for the lottery as we waited for the draw under the foot of the Campanile in San Marco. I remembered Signor Bon's warning about the little house where huge sums were staked.

'I believe we shall find that Darcy has gambled the money away,' I said quietly.

I thought, *Like a snake, she has swallowed all our money alive.* My mind's eye saw Darcy engulfing the coins and notes of our fortune, putting herself outside of it, distended with it, disappearing with it into the dark places of the earth, and then coming back for more, the snake in our Garden of Eden in Venice, the author of our Fall. Credulous as Eve, we had enacted her will.

'You gambled?' Berenice's voice trembled. 'Our money?'

'You scrattocks!' Darcy said quickly. 'Tristan *wants* us to fight to the death! With each other! He counts on us to fall into disarray over this. So we shall not think to blame *him*.'

'Or is it Growant who is our true enemy?' asked Oona, fearful of any more scissoring the shreds of Darcy's good graces. 'Not Tristan at all.'

'Oh, Oona,' I sighed. 'There is a time to show a body understanding, and there is a time to be your own woman.'

We bent over the fluttering pile of Growant handbills and labels. Our years in the business had taught us how to read them better than any merchant's wife. Growant's advertising was more extreme than ours, and yet it appeared that the gullible public was persuaded to believe its claims, some stolen from rivals' handbills, that it would *make hair grow on an egg, If a particle of hair matter exists, it will be found, nurtured, fertilised and encouraged by this Growant.*

There was something familiar about the grandiosity of these words, something that nagged at me. Had I not been distracted by other miseries, I might have listened more closely to Growant's lyricism.

But I was sorely distracted. For by unfortunate coincidence, Mr Rainfleury's doll factory was also struggling. When he wrote, it was without the usual endearments and increasingly in the stark language of business. He no longer painted a world starving for Swiney Godiva hair but informed us of the blossoming fancy in the gentlemen collectors' market for little girl and baby dolls, which had almost overnight eased mature models out of the shops. Suddenly – and not unhelped by a few unpleasant editorials planted by Growant's canny manufacturers – British girls were waking up to the fact that it was perhaps a tint ridiculous, not to say aberrant, for them to be seen cuddling dolls that depicted mature females.

No, babies are the thing now, Mr Rainfleury confirmed. *Any girl might be seen fondling a baby without reprehension. Such a spectacle represents a charming rehearsal of every rosebud female's desire for maternity.*

Within a few months, the Swiney Godiva dolls had ceased manufacture, and Mr Rainfleury's clerk was delegated to write to us of an entire warehouse gathering dust and eating up the rent. In fact, the detail was yet more horrible, as Mr Rainfleury finally brought himself to explain. To save space and recoup losses, the dolls had been decapitated. Once their distinctively Swiney heads were removed, the composition bodies of our dolls were re-equipped with the coveted *bébé* faces. I imagined our severed heads lying in sacks on the warehouse floor.

Yet Mr Rainfleury made it seem as if we Swineys had enacted self-murders in his warehouse:

It is not just the fashion for bébés: *it is your protracted absence that has killed the 'Miss Swineys' dead as Henry VIII. Without your cultivating desire for them, the dolls have lost their retail attraction. Your tangible presence was required town by town, street by street, to keep you visible. By the effort they put in to attend you, by the money they spent on the shows, our customers used to love you. Now they may not put themselves in your paths, they have disinvested their interest and their love for you, and find other objects, closer to hand, to admire and believe in. As you persist in staying in Venice for reasons that cannot be explained to your former customers, you must understand that Rainfleury & Masslethwaite cannot go on supporting you.*

With great regret, I must give you the statutory six months' notice of the dissolution of the Swiney Godiva Corporation contract. If you were sensible girls, you would thank me. By thinking ahead, I have enabled the Corporation to wash its face – we'll not be coming after you for compensation. Now I must think of the company and our employees, poor Irish souls. For their sakes alone, it is only prudent for me to involve myself in other, healthier business ventures at this juncture.

Finally, it had happened, what Alexander had wanted. I was free of the Corporation. But now Alexander did not want me.

Darcy stormed, 'In cold blood! But what about the Swiney Godiva Corporation? Rainfleury's is still a director of that! So he is involved in the essence and the scalp food and all the other poisons. He still has responsibilities to us as long as there's a drop of Swiney Godiva in a shop! He'll just have to intrude into his own savings for a change, instead of filching and squandering ours.'

'Don't be giving up,' chimed Oona. 'He speaks just of the dolls. He has had a setback and is emotional. At least we can rely on Tristan not to be emotionally overwrought and to keep working for the good.'

The next week's post brought us a new letter from Tristan. The Swiney Godiva Marrow and Daffodil Pomade, he told us, was selling too poorly to maintain its properly improper ingredients. O'Mealy was becoming venal. Meanwhile a lamentable fashion was emerging to unmask quack products for ladies. Two laboratories in England had expressed a desire to analyse the Swiney product. Of course it was Millwillis who had drawn their attention to us, Tristan wrote. *It was a dark day you sisters invited him into your house. If only you had not committed that act of folly and brought this storm down upon us.*

360

Rather than have their contents analysed, Tristan advised the withdrawal of every item. He deducted the funds from our accounts for the removal and destruction of the bottles.

He wrote:

It pains me to say so, but we must look at other retrenchments. I have closed the factory, of course. It was bleeding money. But the Corporation's staff must also be thinned. Out of compassion for their plight, I have been looking to find the people work in other establishments.

Darcy had begun to hammer these Corporation missives to the wall, so that she might keep them in constant view and spit at them whenever she passed. Into delicately marbled walls and painted panels she pounded Tristan's and Mr Rainfleury's letters, fragmenting wood and stone.

'That's just stupid!' ranted Darcy. 'The whole world's presently falling to shards and dribbles, and your man's working up a froth about a sliver of the tail-end of a triviality. I will reply at once. Take this down, Manticory! *This is a temporary setback. You are acting from irrational, pusillanimous fear! Be a man, Tristan! For all you dress your ringlets like a milkmaid.*'

No, Darcy, it is fundamentally rational, came the cool reply in his flowing hand, with much more painful detail besides. *You must now force yourselves to dine upon the bitter herbs of truth, and to swallow them.*

'I'll force *them* to eat the truth!' Darcy muttered. 'They have regaled themselves of us like pigs of acorns!' Distractedly, she pulled a hammer out of her pocket and beat it on her left palm with her right hand.

'Darcy honey, a hammer like that is mighty apt to hurt a body. Put it away, there's a good creature honey,' begged Oona.

44

We had always felt rich in Venice – at first, rich in personal beauty and capillary attractions, latterly in our *palazzo* and in our accounts. Venice had seemed poorer than us – we had struggled to find shops grand enough to spend our bounty in.

Now, suddenly, we were rabbit poor, dirt poor, dirty poor, too poor for soap. Darcy was frank on this subject. Not a penny was to be spent without her authority.

Darcy went to war on expense. She dismissed the maids, telling them that 'proper Irish' replacements were en route from Dublin. Pertilly took on all the work of the household. To wash our hair, Darcy had her save the spoileen, as Annora had done back in Harristown. She sold Ida's violin. I did not like the way she eyed my new Remington typewriter and took it into my bedroom each night for safety.

While Darcy saw this new poverty as a foe to be destroyed, the rest of us recognised an old friend. To me, there was a sense of disagreeable rightness about it, as if we had simply risen like a bubble on a droplet, and now the bubble had burst and we were dissolving back into the general swill of poverty, of Irish poverty, of backwoods, backwards poverty, the drabbest and most general poverty in the world. We had known what it was to be poor, with the turf stove and the thin geese and the slow crows. I could find no rampant triumph in parsimony, because I remembered poverty in all its comprehensive boredom, cold and hunger. Perhaps it was inevitable that it would reclaim us. The shock lay in the plummeting nature of our fall.

I retrieved the seashell lamp from its hiding place in my trunk and hung it from the rafters in the dining room, the only place in which we now kept a fire. Darcy had insisted that one candle was all we burned at night; I became accustomed to the spectral vision of my sisters flitting uncertainly through the dark rooms. We sat at the table under the seashell until the candle guttered, and then we shuffled back to our bedrooms in a wretched shadow of our former chorus line on the stage.

'Why is this happening to us?' asked Berenice. 'We haven't done anything wrong.'

'Except spend money like water,' retorted Darcy. 'Now you must take your punishment.'

Except it was you who controlled all the money, I thought. *It was you who did all the spending, you who gambled. The rest of us had pocket money, that is all we had.*

I could see the same thoughts inscribed on my sisters' faces, and the same lack of appetite to voice them.

'Are there *no* savings, Darcy honey?' appealed Oona. 'Something kept back for a rainy day?'

Darcy glared.

I blew out the flame in the seashell lamp, and in the safety of darkness asked Darcy, 'And what of Phelan Swiney, Mariner? Do you remember the money he wrote about, the deposit he made for us in the La Touche Bank in Dublin. Do you think—'

'I do not,' she bellowed. 'That subject shall not be raised again. I told you! That money was merely a honey trap, left by a feathered snake of a faker, a Hair Despoiler even, to buy his way into our lives. I cut him off at the knees. And now he is in prison. There's no more coming from there.'

Or does he lie under crossed spoons in the clover field at Harristown?

Whoever or wherever he was, it was clear as Waterford crystal that he could not help us now.

The smiles of strangers in the street seemed to mask a patronising pity. Pertilly shopped at Rialto at the end of the day, when things were cheap, bringing home distressing portions of animals wrapped in bloodied newspaper. Or she went on long excursions, she told us, to islands where she bought direct from

363

farmers or fishermen. She haggled for fish on the turn, vegetables furry with mould. Everything had a grey tinge, or perhaps our eyes were failing as we rapidly descended into our own private Irish famine on the Grand Canal.

Of course we starved in the utmost elegance, in our extravagantly painted rooms. If paint had been edible, we might have taken ourselves a taste.

Gone were our 4-franc, six-course breakfasts at Quadri in the Piazza and our long suppers at the Cappello Nero in the Merceria. Even coffee at the Orientale on the Riva was 20 centesimi, and we could not respectably linger, for soldiers and sailors played draughts in the big golden room. We persuaded ourselves that we needed to patronise the *caramei* men with their skewers of candied fruit, dropping precious coins on their brass trays – for the sake of our morale and for the sake of the *caramei*'s often-cited starving children. We went to the sideshows and circuses at the Riva and watched the acrobats and exotic animals because the entry fees were so tiny compared with the good they did our spirits.

To support us in these necessary luxuries, we began to sell things: jewels, furs, even our boots, at prices that were a fraction of what we'd paid.

When our breakfasts were attenuated to tea, we copied the street urchins and went to stand next to the three-legged braziers of the roasters of spiced pumpkin, hot pears and chestnuts, to steal a little warmth. They did not give us free tastes: we were already too diminished in substance, a company of rackabones, with a telltale looseness in our clothes. They gave encouraging samples only to people who could afford to be plump.

We hadn't the price of a meal in our purses. The sight of us would frighten a bowl of macaroni, so hungry were we, hungry enough to eat the shell off a snail like the slow crows back in Harristown. As we grew thinner, our skin fitted too tightly to our bodies, and our teeth, like Annora's, became more prominent. I realised now that she had denied herself food so that there was more for her hungry daughters. Our eyes bulged, sometime inadvertently rounding at the sight of an apple, forbidden because of its cost, at a *fruttivendolo*.

Signor Bon, handing me into the boat, observed sadly, 'There is less of you, Miss Manticory. May I do any small thing to help?'

'Call me "Manticory", I beg you. The "Miss" is too much of a mockery.'

His eyes met mine. He knew exactly what I confessed by that. I saw that he hated to know the extent of my lost intimacy with Alexander Sardou. But I saw his face change too, into acceptance, then sympathy and finally back to his usual affectionate approval.

'I do not consider this a mockery, to call you by your name, Manticory. If I ask you to call me "Saverio", shall you consider me as mocking myself?'

I smiled, unwillingly. 'Saverio, then,' I said.

We continued on our journeys through Venice, almost in silence. I sat with my hands on the wooden rim of the boat, feeling the water through my whole body, sweeping cleanly around my kidneys and my stomach.

Formerly Saverio had always been behind me, but now he was not. I could not remember when I became aware of a desire to turn and face him, and watch him row, and see Venice filtered through the silhouette of his long limbs.

But now, on all our boat journeys, I sat that way, and watched him.

There was a story he told me again and again, about a bridge made of glass, and my own journey upon it. He told it as a parent tells a child, and I received it as I would a fairy story contrived especially soothe the ache of my own repertoire of nightmares.

'Manticory, see yourself crossing a bridge,' Saverio told me. 'Close your eyes and feel it under your feet. See it woven of glass, transparent fairy threads from Murano. As you cross the bridge, the steps behind you melt like spun sugar in the sun. It becomes a three-quarters bridge, a half bridge, a quarter bridge of glass. Then turn, and look back and see what you have left behind. See him standing there with his cloud of contempt darkening the ground around him. With the canal between you and him, tell him that he may not pass, that you wish him well, but he is in your past now. Turn and face towards San Marco, and the whole life of this city, and walk towards it, with the sun warming your back.'

The waves applauded Saverio's story, slapping the boat with appreciation.

But I could not. I did not want the sun or life or the fairy threads of glass.

We wrestled bravely with our hunger but it had too many arms and too many pinching fingers, more than all the remaining Swiney sisters' put together. Darcy fought the fiercest, of course. It became the day's triumph if she was able to terrorise more credit out of the shops that still deigned to deal with us, or a jug of milk out of the tall cans of one of the *lattivendole*. We could not afford to wash our sheets – Darcy became adept at stealing clean ones from the laundresses of San Polo, who hung their work from slender poles in the square, which resembled a lake adrift with sailing boats. It was a poor day if she came home empty-handed.

'I tried to knock another chop out of the butcher, but his wife wouldn't have it,' she'd scowl. 'I made her sorry.'

After that, the butcher swore when he saw us coming. '*Che cani dei to morti. Cani affamati.*'

What does that mean?' demanded Darcy.

'That our ancestors were dogs,' I replied. 'Starving dogs.'

We stole our neighbours' pears from their trees.

Darcy went every few days to San Marco to trap a fat pigeon in her skirt and stamp on its head. She rolled it into her reticule with her boot. Too many of our meals were done that way.

'Those pigeons are sacred to the Venetians,' I warned her, 'like the cows of Hindustan.'

'Why should those fat hogs of birds die of overeating while we starve?' Darcy retorted, waving a tiny bare wishbone.

*

366

Pertilly came to us with a story of a restaurant owner who would never let a woman with long hair go hungry.

'How did you find out?' Darcy asked. 'And where have you been all day?'

We took to dining at Signor Pagin's dark *trattoria* after he had closed to the public. Pertilly suffered him to stroke her hair after he had passed around the steaming bowls of *zuppa di peoci* in one hand and dishes of *fegato alla Veneziana* with the other. Without being asked, he poured us glasses of *Vermouth amaro* and even De Luze champagne. He didn't ask for money payment, but if he was allowed to wash our hair for us in one of his vast pastry basins, then we might take home a food parcel that would last for days, even though the whiff of garlic, embedded in his fingernails, also floated about our hair until the next wash. But we were frankly grateful for the hot water on our scalps, as Darcy had forbidden even that at home now.

And it was truly lovely to hear him talk of Pertilly. 'It is,' Signor Pagin told us frequently, 'as if Tiziano painted her hair and Rubens her body.'

And Pertilly blushed and cast her eyes down like a Bellini Madonna.

Darcy allowed him to talk like this because we survived on Signor Pagin's generosity – until the real cold came. Then even his devotion did not suffice to keep us in health and out of absolute misery.

That first winter of poverty: how the wind shook the *palazzo*, how the cold inched up the walls and up our legs to the very core of us.

The rugs had been taken away the previous summer so that the fleas would not colonise them. That winter they did not come back. I imagined that Pertilly had turned the proceeds into soup. Our shoes were not up to the cold of those *terrazzo* floors. We took cushions from the armchairs and placed them on the floor, making islands from which to jump, so that the ice of the floor did not touch our shivering feet.

We were down to one fur, and so we took turns to go out to be fed by Signor Pagin. I hunched over my food in the *trattoria*, grateful that the restaurateur, with frank pity, wanted only to wash my hair and not to stroke it. His hands were brisk and the water was warm, and I was so tired from fighting the hunger that I felt nothing more than gratitude.

The cold grew more extreme. The bora wind descended from Siberia, and worried the town in its wolfish teeth. We did not go out, except for Pertilly, who seemed to stand it better than the rest of us. We wore the fur indoors too, each of us rationed to four hours inside it, like taking turns to be eaten by a bear. We took to the Venetian *scaldino*, an earthenware pot of hot charcoal, which we rested on our laps so that it could warm us from the middle outwards, like the pot we used to place under our scrawny haunches in Harristown. But the fumes gave me a constant head-ache. As did the melancholy weight of gelid humidity and the remorseful chiming of the church bells in the clear frozen air. We let down our hair and wore it like shawls, trailing it in the bitter dust of the frozen floor. We stayed more and more in bed, wrapped in hair cocoons and thoughts made vague by hunger.

Pertilly disappeared for long periods of the day, and returned not just with extra morsels from Signor Pagin but even with a small chicken or sack of polenta or a single candle for the seashell lamp. She refused to say where she had been or how she had earned the food. It seemed unlikely that she had descended into exchanging her body for these items, though Darcy was not slow in suggesting it. I supposed that she had undertaken some menial duties at the restaurant for Signor Pagin, in exchange for some hours of warmth by the fire, and for the food she shared with us.

Darcy seemed to feel the weight of our unspoken recrimina-tions, or at least felt obliged to refute them.

She said, 'I am a victim more than anyone. I had more, so I had more to lose. Did that even occur to you in your heads?'

Oona took her hand. 'Poor Darcy! You just didn't understand the money, did you? You didn't want to show them that you didn't know. Mr Rainfleury ran circles around you.'

'Was I supposed to know anything about money?' sniffed Darcy. 'I thought it was my *vision* that was prized.'

'And your Gorgon-ness, for getting what you want,' Berenice observed.

'For destroying the world,' put in Pertilly.

'Sure Darcy's always been destroying the world, but isn't she so very good at doing it?' said Oona. 'Would you have her do something she's not good at?'

I watched my sisters enclose Darcy in the old tribal interiority. She looked over their heads at me, proud and hard as a stone gargoyle who fully believes that the congregation inside his church is assembled to worship himself alone.

It was just of a piece with the rest of our bad luck that now it commenced to freeze and to snow.

While Darcy was recasting herself as a victim, the snow was like a witch endlessly unwinding slanting coils of white hair. The lagoon froze over and ice floes patrolled the Grand Canal. The squares were white blotters, scribbled with careful footprints. I looked with envy at the *facchini* who kept warm and paid by shovelling snow from the banked-up streets into the canals – cushions of white flumping into the water. Even the boats were softly upholstered with snow and rose up to their bottom seams above the frozen small canals where the ice was pocked with bubbles of fish breath and the tracks of tiny birds.

Then there blew a wind that would hoist a dead sow out of the mud and make it fly the width of the world. The snow settled to a white stitching at the seams of every roof. In the wintry flood tides, the water was the colour of the shadow inside a dying lily. The wooden *bricole* pointed up in desperation like the tips of a dying man's fingers.

I had used to love it whenever the snow lingered a moment on my red hair, spotting it with white. Now I grew to hate the snow and the ice. I hated it for the pain in my chilblained extremities and because it cost me my boat trips with Saverio. Although I had shown him but scant appreciation, I found that I could ill spare the lulling serenity of them and his quiet company nearby.

The cold made the Swineys even more pagan than we had been – we avoided the church at San Tomà where the cold would martyr a polar bear.

Our blood ran slow with cold; we'd do anything that would put a bit of heat in us. It got so that we all slept in Darcy's bed, barely breathing in the icy air that fell down the chimney. Feeling my sisters' bodies beside me under the covers brought cruel memories of being in Alexander's arms. Darcy reported that she had seen him near the *trattoria*.

'With his wife,' she said, looking at me. 'And what would suit the creature but to go charging off in the other direction at the sight of me! Dragging the poor woman behind him, and the belly on her stretched to its giddy limit. Imagine, Manticory! That's what you're good at, isn't it? Imagining?'

I rose and stumbled out of the bed, slipping on the icy floor.

'Darcy, could you not be even a little bit kind?' begged Oona. 'And Manticory suffering so that she'd rather break her legs than stay warm beside you?'

'I'll try,' sniffed Darcy, 'but I'm not promising a great deal. Come back to bed, Manticory. There's no use in lying there like a nun on a church floor.'

Surrounded by the thin bones of my sisters, I dreamed that night of all the Swiney Godivas, even Enda, as seven ice queens in the moonlight. We were standing barefoot and naked in a garden, our loosened hair enfolding us. Saverio might have photographed us like that, I thought on waking, with our hair transformed into a cascade of brittle crystal that joined us to the frozen earth beneath our feet.

Somehow, we lived through that winter and into the next spring. We ate just enough to keep the cruelty of the weather from killing us. We kept ourselves in heart by singing, warming our throats with old songs from County Kildare. Darcy even gained a little weight. I suspected that she had enjoyed some unaccustomed luck at her gambling, but took care to eat it on the way home so as to avoid sharing.

Some time in those bitter months Alexander's child must have been born, a winter baby for a wintry father. If Darcy knew, she manifested her attempt to be kind by not torturing me with the news. As long as I did not know the sex or name of that infant, I could pretend, for whole minutes at a time, that it did not exist.

Pertilly continued to absent herself every afternoon for a few hours and to return with some potatoes or fish. When summer came, we took ferries to the islands and foraged for seaweed and mosses that she turned into soup.

And by that time I was also away from the house by day, employed by Saverio in his *laboratorio*, a graceful room bathed by the light of five tall windows. I did not know if he really needed an assistant to arrange the hands of his portrait customers on the arms of the prayer chair or faux-marble columns. Could he not, I wondered, manage without me standing by him in the small darkened room while he turned the spectral images on his glass plates into living faces? Did he truly require someone else to write the labels for the envelopes that held those plates? Or to trim the blue paper he used to give night scenes their special luminosity? Did he need me to tell stories to his child-subjects in my imperfect Italian, to keep them from fidgeting themselves into a blur?

He paid me the compliment of never requesting me to model for him. Nor did he ask me to animate the eyes of his gentlemen customers by letting down my hair for them.

Feeling guilty for his favours, I offered it to him for some photographs.

'Thank you, no,' he told me.

Even though I often found his eyes on me, they were not on my hair.

However, he taught me things about my own hair I'd never known, demonstrating how to hand-tint one of the old Swiney Godiva postcards.

'Red is not red,' he told me, squeezing a bewildering array of colours onto his palette. 'If someone shaved a rusted pipe – the way a careful girl might pare her orange and roll its single rind around her wrist and let the light make yellow lichen of it in parts with the shadows of the foxes and deer lurking there and the glimmer of churning goldfish, a crab's claw, a brick and a kidney bean besides – if someone did that, they would perhaps *begin* to assemble the colours of red in your hair.'

With a fine brush, he began to apply kidney bean, fox and lichen to his photograph of me.

'But still,' he said gravely, 'this is not your hair. For it would not, forgive me, lie on a lover's eyelids like clover or shuck like cornsilk between finger and thumb or taste as yours must in the morning.'

For the first time since I'd met him, I looked into Saverio Bon's green eyes. And he looked back at me. 'Do I shock you?'

I wanted to say, 'You delight me,' but I could not. How soon before Darcy would be telling him too the story of my incontinent lust? I murmured politely, 'So many stories in one colour. I never knew. Thank you.'

'Do I bore you?' he asked anxiously. 'My love of my work is unreasonable and inexcusable. Yet I do not apologise for it.'

Then the glass plates tinkled in one of the earth tremors that had been frequent in Venice in the last few days, and we rushed to still them before they chipped.

My old hatred and distrust of photography withered and died in that studio of Saverio's. There I learned what kind of evenings you can have with a person of a nature sympathetic to your own, who is not of your blood but is of your business – for now I considered his profession a storytelling one like my own. Apart from the times with Alexander, I had never even known an intimate conversation outside my sisterly circle. Those conversations with Alexander I kept in easy reach on the shelf of my memory, and frequently took them down to peruse again. That alone should have alerted me to how I had craved friend-talk, and how much I would love it. But those exchanges with Alexander had not in themselves constituted a friendship, no matter how I wore those words to shreds with caressing nostalgia.

Saverio's words flowed in and out of my mind, not lingering as there was always something new to be said. Little fumes and gurgles of music often punctuated our conversations: a flautist from La Fenice lived downstairs. Sometimes Saverio made me an alchemical cup of coffee from beans he ground himself or a bread roll with Taleggio cheese drizzled with honey and a heart-shaped red apple sliced in two. With Saverio, I'd sit up all night talking at the retouching table, laughing, gulping tiny cups of his intense *espresso*, cramming my mouth with macaroons he bought from the *pasticceria* in his square. I'd creep home at dawn while my sisters still slept.

In those days and nights in his *laboratorio*, I learned that Saverio had no wife, sister, brother or parent to support. He lived in a spare but elegant style in apartments above the studio.

So he did not need to work those hours we kept so late into the night, except in that his love of the work was stronger than sleep.

But he seemed to need to help us by paying me a wage, and there was often a basket of food and kindling at the door for me to take when I left, and I was in a state to be nothing but grateful. Embarrassment is too rich a commodity for the poor, even for me, even when I imagined Saverio's scrupulously clean fingers handling each tomato, each bread roll, as he placed it inside the perfect white napkin, tying the four corners in a pair of soft rabbit ears.

45

A sealed note was delivered to me at the hand-tinting desk at the studio. Alexander's writing ordered: *Leave the gate and doors unlocked tonight.*

I stood abruptly, spilling my coffee in shameful rivulets. Saverio raised his eyebrows. I looked away from him.

The earth trembled slightly – the substratum of the lagoon had been grumbling noisily for days. The note sailed gently from the desk to the floor where Saverio could see its meagre words.

Having read them, Saverio too looked away, and then walked and quietly left the room.

A few moments later, I heard his footsteps and felt his hand gentle on my wrist. 'I have another letter for you, Manticory. In the last months, I have watched you do battle with love, as if love were an enemy in your house whom you must kill in order to live. You are brave. You have armed yourself and you have only rarely lain down to weep. Every time you give up, you stop giving up and fight some more. I am amazed by you.'

He bent and took my face in his two warm hands, tilting my head up to him.

'No, Manticory, do not look away from me. Do not look down.'

I looked at my small self reflected in his eyes.

'No,' he insisted. 'Don't look at her. Look at me.'

I too rose, but he did not surrender the gentleness of his hands on my head.

He said, 'You have made me think about love between men and women, and how it should be done. I could not say these words aloud to you, so I wrote them down some nights, almost like a story – yes, here I am too with the stories. Perhaps I am infected by your love of words? I did not intend to let you see these writings, these pictorial philosophies of love, these worded photographs, or whatever you might call them. I am not ashamed of them, yet till now I did not wish to place the burden of their longing on you. My mind is changed.'

He picked up Alexander's note and handed it to me.

'Could you read what I wrote, please, before . . . Sardou?'

'Before Sardou,' I promised quietly.

He tucked both his own letter and Alexander's into the basket of food he had prepared for me.

'For later,' he emphasised. 'But before.'

I left immediately, for there would be no more concentrating that day. In my room of Chinese pavilions, I read Saverio's letter.

On the outside, he had written in pencil: *This is all the fortress I can build you for now. I could have wished a sword and a pistol, today. Forgive me. S.*

Inside, the words were penned in black ink, without correction:

If I were permitted to love such a woman as you, Manticory, I would want her in my studio, and in my kitchen and in my boat as well as in my bed. She would inhabit the frame of my vision like a permanent stain on the lens for I would want her in every place my eyes see and every place I am. I would want her inside me. I would need to know each story inside her, including what makes her eyelashes flitter, in the contour and pockmarks of every pebble she picks up from the beach we walk along together, in the seashell lamp that she follows with her green eyes like a pilgrim.

I would want to know why she sometimes looks with suspicion at a bridge. I would want her eyes to open up with pleasure every time she lays them on me. I would want to understand who she is at three in the morning and who she is at eleven the next night, and all the shes she has been in between. Of course, I am greedy: I would want all those shes to have been mine.

I would cherish the imprints of her teeth in an apple and the silhouette of her waist against the light of the window.

I would want to capture her at her desk and see the words growing on her page, knowing that I seeded some of them but that by far the largest number come from places I have never been. There will be days when she will not find one word to pour into my hand; I shall not hate those days because then she will look for the words in my own mouth, and because I know there shall be other days when she drowns us both with her words. I would want those hands of hers to write me in tiny corners of her tales. I would want to start stories that she finishes and I would want to enter her stories at unexpected moments and run down a calle *with them, with her following breathless, indignant, laughing until the picture of us blurs and we melt into one another with hands too busy to write a caption.*

I'd like to run my finger along the tip of her nose when she's in profile, gazing, in that way she has with her eyes far away in the land of what she wants. I would not let her eat her honey from the edge of a knife any more: I would show her that honey is sweeter on soft morning bread in a bed of butter. I would show her how not to break her hand on the locked door of love and instead to know an open door when it smiles at her. I would teach her that the natural motion of the heart is not chafing. Love does not scald, I would explain to her, or cramp, or starve. It fattens and chatters and thanks. It never undervalues and it always senses something marvellous coming.

I would want to lift the covers of our bed for her, only to have her get in on the other side, laughing. At the beginning of the history of our love, I would want her to dispose herself on my body as a boat lies on water, utterly accommodated and yet subject to my tireless rising and falling. I would want her to lie low in me, so that I almost enclose her in my element, but part of her will always remain safely out of reach in the realm of air. I would want to lie beside her and feel her hands on their adventures. I would want to clean my face with the humidity of her skin. I would want to lie against her body, with my mouth

376

fastened on hers, even as we hurtle in a train through the snow. I'd want our heat to nourish creatures who might otherwise die of cold.

I would want her to turn round and come back to me three minutes after leaving me. Indeed I would not survive parting from her unless I knew she was coming back.

But if she had to leave me, even for an hour, I would open drawers and find the smell of her fingers inside. I would bury my head among the spoons and scissors she has touched.

Does this sound mad, or bad, Manticory? I have hated watching you in love with that man, spending your heart like a bird on a thorn bush, bleeding to death, not even noticed.

'Except by you, Saverio,' I said aloud, opening my *armadio* and placing his letter on the top shelf. I inspected my taut face in the kindness of its speckled mirror.

'You noticed everything,' I told Saverio quietly.

But all I wanted that night was for Alexander to behave as Saverio wrote.

That night Alexander loved me in a way that had no love in it. When he groaned, I felt as if a snake had died inside me. My thighs were painfully raw with the violence of the loveless friction. He shrank away from me immediately and sat up on the edge of the bed, as far away from me as possible.

'I did not mean for that to happen,' he mumbled.

'Then why did you come here?' I asked. 'If you have not come back to me?'

'Don't talk,' he said. 'I have things that need to be said.'

'Darcy has horns!' I blurted. 'She lies, I mean. Surely you know that about her. You've always known it. Why do you believe her now?'

'Horns?' he said cynically. 'You'd say anything, wouldn't you?'

The words came out of him then. He told me blandly that in the months since Darcy had shown him what he 'should have guessed', he had been spending time with his wife, and she had reminded him very forcefully of the happy early days of their marriage.

But you told me that you were never happy with her.

I hugged myself to keep the tears inside me.

'She forgave me before, when I ran away to war to avoid marrying her. She forgives me again. It is her nature. Elisabetta has helped me realise that there are just so many things to do and see and enjoy, which I have sullenly and stubbornly ignored, or been led away from, so many parts of my life that could be better integrated and so many plans that could lead to interesting things.'

And I? Am I not an interesting thing?

'I thought we . . . you and I. I thought . . .'

He made an equivocal noise, low in his throat.

'*We* enjoyed—'

You were there too, I wanted to tell him, *when we made love.*

'Maybe we did once. But even before Darcy told me . . . I no longer felt for you the way I used to. I had to put so much of myself away when I was with you, accommodate so much. You will not do, Manticory. You will not do for me. Elisabetta says that it was a part of my low regard for myself that made me associate with . . . *uno scherzo della natura* . . . one of nature's jokes, a circus freak. Don't be offended, Manticory. You are what you are. And Elisabetta has helped me see that you were of course using me to elevate yourself, as is only natural in one of your birth. Your origins dictate that you have a certain native cunning that facilitates those actions in you. Of course, I succumbed out of my own weakness. It's not really your fault, Manticory. I should not have let the thing go on so long. I blame myself for that.'

'Could we not address some of those—'

He spoke to me as he would to a drunk in the street who petitioned him for money, his voice taut with righteousness. 'I would not be a participant in such . . . there is nothing to address.'

The dawn was coming. I reached for his hand and wrenched it out into the light. He wore, for the first time, a ring.

378

I looked at the plain hoop of gold and at his face. He turned his head then, as the room shook with another little tremor from beneath the *palazzo*. When the room stopped being blurred, there was some clarity in my thoughts too. I understood that the reason he was behaving as less than a gentleman with me was that Elisabetta, who had met Swineyness in the form of Darcy, had led him to the understanding that I was less than a lady. I was a thing with hair. And it was my excesses of hair that made me a thing. I was not bred up to romantic love in Venice. I was a Swiney, of the sodden earth of Ireland.

He was speaking to Elisabetta's script. And now, when I thought back to his disdain in our first backstage conversation, when he had decried the quackery of the Swineys – that had probably been scripted by Elisabetta too. He had been under her influence then. He was again now. I had distracted his affections for several years, but now Elisabetta had reclaimed his opinions, with a little timely help from Darcy. His wife already had his ring, so she did not need his love. All that she currently required was that he did not admire me any more.

Alexander took my quietness as quiescence and even praised me for it.

'You do at least know me well, in your way,' he said. 'That's why you will eventually see how things must be. You're a good creature at heart.'

'Creature': that word was a gift from Elisabetta. It was not the friendly 'creature' of the Irish, a word uttered in universal sympathy or commiseration. Elisabetta's was the 'creature' of bestiality and baseness. Elisabetta had defined it, but Alexander had allowed it into his mouth. And she had even wanted him to lie with me, the hair creature, underneath him, but this time it was to be with the intention of proving just how base I was. Instead of showing him pride, or anger, I had been compliant, adoring his skin on mine. By taking him into my bed, without hesitation, I had shown myself again a creature of flesh, not of character.

Another tremor made the cupboard door swing open. Saverio's letter fell from the top shelf. Alexander eyed the paper without curiosity. Instead, he looked at himself, for the mirror inside the *armadio* door showed us lying together, Alexander sitting hunched, me on my stomach. I followed his gaze. My body was covered almost entirely by my hair, with only my ankles peeping through. I looked like a pelted animal. I asked Alexander if he thought I should cut it off.

'I have no opinion,' he said. 'You show it to strangers. You subject it to scabrous innuendo that you write yourself. I've never been impressed by your hair. And it's your business, in every sense.'

In my inner eye, the lovely nymph Elisabetta had grinned down on me, silently mouthing the words he had spoken and flapping her iridescent wings at me.

'Business,' I echoed. 'Is it a coincidence that this business of not loving me arose exactly when Darcy told you that my fortune is tied up in a contract? That your eyes suddenly cleared, and you saw my baseness just exactly at the moment when you knew that I had no money to call my own?'

The relief of saying those words died as they skidded off my tongue.

'Insult me,' he said coldly, 'as someone of your kind would. I came here prepared for it, knowing what you are.'

I picked up his ringed hand and kissed it, wanting to end this bitter talk with the sweetness, at least, of nostalgia. He could not deny me that.

'Remember this?' I asked.

'Yes,' he smiled cynically, shaking me off. 'I remember.'

That was my own weakness that hurt me there, I told myself, taking my hand back for comfort into the warmth under my arm. *Of course he must deny the past to square up the present.*

'We have a useful proverb in Ireland,' I said aloud, 'which advises that though the honey be heavenly sweet, one should not lick it off a briar.'

'You know why I came here—' he began, but I cut him off with my scorned hand held up.

Wordlessly, he rose and dressed with his back to me, steadying himself against the wall when the room shook with yet another earth tremor. I watched him leave in the silence I had carved with the hand I still held up against him. He kicked Saverio's small pictorial philosophies of love, his careful worded photographs, out of his way as he passed. I wanted to call after him, 'No! Take that letter and read it for yourself!' but there was no hope of that sentence making its way out of my mouth.

Next door, Berenice sighed loudly in her sleep. The tears came at last, as I thought of her, lying lonely in her bed, even her twin's ghost preferred by Mr Rainfleury. However, unlike Berenice, I would never again be allowed anywhere near my rival. I had no business in the same rooms he frequented. A circus freak, a joke of nature, would never be admitted through Elisabetta's noble *portone*.

I had a sudden vision of myself erecting a small tent in the centre of San Polo, and charging people a paltry sum for a look at my creatureness. My hair grew visibly as they came to stare at me. Even from my eyelids it grew, like hundreds of horned tears rushing to the ground with their own weight in misery.

46

My eyes, swollen and sealed by tears, were opened by a shower of stucco on my face. The rounded doors of my cupboards were swinging open and shut. The chandelier tinkled like the percussion section's moment of glory in a symphony, dispersing light and shadows on the marble floor, and soon flakes of coloured glass too. Oona was screaming in her deep bass voice from her room on one side of me; Berenice shrieked on the other. My bed, the floor, the whole *palazzo* shifted and shuddered.

The roar and grind of living and unliving things lasted perhaps a minute. When it stopped, my sisters were still howling. Darcy stumped into my room, her hair terrifyingly askew, her horns visible. She rapped the floor reprovingly with a parasol tip, saying, 'And now I suppose we'll be sinking into the mud and all our things destroyed, and all the steamers sunk so there'll be no escape. And—'

I was not listening.

When the earthquake struck, Alexander had only just left, or so it seemed. It was dawn. I had been dozing stickily, pretending he was still there – as the person he had once been – to accompany the haze of him on my own skin.

I rolled over and sat upright.

If he had only just left, Alexander would not yet have reached Elisabetta's house in the Corte de la Vida. He would not even be at Mr Neville's iron bridge near the Accademia.

As I wrenched on my clothes, I was struck, like a sword in the ribs, with a sense of a new species of loss to add to all the other things carved out of me that night. For a moment I paused, thinking to delay the moment of too painful certainty.

Let the news come to me, when it is ready. Why should I rush towards it?

I twisted my hair into a loose topknot like the Venetian women wore. I slammed through the servants' corridor to the main hallway, pausing to look at the ruin of our blue sky fresco. The sky had fallen in, and presently lay on the banisters in cakes and crumbs of mocking azure. Behind me, in the dining room, the seashell lamp still rocked crazily from the rafters.

I ran down the stairs, tugging the ropes from the green lion heads, through the *androne*, the garden and the front gates, down the *calle* and left towards San Polo, just as Alexander must have done.

Was it really ten minutes ago he left me?

The quake was over but its depredations continued. Bricks were still leaping like live things out of walls and tiles shearing off undulating roofs. A stone grazed my wrist. The bridge of the Madonetta had taken a fearful blow. Its humped centre had fallen away into the water. I skirted the edges, threw myself into the *sotoportego* of the Madonna and reached Campo San Polo, where terrified residents in their nightshirts were milling about, pointing to fissures in their walls, drunken lamp-posts and water spouting from broken pipes. A man powdered with dust was sobbing on his wife's shoulder. He cried out loud to everyone that he had escaped death by the black of his nail.

I ran through the square, mouthing Alexander's name, my cries mingling with those of the Venetians. I fell silent when I saw the cairn that had once been the bell tower of the church of San Polo, and the people crawling over it. A man called shrilly, 'I can hear screaming. There's someone alive under this!'

'For a moment,' mumbled an old woman beside me. 'No one can survive that. If he has a leg or an arm left, it'll be done for by gangrene and—'

I borrowed one of Darcy's looks for her, and threw myself to the ground at the foot of the cairn.

'Alexander?' I called.

'Manticory.' His voice came faintly from deep within the rocks.

In the silence that followed, I was remembering how I had once imagined him mortally wounded on his way home to his wife.

Alexander was just two feet from the surface, both legs crushed under a beam and only one arm unbroken. He could still talk from time to time.

'My right arm is gone,' he told me. 'I can move my left hand. It's by my head. My legs, I think they are on the other side of the beam. There is a shaft of sunlight above my right eye. It almost blinds me.'

The stones and beams were stacked in such a way that to move one would force the others to give way and crush him. An engineer had been summoned from the mainland. Meanwhile, the air rang with a sound like a swordfight: narrow iron bars were being sharpened for a perilous game of fiddlesticks.

'You are to move away now,' I was told by a man holding a slender pole. 'We shall care for your friend.'

The rescuers started by inserting laudanum-soaked sponges on long-handled tongs into the precious fissure that connected Alexander to the world. A sponge soaked dark with water followed, and then, after some whispering at the crevice mouth, another sponge soaked with brandy.

'For the pain,' people whispered. '*Poverino.*' A crowd had gathered now, having run out of other tragedies and ruins to remark on. They had settled on Alexander as the most spectacular victim of the earthquake.

'*Chi è? Chi è?*' they asked one another. '*Il vittima?*'

Then there was an earnest conversation among the men who had taken charge of the ruin. Mouths were held over the small crack that gave access to Alexander. A slender pipe was inched through the crack. Through it they passed more laudanum-sopped sponges on sticks. News filtered back: it seemed his hip was broken, and another beam rested on his breastbone.

A man impatient with the delicacy of the operation ran to the rubble, reaching to lift a heavy block with both arms.

'Don't stand in his light!' I shrieked.

'He has no more light, *signorina*.' An old lady tugged at my sleeve, and handed me her rosary. 'He was given to the light by his mother and God. Now he must go back to the light.'

My stomach sang with pain. As every daughter of Annora knew, the Virgin Mary gave birth painlessly while kneeling in prayer. Yet she suffered searing birth pangs when she watched Christ dying on the Cross. Those pains rent my stomach now, so that I bent over and retched. The old lady patted my back. 'You are young. When you are older, you will accept it as God's will.'

An ominous shifting of stones and wood announced a new settling of the masonry. The crowd groaned. This was surely the end for Alexander.

A man pressed his ear to the tube and listened intently.

I saw him recoil. Then he rose and whispered to a grave-looking man, who flinched, then nodded and departed. The crowd divided to let him pass.

'He has one at home,' said the old lady. I could not form the words to ask what he had at home, but I was beginning to suspect.

'Is the pharmacist still here?' called the man. 'With his bag?'

Another sponge on a stick was pushed down the tube.

When the grave-looking man returned it was with a small burlap bag slung over his shoulder. From it he drew something small swaddled in a red cotton cloth.

'Please let it not be that,' I whispered.

But it was.

He bent to the tube and spoke into it. Then he nodded. He put the tiny gun to the mouth of the tube, angling it so that it would slide down into the narrow void that led to Alexander. I could not keep still any more. I threw myself towards the rescuers, searching for the wrist of the grave-faced man, trying to force him to withdraw the gun from its passage towards Alexander's one functioning hand.

'You know him?' asked the man. 'La Signorina Manticoree?'
I nodded.

'*Vi voleva.*' He wanted you. 'He just said so.'

'*Non è morto!*' I protested. 'Do not use the past tense, sir!'

'*Vi voleva, ma ora vuole la pistola.*' He wanted you but now
he wants the gun.

'*Dovrebbe capire, signorina, non c'è più speranza, salve che . . .
solo dolore e una lenta morte.*' You have to understand, miss,
there isn't any more hope, unless . . . only pain and slow death.

'Sweet Jesus, I am killed,' I told the crowd.

'*No*, signorina,' said the man in English, 'It is he who is killed.'

As he spoke, the report of a bullet brought down a new
shower of purifying, scarifying raw white dust.

47

The he who was killed lay yards from me.

I stood in the square. It had always been a cosy place, but suddenly, with its bell tower gone, it had a dangerous edge. Now the jutting corners of the buildings looked like the shoulders of bullies, blocking out the light, moving in for the kill.

I hurried away towards the *sotoportego*, only to meet Darcy and Oona rushing through it. Oona took my hand.

'Alexander?' she murmured into my hair.

'He is dead.'

Darcy said, 'He was already dead to Manticory.'

Oona pushed herself between us and wrapped her arms around me.

It would be two more days before they could excavate Alexander's body, and I was not allowed to attend although I haunted the fringes of the screened-off site, sitting on the torso of one of the two stone beasts that used to crouch at eye level on a cornice of the fallen tower. Each of them nursed a human head in its front paws.

Gossip in the square told me that Alexander's widow was away in Paris, and had only just received the news.

That would explain his timing, I thought, in coming to see me when he did, and his passing the whole night with me.

The men excavating the site had handed me Alexander's ring but I did not want it without his hand. I put it in my pocket, anyway, and left. I did not wish to see his body carried away.

A week after Alexander died, I realised that I had been rehearsing his loss ever since I met him. I had never been in true possession of him. The loss of Alexander was larger than Alexander had been because he had never taken the full role in my life that I had desired for him. There was as much potential lost as reality, as much longing curtailed as fulfilled.

My heart was a fist. There was a sourness snapping around my teeth. My sinuses were burdened with salt. Alexander's death, juxtaposed with the passion and cruelty of our last night together, left me homeless; nothing inside me was at home any more, I could not be comfortable with the separate organs jostling under my skin and my skin felt unequal to its statutory task of assembling and containing all the parts of me in their proper order.

I left my apricot room where I had passed those last hours with Alexander. I moved to Enda's forsaken apartment and found an anonymous bed, with no memories scribbled on the sheets, to lie on at night, with my eyes open, burning, sometimes widening in disbelief, sometimes narrowing with anger.

Days passed and I was not able to tell anyone about what I felt. My sisters knew not to mention it, for they had seen what happened if they did. I couldn't talk about it, because it felt as if I was killing Alexander each time I acknowledged his absence. Flowers arrived from Saverio, making me black angry. I tore up those roses, muttering, 'You have no idea of the enormity of the thing. It cannot be contained inside a rose, you imbecile.'

And then I went to my bedroom and tore his long letter in half, and then quarters, and strewed the pieces in the Grand Canal along with the mutilated roses.

I did not return to the quiet discipline of Saverio's studio. I had no need of his coffee or his kindness. Accepting his sympathy would denote believing in Alexander's death, and that was not acceptable to me. And I feared my rage would cause his glass plates to explode if they caught my reflection in the sun.

Whenever Oona or Berenice pressed platitudes about time healing, I wished sudden, multiple and cruel bereavements on them. I did this silently. They would never guess that my eyes glittered with the acid of hate and not the softness of tears. I refused to light candles for Alexander or mutter prayers in memory. It was a sight too fierce and dirty for that, what I felt. This was a rubbishing, roustabout, rabid, untidy kind of grief. It was more like what I remembered from the Famined days in Ireland, when those about to perish from their hunger had laid themselves down in the street to be walked over, so that some-one could witness them dying. I too felt that my grief required acknowledgement, but I did not know whose – I just knew that it was not that of the tourists, nor of the quiet-eyed Venetians, nor of my sisters. I strode the streets, my eyes scanning the people I passed as if one of them might provide the witness I needed.

Whenever Pertilly or Oona gently asked me how I was, I couldn't very well answer the truth: *I hate everyone who is alive who is not Alexander, and that includes myself. And nor can I escape the fact that Darcy is right and I was dead to him before he died himself.*

So I murmured that I was doing well and soon hoped to be better.

'Why don't you take yourself back to the studio, Manticory?' Oona asked. 'It would do you some good, honey. Signor Bon has been asking for you.'

'I'll eat less, if you need the money,' I snapped.

We Swiney Godivas had once made a pretty thing of mourn-ing, piously picturesque around Darcy's coffin and stuffed black cat; decorative and expensive with Ida's hair and mourning jewellery. Enda's ugly death had emptied these things of decency. The image of her last fall and of Alexander pointing the little pistol at his brain intertwined in my mind with the memory of Ida waiting for love at the railway station and her abrupt removal from us. If Ida were with us, I thought, she would understand the simple butchery of my feelings. She would understand that death had little to do with the songs that the Swiney Godivas had warbled in our day. It had no busi-ness with delicate jet earrings, or willows or wreaths, or weeping angels. There was nothing pretty about it, or gentle. Death was like a kick in the belly from a vicious horse, its withers dripping with yellow dung. Death was the ugliest brute in the bar, the one with his wife's blood on his knuckles, the most stinking clot of sawdust on the butcher's floor. Death was someone taking your hair and tearing off your scalp without a blade to ease its passage.

I suddenly saw the point of wine, and brandy, and even beer, or any liquid that would help the pain flow out of my brain in long dribbles of tears. After some days, Pertilly said mildly, 'Will you have a morsel of food with your supper, Manticory?'

'You were snoring like bagpipes last night,' reported Darcy. 'It floated right across the garden like a bear roaring. I put it in my black book.'

'Will you have a tint of feeling, Darcy honey?' reproved Oona. 'Or at least pretend.'

'You wouldn't want to mind me,' said Darcy. 'You don't, do you, Manticory? Good, I knew you didn't. Carry on acting the tragedy queen till your heart bursts and showers us all with its giblets. But not in public, please. It's not as if you were married. Even if he was.'

God rains on the wet, they say, somewhere with a superior line in proverbs. So there were pictures of Alexander every-where, to remind me of the pale hair on his head, the slanted shadow under his lower lashes, the perfect kite of his torso.

Artist slaughtered in earthquake, wrote the *Gazzetta. Young widow and son, distraught.*

I should have expected the *and son*, yet it hurt me like a fall on ice.

Out of respect, no one overpasted Alexander's billboards, and indeed many became shrines, with flowers and candles left underneath to remind me that I was of the common herd of Alexander's worshippers. I did not attend the funeral. I did not wish to see Elisabetta playing his grieving widow any more than I had relished the thought of her being his wife.

Did Elisabetta wonder what had become of his ring?

I took the ring out of my pocket and slipped it on my thumb, the only finger it would consent to stay on. It had an attraction to plugholes and drains and would slip away from me if it could.

By night now I dressed like a Venetian woman in my fringed *sial* and went to cafés and wine shops, begging credit so I could nurse a glass of sullen red wine at a corner table, watching how life was lived by those who thought it worth living. I looked at real families in which the men were little sultans surrounded by adoring wives and children. If any man tried to approach me, I showed him Alexander's ring, and laughed until he skulked away.

Until one night it was Saverio whom I saw when I looked up.

'Come,' he said quietly, holding out his hand. 'There are better places than this. And there is work to be done.'

48

A month after the earthquake, the post brought Matron Tar's quarterly report about Ida.

I was reading it aloud, over a supper I had brought home from Saverio's studio, when I reached an item on the second page that stole my voice and made my hand tremble. The matron mentioned a visit by that kind gentleman, our cousin Matthew. I forced myself to read on.

'The dear man was most distressed to discover your sister Ida in a condition of what he opined to be 'lonely, cruel and humiliating' confinement, and felt that you should have informed him. He considered her elegant accomplishments in the creation of hair ornaments to be 'outright slavery' and demanded to see the receipts of sales.

I regret to say that Ida is at present in a state very much removed from reality, and she did not even recognise her own cousin. But he bravely persisted in his visit, and eventually she quietened, and listened to him, though she did not talk. However, I am afraid he also persuaded her to show him her work in the butcher's kitchen. By the way, may I remind you that the quarterly fee is overdue by six months?'

Darcy spluttered.

'What Cousin Matthew?' asked Oona.

'You imbecile, it is either that wheedling fortune-hunter, the so-called Phelan Swiney, Mariner, or the bastardly Millwillis, impersonating a member of the family,' snarled Darcy.

'I thought you said Phelan Swiney was in prison,' I reminded her. 'For despoiling Pertilly's hair.'

'So it must be Millwillis then. The one time he came to Pembroke Street, Ida was in the music room. You and I were the only ones who laid eyes on him, so Ida wouldn't recognise him now. At least Ida did not talk. He will have gone away without any fresh muck to spread. He won't waste any more time with her.'

'Shouldn't I write to Matron to say that he's an impostor and make sure he's forbidden access to her?' I fretted.

Darcy snapped, 'Ignore the letter. We are supposed to be in Russia again anyway, so how could we have received it yet? He'll be long gone by now. Millwillis has no patience, and he'll not want to spend hours in that hideous place, without heat, wretched and dirty, in danger of his life from twenty shades of homicidal delusionists and rapists.'

Oona cried, 'But, Darcy, you always said it was a lovely, gentle place there, with no dangerous patients, and no men, and just poor nervous ladies like Ida. You said we shouldn't visit because she needed to remain in absolute tranquillity—'

'I was thinking she was lucky to be there while we starved in Venice,' said Berenice. 'It was a comfort to think of her in luxury.'

'Well, I didn't want you in a state too, did I? Yes, it has its share of murderers, like any other establishment of that kind. And it doesn't do to make these places too cosy, or the lunatics get used to it and think of all kinds of excuses to stay, putting a burden on their families with the expenses,' Darcy said firmly. 'No, old Millwillis won't go back a second time. Was I ever wrong yet?'

'We should fetch her away here anyway,' said Oona. 'She does not chew her hair any more, does she?'

'No,' admitted Darcy. 'But where would I find the cost of train tickets at this time? When our luck turns, and when Millwillis has given up haunting Ida, I'll fetch her.'

But 'Cousin Matthew' proved most devoted. Matron's next letter told us how he made a point of visiting once a week. Ida had begun to recognise him, or at least acknowledge him as her 'old new cousin'. Her sense of time, Matron told us, was distorted by her illness.

She has accommodated him as part of her childhood, and prattles to him of mutual memories that seem to make her happy.

'God, there's no knowing what she will spill. Once she starts talking, she's as flowy as the cholera,' moaned Darcy. 'Manticory, write something to Matron that will have him chased away.'

Dear Matron Tar.

[I wrote.] *As ever we remain grateful for all your kindness to our afflicted sister. I apologise for my slow response. As you know, we have been touring in Russia, and a Venetian acquaintance has only just brought us our post including your longed-for news of our dear Ida. I hasten to warn you that no 'Cousin Matthew' exists in our family. The impostor is known to us. His only wish is to do poor Ida harm. In the name of all my sisters, I formally request that you deny him access to her. But kindly do not unmask him. That could be dangerous. Please feign to respect him. If she has talked to him, you must assure this man that she is not capable of recounting the truth, and that he must not use her fantasies for any of his purposes, which, we suspect, are malign.*

Matron replied by telegram:

REGRET FALSE COUSIN. BUT HAS NOW WILLINGLY REVEALED TRUE IDENTITY. SAYS HE IS IN POSSESSION OF ALL CRUCIAL FACTS. ON HIS WAY TO VENICE TO WAIT FOR YOUR RETURN FROM RUSSIA. DEEPLY SORRY FOR ANY INCONVENIENCE BUT FELT IT CORRECT TO SUPPLY YOUR PERMANENT ADDRESS. YOU MUST MAKE OTHER ARRANGEMENTS FOR IDA PRESENTLY. DO NOT WISH PUBLICITY.

From the cold tone, we understood that Millwillis had shared 'the crucial facts' and that they had not been to Matron Tar's liking.

So now Mr Millwillis knew it all, the whole terrible sight of scandals, from the seven nit-ridden fatherless sisters to the fake Pertillys. From his first articles, it was clear he already knew about the fake locks sent out and the letters written as if from us in Mr Rainfleury's factory. He knew about the ringworm. He knew what was in the essence, and the scalp food. He knew about the adulterous marriage of Mr Rainfleury and Enda. Now that he had talked to Ida, he knew the facts about Enda's fiery end and even, perhaps, what and who had caused it. He knew we had fled to Venice to save ourselves from him. He would write of the seven sisters, who weren't really sisters and who had not been seven for some time. He would write about the hair that wasn't all theirs. Of course now there was the extra shame of poor Ida being confined in a sordid madhouse for him to gloat over. Ida had read Darcy's black books – perhaps Millwillis would know what was in them now too.

And there could be but two possible reasons why he had wished to empty Ida's rattling head of all these matters – he wanted either to expose us or blackmail us. He would write the Swiney Godivas up as quacks, adulteresses, liars, fakes and even murderesses – or we would pay him for his silence. He would no doubt plan to live off us for the rest of our lives. The one thing that Millwillis did not know about us was that we were now paupers who could never pay his price. About that one small fact he was crucially uninformed.

As for Mr Millwillis himself, well, we could be expecting him in Venice at any time to put his torment on us, thanks to Matron's idea of what was correct, which now also had Darcy tongue-cudgelling money out of Pertilly's savings to pay for train tickets so she could rush off to England and fetch Ida back to us before she let loose any more candid recollections.

Even as Darcy and Ida churned third class on bare benches across the Continent in the train, the next week's post showed a taste of what was to come. Millwillis had already started publishing his new articles about us. He'd allied himself to an Italian psychologist, Cesare Lombroso, who was writing essays in which he argued (with deft and cunning recourse to the harmless Mr Darwin) that thick dark wavy hair was a sure sign of backwardness and a signpost to a subhumanly criminal, morally debauched nature. Abundant hair in women was condemned as a virile growth, revealing the hirsute female as nearer her ape origins than to civilised man. There were other psychologists ready to associate hairiness with madness, sexual incontinence, insensibility to pain, infanticide and degeneracy. Mr Millwillis found illustrations for all these phenomena in the Swiney Godivas.

'Who is translating Lombroso for him?' I asked. '*Who?*'

For Millwillis was able to classify, compartmentalise and label each 'criminaloid' Swiney sister. Low-browed Neanderthal Darcy was sensual and violent, Berenice impulsive and vindictive; Pertilly had ears of a criminally large size; Enda had been guilty of a monstrous vanity; pale Oona was congenitally frigid; Ida was the passionate imbecile with a sloping forehead who played the fiddle as if the Devil were dancing for her. I myself was a monster of red-haired lust and cold rapacity. Millwillis also used Lombroso to argue that the Swineys, like all women, were more cunning and vicious than any murderer.

Those girls have never drawn a breath, he wrote in the *Pall Mall Gazette, but that they've used it to poison someone.*

Ida and Darcy had been home only two days when I caught my youngest sister waving out of the back window.

'There's Cousin Matthew!' she told me. 'Come all the way to see us. Shall we wet a pot of tea for him?'

49

'I'd like to see him at the bottom of a lime pit,' growled Darcy. 'I'd pour the lime myself.'

Berenice envisioned his skeleton prodding the mud at the bottom of the Grand Canal. Pertilly wanted him staked on a bonfire. Oona opined that Millwillis should be struck down by a highwayman. I kept my imagination away from him. My imagination had already done too much damage.

'You're very quiet, Manticory,' hissed Darcy. 'Got a scruple, have you? For a change?'

'She is sad,' said Ida. 'Not in a killing mood, but a dying one.'

When I embraced her at the station, Ida had given me a long look. She'd whispered, 'I heard about Alexander.' And she had offered the only consolation that seemed to stick for a moment because of the hideous sense it made: 'You have been took bad by bad love and you'll be a dirty long time dying of it. He was more lucky than you. *Minutes*, he had of pain, and then a clean ending. But Manticory, you should be happy. You have been dancing with a broom like the last spinster left at the ball, like the last spinster left on earth. Alexander, he was a broom; he had no more life than that, even when he was alive.'

'The hack's still here.' Darcy was at the back window taking another look at Millwillis. 'I hope your knives are good and sharp, Ida.'

'Don't be talking of knives, Darcy honey,' pleaded Oona. 'Or thinking of them.'

The journalist passed unhurried hours in the *calle* outside our house waiting. His self-possession was admirable, especially in the heat. Besieged, when necessary we used a different exit, through a neighbouring deserted garden, past the lime pit that housed the bodies of the neighbourhood's dead animals. It was necessary at least to get to the post office for our correspondence with Tristan.

In defiance of Millwillis's articles, or perhaps inspired by our new notoriety, Tristan was engaged in 'one final bid to save your fortunes, ladies'. Given that Growant had entirely killed the market for Swiney Godiva Scalp Food and Hair Essence, he wanted to market a Swiney Godiva depilatory cream: something to remove those hairs where hairs should not be. He'd not so much asked our approval as informed us that the Swiney Godiva name was now doing the opposite of its normal work.

AWAY! FROM ARABIA, Tristan called it. *The Latest Swiney Miracle*.

And it was advertised as containing sandalwood, cloves, musk, red Cyprus and roses. When he threatened to use an image of the Baboon Lady, Julia Pastrana, to advertise it, we agreed to let him Swiney *AWAY!* instead. Saverio was invited to the *palazzo* to take some photographs of Oona and Berenice to illustrate Tristan's caption: *Will you run the risk of alienating the affection of a husband by not attending to the few unsightly hairs that have sprouted above those lips he once loved to kiss?*

Saverio Bon pursed his lips, asking me, 'Is this really necessary?'

But neither Tristan's sudden slight rekindling of interest nor his enclosures of handbills could distract us from the unwelcome visitor who haunted our gates.

'That wants solving,' muttered Darcy, staring out of the window in a speculative way. Then she suddenly hunched her shoulders and cried, 'No!'

'What is it?' I asked, for her face was contorted with fury.

But all my response was the winnowing noise of her skirts as she rushed to the kitchen. Following her, I saw her grasp Ida's carving knife, which she tucked into her pocket alongside the hammer she used for nailing up the letters from Tristan and Mr Rainfleury.

'Go,' she hissed. 'Look outside, and you'll want to be fitted up with weapons too.'

Hastening to the hall window, I saw what Darcy had seen.

Mr Millwillis had a companion walking arm in arm with him, back and forth in front of our home. And that companion was the Eileen O'Reilly, every inch of her, no longer runtlike but quite the shiniest and most prosperous little piglet of a girl you ever saw. She would never make a fat corpse, and yet above her slender waist she had grown a prosperous pair of breasts, which displayed themselves at a jaunty angle inside a plaid waistcoat. Millwillis and the Eileen O'Reilly paused together in front of our garden gate, a few yards away from me.

And the most amazing thing of all was to hear the very Eileen O'Reilly herself chattering loudly in Italian to a passer-by. Hers was much more fluent than my own. Of course it was! She was a lady of business now. Her uncle must have invested in her acquiring the tongue so that she could deal with the Italians from whom he bought his delicacies.

We already knew that Millwillis had encountered the Eileen O'Reilly on one of his sleuthing visits to Harristown, where she still spent her Sundays, as Mrs Godlin regularly reported. Of course, the butcher's runt would have thrust herself forward, being only too happy to share her many colourful old stories about Darcy. She'd probably embroidered on them. And now he'd rewarded her long tongue with a trip to Venice!

No doubt she was the one who'd translated Lombroso on hair as a diagnostic of feminine depravity, feeding him information that served to fatten his mock-scientific theories. The Swineys, he had just written, *show just that absence of self-control and civilisation that we regret in the savage beasts.* Yes, he could see it that way and he would keep writing it that way, and there would be nothing we could do to stop it being printed in a book, a thousand times over. A book raised the stakes. A book was like a tombstone, for ever. Millwillis would be washing our hair in public for years to come; the filth of his insinuations would be indelible. People might dismiss newspapers as entertainment but everyone believed what was in a book.

399

Darcy put her hand on mine. The veins on it were raised and livid. She said, 'There *is* something we can do about it. Call everyone to the dining room.'

Darcy treated us to an hour of the inside of her mind, as dark a place as you might imagine. There was a fairy-tale quality to the way she spoke of murder. It had a lulling effect on the rest of us. My sisters listened to her as they had so many times before, believing the worst of her violence to inhabit her tongue and just occasionally, these days, her hard hands. Only I thought again of *PS* buried in the clover field at Harristown. Had Darcy killed a man, in real life, not just in threats? I believed she had. Even as a very young girl, she had somehow contrived it. And then there was Enda, who had tried to use her influence with Mr Rainfleury against Darcy, and had not survived it.

The lime pit was in the end dismissed by Darcy as impractical. How would we push Millwillis down it?

'We?' said Oona. 'Darcy honey—'

'It's too shallow. Would he be buried *enough* down there?' Darcy asked herself. She specifically wanted him wrapped in a winding sheet, coffined, lead-encased, with earth packed down around him. An open grave, even if a relatively deep one, would not be sufficient. And the other problem was, as ever, the Eileen O'Reilly.

'Even if we manage to separate them, and to dispatch him,' Darcy insisted, 'the butcher's runt will never leave off looking for her fancy man. She'll be battering at our door in a hog's grunt.'

'Oh no!' said Oona. 'That just shows—'

'She would follow us to Hell but she'll have something out of us,' muttered Darcy. 'The corpse must not be found in our proximity.'

'Better if not even in Venice, really,' observed Berenice. 'You're still quiet, Manticory.'

'Wait,' said Darcy. 'I've thought of that too.' Her eyes were glittering with that dark light that they emitted only when she was in possession of an idea.

'Do you remember your stupid ballad, Manticory?' she asked.

'Which stupid ballad?' I asked bitterly. 'They were all condemned by you at one time or another, even the songs in *The Cruel Sister*.'

'The one about the evil hack suffocated by the bales of Venetian laundry dropped on top of him,' she said. 'In a boat. After being hit on the head and pushed in.'

'Leave it be, Darcy,' I said.

I had not remembered it until this moment, but now I did, in every detail. How could Darcy have kept it in her mind all this time?

'A crueller death than slow suffocation is hard to imagine,' Darcy said happily. 'Your Mr Sardou preferred a quicker end. And *this* death will come with a mighty headache on top, and no laudanum or brandy or a gun to speed and ease the end! The beauty of it is that we don't even have to kill him,' gloated Darcy.

'Fetch it from your desk,' she ordered me. 'That ballad of the laundry, I know you keep all your little productions. No, I don't trust you not to tear it up. I'll get it.'

She returned a moment later with the paper folder I had marked *Unperformed Drafts*. How easily she'd located it! How often had she spied on my writing?

Reading it aloud, she stopped frequently to embroider my ballad. Instead of 'the hack', she substituted Millwillis's name, lending a dreadful reality to the fiction I'd composed that long-ago evening in Venice when I had thought existence was properly perfect, our first night in this *palazzo*.

Darcy's commentary ran on and on, substituting reality for fantasy. She was anxious to ensure that Millwillis was briefly stunned long enough to be covered with bales between the men's departing with the clean sheets and arriving with the dirty ones. 'We can let the bales' weight do the rest.'

Oona said, 'Well, Darcy, I am sure it was a great relief to you to picture all that murdering in detail, but what are we really going to do about that dreadful man so?'

'It will be a great relief,' repeated Darcy. 'A very great relief.'

*

401

It was an August dawn already pulsing quietly with heat and the heat's whining handmaidens, the mosquitoes, the morning that the deed was to be done. I sat on our slender terrace, with my hands around a cup of coffee I had made for myself. This was a skill I'd had a care to hide from Darcy lest she delegate me to serve it to her hourly and somehow produce the funds for the precious beans too. Below me men were already in their boats bringing *'il latte, il burro e il formaggio'* to the shopkeepers of Venice. I loved those proper namings – not just any milk, butter and cheese but *the* milk, *the* butter and *the* cheese. None other would do.

Shirtless men rubbed their torsos with rags to blot the sweat. As the sky lightened, a suggestion of a breeze teased the hairs on my arms, but soon disappeared. Even the water did not pretend to be cool. Its feverish surface borrowed hot terracottas and molten ochres from the *palazzi* hovering above.

Our assignation was for six. Darcy had dictated the letter I had written to Millwillis at his hotel to say that I was ready to talk, but that this meeting must be out of doors and secret: *My sisters are against this. So I must do this discreetly. I know every-thing, and anyway – better one visible, speaking, cooperative sister than seven invisible, silent ones.*

He had agreed. I had not counted on that. I had been sure that Darcy's mad plan would stop there, with the newsman too canny to fall for the bait.

After all, he knew what we Swineys were like. Or at least he'd written the words that defined us: savage, primitive, violent, backward.

You must come alone, but bring the manuscript, I had written. *So I can help you with the material points.*

He had agreed, so sure was he of himself. None of the Eileen O'Reilly with him, he assured me in his note. *Of course I'll bring the manuscript, and an open mind.*

Not a steel-tipped knife or loaded gun, or a lifebelt, or a stout pole: just the manuscript and an open mind.

I could not believe it. I did not want to do so. I told myself he'd bring a guard with him.

One by one, Darcy, Oona, Pertilly and Berenice joined me silently on the terrace. The others were still in their wrappers, but Darcy was dressed and ready.

She raised an eyebrow at the empty cup of coffee.

Perhaps, I thought, *there will come a day when I'll feel strong enough to say no to her, to her face, instead of subverting her will only in secret, only in subplots, only for my own satisfaction and not for the good of the world.*

It was our old routine – and it had never yet failed to stun.

I tried to tell myself that Millwillis was scarcely human. I had stood inches from him in Dublin; I had breathed the corruption of his breath, seen the misery he spread, not just to us but to the living and the dead, to living women in Paris to St Petersburg, to the corpse of poor Julia Pastrana.

When Millwillis approached the end of the *calle* he would find me waiting for him, just as he expected. He'd have his manuscript with him, of course, swinging in that greasy leather case of his. What he would not expect was Darcy, quietly walking behind him with her hammer in her pocket. I would keep my back to him, gazing at the shimmering spells the sun cast on the water. The glare would dazzle his eyes and make a debatable silhouette of me. As I heard the footsteps of Millwillis approach, I would let down my hair. It would be the first time he had seen it: in spite of all the reams he'd written on us, he'd never bothered with attending a Swiney Godiva show.

'Come a trifle closer down the alley,' I was to urge him, casting one of our famous looks over my shoulder.

And Millwillis would come closer, his eyes fixed on the red rivulets of hair. His sensibilities were too coarse to read a bloody warning in them. Millwillis was never a Brother of the Hair, but *Swiney* hair was now the meat and milk of his life, was it not? Whatever our hair made for us, it also made for him. He would want to get closer, to touch, even better to claim he'd had his fingers among us, and could write with palpable experience. He'd be happily fashioning the heat-charged adjectives even as he approached.

403

And as he leaned forward with an eager hand, Darcy would come behind him and deploy the hammer with one hand; with the other she would grasp his leather case containing the manuscript. Then, with her Gorgon's strength, she would push him into the boat, covering him with an old sheet I'd carried folded against my chest all the way from our *palazzo*, cradling my frantic heartbeats in its softness. The sheet would make Millwillis invisible. Darcy and I would withdraw to the courtyard of the hotel, where the door, I knew well, was always open. The men arriving with the bales of dirty laundry would heave their burdens gratefully into the boat and turn their backs. They would bury him.

I imagined Millwillis waking at some point before he died, sucking the sheets into his lips, gasping on soiled white cloth, the damp bubbles of linen blowing inside his mouth. I imagined him remembering what had happened to bring him to this pass, and by whose hand it had been done. As he started to lose his sense of himself, he would realise that this was just what he had wanted to do to the legend of the Swiney Godivas. He had sought to bury us under dirty laundry, pulling endless soiled sheets of it from his imagination to swaddle and shroud us in sneers and lies.

And so he might muse and picture for a while but not a very great while. Every breath would be expensive and his little stock of air would soon be spent.

By the time they arrived in the laundry at Mestre, there would be no breath left at all in Millwillis's body.

50

I had done nothing more than write the letter and let down
my hair in front of him.

Well, yes, I had also, at the last moment, been forced to help
push Millwillis into the boat. I'd barely touched him. Yet none
of my senses would permit me to conceal from myself that I
had by the indiscretion of my imagination helped to author a
man's death and that it might have been for nothing, for
Millwillis had arrived without the manuscript of his Swiney
Godiva biography, even though he had left us exactly the way
Darcy had planned it and I had scripted it.

All the way home, walking through a world vacated by
Millwillis, the heft of his shoulder clung to the tips of my fingers.
I could feel the grease and harsh linen of his jacket still. I continued to breathe the sweat and stale breath of him, closer than
they had been since our first encounter in the parlour at
Pembroke Street. Nor could I forget the dull thud of Darcy's
hammer and his quiet grunt, the juddering of the boat as he fell
into it, the waves that sniggered around the prow then, the air
seizing the sheet as it sighed over him, so that his left foot
remained visible, my wrenching off my white petticoat to throw
over it just as we heard the *portone* of the Hotel Squisito open
for the returning laundry men. I remembered Darcy's breathing, and mine, as we waited behind the courtyard door, counting
the fourteen heavy bales as they slumped on top of Millwillis
and then the men leaping into the boat, the ropes slithering
back onto its deck and the oars casting away from the shore.

My reliving of those moments was punctuated with a recurring
vision of the incriminating manuscript in his hotel room, where

the Eileen O'Reilly, who probably knew every word by heart, no doubt still had the wits and the malice to use it against us.

Millwillis had died for something he had not even delivered.

Yet Darcy refused to countenance the idea that our trouble was anything but over. She repelled my worries with ferocity. She forbade mention of Millwillis in the *palazzo*. Oona, Pertilly, Ida and Berenice were silenced with individual threats. The rest of the day passed in an awed hush. None of us ate.

Unable to talk about what I feared, the fears accumulated inside me. By bedtime they had bred new fears – about the contents of the manuscript, about the Eileen O'Reilly, about some witness to the crime hiding behind curtains at an unknown window of the Hotel Squisito. I couldn't sleep. I rose and took to the streets, haunting the pharmacies until I found one where a lamp still burned. I would have spent everything in my purse to buy myself three hours away from my own brain. It was not just unconsciousness I craved but deep, bone-knitting, muscle-smoothing, skin-loosening sleep.

Millwillis's death had solved nothing.

Nor had it solved the problem of what we were to eat, or of what we were to do with the Eileen O'Reilly the very next morning when she sent her card up the stairs to us.

We descended in a long silent row to meet her in the *androne* where Pertilly kept her under bare control by blocking the way to our stairwell with her entire body.

Darcy had quickly handed out various items of her own before we went down – a good shawl to me, a velvet jacket to Oona. Berenice and Ida were hustled into unpatched skirts.

'Let your hair down!' she ordered us. She might as well have said, 'Gird yourselves for war!'

Then she rifled in a box and produced a single earring for each of us. 'Just stay in profile,' she warned.

The Eileen O'Reilly saw through our bare finery in a moment.

'Darcy Swiney,' the butcher's runt marvelled. Her Italian might be polished, but when she spoke our native tongue, it still rasped with all the rough of Harristown. 'Arsey Swiney and all her bastely little swine. It's long years since I last laid eyes on ye and your nits. Those years' – she looked us up and down – 'ain't been good to ye Harristown sows, I belave, not to look at ye anyways, Darcy Swiney, no they have not. I believe your guts are a thrifle thinner than a goose's neck! Look at the great affluence of your hairs aich standin' on end wid the hunger! I see grey, and thinning like the thinness of death there. And for your clothes, can I borrow ye the loan of a few rags?'

We stood wordless. The Eileen O'Reilly had not really changed – in spite of the tight dress in grey Scotch cheviot and the high breasts, she still had the small blue eyes, the meat-fed complexion and the freckles of a butcher's runt.

She had not brought the manuscript with her.

She had eyes only for Darcy. She did not cast a single glance in my direction. Taking Darcy's silence for defeat, she mocked, 'Ye'll not be showin' me any splendid Irish hospitality then? Where is all the urgin' for me to come up and take an *air* of the fire in this damp hole? Perhaps ye cannot afford a fire these days? What did ye dine on today? Air pie and a walk around, by the looks of ye. And I don't hear ye askin' if I have a mouth on me that might be moistened by a cup of tea? I'd pay ye a penny for it, Darcy Swiney – if I didn't think ye'd murther me for it in your desperation.'

I exchanged a glance with Oona.

'What do you want?' demanded Darcy. 'We'll not be entertaining a butcher's runt in our palace. The servants' entrance is presently occupied by a dead pig for a local feast, which is the only reason why the likes of you is permitted this grand threshold and even its dust is too good for you to choke on.'

'I want to know what happened to my employer, Mr Millwillis,' declared the Eileen O'Reilly, quite uncowed. 'I'd not put anything pasth ye, Darcy Swiney, even a kidnappin'. I picture the poor felly thrussed up in ropes, mumbling on a gag. I told myself, "I'll see to that." '

'Is Mr Millwillis in Venice, then?' asked Darcy airily. 'Fancy! And has he taken to his dotage, employing a brutal-looking

407

thing like you about his business? That was an unlucky day for him entirely, for you've not the apparatus in your head to sustain a good lie like he has.'

'Ye are standing in a grave shovellin' dirt over yourself, so ye are. Now that ye're poor and old, your ballyraggin' is grown feeble wid ye, Darcy Swiney. It's hardly worth liftin' my tongue against ye. So enough of that. Ye know very well that Millwillis is gone missin', so ye do. And where else would he be but here?'

Her voice had risen to the shrillness and phrasing of her schoolgirl days. She cast the arc of her blue eyes around our faces. 'Tell me where ye've got Millwillis. Tell me, Manticory Swiney!'

I looked at the ground.

'Haven't seen hair nor skin of him.' Darcy crossed her arms. 'Nor smelled a whiff of him either. And we'd have noticed *that*.'

'Do ye see the mark of a fool about me?' ranted the Eileen O'Reilly. 'I *know* you've done somethin' wid him. I know the very thoughts of ye, Darcy Swiney, as well as if I was inside of ye. You're holdin' him against his will, so ye are, and it is a great shame, so it is. It is off to the police I am goin'. I give ye my hand and word I am on my way to them prasently. And if ye've done somethin' to the man, Manticory Swiney will have to weave an enchantment of a story if your necks are to be saved from the noose.'

Then she drew herself up proudly and allowed a smile to spread over her face. She turned her smile on me. It was a smile from Harristown, from the days of our poverty and abasement, a time when we were prey for all hard tongues, and most of all hers. It was the smile of someone about to pour herself a bowl of cream and drink it. It was a smile that begged a blow, even with a hammer. But I did not, I truly did not want that to happen. I still remembered her small fingers handing me a corner of her smock to sob into. I remembered her kindness to Annora, our lessons in the hedgerow, the misplaced loyalty that I had allowed, by my silence, to grow into an enmity I'd never wished for, which had stretched through the years and found Millwillis as its last instrument of war.

Turning, I saw the vertical cemetery of the lime pit dilating in Darcy's eye where her pupil should be. She took a step towards the Eileen O'Reilly. I put a hand on Darcy's arm and a foot on the skirt of her dress. I could still tell myself that we had not killed Millwillis: the laundry had suffocated him. If Darcy moved on the Eileen O'Reilly, there were no sheets to do our work for her.

But the smile did not deliberately beg a blow. It was a smile that leaked out of a secret that the Eileen O'Reilly now chose to divulge. She *chose*. She chose to divulge then, when, if she'd had any desire to live at all, she would have backed away from Darcy's glittering eyes and hard hands and desperation. But no, the Eileen O'Reilly insisted on saying what she said next.

'Did ye bastely sisters ever hear of a product called "Growant"?' she asked. 'Such an excellent thing in a bottle. If it's not delightin' the whole feminine public, makin' them grow shags like bullocks off their heads, it's no matter! No blazin' wonder it has undercut the market for—'

'The market created by us!' barked Darcy. 'Growant would not exist if not for the Swiney Godivas. I've heard it's swill, too, so.'

'True,' simpered the Eileen O'Reilly. 'True, 'tis arrant, arrant swill. And true it is too that I'd never have thought it up were it not for you Swineys and your great success. Growant would not've happened, 'twere it not for the thought of ye seven sisters aich seated on your great hairy curabingos upon velvet chairs in rooms where there was nothin' but heaps of gold and silver snuffboxes, amoosin' yourselves with apples and nuts and hot boileds and roasts while the rest of us starved back in Harristown. The vision of *that* has kept me company for years. *Your success*, we should toast it! For without it my uncle would not have been persuaded to put money into Growant. And I'd not have spent these years studyin' how ye've done what ye've done, in order to do it betther than ye.'

Our silence seemed not to trouble her. She rattled, 'It's so long since ye've been back to Harristown, ye've never even seen our smart new Growant factory at the back of the estate. Your old hovel – it's our stables now! The clover field – it's where we turn the drays.'

A picture sprang into my mind of the horses trampling on the crossed spoons, crushing all evidence of the life and death of *PS*.

The Eileen O'Reilly continued, 'We employ the boys ye used to enterthain. One of their first jobs was to paint a big sign on the wall of the factory. Do ye know what it says?'

We failed to answer.

'It says,' she chanted:

> 'HARRISTOWN.
> HOME OF HAIR.
> MUST BE SOMETHING IN THE RAIN.
> AND PURE HARRISTOWN RAIN'S WHAT'S IN
> GROWANT.

'And there's a picture of the Swiney sisters painted on the wall, jest in case someone misses the point. It's a copy of that ridikelus portrait ye had made of your piggy selves, like ye was the royal family sittin' in state! Some scamps have added some amoosin' detail to the picture, and we've somehow never found time to clean it off. That's how busy we've been.'

'I'll break every second bone in her unlucky carcass,' whispered Darcy.

'You've grown rich on us so?' asked Oona faintly. 'Rich there?'

'We've been trading oft the back of ye something fierce. Every time ye thought ye was risin' above me and Harristown, ye was simply helpin' me and Harristown on our way. Like Growant were the nit and ye was the Swiney Nitsters,' she giggled, the high little breasts on her jiggling with merriment above her neat breastbone.

My first thought was that Tristan and Mr Rainfleury had been negligent. They had told us they were doing every possible thing to find and do down the Growant people. But they had not thought to look all the way back to Harristown, where it all began. The Eileen O'Reilly and her uncle had had the run of the place, free to exploit us – even as Tristan and Mr Rainfleury had.

But Tristan and Mr Rainfleury had not been diligent on our behalf in any way at all recently. I realised something that I should have understood an age past. It was a long time since either of them had been truly interested in us. The two men had made their fortunes on us and moved on, and they had colluded in so doing. Their betrayal had been orchestrated and symphonised. They relied on our not noticing – and our stupidity had been reliable. They had not traced Growant because they didn't care that we failed. They had seen to it that they themselves were no longer contaminated by our failure.

The faces of my sisters showed the hurting passage of those same thoughts across their minds. Darcy muttered, 'They're just a pair of scuts and nothing better! Damn them and the dogs who gave birth to them.'

'Ye've been as dead in the brain as *seven* Julia Pastranas, wid two smart fellies sellin' the use of your bodies,' crowed the Eileen O'Reilly. 'Rainfleury and Stoker didn't even wait till ye was dead. The world is laughin' at ye.'

Ida said, 'I don't care what people think about us. When we were just Swiney girls in Harristown, no one thought about us at all.'

But I flinched, and most of all for Oona. How long was it since she had received a tender private letter from her hero? Weeks, I knew it. How long since Mr Rainfleury or Tristan had been to see us? I counted back the months and found myself in the middle of the previous year. They'd not even had the courage to face us, to see our starving features and our shabby clothes.

Darcy, Pertilly, Oona, Berenice and Ida stood quietly, though they let the air out of their chests simultaneously, with an audible noise. It was Berenice who asked, finally, 'And your partners in this Growant business? Is it just your uncle?'

'Well, until recently, so it was. But we've lately been joined by two gentlemen with a heap of practical experience in the field.'

411

I remembered Tristan's letter: *Out of compassion for their plight, I have been looking to find the people work in other establishments.*

The Eileen O'Reilly's face was avid as she watched Darcy grasp the sharpness of the truth. Tristan and Mr Rainfleury had simply transferred the material benefit of the Swiney empire into the realm of Growant. The Swiney Godiva Corporation had been dissolved at their convenience, leaving them with no responsibilities towards us, apart from those one might think moulded by years of tender connection with Enda, Berenice and Oona. They had realised that they might be rich on hair without paying the Swiney Godivas for the privilege. And they had not let sentiment or loyalty get in the way of their profits.

'They was false to ye from their mouths to their marrows!' guffawed the Eileen O'Reilly. 'Pure poetry, ain't it, poor Oona? Ye'd be the most unpoethical of girls not to see it.'

She hesitated, her face rueful at the sight of Oona's tears. She turned to Darcy. 'Yet don't be givin' them fellies too much splendour for their cunnin' and their cruelness. *You* helped desthroy yourself, Darcy Swiney, so ye did, draggin' your poor sisters down beside ye. It wasn't just meself and Mr Stoker and Mr Rainfleury who piled the bastely ignominy on your foolish Swiney heads.'

She pointed at Darcy. 'Look to your own black-eyed, black-tongued sister, girls! She's the one who's cut all your seven throats with her black tongue and her suppuratin' bitter mouth. Aich person Darcy Swiney ever offended has lined up to take their revenge. Is there a child in Harristown, who Darcy Swiney once beat the lard out of, who has not grown up rejoicin' in a chance to do her down by workin' in the Growant factory? I see 'em grinnin' at their work all day, even when the stuff burns their fingers.'

She took a step towards Darcy. 'Did ye not treat Stoker and Rainfleury to the length of your snaky tongue all these years, Darcy Swiney? Did ye not offend the poor auld hairdresser, Miss Craughn? Did ye not put a great trouble on her? Did she not get bastely disobliged by ye? Well, hairdressers make good spies, Darcy Swiney. Miss Craughn has become a friend to me, and do we not enjoy a good chat about past times, and does she mind at all if I have a shred of paper handy with a pencil on the side? She does not. Your groom in Dublin, who ran back and forth with the brown envelopes to place your bets, did he ever get anythin' but a sour look for his pains? He's only too pleased to remember your great run of black luck for me. And what of those poor fake Pertillys? Did ye not bully aich one on them till they ran away on ye? But for your behavin' against good manners, Darcy Swiney, your sister Swineys would have no enemy in the world.'

Darcy spat on the ground. 'Were you so tenderly brought up yourself? Weren't you just the biggest splash in the puddle, with your greasy crubeens to give out?'

None of my other sisters had words for her feelings.

'Ah!' said the Eileen O'Reilly into the silence. 'Why do ye let that Darcy make people hate ye, girls? Ye're big enough to look crooked at me in the great mob ye are, but one by one ye aich have mouse hearts.'

So Alexander had said, I thought, *mouse hearts*.

'Mouse hearts, you say?' Ida smiled. 'No, a mouse heart is *this* big.' She pinched her thumb and index finger together. 'You must take the very smallest knife to divide it. A lamb heart is also but a morsel. A goose heart even less.'

'What is it at all that ye are talking about? That Ida's as deminted as ever,' the Eileen O'Reilly laughed. 'Ye must be proud of her, Darcy Swiney, for the Devil is. I am sure ye fashioned Ida that way by your cruelty to the poor creature.'

The Eileen O'Reilly tapped her finger on Darcy's breast. 'And in speaking of poor creatures, do ye know what we found when we ploughed the clover field near your hovel? We found a little skellington of the tiniest dead babby. No bigger nor a doll. There was one of those awful shoe dollies of yourn buried wid it, jumbled up inside the shreds of a linen pillowcase, wid the name "Phiala Swiney" sewed on in red thread. Very rough, it was, that stitching. There was a date, too, somethin' in 1854. Do ye know somethin' about that, Darcy Swiney?'

Darcy's face was set in pale sweating stone.

The runt looked around the rest of us. 'I see none of your sisters do. In fact, Manticory has a partikeler startled look about her.'

'"Phiala",' I said. 'That means "saint's name".'

The name Annora always called so longingly into the twilit garden, the name she always gave her favourite goose.

The butcher's runt asked, 'What were ye, Darcy, eight year old, was it? When that babby met its death. The same year ye tried to poison me. Are ye tellin' me ye had nothing to do with that skellington?'

Oona and Berenice held one another's hands, mouthing the word 'Phiala'. Unconsciously, they shaped the syllables to sound like Annora's all those years ago, back in Harristown, when she had keened the words into the dewy night.

Darcy's face was stiff with rage. She said nothing. I thought again of all those letters from Phelan Swiney, Mariner. Our real father did not lie dead in the clover field, so was our correspondent really an impostor? Had we kept him away from us all these years? Had I tacitly helped Darcy to do that, by believing him in prison for hair despoiling or, more likely, killed and buried?

'Your dark hair was inscribed wid crime from the day ye was born, Darcy Swiney,' cried the Eileen O'Reilly. 'With nits and shame and bashings and doing away with innocent creatures, so it was! In love with death, your whole black life, a great black witch, ye are. But I'm not freckened of the likes of ye! *Where's Millwillis?* Do ye not know that the police will be here shortly to ask the same?'

Despite the solidity of her victory, there was something slightly ill at ease about the Eileen O'Reilly. Why had she needed to seek us out in such a paroxysm about Millwillis? She'd not been able to resist the deliciousness of telling us about our own betrayal by Rainfleury and Tristan, but there was something frayed about her own manner. She might have enjoyed unravelling the Swineys, but she surely remembered that she was putting herself at risk by dealing so with Darcy.

'Do your people know you're in Venice?' Darcy asked.

The Eileen O'Reilly blushed a shade of late-autumn plum.

'No one knows? I thought as much. So your relations with Mr Millwillis were not quite respectable then?'

She did not meet Darcy's eyes. Darcy visibly rallied. She walked around the Eileen O'Reilly, inspecting her tight dress from all angles. '*That*'s knocked the indecent rejoicing out of you, hasn't it? Is this the hysterics of an abandoned harlot herself that we are being forced to witness here? Did the dirty hack amuse himself with you, pretending to be interested in your old secretarial skills, in your Italian tongue, maybe even taking advantage of them too? But did he pay you in wages, or in kind? Do you lack a decent explanation for your absence? Perhaps it would be better if you *never* went back to Ireland? Perhaps you'd like to join him, wherever he is?'

The Eileen O'Reilly took each blow as it came, screwing her blue eyes closed for a second, and then returning to her defiant stare. But her skin coloured its way through every shade of blanched and blushing.

'A red face is not becoming to the complexion, although it matches that unpleasant pale red on your head,' said Darcy tranquilly. 'A colour indeed thought to be the sign of a fool in many parts of the world.'

The Eileen O'Reilly's eyes skittered over the many doors that led from the entrance hall and fixed on the one to the back garden. She spun round to face the water-gate. Could she even swim, the poor little butcher's runt?

Berenice and Oona were behind her. Darcy and I stood in front. Ida was to her left. The vastness of the ship's lantern barred her right. And from the large pocket of Darcy's housecoat protruded the handle of the hammer that had already delivered us from Millwillis.

I said to Darcy, 'Best step away. Best leave her.'

But Darcy's eyes were fixed on the girl in front of her.

The Eileen O'Reilly uttered a moan, high-pitched like a shrew in a cat's jaws.

'You have lost the run of yourself, runt,' replied Darcy. 'And just think, if I'd murdered you the first time I'd wanted to, I'd be out of prison by now.'

She took a step closer to the Eileen O'Reilly.

'Cover your eyes,' ordered Darcy. 'All of you, now. Ida! You—'

51

Darcy lay on the floor, a thin snake of blood coiling out of her left ear. Her mouth was open, and her black eyes too, but there was no light in them. Her left temple bore an angry contusion embossed in the shape of the head of the hammer Ida had snatched from her hand.

The Eileen O'Reilly was kneeling on the floor, cradling Darcy's broken head in her arms. She shrieked at Ida, 'What has took ye? For why have ye murthered your own sister?'

Ida said, 'She shouldn't have drowned my cat. She shouldn't have pulled my hair. She shouldn't have sold my violin. She shouldn't have put me in the madhouse. She shouldn't have said what she did. All the things she said. For years and years, she said and said. She made bitterness out of sweetness and hardness out of softness. She was as crooked as the Devil's hind foot. She spent all our money that we worked so hard and horrible to get, and she spent it on her bedlam tricks with the lottery. She should not have pushed Enda on the stairs. I was behind her. I saw it. She should not have made Alexander hate Manticory. She should not have killed your friend Mr Millwillis, no matter how bad he was. She should not have taken us away from Harristown. Do you remember what you used to say about her, back in Harristown?'

'That she was a Divil, and the Divil's creature, a snake, with all God's curses on her,' whispered the Eileen O'Reilly. 'That Darcy Swiney had a forked tongue on her. Beyond anythin', she was. There was no beating her; she had got the gift of getting one over ye, no matter what. And since we found that little skellington in the clover field, I've been sure she was a murderess besides. Did she kill Millwillis?'

'Yes, she got him. Even our mother said that of her,' declared Ida, 'that she was a devil. Now may the Devil sweep Hell's floor with her and burn the broom after.'

Still holding the sticky hammer in her right hand, Ida bent over and closed Darcy's eyes with her left. Then she wrenched out the six hairpins that held Darcy's frizzled fringe in place and flung the thing across the hall. She pointed to the horns on Darcy's naked forehead.

The Eileen O'Reilly reached a trembling hand to assure herself of the reality of those horns. They had grown an inch since I last saw them. I felt them under her fingers, remembering the ragged toenail roughness of them. She pulled her hand back as if burned.

'Hot like hellfire! You see,' remarked Ida, 'a hard-faced, dry-skinned Devil-snake Darcy was all the time, as strong as a python.' She added, consideringly, 'Though the skull was surprisingly soft on her.'

She looked straight into the Eileen O'Reilly's eyes. 'And you knew it too that she was the Devil, for *you* held her fast while I did what needed to be done.'

She straightened and acknowledged the rest of us, one by one. 'And you did not stop me, Berenice, nor you, Oona, nor you, Pertilly. Nor even you, Manticory-the-timid-deer. And in your deepest hearts, are any of you sorry now?'

Was I sorry? To see Darcy extinguished brought on a dizzying emptiness in my mind, my bones, my heart. Grief swayed me next, but it was not for Darcy. It was for Enda. If Darcy had died earlier, Enda would still be alive. And, perhaps, so would our secret sister Phiala.

My sisters' faces showed the same undulations of emotion that I felt. But I did not see the smudge of guilt on any of their features, or the softening of sorryness.

Finally, Berenice said, 'We must put her in the lime pit.'

Ida insisted, 'Not till it's dark, silly. Someone might see. Until then, we clean.'

We acted in strict obedience to Ida's orders. We were curiously slow and heavy in our movements. It was as if, if we deviated a moment from her direction then we would no longer be safe inside the shelter of our old tribal interiority, which had simply opened for a moment to eject Darcy and to admit the Eileen O'Reilly in her place. It seemed natural that the Eileen O'Reilly should help drag Darcy's body to our storeroom by the water-gate, scrub the floor, burn her bloodstained clothes in the fire along with ours, take her turn in the bath. She too, I observed, followed Ida's instructions without comment; she too, I supposed, kept from screaming and weeping only by virtue of a strictly somnambulatory way of going about these things.

Ida brought a day dress for the Eileen O'Reilly from Darcy's armoire; it fitted neatly, apart from the length, which Pertilly quickly amended.

'Nothing runtish about her after all,' said Ida with satisfaction.

I found my eyes dwelling on the Eileen O'Reilly. I hurried to sit next to her when we ate the porridge that was our evening meal, for Pertilly had not left us to go foraging.

I wanted to follow the Eileen O'Reilly when she moved from room to room, touching the gilding, the mirrors, the damask. I wanted to hear her Harristown voice, and I wanted her to talk about the slow crows and sodden fields, which she did, on my requesting it, keeping us spellbound for an hour.

'Will you stay?' I asked her, as the moon rose.

You are already a part of this; you cannot denounce us now, I meant.

'I will stay,' she answered.

I said, 'Would it not be difficult for you to go back, after what happened between you and Millwillis? When they find him, it will all come out, about the room you shared.'

I do not blame you for that, I thought. *I know what it is to share a room with the wrong man, and to pay for it.*

'She will sleep in Darcy's bed,' said Ida. 'Tonight. And from now on.'

She rushed to hug the Eileen O'Reilly, who stood quietly in Ida's arms, while I told her exactly what had happened to Millwillis.

'Did you love the man?' I asked finally. 'He did not seem to be made for loving.'

'No. I never even thought that I did,' she said quietly. 'It was a great curiosity and a bad behaviour of me to do what I did with him.'

'*This* is where you always wanted to be, isn't it?' Ida told her. 'This is for why you pranced around us so much in Harristown, and followed us, and talked about us, and tried to keep all the other children away from us so you could have us for yourself. This is for why you tried to take our places with the Growant. This is for why you followed Millwillis. Helping him made you *matter* to us. And then it brought you here to us.'

The Eileen O'Reilly wept long trails of tears. Ida kissed them away.

'Once we were seven and we thought we did not need you,' she said. 'Now we are fewer. Well, here you are among us, and here you shall stay.'

The Eileen O'Reilly looked at me, taking deep shuddering breaths.

I handed her my handkerchief, clasping her hand inside my own as I did so. It was small and soft, and it clasped me back.

We waited expectantly for Ida's next pronouncement. She told us, 'Now the moon is high and our neighbours are at their tables, not at their windows. We shall put Darcy to bed beneath the lime and above my poor Kitty, and then we shall go to bed ourselves.'

I lay sleepless on my mattress, letting images of the day dilate and shrink back inside my head. When my mind had eaten the colour and shape out of those pictures, I began to think of what had led up to them, and my own part in them, not just in the last days, but in all the years since my childhood. I had allowed

Darcy to make money out of the troll who had tried to degrade me on the bridge. Thinking to escape, I fell in with Darcy's desire to leave Harristown, but I had been more degraded than ever – letting Darcy take money from people who wanted to fondle my hair or own it or steal from innocent people using the image of it. Then I had found love but Darcy killed that too. Yet if she could kill it so easily, then it probably had not been worth having. Had I really loved Alexander? Yes – my pain alone proved it – but was there not a deeper attraction in the prospect of him? Was it not really the case that all I had ever wanted or needed was to *get away from Darcy*? And even now that she was dead, I was still trying to get away from Darcy, but my thoughts continued to settle on her like bats that return to flutter in the dark of their cave. I had watched Darcy kill Millwillis; now my mind's eye saw her murdering our youngest sister, little Phiala, no bigger than a shoe dolly, and just as breakable. Had she thrown the baby against a tree, as I'd once watched her do with a rabbit?

I must have willed myself unconscious simply to escape the image, because in the early hours of the morning, I was woken by uneven footsteps on the stairs.

My mind, like a tongue to an abscess, flew to Darcy as I'd last seen her, head down, her legs up against the side of the well, the lime heaping over her.

It is Darcy come back, I thought in terror. *She will never be finished with us. I should have known that Darcy would be stronger than death.*

The steps grew louder and closer, and were accompanied by rasping breath.

The candle in my shaking hands threw canyons of shadow around its faint light. I hurried to the main hall in time and lit its pink-globed gas lamp.

Ghosts hate light, I told myself.

It was not Darcy but Ida whom the lamp illuminated – Ida stumbling through the *portone*. In her left hand she held the cleaver she had brought back from the asylum. From her right hand dangled a mass of dark bone, clotted blood and white powder.

'I hope that's not the poor cat's bones, Ida.'

'It's not at all the cat's bones,' she replied. 'We forgot! Of course we must have a harp of Darcy's breastbone. I shall curve the spine over just so, and tie it to this thigh bone once I have cleaned the meat and washed off the lime. Oona will give me some hair for strings.'

She took a step towards me. 'Manticory, there was something wrong with *The Cruel Sister*! I mean the operetta you wrote, *The Cruel Sister*. It was wrong that the good sister died and that the cruel sister won. We have made it right.'

The Eileen O'Reilly appeared, ghostly in Darcy's nightdress. Quite a creditable cascade of light-red curls fell down her back. I wondered if they had started growing faster in the night as she lay in Darcy's bed, breathing the air of Darcy's pillow.

She pointed her candle towards the stairs where splashes of blood descended down to the *androne*.

'Will ye be showin' me where the scullery is? And the buckets and rags?' she asked. In her other hand she held up Darcy's frizzled fringe.

'And a spade for buryin' this in the garden? To do the business complete.'

I was uneasy with Eileen O'Reilly in the *palazzo*, yet absurdly happy with her company too.

My sisters clustered around her, seeking her conversation, especially about Harristown and all the other places of our childhood. I was afraid of claiming too much of her time, but her eyes always followed me over the tops of their heads.

Ida had insisted on cleaning the bones and stringing the harp with Oona's hair. The articulations of Darcy's spine curved just as Ida wished. The thigh bone stood straight, white, virginal. Of course it made no music. Oona's hair was silent under Ida's fingers, but she hummed nasally, impersonating the harp's voice. Finally, she had been persuaded to put the gaunt instrument away in a cupboard. From there I quietly extracted it and hid it under a fringed armchair.

It thundered all through the next day and night, with the

wind hurling the shutters against the walls. The Eileen O'Reilly stood at our window, transfixed by the drama on the canal, following the creaming tip of each wave with her blue eyes.

'The Divil wouldn't send out his dog on such a day as this,' she whispered.

That night, when I closed my eyes, I imagined Darcy's hollowed corpse struck by a long dry shaft of lightning all the way down in the lime pit. I saw her sitting bolt upright all white and powdery with the lime, and climbing up the stone shaft, while the moon shone through the gap in her upper torso where her breastbone had been. I saw her walking across the garden and then passing through our great oak door – as all doors are permeable to the dead – and mounting our lion-studded stairwell with dragging steps to arrive in my own chinoiseried bedroom. She stood over my bed. Her skull, the house of her bad brain, was broken. Its horns were fused to its bone.

At last, lying rigid with terror in my bed, I took responsibility for the words that I had written: I felt that I deserved Darcy's retribution thick and threefold, more than any other Swiney, far more than Ida who had simply applied herself with pure literality to the story I had set up with my conniving, heartless words in the name of entertainment, to make money, to sell lies.

The Cruel Sister, I thought, *she is me*.

The next day passed in a sick swoon.

Deserving my punishment, that night I turned myself out of doors; I turned myself into bait to draw. Every sliver of innocent noise was the scrape of a blood-dripping shoe; every creak, the crack-knuckles of Darcy, the accomplished ghostly hammerer and filleter of Irish Goose Girls who pretended to be writers. Every gurgle of every wave was a mocking thing, the giggle of a murderous dead sister happy in her work of hunting down her real killer. Every knock was the dropped knot of Darcy's hand-kerchief garrotte, every breeze the final breath I might draw before Darcy took me at last. I felt the rush of her hammer and knife at my neck.

But when I looked behind me, the only person I saw was the Eileen O'Reilly, finding me in the dark, just as she found me by the privy midden all those years ago. And just like that, she said again, 'What is it, Manticory Swiney? Is ye took sick on yerself, is it?'

She was carrying a shawl for me and an umbrella. She wrapped the shawl around my shoulders.

'Don't be infuriatin' on me for following ye on your private walk, Manticory. All day ye've looked haunted out of your seven senses and I was afearin' for ye. I know ye do not sleep. How could ye? Ye're so tired and kilt ye can hardly think, can ye? Let us be goin' home. I wouldn't be sorry for a cup of steamin' tea in my hand, nor a toasted bun neither.'

'No more would I,' I agreed.

We linked arms and walked silently. Her side aligned against mine was warm; her hand on my wrist was firm. She did not press me for explanations.

She said, 'Manticory, I have me own hauntin' to keep me awake – I jest remembered I must go and fetch Millwillis's ghastly manuscript, or desthroy it.'

'How could we have forgotten that?'

'I will go in the early part of the evening. I made a friend of the maid who turns down the sheets. She'll let me in on the quiet.'

'How will we live through the day?'

'As we have done till now,' she said. 'In agony. As if in a dream.'

When we arrived at the *palazzo*, it was to the sound of nasal notes haunting the upstairs apartments. The music trickled down the stained steps to the *androne*, where I paused, and cursed.

No matter where we hid the harp, Ida always found it again.

'Play the fiddle, Ida honey,' urged Oona, 'not that thing.'

'You forgot,' said Ida. 'Darcy sold it to buy a lottery ticket.'

Ida lifted the harp. Of course, it made no music. But keening, shrieking sounds poured out of Ida as she plucked on it, flooding the *palazzo* with the memory of blood.

52

The next day the *Gazzetta* ran a story about an English newsman discovered dead at the bottom of a laundry boat in Mestre. The police, it reported, had no credible leads in the case.

I fed on the sentences that said:

Although the gentleman bore signs of a contusion to the back of the head, this probably occurred when he fell against the hard surface at the bottom of the boat. The post-mortem has confirmed that he died of suffocation. All signs point to an unusual and unfortunate accident.

We had not killed him. The sheets had done it. My brain fell in love with that fact, finding all kinds of corners to hide in. The body had been made away with and had not been found in any proximity to us. I tried to give it similar distance in my mind.

That was not to be allowed.

For that same afternoon, before the Eileen O'Reilly could retrieve the manuscript, a policeman came calling at our *palazzo*.

A tall man, his jowls and his dramatic widow's peak gave his face the look of a seven-pointed baroque shield. He introduced himself as Capitano Viaro.

He had some pretensions to English. So it was in broken English that he told us that he knew that '*il giornalista morto*' had been writing about us.

'The manuscript of a book,' he said, 'it was found in the hotel room, abandoned with all his possessions.'

As he spoke, he ran his eyes around, noting our poor clothing and the grandeur of the drawing room where we sat. He was no Brother of the Hair, this sober middle-aged man: he looked at our heads without wonder.

From his disapproving expression, this Viaro had taken a deep dip into Millwillis's pages, and the writing had not been too sophisticated to withstand his linguistic skills.

Berenice said defiantly, 'I still cannot for the life of me understand why you should want to talk to *us* about his death. I've never even been to Mestre. I believe none of us have.'

'None,' we chorused.

'Mestre,' I added hastily. 'We know he was found at Mestre because of the *Gazzetta*.'

I held it up, blushing at its finger-worn pages, which betrayed the intensity of our interest in the death.

'Signorina, I come here for information. We are afraid that there may be another victim. It is discovered that a young lady had been travelling with Mr Millwillis. She had been seen in the hotel, though she *had no room of her own there*.' He paused significantly. 'And we are finding that she disappeared a short time after the man's death. Her clothes, they were still in that room. The hotel owner called us to take them away.'

In rapid Italian, the Eileen O'Reilly spoke to him. 'I believe,' she said, 'that you speak of myself. I am she, Eileen O'Reilly of Brannockstown, County Kildare, Ireland. And I am here and perfectly safe and well.'

'I took you for a Swiney sister,' said Viaro. He counted on his fingers.

She interrupted, 'I had been working with Mr Millwillis, it is true. But I discovered that Mr Millwillis was a bad man, a corrupt man, and I forsook his company—'

'So you came here?' The policemen frowned. 'But I understand that you spoke very badly of these ladies to Signor Millwillis, and that he wrote down what you said, Signorina O'Railli. To *sell*, Signorina O'Railli.'

'That is the very reason why I am here! I came here to explain to these ladies, and to apologise to them.'

I said quickly, 'Of course we are old schoolfellows, with a friendship going back to our childhoods—'

Viaro was half listening, distracted. His eyes continually returned to Ida. Finally, he asked, 'Where did you get that most unusual harp?'

Darcy's breastbone, now grey and creamy white and strung with Oona's hair, sat in Ida's lap. She strummed a silent note.

Viaro asked again, 'The harp?'

'It is a part of our singing act, of which you've read,' I told him.

'*The Cruel Sister*!' explained Ida.

'This *model* of harp is called "The Cruel Sister" from an old Irish folk tune,' I said hastily.

Ida said, 'And doesn't it look *fierce* like the breastbone of a sister?'

'I could not say against that,' said Viaro. He tore his eyes away from it with reluctance. 'Now may I confirm this list of all the Swiney ladies who are here, for my records?'

'Miss Ida, aged twenty-two? Ah, it is you with the harp, thank you. Miss Oona, aged twenty-three? Yes. Miss Pertilly, twenty-four? You dress as a maid? Very well. Miss Manticory, aged twenty-five? Good. Miss Berenice, twenty-nine years? Thank you. I know your sister Enda is departed. My condolences.'

He frowned at his notebook. 'So where is your sister, the eldest, the Signorina Darcy, aged thirty-one?'

'She has been away in Dublin some weeks,' the Eileen O'Reilly said quickly. 'She's contriving a new show.'

'She's a very contriving sort of girl,' said Ida, strumming the harp, 'with a very contriving heart inside her. Of course, that was in the old days, when she had a heart inside her.'

She laughed loudly.

The policeman persisted. 'When exactly did the Signorina Darcy leave? Is she coming back to Venice?'

'A bit of her shall always be among us,' insisted Ida.

Oblivious to the rictus of anxiety clamping her sisters' faces, Ida let her tongue clatter on, very far from sense, but close enough related to it that the policeman pulled out a notebook

427

and began to make himself some tense little scribbles. The sun was setting but we made no move to light a lamp.

'Our sister Ida,' I said confidentially, 'has episodes when she is not herself, as you can plainly see now. Do not let her distract you from your proper urgent investigations about the terrible fate of Mr Millwillis. Let me see you to the door—'

Ida interrupted, 'For it's getting evil dark outside and I am sure there are devilish crimes happening that need to be solved. You know what they say, the longer the hair, the closer to Hell.'

The policeman allowed himself to be guided out of the room.

'I shall return shortly,' he said on the threshold.

Ida cooed, 'We thank you for your visit, and fair weather after you.'

'Expect me tomorrow,' he said, bowing, pale, determined.

'Is that so at all?' I asked but my voice wavered on the words.

53

'He knows we killed Darcy, the creature,' wept Oona. 'And he will work it out about Millwillis, too.'

'We're corpses,' keened Berenice. 'They have done for us. They have taken everything now.'

'It is not all of us who are implicated,' I said. 'Only Ida and myself have anything to fear. At worst, the rest of you are just witnesses whose tongues were temporarily frozen by fear. If we devise a confession—'

'But you and I shall not go alone, Manticory,' said Ida. 'The Swineys do everything in perfect synchronicity. We shall drop from our gallows at the same time. The Harristown crows will be calling for us soon.'

I looked into Ida's eyes, seeing only clouds and shadows.

'And we shall have our names to the very last!' she said. 'Our beautiful names! Berenice! Pertilly! Manticory! Oona! They never took those.'

Ida had uttered a truth. Our paternal gift of names had been almost the only thing about us that had not been changed along the way by those who had profited from us.

'Better to hang than to starve,' laughed Ida. 'Quicker that way.'

'Ye are starving,' said the Eileen O'Reilly. 'It is true. I took a look inside the kitchen cupboards. What have ye eatable? Only a few grains of porridge in the house, is it not? Rainfleury and Stoker did this to ye? And Millwillis did his part, too, I know. With my own help.'

She looked down.

Pertilly said in a clotted voice, 'We are not without a cup of comfort; I'll fetch us something from the kitchen.'

I rose abruptly and went to stand by the window, on the edge of our declining Swiney world and the other place beyond it, with just a pane of glass between our desperateness and its indifference to us. The Eileen O'Reilly joined me. Oona and Berenice linked arms with me. Ida came last, and she gave her hand to Berenice, inserting herself between Oona and myself.

That evening, Venice was in a state of furious beautifulness, as perfect in herself as one of Darcy's pure rages. The work boats were gone and the gondolas had not yet commenced their trysts. The steam *vaporetto* had retired for the night. The Grand Canal was onyx, stippled with rare shafts of white light from gas lamps and lanterns. It was the moment of dead tide, the turning point between ebb and flow, a sinister, passionless moment, a lost no-time.

'Something to drink?' Pertilly arrived with the only silver tray that had not yet been sold. On one side were glasses brimming with wine, and on the other a whole quire of blank paper. In the middle was a salver piled with coins and banknotes.

'The money,' she said, 'I held back till this moment. I have something to explain. It is that—'

Her eyes flickered nervously from face to face.

'I have been working at Almoro Pagin's *trattoria*—'

'While we were starving and starving?' Berenice asked. 'With a single candle between us?'

'I fed you as much as I could,' said Pertilly, 'without making you suspect me.'

'Why did you not tell us?'

'Almoro made me promise. He was afraid that Darcy would gamble it away if she knew of it. I did not like to lie to you all, but I wanted to save enough to feed us while Manticory writes the book that will feed us better than I can.'

'The book?' Berenice frowned.

'The book that Darcy told Millwillis about, the one that is the story of the Swiney Godivas but by us. Darcy would not permit you to write it, Manticory, because she knew *she* would come out of it badly. But Darcy cannot stop you now.'

A silence fell among us.

Pertilly added, 'And if there is anything you're not remembering, Manticory, I am sure you can take yourself a look in Darcy's black books. I had to burn a few for kindling but they're still massed in the press in her room.'

I asked, 'And how will the most recent chapter with the True Revelations about the deaths of Millwillis and Darcy be received by the public? And how will it keep us from dangling off the end of our nooses?'

'And a book will take for ever,' said Berenice, 'and the policeman will be back tomorrow morning.'

'I belave,' said the Eileen O'Reilly, 'that I have the means to hurry things on their way. That was an ugly turn I did on ye, when I spoke of ye to Mr Millwillis. Let me be makin' it up now.'

She took hold of my hand. I sniffed the scent of her – soap, Irish skin, sweet and salty like rain. She smelled like a Swiney.

'If I talk to the policeman, will ye trust me?'

I nodded. Berenice, Oona and Pertilly breathed as one. 'We will.'

'And Manticory, would ye not let me be discoorsin' an' discoorsin' without ever coming to a point?'

'I could,' I told her.

'And if I falter and fail, will ye lend me the gift of yer tongue to save me, Manticory? It would be like an amulet for me to know that ye were with me on that.'

'I will be with you on that.'

'And Ida,' she asked, 'will ye hold your tongue?'

Ida smiled. 'I shall hardly speak a word.'

'Let us be havin' this drink now.' The Eileen O'Reilly raised one of the glasses that Pertilly had brought in.

'To your Ma,' she said. 'Who I wisht could've been mine.'

54

The next morning's *Gazzetta* plunged us into a new abyss. The Venetian newsmen were assiduous in investigating the death of one of their own tribe. They knew Millwillis had been writing of us and that we had been visited by the police.

The headline read: *Irish Sisters 'Persons of Interest' in Laundry Death*.

I was still reading the article aloud when the doorbell rang.

Ida shouted at the bell-pull, 'Go away, Mr Policeman!'

'No, Ida,' said the Eileen O'Reilly. She looked at me. 'Don't be lettin' the heart fail inside ye, Manticory.'

From the red rims of her eyes I had already deduced that she'd passed the night rehearsing word and gesture. I had heard her voice from Darcy's room, trying out different levels of emphasis, but I could not make out the phrases.

The doorbell chimed again.

'Lay him on,' said the Eileen O'Reilly. 'I am ready.'

Viaro came puffing up the stairs, his face moist from the heat of the morning. The polite salutations tensely achieved, he opened his notebook, in which he had written a list of questions.

The Eileen O'Reilly stood herself next to him. Boldly, she reached out and closed his notebook.

'*Le Signorine Swiney*,' she told the policeman, 'have asked me to speak for them.'

We nodded vigorously. Pertilly clasped her hands together in a thank-you.

'Ye may be wanting to take a seat for yourself,' the Eileen O'Reilly told Viaro. 'This will be some time in the telling.'

I offered him the least lumpen of the armchairs, and he sat upon it delicately.

The Eileen O'Reilly commenced to pace, and to talk. 'It was only after ye left yesterday, Capitano, that the workings of my mind began to put the pieces together. Ye yourself may have already gathered all the facts – sure ye have – but I may have somethin' to add. Where to begin, where to begin? The whole story is like a string danglin' in front of a cat. I am fair exhausted from battin' it around all night on my sleepless bed.'

She made a vague and helpless gesture with her hand, to indicate the great business of innocent disorganisation in her thoughts.

The more dowdy her presentation, the surer I grew that she had scripted herself perfectly.

It is the Eileen O'Reilly who should have been up on the stage, not myself, I thought. *All these years, she should have been up there, the Swiniest of us all.*

'So.' She stopped still and looked her man in the face. 'No doubt ye have found out since yesterday, with the great thoroughness in ye, that I am here in Venice on behalf of the alimentation business of my uncle Declan back in Ireland? I expect no less of ye, great man that ye are.'

Viaro shook his head. She feigned surprise. 'Ah, then, here is the nub of it. My uncle Declan's a grand importer of your Italian white wine and your stuffed olives and your white anchovies that are a wonder in themselves. So I am here that the wine and olive merchants may meet with me with greatest convenience and for to keep an eye on our Venetian agent and stop him palatherin' at girls when he should be doing the books.'

With the policeman's eyes engaged on the expansive gestures of her hands, I was able to make a cutting motion with my hand across my throat without his seeing me.

She nodded. 'But there's me discoorsin' and discoorsin'. The point is that it suited me to be in Venice at this particular moment because I had . . . *business*' – she seemed to falter – 'with the newsman St John Millwillis.'

433

From somewhere, she produced a blush.

'Mr Millwillis was not a good species of a creature. In fact, I must confess that he was a very sordid thing of a man in my own respect, and abused my own trust in ways that bring shame on our whole family. It'll look bad on me, I know. But I must confess it, for there's no denying it.'

She squeezed a tear from her blue eye. The policeman made soothing noises like a pigeon in the back of his throat. 'Dear *signorina*,' he said paternally, 'when one's blood is young and fierce, these things happen. It need not stain your life for ever.'

'It is true,' she sniffed, 'that I cannot hold hatred against Millwillis any more, for the man died a terrible death.'

'And you have something to tell me about that, my dear?'

'Millwillis was wantin' to be here in Venice on his own account, about the nasty book he was writin', the one about the Swiney sisters. I was black afraid of the use to which he'd be puttin' my own nigglety words. I had spoken rashly to him and I was full to the neck of regrets.'

She looked into my face. 'It is true, full to the neck,' she said sadly.

She turned back to Viaro. 'So I . . . travelled with him to Venice. In the train, on the way, he was only too happy to let me read all those pages he had written. He was proud of it, the dirty dog, so he was. Like with the articles, he had twisted my ignorance to suit his purpose, which was to denounce the Swiney girls as a shameless sack of charlathans in themselves. He twisted my memories from old ages ago! Millwillis was a *journalist*. He hated the truth. He lived off manufactured sensation.'

She shook her head sadly. She spoke in quiet tones now, as if in a confessional. 'For the way I had helped him in that, I am sorry with all the veins of my heart, for they are good creatures, the Swiney sisters, for the most part. And it was only ever Darcy Swiney who deserved my raggin', with the bitter hand she had and her black tongue, a livin' terror she—'

'Perhaps enough about Darcy?' I suggested quietly. She nodded.

434

'Millwillis was like a gravedigger, so he was. He tookt my little words and used them as a spade to dig deeper and to find more darkness. And the more he delved, the more he had changed his mind about the root of the evil in the Swiney Godiva Corporation. Through Mr Millwillis's investigations, I have discovered that my uncle and I—'

'Wait! Your uncle is involved with Mr Millwillis?' Viaro had opened his notebook and was furiously scribbling.

'No indeed. He's a decent man himself. But aside from his importin', my uncle Declan has a business called Growant. For the hair.'

'You too are in the hair business?' the policeman said. 'It is an Irish thing, this great interest in the hair?'

'It was a dark and revengeful thing, my own interest in the hair,' admitted the Eileen O'Reilly. 'Growant was set up to destroy the Swiney Godivas' business. But that is not material to the case, as I am not, except to tell ye things that matter. And that is . . . that my uncle Declan and I have been very much mistaken in the characters of our two chief investors in the Growant business, the Misters Rainfleury and Stoker.'

'The same men who are the patrons of the Swiney Godivas?' Viaro waved his pencil. 'It seems far from scrupulous that they should invest in a rival?'

'That is the least of it!' cried the Eileen O'Reilly. 'Those two scuts of men have dealt unscroopilessly with the Swiney Godivas, embezzlin' the profits out of the poor ladies—'

She put her hand on my shoulder and said, 'And forcing them into unsavoury situations.'

I nodded and she continued. 'Ye'd not be believin' how they abused and exploited the trust of those fatherless girls. Gave them neither peace nor ease till they consented to all sorts. Manticory, can ye explain more?'

'Indeed, sir, it is true. We were tricked, kept in the dark' – I looked at Oona – 'seduced' – I turned to Berenice – 'betrayed. We were unwittingly forced into the filthy human hair trade. And into quackery. How for *years on end* we Swiney sisters were nothing more than dolls animated by Mr Rainfleury and

435

Tristan Stoker to enact their corrupt commercial desires. They always acted as if we were devoid of souls of our own. And finally, they were the ruin of us.'

'I am sorry for all that,' said Viaro gravely. 'But the death of the newsman remains unexplained. And there is every reason . . .'

'Now here is the material point at last,' announced the Eileen O'Reilly. She bestowed on the policeman a gaze as unwavering as a Madonna's. 'Before he disappeared, I saw with my own eyes that Millwillis was livin' in a terrible fear of his life. And the people he feared was not the Swiney girls but the two men, Augustus Rainfleury and Tristan Stoker. For Mr Millwillis was on the point of exposin' Rainfleury and Stoker and *all their evil doings*. In his book.'

The policeman agreed. 'It is true that these men's characters would be ruined by that manuscript, if it were published.'

Eileen commenced once more to roam about the room. Her gestures amplified. Her hands described wider circles. One long lock of hair loosed itself from her chignon and tumbled down her back.

'Millwillis's murtherin' lies on the consciences of Rainfleury and Stoker,' she said. 'Think on it. *They was the ones who had every motive in the world* to destroy Millwillis. As for the Swiney girls, well Millwillis was the best thing that ever happened to them, for he was the first person to open their eyes to the ways those scoundrels had abused their innocence.'

'And yet the Swiney girls are here in Venice where Millwillis died,' Viaro pointed out. 'But Rainfleury and Stoker are in Dublin. My colleagues there have ascertained their whereabouts. Securely.'

The Eileen O'Reilly blustered, 'Of *course* neither of those criminals was here in Venice when it happened. They are too cunnin' in themselves for that. Mr Millwillis knew this was so. But he was black afraid of a man he thought the minion of Rainfleury and Stoker. He had seen the man outside his house in Dublin many times, he told me. And also near his place of work.'

I mused aloud, 'Could he have been that same man who had written threats against him in letters to the paper?'

The Eileen O'Reilly looked at me with wide eyes.

Viaro said, 'Yes, there was a man who signed himself *PS* who promised a beating to Millwillis. Did the journalist say what he looked like?'

'Indeed. He was a large, hairy man who would terrify a rhinoceros with his sideburns hangin' halfway down to his knees and the evil expression on him enough to scare a Medusa.'

'What a horror!' cried Oona.

I shot the Eileen O'Reilly a warning look. She had gone too far. I wanted to tell her, *You cannot invent such a man. He sounds like a thing from a fairy story. You must make him seem more comfortable, like a common murderer.*

As if she had heard me, the Eileen O'Reilly insisted, 'No, I *really* saw him, and he really was a monsther of hair. I saw him myself, exactly two days after Millwillis disappeared. I recognised him from Millwillis's describing straight away. It is only now that all these things are fallin' into place in the scattered brain on me.

'On the day of his death, Mr Millwillis received a message from Rainfleury and Stoker. They wanted him to meet with their minion, a man he would recognise, they said, by his extreme hairiness. Millwillis suddenly realised why the hirsute fellow had been a-following him. His love of money were stronger nor his fears and he decided to meet with the hairy minion.'

The Eileen O'Reilly paused, clearly exhausted by her inventions. I admired her wholeheartedly. I'd never had to compose any of my fictions under the view of a policeman.

'So,' she continued, 'that Rainfleury and that Stoker was dangling the prospect of a rich reward, if Millwillis would only leave their two names out of his Swiney Godiva book. That pair of beasts did not mind if the newsman destroyed the Swiney girls at all. The point they made was that Millwillis would still have a sensation on his hands, but he'd earn the double on the quiet. Millwillis went after the bait. And he ended up dead at

437

the bottom of a laundry boat. And I'd be guessin' that the hairy monster of a minion is at the bottom of that black deed.'

'It is true,' said Viaro, 'that at the end of his book Millwillis was speculating that this man *PS* was a danger, and that he was employed by Rainfleury and Stoker.'

'The manuscript is your evidence. From the victim himself. Ye have seen that Millwillis had not yet had time to erase their two names when he went to get his reward – he wanted his money first.'

The doorbell chimed again.

'It's Signor Bon,' Pertilly reported.

An unaccountable smile stretched across my mouth, and it did not escape the Eileen O'Reilly.

'From all I've heared told of that Bon since I've been among ye,' she said, 'he sounds any amount of a quality gentleman and can only do us good.'

I smiled at her 'us' and then my skin warmed with relief at the sight of Saverio's sweet face.

'Dear ladies,' said Saverio quickly, 'I was so worried when you did not come to my studio for the photograph that your *friend and saviour* Mr Millwillis had commissioned of you specially for his book—'

Dear Saverio, I thought, *you have already contrived the same story as our own. Only you could do that; only you would offer yourself as our accomplice now. Only you and the Eileen O'Reilly.*

He stopped, noticing the Eileen O'Reilly. I saw him take in the absence of Darcy. His eyes met mine. I shook my head slightly.

Introductions made, he continued, 'Then I saw in the *Gazzetta* this morning the reason for your absence: that the *Capitano* has somehow got to thinking of you ladies as persons of interest in the death of the foreign newsman. And so I made my way to the Questura to make certain facts available to him about your patrons Rainfleury and Stoker, who are the only ones who would really have a motive to silence that poor gentleman who was about to reveal *their* evil ways to the world.'

438

The Eileen O'Reilly said enthusiastically, 'Indeed I'm after tellin' the *Capitano* exactly the same thing!'

Saverio said, 'I deduce from this terrible story that the poor Swiney sisters suspected it too but they were too afraid to denounce the two dangerous men who had held them in thrall all this time.'

'Indeed,' said Viaro, rising. 'My investigations shall continue in this new direction.'

'I shall accompany you,' said Saverio, speaking in Venetian, 'and perhaps I can confirm any matters that are still uncertain in your mind.'

'I shall be in your debt,' replied Viaro in a rush of mellifluous dialect.

When the doorbell chimed a few hours later, Pertilly reported from the back window that a tall man with beautiful hair stood at the gate.

'The hairy man! Come to finish his murders!' cried Oona. 'God save us all!'

Pertilly called, 'No, he is not like that. He has a look of kindness about him. In fact, I cannot say for why, but I very much like the look of him.'

From the rear window, we all – Oona, myself, Berenice, Ida, Eileen, Saverio – looked down on the man. Unaware of our scrutiny, he made his way along the garden path with an easy, rolling step. He was tall, prosperously attired. Most prosperous of all was his hair. His sideburns curled, his auburn head hair curled and his beard curled in dense luxuriance.

He was the man I had seen at Enda's funeral.

Ida cried, 'He has legs as fine as Oona's inside his trousers. Let him come up.'

When Pertilly ushered our gentleman-caller into the dining room, I was the first to take his hand.

'Phelan Swiney, Mariner?' I asked.

55

'The same,' said the man. His accent carried the salt of the docks of Philadelphia and the mist of the fields of Kildare. A grin flowered over his face, a grin of Swiney dimensions, a grin of Ireland, of green fields shimmering with dew under the shadows of the slow crows. There was a musicality to his voice that recalled Oona's, and a look of Enda in his elegance. I saw Ida in his brow, and Pertilly in the outline of his head. I saw myself in his eyes, green as glit.

'Will you be giving your father a hug?' asked Phelan Swiney. 'Let me see, I know you, surely. Berenice of the brown hair? Oona the fairy? Idolatry, my youngest. Sweet-natured Pertilly? And Manticory, of course you must be Manticory.'

We were all grinning now, the family grin. Phelan Swiney pointed to the Eileen O'Reilly. 'Who is this? I know the sad fate of Enda, but where is Darcy? This is not Darcy, though she is a lovely girl in herself, I am sure. Where is –?'

Without a moment's hesitation, all of us, including Eileen, threw ourselves into his arms and there was no more talking, only weeping and laughter.

I buried my head in Phelan Swiney's waistcoat, and did not want to look up from it.

Our father smelled of fine laundering, of good tobacco, and infinite comfort.

In the light of the seashell lamp, we were finishing a master-piece of a meal cooked by Pertilly. A great spending of emotion had kindled a fierce famine in our bellies, as well as an unself-conscious desire to break bread together as a family. Pertilly had rushed to the market, her pockets heavy with the money Phelan had forced into them.

Now, when we could eat no more, the conversation turned at last to Millwillis, and to Darcy.

'You know I was on his trail,' said Phelan Swiney, 'frankly wishing to do him a disservice if I could, and indeed make the great weasel of a creature know the meaning of fear. So imagine my surprise when I found someone had already avenged my daughters for me. And more emphatically than I was planning. I cannot say I am sorry for it, either.'

'I cannot believe anyone is,' I told him.

'It is a credit to you, my sweethearts, that not one of you has for a second questioned my innocence in this matter of Millwillis's death,' Phelan Swiney said.

'There is a reason for that,' remarked Ida. 'We know you did not do it.'

'How?'

'Because Darcy did.'

He swallowed. 'I had always been afraid that she would turn in that direction. I should not have called her by the name of Darcy. You know it means 'darkness'? And then there was the truly dark thing that befell the poor girl when she was eight. It cannot but have damaged her mind. Your dear mother always feared – but where is Darcy? Does she hide? Is this why? I did not want to ask—'

'Yes,' said Ida. 'She is hidden. Very much so.'

I interrupted. 'What happened to Darcy when she was eight?'

'It is the saddest of sad stories. Your mother gave birth to a little girl in November of that year. A new little daughter would normally have been a matter of joy for me. But I still feared my Fenian shenanigans bringing the law down on my family. So I was away in America then: I made my secret visits back only when I knew I might see my latest sweetheart of a daughter and choose her name for her. However, this little baby decided to arrive three months early and in a tearing hurry. When your mother saw how it was going with herself, she sent the twins away mushrooming, so that they would not hear the screams.

441

She shut the younger ones – I suppose that would be you, Oona, Pertilly and Manticory – in the barn with a blanket and some buttermilk. Ida, of course, was not born yet.

'Your mother locked Darcy in the room with her, in case she would need help with the little one. She blamed herself for what she imposed on our eldest. You know she ever after denied herself the consolations of Mass by way of a penance, poor creature?'

We nodded.

'When Annora started screaming with the birthing pains, Darcy hid under the bed. Your mother was delirious, nearly dead from pain and loss of blood, but afterwards she always remembered the curses she screamed. Darcy must have thought they were directed at her, for tucking herself away. But there was nothing to be done anyway. The baby was born dead. It was not her time.

'In spite of her fever and her pain, your mother's head was full of the thought that, without me there, she herself was to come up with a name for the dead child. She called her "Phiala". But of course little Phiala, being stillborn, was in Limbo.

'The bleeding went on. Annora fainted more times than she could remember. She thought of the little ones shut in the barn, but she was too weak to rise. She told me that all she could do was ask Darcy to take the poor creature in a bucket and to bury her before the twins should return and be terrified by the sight of the corpse and all the blood. Annora had the strength to scratch the initials of the baby's name and the year on a wooden spoon, which she fashioned into a cross with another spoon tied with rags. She sewed the baby's name on a pillowcase that she wrapped around the body, to spare Darcy the worst of the looking. And then she fainted again.

'When she awoke, Darcy was in the room with her, mopping up the blood. The bucket with the baby had vanished. So had the cross. She asked Darcy where she had buried the body, so that she might give the infant a proper burial in time, but the girl refused to answer her. In fact, Darcy would never talk of it again, and pretended that it had never happened. She denied all knowledge of it. And eventually, I suspect, she forgot what had happened, and where the corpse had been laid.'

I pictured Darcy's fat childish fingers digging with a wooden spoon into the sodden soil. I told him, 'Darcy never forgot. She buried the baby in the clover field. And she hated anyone to go there. She would punish you, if you did.'

'From what I heard, Darcy was quite a one for punishing,' said our father. 'Your mother said that Phiala's death changed her. Darcy had been a whole-souled child then. Somewhat inclined to contrariness, but no great harm to her. After that, she grew morbidly interested in all things to do with death. But she also became more angry, with more violence about her too. Your mother worried about how she would beat the rest of you, how she seemed to lack any human sympathies—'

'The baby was found with a shoe dolly,' I remembered.

'That must have been Darcy's own idea,' he said. 'And it must have been her own dolly. Perhaps it was the last time she showed anyone a kindness. I would say that she buried a part of herself with Phiala.'

'The better part,' said the Eileen O'Reilly, holding one side of her head against the remembered blows of Darcy's fists.

'Your mother tried her hardest to tame Darcy's blackness. But it only grew the worse. Annora claimed that a devil had jumped out of the hole where Darcy buried Phiala, and had climbed into her breast.

'She longed to put it right, your poor mother. She wanted to console Darcy, but Darcy would not consent to be consoled for something she could not admit to. Your mother tried to find the grave, hoping she could draw Darcy's memories back to that day, and correct them. Annora never stopped looking for it. She would call for dead baby Phiala around the place when she could, as if her little soul might hear her in Limbo.'

'The goose!' Oona said. 'That was why she always called a goose "Phiala". So that she might call the name to her heart's content, and no one would think her mad.'

'Darcy always liked to strangle that goose, when she could,' Ida remembered.

Phelan Swiney nodded. 'Don't be thinking that Annora didn't notice that thing too. And then when you began to talk of going off to Dublin in all your grandness, she told me that she would never leave her lost baby, not until she found the grave. She never did. And now she's gone too, leaving you motherless, one and all.'

Footsteps rang in the corridor. Saverio's tall body, Saverio's kind face were approaching.

'Who is this fine gentleman?' asked Phelan Swiney. 'He has a great look of family about him. Did I inadvertently sire a son?'

Oona looked at me. 'If you want Saverio,' she said quietly, 'and if you promise you can recover if he is not after all what you want, then have at him.'

Ida and Berenice smiled at me. Eileen nodded.

Then Saverio was with us, his eyes on me.

'Manticory,' he said, in that voice that always said twice as much as words.

I rose and kissed him on the mouth, long and tenderly, until we both remembered to breathe, at the very last second. Otherwise I believe we would have died happily like that.

When we stopped, I saw that Phelan Swiney, Mariner, was weeping.

'Your mother used to kiss me that way,' he told me.

56

Each time I had bent my body under Alexander's, I wondered if he still found in me what he wanted. And I had feared that he would not. But I was sure of Saverio's esteem. I had never needed to wait for rationed portions of it. It was always there. For months, I had worn it as a garment, like a better, more hopeful version of my own skin. I had accustomed myself to its warmth without even knowing that it was Saverio who was making me feel less cold.

So we did not go at it raw, this business of kissing, Saverio and I. We went at it with the kiss half entered already, and I was free to think only of my senses, because Saverio, with that letter he had given me, had already made sense of love – love not as Alexander practised it, tactically and selfishly, but love as human animals properly make it – untidily, thoroughly, with the feelings spilling over into the thinking and the tasting knitted to the touching.

Saverio had named all the parts of love in that letter of his, in which he had written Irishly as the Harristown rain, scribbling his words all over me, in a sheer profusion that should have drowned my loneliness, if I'd only let it.

I had not listened then. But I was listening now.

'I'm feeling newborn,' I told Saverio, in the bedroom of the apartment above his studio.

We had walked there from the *palazzo*, as if deer-stepping over liquid crystal in glass slippers, so beautiful and fragile was the tiny space between us.

His room was large and light, empty of ornament, except the shifting reflections of the canal, Saverio, his bed and his voice. I asked him to lie down with me.

We lay face to face, kissing, breathing, looking, and kissing again. My fingers explored his face, and his traced mine. Our lips followed our fingers.

'What do you want of me, Saverio?' I asked him, and I was not afraid of the answer.

'You have given me such a long time to think about that question that the answer has regretfully become rather long.'

'What shall you want in the end, I mean?'

'This is all I want,' he told me. 'To have you in my arms, looking at me as if there is nothing else you'd rather see. For the rest, ask me again in two hundred years.'

After a long slow while, I asked, 'May I borrow your hand, Saverio? It would be the shame of the world if I knew how only your mouth and eyes taste.'

'The shame would indeed be killing. Yes, you may, if I may borrow yours.'

We tasted the different flavours of each other's fingertips, concluding that our thumbs were the saltiest, and the little finger of my left hand was the sweetest.

I asked next, 'Could you turn a little?'

'I am unwilling to lose the sight of you.'

'Just for a moment.'

In a moment I had found the musk tucked in the tiny creases of Saverio's neck. I thrust myself full length against his back and wrapped my arms around the great warmth and firmness of him, nibbling on the little curls at his nape. I could not help my hips pushing against him, withdrawing, and pushing again.

'Come back to me,' he moaned, turning to face me.

'Very well. But would you greatly mind removing your shirt?' I asked him. 'Linen and buttons are rough, and you'd not like to be kissed by a cat's mouth, would you?'

Saverio said, 'No. Why do you sigh, Manticory?'

I was sighing because I understood at last. *Your skin's supposed to feel like soap shedding its veils in warm water and the space between the blades of your shoulders is meant to feel a surge of feathers and your mouth is bound to fill, over and over, like an oyster, with salt and sweet.*

446

Saverio, I did not need to tell those things. He had as much human nature in him as I did.

We began to rake off our clothes, helping one another with buttons and the progress of linen over our knees and ankles, scrabbling with feet and toes.

When that was done, we lay flat on our backs, breathing quietly like lizards, looking at the water's shadows dancing on the ceiling.

'Let us not be solemn now,' Saverio said at last. 'It is the most inappropriate time to be solemn.'

'So it is,' I agreed softly.

Unable not to look at him, unable not to be closer to him, I burrowed my shoulder under his and kissed my way over the hairs of his chest till I found his nipple and fixed my lips on it. My tongue knew exactly what to describe upon it, and there was nothing solemn in that at all. My hand took his and asked it what to do and where to go, and was quickly helped there.

I held him quite tranquilly, despite the heat and hardness of him growing under my fingers and the audible clatter of the waves in my own blood, quickening and muting, quickening more.

When they were too much for me, I half rose and crawled to the centre of the bed, placed my forehead against the pillow and raised my hips, as I had always done.

Saverio climbed up on the bed too. But he eased my body round and laid me upon my back, so that I looked up at him, his skin filling the frame of my view entirely. Carefully, he placed his long thighs between mine, and grazed my face with his own.

'I would rather not go on with this,' he said sadly, 'than do it without looking at you.'

I drew his mouth to my lips, and then to my breasts, each in turn.

He looked up at me. 'You have not been sweetnessed here before,' he told me. I nodded. 'Or this way.'

It was I who shifted and gyred till he was inside me and above me.

447

I had thought it would take years to settle my skin into someone who was not Alexander, but it took less than seconds. With Alexander, desire had been like a bird that flittered through my body without alighting, leaving a tickling feather behind. Now desire fell on me as the swan fell on Leda, as a hawk falls on a rabbit, and it held me down, despite my writhing, intent on inflicting pleasure until I was utterly spent. And Saverio never stopped kissing me until I had to pull away from him so as not to cry into his mouth. And even then I wanted him back, because I wanted his voice, his nest of a voice with beating wings in it, inside me as well.

Afterwards I lay on Saverio's shoulder, encircled by his arm, his lips pressed against my hair, my skin. I breathed the sweet sweat I had generated on his skin. My heart still beat mightily, like a great festival rampaging through a village. I had never been so tired, I thought. I could feel the marrow seething inside my bones; my teeth felt raw and tender; my fingers seemed to have elongated by inches with all they'd encompassed. I wanted to sleep like a fisherman's cat, fat and slick with all I'd desired inside me, but I wanted to be awake too, to see what words could do to polish the afternoon's perfection, sidelined and forgotten, as the words had been these minutes numberless without number, Irish minutes tumbled with Venetian ones, minutes that grew to hours.

And Saverio began to talk then, of things past and to come, and I began to answer. Eventually the words grew quieter, our breaths longer and deeper.

Untangling

It is one year now since that day and the soft night that followed it.

The next morning there came a brief interruption to our pleasures when Viaro returned to the *palazzo* wishing to interview the Phelan Swiney, Mariner, who had written threatening letters to the dead journalist Millwillis. While the policeman was committing our father to a holding cell – showing him every courtesy and expressing his regret – Saverio took himself quietly to Mestre and examined the books of the carriage company that had brought our father to Venice on his mission of revenge. They proved that Phelan Swiney had indeed arrived in Venice the day after Millwillis met his death. This information chimed happily with the persuasive scenario the Eileen O'Reilly had in the meanwhile embedded in Viaro's mind of a hairy gentleman who looked entirely different to Phelan Swiney, Mariner, in every manner except regarding the quantity of hair. The policeman announced himself delighted to release our father with no taint to his character. Our father walked out of the prison immediately, and was again praising Pertilly's cooking three hours later.

Pertilly has married her Almoro Pagin. We dine better than we have ever done. Pertilly dresses the hair of Saverio's grand clients; Berenice teaches English to children from the church. It is enough to pay our rent, and a little – a grateful little – more. And Pertilly expects her first child, a Christmas gift for us all.

Ida is at peace. She assists Signor Pagin in the kitchen, dressing his cutlets and joints.

Not one of us has ever feared a thing from Ida. That one death was all she had ever needed to commit, and she is calm now, which we read in the thick dark-brown hair that has lately reached her knees once again. Ida still strums on the breastbone harp, supplying the mournful notes with her voice, when the mood takes her. And we do not stop her. That harp, that song, like our hair, occupies that liminal country between a sentient being and stuff, between living and dead, between the imperatives of nature and of conscience, between sister and enemy, between culture and biology. Who are we to decide what must be forgotten, and what can be?

No one expects to see Darcy in Venice – or in Dublin. We tell our Venetian friends that Darcy disliked Venice, and that she has returned to keep house in Dublin. On our rare visits to Dublin, we tell people that Darcy prefers to stay in Venice, being so wedded to the place with her heart, as we say.

My first book, now six months old, sells well and better than well. Readers love a scandal, especially one with love-making and immorality and young girls led astray by men for money. And yes, the public's imagination will always thrive on super-abundant quantities of hair.

Whoever owns the words tells the story – that old lesson of my childhood comes back now with a new flavour of truth. I have owned the words and told the story. And I have discovered my red wildness lies not in my hair, nor in the love I made with Alexander, but in my writing, and in the nights I spend with Saverio.

Of course the ends of Millwillis and Darcy have no place in my book, though the return of Phelan Swiney is a great episode in it, as in life.

The Venetian policeman's suspicions have put Rainfleury and Tristan under a charge of conspiracy to murder. My book has left their characters shattered. The Eileen O'Reilly wrote persuasively to her uncle Declan that they must separate Growant and themselves from the filthy contamination of Messrs Stoker and Rainfleury. The gentlemen were made to surrender their Growant shares at the tiniest of prices. Declan O'Reilly has kindly diverted the proceeds to the Swiney sisters who had been so black betrayed by way of moral recompense for the frauds practised on them.

Rainfleury and Tristan were last heard of in Australia, where they had fled under false names. The outlaws were trying to train a native woman hairier and more simian than the poor Baboon Lady Julia Pastrana. I have written to the 'Australian Monstrosity' with a copy of my book, and some newspaper cuttings about the alleged murderers, to ensure that the expense of their travel will not be rewarded. They may not return to Europe, as they have rewards on their heads in both Italy and Ireland.

It was my idea to spend a small part of the Growant money improving the formula with genuinely health-giving ingredients.

Oona has stopped pining after Tristan. It was one more blessed thing that came from my book. When she read my account of what had happened, she could not avoid seeing what he was and what a beguiled innocent she had been. Because she truly loved him, she knew immediately how to hate him, cleanly and thoroughly. It is a joy to hear her stretching her vocabulary with denouncing him.

'It is a woeful dry shrivelled thing that Tristan has inside himself,' she says now, 'where you'd expect to find a poet's heart, all moist and mighty there.'

Now there is a handsome Venetian merchant who pays Oona court and treats her like a princess. He has made a better offer at love than Tristan ever conjured in his shabby verse.

Berenice has likewise recovered from her passion for Augustus Rainfleury. She had wanted him because Enda did, not for the man he was. So now she manages a little regretful tenderness for him, wondering if the Antipodean sun has crisped his delicate pate. She has become religious and says her rosary daily for Enda, especially the Sorrowful Mysteries. I have never asked Berenice if the candle flame on the Pembroke Street stairs was deliberate, because I know Darcy's push over the banisters was.

We see our father often, though it is never often enough. The road did not fly under us to bring us together. There is too much time, and too much loving, to be caught up with.

His love for the joyous multiplicity of Venetian boats is a thing to see. We are looking into buying him a stake in a shipwright's business in Pellestrina as a way of keeping him more often among us. He has taken to Eileen with delight, pronouncing her his lost daughter. Indeed, looking at her hair, which grows ever more luxuriant, I sometimes wonder. Her butcher father loved his gin more than he cared for his scrawny daughter. Was Eileen the fair sister we should have had, instead of the cruel Darcy all along?

And it was Phelan Swiney, ex-Mariner, ex-Fenian, who arranged our last trip to Harristown, where we reburied baby Phiala and Annora side by side in a grave by the old chapel, while the slow crows wheeled overhead, mourning the world, the Swineys and all that had passed, all that has been lost.

The Eileen O'Reilly made sure that Phiala's little coffin held her shoe dolly too. The crossed spoons with her initials – I brought them back to Venice and I have planted them in the garden here, near the clover-sweetened grass where I like to read and write in the perfumed shadow of the wisteria.

Eileen spends her days among her uncle's purveyors of food-stuffs and brings home a comfortable spread of samples. Her evenings and nights she spends with us.

Venice has become our village more than Harristown ever was. We have friends in every *sestiere*. We have the foreigners' freedom to mingle between the classes and we are welcome everywhere.

'*Dénouement*' – that is the French word for 'untangling'. The Swiney Godivas are all untangled now, and each sister wears her hair as she pleases. Strangely perhaps, I have not cut mine. I find that I still love the whisper of it about my ears and the cloak it makes around my body, and its fierceness that would spring out and ambush you at any minute were it not plaited or caged inside a snood trussed with a stout pin. Although my book has brought us many requests, we shall never go on the stage again; for us, it was a place of servitude and uncomfortable exposure where we were sent, by Darcy and by our so-called protectors.

As for the original 'Miss Swiney' dolls, they too have come to rest in Venice. But they sleep day and night in the dark, in a large trunk never opened, up in the hot eaves in the attic. But those dolls are not as they once were, stiff and splendid. For each doll's body is inscribed with the fate of the girl she so hollowly imitated.

Enda's doll consists only of ashes in an urn. We cremated her in the fireplace. Pertilly's doll is shaven, and Darcy's has a great dark hole in the breast.

You might think 'Miss Manticory' would have a hole there too, since the heart was ripped out of me when Alexander died. Or rather, that the cavity opened when I discovered his betrayal. But I left the 'Miss Manticory' doll intact because I intend to heal. And because Saverio is helping me to forget what it is to be disdained and know what it is to be cared for, gently but passionately well. As he rows me around Venice in our green boat, I sometimes see a pale face on a bridge that reminds me of Alexander's. There is no pain to that vision. With the waves infinitely creative beneath me and love infinitely kind beside me, I think of Alexander as a land creature, and in the end, prosaic.

Land creatures – I'm not sorry there are no foxes in Venice. I still don't believe I could see one without thinking of Darcy swishing her hand behind her back and in front of her thighs, snatching my memory backwards through the years until it arrived dishevelled, terrified and helpless at the copse by Harristown Bridge.

Venice is full of bridges and maybe a few trolls. But I am up to meeting a gentleman troll now on any bridge and would not hesitate to knock him into the water. It's the ghosts who still trouble me occasionally. I have moved back to my room of peach and apricot and Chinese pavilions. On hot nights I see the face of Millwillis on the pillow beside me, flattened, with the breath pressed out of him. Then I realise who really lies there, fond and tousled and soft with sleep. Relief and gratitude course around my body like liquid sugar.

Some nights I see Darcy walking through the enfilade of bedrooms, restlessly shuffling the *cartelle* from the *tombola notturna*, which she never once won. I can look right through the hole where her heart should be. Other times I wake with a vision of my beloved Enda filling my eyes with liquid regret. She is lying broken and burning at the bottom of the Pembroke Street stairs. Saverio knows what my tears recall, and he holds me until they are all spent.

I even glimpsed Annora once, rising like a mermaid out of the water, with her stringy hair hanging down, waving a hand wrinkled from washing a yoke-necked smock in the greenness of the Grand Canal. She smiled at me with her long teeth, and offered me a salt-encrusted penny, as if to say, 'I told you it was true about your father.'

And then she slowly melted into the mist that rose forgivingly from the sweet soft water.

I don't believe I'll see her again.

They say that the Irish don't understand irony, but in fact we're teeming with it, like a head full of hair, like a head full of memories, like a moth in a mousetrap, like a sack of shame that empties itself into a book and finds itself redeemed.

For all I wished to put behind me, my book will keep the sodden earth of Harristown wet and the bodies in the Famine pits close to the surface, with only an inch of grass between us and death, only a long red curl between me and you.

One long red curl, partly inside me, partly outside.

HISTORICAL NOTES

All the characters in this book are invented apart from the La Touche family, Marcel Grateau of the Marcel waves and Julia Pastrana. London, in 1857, was convulsed by the spectacle of Julia Pastrana, the 'Baboon Lady' or 'the Missing Link', who danced and sang on the stage. Her face was simian and hairy with extra sprouts of growth in the form of a moustache and a beard. Five years later, her embalmed body was displayed at Piccadilly's Burlington Gallery.

'Captain MacMorris' is the name of Shakespeare's only Irish character.

My sisters' story has elements in common with that of the long-forgotten Seven Sutherland Sisters, who were once household names in America.

I would never have heard of the Seven Sutherland Sisters of Niagara County, New York State, if my friend Bill Helfand hadn't mentioned them over lunch a couple of years ago. Bill, an eminent medical historian, has advised me for the last three novels. He had an inkling I'd be interested in seven hairy sisters who took to the stage to peddle a quack hair restorant, made a fortune, spent it eccentrically and fell into obscurity with the advent of bobbed hair.

The Sutherland girls were born in rural poverty. There was also a brother, Charles, born in 1865, and possibly two other sisters who died young. It is said that their father, Fletcher Sutherland, a preacher and politicker, was exceptionally well endowed with hair, and that their mother had prepared a homemade ointment for her daughters' hair, the smell of which made them unpopular at school. But the girls' singing voices were popular in church. Their father cultivated their stage career from their early childhood. The Sutherland Sisters joined Barnum and Bailey's Greatest Show on Earth in 1883, with Charles working as a gatekeeper. Naomi married J. Henry Bailey, then employed in the dining tent, in 1885. By this time Fletcher, with Bailey's help, was marketing a Seven Sutherland Sisters 'Hair Grower'. The Seven Sutherland Sisters Corporation was based in New York. It all worked like a well-oiled machine: the circus made the sisters famous, helping their Hair Grower to earn $90,000 in its first year. Soon they added a Scalp Cleaner Comb and Colorators in eight shades.

The Sutherlands eventually made at least $3 million from their products, with 28,000 sales dealerships in the USA. Their best years were between 1886 and 1907, but they continued until 1917, with factories in New York, Chicago and Philadelphia.

They spent their fortune at a ruinous rate, especially on a grand Gothic mansion in Lockport, built in 1893 and fitted out with turrets, cupolas and chandeliers. The sisters were notorious for exercising on their bicycles on a circular cinder path in the garden, wearing nothing more than bathing suits. They owned at least seventeen cats and seven dogs, the latter arrayed in handsome handmade collars. One dog, Topsy, wore dresses of silk and cotton in the summer and wool or plush in the winter. Whenever travelling, the sisters sent fresh steaks to the dogs (which generally arrived already putrid). The cats dined on fresh liver. Expensive funerals were held for the pets. The sisters also commissioned a group portrait, and kept seven individual portraits mounted on easels.

But this lifestyle could not be maintained. They outspent their massive income, and the hair products lost popularity, leaving them destitute. The mansion was sold, with much Sutherland Sisters ephemera abandoned in the attic. Far from the days of the lavish pet funerals, sixteen of their cats were mass-chloroformed and buried in burlap sacks.

Four sisters never married. Isabella married twice, both times to men much younger than herself. Her first husband, twenty-seven years old to her forty when they wed, was Frederick H. Castlemaine, a colourful, cultivated morphine addict, and obsessed with guns. Castlemaine was said to shoot the heads of turtles basking on logs, the spokes out of the wheels of passing buggies, the bowls out of his hired men's pipes. He died of a morphine overdose in 1896. Isabella built him a $10,000 mausoleum, which was ransacked by thieves hoping to sell the body back to the grieving wife for a ransom or in search of the jewels allegedly buried with Castlemaine. They failed. Isabella grieved passionately for Castlemaine, until, at forty-six, she married Alonzo Swain, aged thirty. Victoria Sutherland married a preacher's son of eighteen when she was fifty. Only Naomi bore children – four of them.

The youngest Sutherland sister, Mary, died in the State Institution for the Insane in Buffalo in 1939. Grace Sutherland lived until 1946.

Each Sutherland sister had a single doll made in her image (and using her own combings) – but these dolls were not mass-manufactured for sale. Instead, they were used in window displays of Sutherland products. Victoria was offered $2,500 (sometimes reported as $1,500) for her hair by a drugstore owner or hairdresser, but instead sold a single strand to a jeweller for $25. The seven-foot strand was strung with a ten-carat diamond in the jeweller's window.

The Sutherland archives – including five of the dolls – were destroyed by a fire in their former mansion in 1938, seven years after the remaining sisters – Grace and Mary – had been forced to move away. A film about their lives was proposed, but Dora Sutherland was killed by a car when three sisters went to Hollywood. A script has never surfaced. Ephemera from their products still exists, but little published matter, the most interesting of which is Clarence O. Lewis's *The Seven Sutherland Sisters*, a 60-page pamphlet published by the Niagara County Historical Society.

The coldness of the trail might have been a gift for a novelist, leaving wide-open tracts for the imagination to work in. But the Sutherlands had left numerous advertising photographs and they still loomed larger than life. Their campaign of celebrity endorsement, rags, riches, rags was a parable. I decided I could draw on the dynamics of the Sunderlands' medical history, but set my novel in Europe, in the context of contemporary Victorian writers' and artists' obsession with long hair.

There are other issues explored in this novel. The Sutherlands appear to have enjoyed fairly harmonious relations with one another and frequently chose to live together. They also had a brother. But I was interested in portraying a large set of sisters at war and peace among themselves – so I decided to create my own hairy family and to make them Irish – and much divided in nature and temperament – and to bring them to Venice for the denouement of the story. And yes, there is indeed also some reference to Henry James's *The Aspern Papers*, in which the aged former lover of a celebrated romantic poet is stalked by an ambitious writer, for I also wanted to write a parable of one of the key moral debates of our own time: where does freedom of the press cross over into criminal intrusion, character assassination and simple venality at the expense of the prey?

There are other similarities between the Swineys and the Sutherlands. Like my Pertilly, Naomi Sutherland (who died in 1893) and Victoria (deceased 1902) were replaced by fake sisters. Naomi, like Oona, sang with a bass voice though her hair was brown. Both sets of sisters, Sutherland and Swiney, were born in grinding rural poverty and broke into the lime-light with singing shows in which their hair was the star attraction. Newspapers claimed that the Sutherland Sisters were obliged to be vigilant against frequent attempts to steal their hair. Mary Sutherland, like Ida Swiney, suffered from mental health issues. There was also a rumour that Isabella Sutherland's husband Frederick Castlemaine may have been in love with her sister Dora.

'Swiney' is a version of the more common name 'Sweeney'. In some slang usages, it means an unsophisticated person. The story several times refers to a Swiney who threw a psalter in the sea and later went mad: this ancestor of my characters was the hero of a legend entitled *Buile Suibhne* or *The Madness of Sweeney*, which began to take form in the ninth century but appears to refer back to the time of the Battle of Moira in 637. The story reflects tensions between Christianity and earlier Celtic faiths. Suibhne or Sweeney was king of Dal Araidhe, now County Antrim and north County Down. Sweeney was enraged when he was informed that the sound of a bell told of eminent churchman Ronan Finn marking out the site of the church in his kingdom. His wife tried to hold him back but was left holding his cloak as he tore away, completely naked. And so he arrived to find Ronan singing from his psalter. Sweeney flung the precious psalter into a deep lake and was about to deal harshly with its owner when he was summoned to do his duty at the Battle of Moira.

After a day and a night an otter raised the psalter from the water and carried it to Ronan, who then cursed Sweeney to wander Ireland insane and naked, and to be killed by a spear. As the armies gathered, Sweeney again encountered Ronan; this time the intemperate king killed one of his psalmists and struck the cleric's own holy bell with his spear. Ronan uttered his second curse, condemning Sweeney to live bird-brained in the trees, terrified by any noise, mistrustful of all, even those whom he loved. And Sweeney exploded into a madness that had him floating all over Ireland and eventually taking up residence at Glen Bolcain where the insane congregated, eating cresses. He lamented his loneliness, the absence of music and a woman's touch. He took to wandering for another seven years. After periods of sanity, he took again to the air, and crossed to the land of the Britons where he met the royal lunatic Alan, and they became friends until Alan drowned himself. Sweeney returned to his wanderings, finishing at Moling, where Ronan's first curse was fulfilled when Sweeney was speared by a jealous husband.

This story has in modern times been adapted by Seamus Heaney (*Swiney Astray*) and Flann O'Brien (*At Swim-Two-Birds*).

The natural selection theory of long hair in women was posed by Dr Beddoe, quoted by Daniel John Cunningham in a pamphlet published in 1885. Dr Cunningham himself observed

461

the statistical matrimonial preference for women with brown hair. (His statistics, mysteriously, list three 'social states' for women: Married, Single and Doubtful.)

The poems declaimed by Oona in Chapter 21 are as follows:

As Belinda in Alexander Pope's *The Rape of the Lock*:

> *Love in these Labyrinths his Slaves detains,*
> *And mighty Hearts are held in slender Chains . . .*
> *Fair tresses Man's imperial Race insnare*
> *And Beauty draws us with a single Hair.*
>
> (Canto 2, lines 23 – 28)

As Milton's Eve in *Paradise Lost*:

> *Shee as a vail down to the slender waste*
> *Her unadorned golden tresses wore*
> *Dishevel'd, but in wanton ringlets wav'd*
> *As the Vine curles her tendrils . . .*

She would also have been forced to writhe her way through Dante Gabriel Rossetti's poetic incarnation of Lilith – in 'Eden Bower' – as a rippling Godiva of a serpent-woman, the fairest snake in Eden before she became Adam's first human wife. This was first published in Rossetti's *Poems*, 1870:

> *Not a drop of her blood was human*
> *But she was formed like a soft sweet woman.*

The contemporary scholar Galia Ofek divides Victorian depictions of long-haired women into two types: golden-tressed Rapunzels and angels who were sexually innocent and decorous and needed saving; and Medusas, women who had already fallen into sin, were knowing and dangerous and out of control, but who were also in their way victims of representational codification inscribed in their dark hair.

James Frazer devoted many pages to hair in *The Golden Bough: A Study in Magic and Religion* (1890). He recorded the widespread belief in the sympathetic magic invested in hair (and nail clippings). Hair was sacred to the spirit of the head and was to be molested at peril. It was a matter of anxiety when it was cut. 'The chief of the Namosi in Fiji always ate a man by way of precaution when his hair was cut,' wrote Frazer, who also recorded that among the Toradjas a child whose head was shaved to rid it of vermin was always required to keep a lock on the crown as a refuge for the head's separate soul. He wrote that men who have taken a vow of vengeance may keep their hair uncut till they have fulfilled their vow. Some ancient German tribes would not allow their young warriors to trim their hair or beards until they had slain an enemy. Hair clippings were often protected. The Huzuls of the Carpathians feared that if mice were allowed to make nests of human hair then the donor would become cretinous or plagued by headaches. In Swabia, cut hair had to be hidden in a place where neither sun nor moon could shine on it. Some African tribes buried hair to stop it from falling into the hands of witches. In the Tyrol, some people burned it lest witches used it to raise tempests. Armenians hide their hair in the cracks of church walls, the pillars of houses or in a hollow tree because all severed portions of themselves will be required for reassembly upon resurrection. The Incas of Peru also believed in keeping cut nails and hair handy for that event; additionally, they were careful to spit in one place. Hair should be combed strictly inside the house, according to some cultures, as cutting and combing were thought to bring on thunder and lightning. In the Scottish Highlands no girl might comb her hair at night if she had a brother at sea. It was a traditional belief of the Irish village that, as Annora claims, the hairs on our heads were all numbered by the Almighty, who would expect us to account for each one on the Day of Judgement. Village women would wind hair into the thatch of their cottages for safe storage until then.

The Pre-Raphaelite Brotherhood's obsession with hair is too well documented to be explored here. But it is interesting to note that Rossetti's now iconic 'stunner' paintings like *Lady Lilith* and *La Pia de' Tolomei* were not initially seen in public

463

and went straight from the artist's studio to the home of the buyer. Rossetti was secretive about his work, and rarely exhibited it in public. Both of these paintings were owned by the shipping magnate and art collector Frederick Richards Leyland. Although not exhibited, *Lady Lilith* was described in Algernon Charles Swinburne's *Notes on the Royal Academy Exhibition 1868*, alongside Rossetti's poem. In 1870 the artist's poem was published again in his *Sonnets for Pictures*.

Nor would his drawing, *La Belle Dame sans Merci* (1848), in which the fatal fairy lassoes her knight with her hair, have been seen in public, but I had the Swineys simulate the image with the gondoliers in Venice.

Bram Stoker, a Dublin-born writer, published a story in 1892, 'The Secret of the Growing Gold', in which a certain Geoffrey Brent murders his wife Margaret Delandre and hides her body under the floor of his castle, Brent's Rock. But the hair continues to grow. Hair forces its way through the hearthstones. He tries to burn it but still it grows. Eventually the golden hair, horribly streaked with grey, strangles Brent and his new Italian wife, revealing the secret of the murder, while at the same time avenging it. The uncontrollable anger of the hair, a material, still-living part of a dead body, a spectral but corporeal manifestation: Margaret Delandre's sullen passion, voluptuousness and recklessness were all expressed in her hair.

Hair has become a highly charged subject in academic and artistic circles, with some writers arguing that hair represents the aggression of the id, or drawing upon the concept of weaving in Freudian theory as metaphor for the dream-work of the subconscious. (Freud also saw weaving as a mask for 'genital deficiency'.) Others speak of hair as a metaphor for the umbilical cord that joins mother and unborn child, or as the embodiment of boundaries between the inner and outer (hair grows from inside but exists outside too). The cutting or plucking of hair connotes bodily and metaphysical separation. All agree on its power as a sexual totem. The Anglo-French artiste Alice Anderson works with both dolls and doll hair and explores several of the issues raised by this book. Her website includes some films about her work. http://www.alice-anderson.org

Canadian surrealist Mimi Parent used two of her blonde plaits to make a two-pronged whip when she discovered she had been betrayed by her partner. The work, made in 1996, was entitled *Maitresse*. And the cutting of girlish plaits could also indicate a severance from childhood and innocence.

Ida's gesture of cleaning the floor with her hair has reference to Janine Antoni's *Loving Care*, in which the artist dipped her hair in buckets of black dye and used it as a brush to paint or wash the floor of a London gallery in 1992. But most modern hair art by women refers to cutting it in order to sever connections with feminine stereotypes, or to signify grief upon loss of a lover.

Other artists who have worked with hair include Hannah Wilkes, who used hair that fell out during chemotherapy, and Mona Hatoum, who has deployed hair extracted from hairbrushes, and Esmé Clutterbuck, whose delicate drawings of hair give it a life of its own. Hair art by women was the subject of *Braided Together*, an exhibition in Cambridge and London in 2012, featuring the work of Samantha Sweeting, Elina Brotherus, Marcelle Hanselaar, Tabitha Moses, Karen Bergeon, Marion Michell, Mary Dunkin and others. Some of the images from this exhibition made their way indirectly into scenes in this book. Mika Rottenberg has produced a film called *Cheese* that was loosely inspired by the Sutherland Sisters. Kate Kretz embroiders with human hair. M.K. Guth creates installations of long hair. Their work, and that of many artists who deploy hair, can be seen on the excellent http://hairisforpulling.blogspot.it/. An exhibition opened at the Musée du quai Branly in Paris in 2012 entitled *Cheveux chéris, frivolitées et trophées* – containing 250 works of photography, painting, sculpture and ethnographic objects. Hélène Fulgence, the director of the exhibition, wrote: 'Everything that is to do with hair is important because it is related to the head, and the head, in all civilisations, is sacred.'

ACKNOWLEDGEMENTS

First of all, thanks as ever to Bill Helfand, who opened my eyes to the possibilities offered by hair as a subject in medical history and literature.

For information about Kildare, Wicklow fairy beliefs, the Famine and many other details, I am indebted to Chris Lawlor, who not only provided a wealth of information in his excellent and comprehensive book *An Irish Village: Dunlavin, County Wicklow* but who also went out of his way to help, generously offering insights from his own encyclopaedic knowledge and also finding me copies of rare materials. Thanks also to Nessa Dunlea and Catherine Mackay at the Kilcullen Heritage Centre, and, for help with local newspapers in County Kildare and Ireland, Mario Corrigan, Executive Librarian at Kildare Collections and Research Services. As usual, many thanks to the Wellcome Library staff, particularly Ross MacFarlane and Phoebe Harkins.

To my agent Victoria Hobbs and my editor Helen Garnons-Williams, so much gratitude for their infinite patience and care; also to Kristina Blagojevitch for her help; Mary Tomlinson for her painstaking editing work, especially after I telescoped the timeline. For invaluable writing advice and support, *grazie infinite* to Mary Hoffman, Lucy Coats, Louise Berridge, Tamara Macfarlane, Jill Foulston, Sarah Salway, Ros Asquith and the Clink Street Writers Group. For advice on Pre-Raphaelite hair, many thanks to Dr Lucetta Johnson and for all medical advice, my father Dr Vladimir Lovric.

To Principessa Bianca di Savoia Aosta, Giberto Arrivabene Valenti Gonzaga and Sabine Daniel, *mille grazie* for precious private access to the Palazzo Papadopoli at San Polo.

For countless journeys round Venice in an old green boat, and for showing me the ways of true kindness – *mille baci* to Bruno and Susie Palmarin.

And an *abbraccio forte forte* each to Jenny, Tony, Cathy, Greg, Hin-Yan, Kate, Sarah, Carole, Emma, Kaitlin, Laurie, Claire, Jack, Ornella, Elena, Ross, Irene, Jane, Rebecca, Claire, Melissa, Harriet, Thomas, Nick, Adèle, Marie-Louise, Dianne, Penny, Annabel, Paola, Carol, Fiona, Pat, Alan, Sybille, Paulina, Steve, Erik and Aidan.

They know why.

A NOTE ON THE AUTHOR

Michelle Lovric is the author of four novels – *Carnevale, The Floating Book, The Remedy* (longlisted for the 2005 Orange Prize for Fiction) and *The Book of Human Skin* (a TV Book Club pick in 2011) as well as four children's books. Her book *Love Letters: An Anthology of Passion* was a *New York Times* bestseller. She lives in London and Venice.

www.michellelovric.com

A NOTE ON THE TYPE

The text of this book is set in Berling roman, a modern face designed by K. E. Forsberg between 1951 and 1958. In spite of its youth it does carry the characteristics of an old face. The serifs are inclined and blunt, and the g has a straight ear.